JOE PEPPER

— AND —

MANY A RIVER

Elmer Kelton

FORGE®

A TOM DOHERTY ASSOCIATES BOOK | NEW YORK

This is a work of fiction. All of the characters, organizations, and events portrayed in these novels are either products of the author's imagination or are used fictitiously.

JOE PEPPER AND MANY A RIVER

Joe Pepper copyright © 1975 by Elmer Stephen Kelton Estate

Many a River copyright © 2008 by Elmer Stephen Kelton Estate

Joe Pepper was originally published under Elmer Kelton's pseudonym Lee McElroy.

A Forge Book
Published by Tom Doherty Associates
120 Broadway
New York, NY 10271

www.tor-forge.com

Forge® is a registered trademark of Macmillan Publishing Group, LLC.

ISBN 978-1-250-17807-7

Our books may be purchased in bulk for promotional, educational, or business use. Please contact your local bookseller or the Macmillan Corporate and Premium Sales Department at 1-800-221-7945, extension 5442, or by email at MacmillanSpecialMarkets@macmillan.com.

First Edition: January 2020

Printed in the United States of America

0 9 8 7 6 5 4 3 2 1

CONTENTS

JOE PEPPER

1

Well, preacher, if you've come to pray over me in my last hours, I'm afraid it's too late. I've seen a few of them last-minute conversions, and I never put much stock in them. I doubt as the Lord does, either. But I'm grateful for your company anyway. Looks like they're going to hammer on that scaffold out there all night, so I won't be getting no sleep. Far as I'm concerned they could put it off a day or two and not work so hard.

Don't be bashful. If you want to hear my story, all you got to do is ask for it. It can't be used against me now. I've seen what they said was my story lots of times, written up in the newspapers and penny-dreadfuls. Lies, most of them. Some reporter listens to a few wild rumors, gets him a pencil, some paper and a jug, and he writes the *whole true story* of Joe Pepper, big bad gunfighter of the wild West. Damn liars, most of them newspaper people. Tell one of them the time of day and he'll set his watch wrong.

I think I know what you're after . . . you'd like

to have the story straight so you can tell it to your congregation. Maybe it'll scare some of them twisty boys and turn them aside from the paths of iniquity. It might at that, though I can't say I've wasted much time regretting the things I've done. My main regret has been over some men I didn't shoot when I had the chance.

Don't expect me to give you the dates, and maybe I'll disremember a name or two. I figure a man's head can just hold so much information, and he'd better not fill it up with a lot of unnecessaries.

I've always liked to tell people I was born in Texas, but since you're a preacher I won't lie to you. I always wished I *was* born in Texas. The truth is that I was born just across the line in Louisiana. My daddy and mama, they could look across the river and *see* Texas; they was of that old-time Texian breed, and it was just an accident of war that I wasn't born where I was supposed to be. You've heard of the great Runaway Scrape? That was after Santa Anna and them Mexicans wiped out the Alamo and massacred all of them soldiers at Goliad. The settlers, they lit out in a wild run for the Sabine River to get across into the United States before Santa Anna could overtake them.

Now, my daddy was in Sam Houston's army for a while, leaving my mama with some neighbors on the land he had claimed in Austin's colony. But when the Scrape started, he got to fretting about her, knowing she was nigh to term. Didn't look then like Sam Houston intended to fight anyway; he just kept backing off, letting Santa Anna come on and on. So my daddy deserted and rushed my mama across into Louisiana where she would be safe. While he was there, Sam Houston and his bunch whipped the britches off of

Santa Anna at San Jacinto. Daddy missed out on that. He also missed out on the league and *labor* of land that the Republic of Texas granted to all the San Jacinto soldiers. If he'd of been in on that, we'd of been a lot more prosperous than we ever was.

The rest of his life he always told people he had been a soldier under Sam Houston. He didn't tell them about the deserting, and the Runaway Scrape.

When the war was over my folks went back to the farm, and of course I was with them by then. You'll hear people who don't know no better bragging about what a wonderful grand thing it was, the Republic of Texas. Either they don't know or they're so old and senile that they've forgot. It was a cruel, hard time. There wasn't no money to be had, hardly, and most people had to grub deep just to hold body and soul together. Seems to me like the first thing I can remember is following my mama and daddy down the rows of a cottonfield. Time I was old enough to take hold of a hoehandle, they had one ready for me. Only time I ever laid it down in the daylight was to take hold of something heavier. I remember watching my folks grow old before their time, trying their best not to lose that little old place.

I was grown and hiring out for plowman's wages when the War between the States come on. I was a good marksman like everybody else in that country then; most of the meat we ever had on the table was wild game that I went out and shot. There was people that used to run hogs loose along the rivers and creeks, living off of the acorns and such. Every once in a while I would shoot me one of those and tell the folks it was a wild one. They wouldn't of eaten it no other way. Religious folks they was; they'd of taken a liking to you, preacher. But I always felt like the Lord helped them that helped theirselves, and I helped myself any time it come handy.

Well, like I say, the war started. Right off, I volunteered. My old daddy, he joined up too. It had always gnawed at him, I reckon, that he wasn't there when Sam Houston won that other war. He wanted to be in on this one. So he left Mama and the kids to take care of the place, and him and me went off to war. He never did get there, though. We hadn't been gone from home three weeks till he was taken down with the fever and died without ever seeing a Yankee. We gave him a Christian burial three hundred miles from home. I always wanted to go back someday and put up a stone, but I never could find the place, not within five miles. Probably fenced into somebody's cow pasture now.

The war wasn't nothing I like to talk about. My part in it wasn't much different from most any other soldier's. I taken three bullet wounds, one time and another. I killed a few men that had never done nothing against me except shoot at me. Maybe that sounds funny to you, but it's true. There wasn't nothing personal in it; they was shooting at *everybody* that wore a uniform the color of mine. They didn't know me from Robert E. Lee. It was our job to kill more of them than they killed of us.

Everybody seemed to feel like it was all right for me to shoot strangers in the war, but in later years they got awful self-righteous. Some wanted to hang me when I'd shot a man that *did* have a personal fight with me, men that wanted to kill Joe Pepper, only Joe Pepper beat them to it. Folks would say I'd forgotten the war was over. Well, it never *was* over for me. Seems like I've been in one war or another most of my life. I never could get it straight, them changing the rules on me all the time.

I was way over in Pennsylvania when the war was over and they told us to go home. I had taken a good sorrel horse off of a dead Yankee, but that chicken-brained captain of ours led us into an ambush that a blind mule could've seen, and the horse got shot out from under me. The best officers we had got killed off in the first years of the war, seemed like, and mostly what we had left in the last part was the scrubs and the cutbacks. The night after they told us to go home, I slipped along the picket line and taken a good big gray horse of the captain's. I figured he owed me that for getting my sorrel shot. I knowed he wouldn't take the same view on it, though, so I was thirty miles toward Texas by daylight.

That horse was the making of my first fortune, in a manner of speaking. Big stout horse he was, about fifteen hands high, Tennessee stock. Once I had schooled him, I could rope a full-grown range bull on him and he'd bust that bull over backwards. But that was later on, of course. That was when I was still known as Joe Peeler. The Joe Pepper name came later.

When I got back to the old homeplace I found out Mama had died, and the kids was taking care of the farm themselves. Couple of the boys was grown and plenty able. They didn't have no need of me, and one thing they *didn't* need was an extra mouth to feed. So I taken off and headed south with an old army friend of mine, Arlee Thompson. He had come from below San Antonio in the Nueces Strip country. That was a rough territory them days, Mexican outlaws coming across the line to see what they could take and run with, American outlaws settling there so if they was pressed they could always run for Mexico. The honest people—what there was of them—had a hard time. Even the honest ones fought amongst theirselves a right smart, *Americanos* against Mexicans and *vice versa*. You'd of thought they had trouble enough without that, but they didn't seem to think so.

The ranches had let a lot of their cattle go unbranded through the war because there just wasn't enough men to do the job. There was grown cattle there—bulls three and four years old that had never felt knife or iron—cows with their second or third calf at side, their ears and hides as slick as the calves' were. Cattle wasn't worth much in them first times after the war, hardly worth anybody fighting over. People fought anyway, of course. Men'll fight when they can't even *eat*. Me and Arlee, we figured there'd be money in cattle again. We set out to claim as many as we could. *Mavericking* is what we called it them days, after a man named Maverick who said all the branded cattle belonged to the man who registered the brand, and all the unbranded cattle belonged to *him*.

Now, there was some people who didn't take kindly to what we done. You ever hear of Jesse Ordway? He was a power in that lower country. He didn't go to war himself, so he was sitting down there putting things together while most of the men was off fighting Yankees. He gobbled up a lot of that country, taking it away from the Mexicans, buying out war widows for a sack of cornmeal and such like. He didn't object to people branding mavericks as long as they was working for him and burning *his* brand on them, but it sure did put the gravel under his skin to see other people doing it. He thought he had him a nice private little hunting preserve. The rest of us was poachers.

But damn good poachers we was. Inside of a year me and Arlee had us a pretty good-sized herd of cattle apiece. We didn't own an acre of ground, either one of us, but half the people down there didn't. Jesse Ordway didn't actually own a fraction of what he claimed. Most of it he just squatted on and used because he was bigger and stronger than anybody else and had the gall to hold it.

I didn't tell you yet about Arlee's sister. Millie was her name. Arlee wasn't much to look at, tall and thin and bent over a little, and had a short scar over one cheek where a Yankee bullet kind of winked at him as it went by. But Millie, she must've took after her mother's side of the family. I've got a picture of her here in the back of my watch. See, wasn't she the prettiest thing ever you laid your eyes on? Picture's faded a little, but take my word for it. She wasn't much bigger than a minute, and had light-colored hair that reminded me a little of corn silk. And eyes? The bluest eyes that ever melted a miser's heart.

She was living with her old daddy on the place he had claimed as his share from the revolution. It was a league and a *labor* just like they'd of given *my* daddy if he had stayed with Sam Houston. But the old man Thompson had had his share of hard luck and had lost most of his country one way and another. He was down to just a little hard-scrabble outfit about big enough to chunk rocks at a dog on. Time me and Arlee got there, he was most blind, and it was up to Millie and a Mexican hand named Felipe Rios to take care of the work. Jesse Ordway had branded up a lot of the old man's calves for himself, and there wasn't much the old man or that Mexican boy could do about it. The old man prayed a good deal, asking the Lord to forgive Ordway because he knowed not what he done.

You'll have to pardon me, preacher, but that's one thing I never could accept about these religious people, always asking forgiveness for their enemies. Ordway knew what he was doing, and he didn't need forgiveness; what he needed was a damn good killing.

First time I seen Millie I couldn't believe she was Arlee's sister. But there was a resemblance; they both had the same big blue innocent eyes. You could've told either one of them that the sun would come up out of the west tomorrow and they'd believe you. I told Millie a good many lies at first, till my conscience got to hurting. People will tell you I never had a conscience, but they don't know me. It always plagued me when I done something I thought was wrong. So most of my life I've tried not to do them things. Other people might've thought I done wrong, but I don't have to listen to *their* conscience, just *mine*.

The old man died a little while after I got there. I reckon he had been ready to go before but had waited till Arlee was at home to take care of Millie. Old folks are like that sometimes, you know; they just keep the door locked against death till they're ready to go, then they seem to walk out and meet it of their own free will. I've seen some that greeted it like a friend.

The day came when we got news that the railroad had built west into Kansas, and people in South Texas began to round up a lot of them cattle and drive them north to turn into Yankee dollars. Me and Arlee had us close to two hundred steers apiece over and above the maverick heifers we had put our brands on. The heifers had to stay—they was seed stock for the future. But them steers was excess, a liquid asset like the bankers always say. During our mavericking time we would split them fifty-fifty. We worked together, me and Arlee. We would put his brand on one and mine on the next. Felipe Rios helped us, but he didn't get no cattle. He was working for wages, when we had any money to pay him. Anyway, he was a Mexican. They let Mexicans maverick cattle for other people, but they was stealing if they mavericked for theirselves. They would get their necks lengthened. Sounds rough, but that's the way it was, them days.

Four hundred steers wasn't enough to make up a good trail herd, so we throwed in with some more smaller operators and put together something like thirteen hundred head of cattle.

Jesse Ordway tried to crowd us. He brought in a couple of Rangers and claimed we had stolen a lot of the cattle—me and Arlee and some of the others. He bluffed and blustered, and I reckon he thought he had them Rangers in his pocket, but he didn't. They listened to him real polite, then started asking him to show the proof. That was one thing he couldn't do. The Rangers cussed him out for wasting their time and rode off and left him.

Then he tried to bluff us. He brought a gunfighter he had used to run some of the Mexicans off of their country, a *pistolero* name of Threadgill. He was before your time; you probably never heard of him. He was just a cheap four-flusher anyway. He got by on bluff, not on guts. The only thing game about him was his smell.

Ordway brought Threadgill and some others up to stop us the morning we throwed our herd onto the trail. Threadgill was the man out front. The way they had it made up, he was supposed to kill one or two of us and the rest would turn tail and run.

I used to carry my pistol stuck into my belt them days. I never did fancy a holster much. I watched

Threadgill's face. Just before he reached for his gun, I could see it coming in his eyes. I didn't try to draw my gun; that would've taken too long. I just left it in the belt and twisted the muzzle up at Threadgill and pulled the trigger. Bullet caught him at about the second button on his shirt. One of them other toughs tried to draw his gun, but a shot come from behind me, and he was already falling before I could get my pistol pointed in his direction.

It was over in about the time it takes a chewing man to spit. There was that big Texas gunfighter Threadgill laying on the ground at Ordway's feet, dead enough to skin. The other one was laying there coughing, going the same way only taking a little longer. I looked around and seen smoke curling up from Felipe Rios's pistol. He had one of them old-fashioned cap-and-ball relics that must of weighed forty pounds.

It would've shamed that hired tough considerable to have knowed he was killed by a Mexican.

I kept my pistol pointed at Ordway's left eye, where he couldn't hardly overlook it. I hoped he would do something foolish, so we could adjourn court right then and there. But he decided not to press the case. He taken the rest of his men and went home, looking like a scalded dog.

The story got noised around, and nobody else in that part of the country gave us any argument. If anything, them old boys came out to help us push our cattle along. A lot of them was glad to see anybody get the best of Jesse Ordway.

I could of shot him right then and there, and later on I wished I had. It would've saved me and lots of people a right smart of trouble. It taught me a lesson that I didn't forget as the years went by: when in doubt, *kill* the son of a bitch.

We had a pretty easy drive, as cattle drives went; there wasn't none of them real easy. We caught the Red River in flood and lost one of the cowboys there. The average cowboy couldn't swim a lick.

We could've easy had some Indian trouble up in the Nations, but as it turned out we didn't. We run onto a bunch of Indians that thought we ought to give them some of the beeves just for trailing cattle over their land. Arrogant bunch, they was. The only reason they had that land in the first place was that the government gave it to them; they didn't have any business charging taxpaying citizens for traveling across it. Couple of the boys gave them a steer apiece, but they didn't get any of mine.

Nearest we ever come to a real fight was amongst ourselves. There was a fat boy with us who owned something like four hundred head—more than any of the rest of us. Name was Lathrop Nettleton, and he figured that as the biggest owner he ought to ramrod the outfit. None of us paid him much mind. We each of us went about and did what we could see needed to be done, and we mostly just ignored him. He got to mouthing at me one time, and I had to knock him down. I invited him to pull his gun if he was a mind to, but he wasn't. Time we got to Kansas we was all mighty sick of him. I'm proud to say he was just as sick of me.

We pulled into Abilene and got the cattle sold and split up the money according to the cattle count. You ever see one of them trail's end celebrations, preacher? No? Well, that's probably a good thing. I'm here to tell you it's no place for a man of the

Gospel. There was other cow outfits in there besides
ours, so the whole place was overrun with Texas
cowboys trying to wash three months of dust out of
their throats with the most damnable whiskey you've
ever drunk—begging your pardon again, preacher.
And then there was the girls over there on the tracks.
I didn't go for none of that, you understand; by that
time I had made up my mind I was going to marry
Millie Thompson even if I had to carry her off like
some Mexican bandit. Her brother Arlee was with
me, and I sure didn't want him telling her no tales out
of school. So I stayed with the whiskey and played a
little cards.

There was a small saloon over next to the railroad
that seemed kind of comfortable. It was run by an
old-time Union soldier who had lost an arm in the
war. I kind of taken a liking to him; I reckon he was
the first damnyankee I had ever seen that was cut up
enough to suit me. There was one of them Eastern
gamblers, too, the kind that always wore a swallowtail coat and a silk hat. I figured he had to be crooked;
I never did trust a man that had slick hands and wore
a coat in the summertime.

I ought to tell you that I wasn't just the average
run of-the-mill cowboy when it came to cards. In the
army I'd spent some time amongst a bunch of Missis-
sippi River boys who could make a deck of cards do
just about anything but sing "Dixie." I had learned a
right smart from them, at no small expense to myself.
Still, I didn't think I wanted to try that Eastern gambler on for size. I never could understand them cowboys that knew they was outclassed but still would go
up against one of them sharps. Playing for matches
on a saddle blanket is a lot different from playing for
blood on one of them slick tables.

Some of the boys from our drive wanted to play him. Normally I'd of tried to talk them out of it, but Lathrop Nettleton was amongst them, and I figured it would do me good to see him nailed to the wall. So I just sat there and watched them play. I knowed sooner or later that gambler was going to suck them boys under and drown them like a coon drowns a hunting dog.

He was smooth about it. He taken his time before he set the hook. He'd win a hand and then let one of the other boys win one. Seemed like for a while he was losing more chips than he was taking in, so pretty soon some extra hands from other outfits sat in on the game. Gradually he got to winning. Along about midnight he was taking all the chips. Some of the boys had sense enough to draw out before they lost it all, but Lathrop Nettleton just hung and rattled to the bitter end. Before that gambler got through with him Nettleton had lost everything those four hundred steers had brought him. He was lucky to have a saddlehorse to ride home on. The gambler gave him back twenty dollars' worth of chips. "For seed," he says. "I want to see you back here again next year."

I might've felt sorry for Nettleton then if he hadn't started to beg. That was one thing I never could stand to see a man do. The one-armed barkeep finally had to put him out of there; told him if he couldn't afford to lose, he couldn't afford to play.

I didn't interfere. I could of told Nettleton if I'd wanted to that I had been watching the gambler palm cards all night.

The boys was pretty well whipped down. The gambler set them all up to a drink at the bar before they went back to their wagons. Nettleton was already gone.

I just sat there at the table by myself, glad Arlee hadn't been in the game. When the boys finished their drink and started for the door they asked me if I was coming with them, I told them no, I wasn't quite ready for the bedroll yet.

That gambler knowed I had money on me. When there was just him and me and the barkeep left in the place, he says to me, "The night's still in her youth. Like to play a few hands, just me and you?"

I slipped that pistol out of my belt and pointed it up in the general direction of his Adam's apple. It got to working up and down. "So that's it," he says. "You're going to rob me."

I says to him, "No, the robbery has already taken place. If I'd of told them boys they'd of tore you to pieces and fed you to the dogs. I thought the best thing was to stay here till they was gone and give you a chance to square things up without throwing your life into forfeit."

He blustered and bluffed about not being a cheater, but I had him cold, and he knowed it. He finally caved in. I told him the only fair thing was for him to give back all the money he had won from the boys. I said it might help their feelings if he throwed in a little extra for interest. He turned kind of clabber-colored, but he shoved all the chips across the table. I got the barkeep to cash them.

I told that gambler if I was him I wouldn't wait around for daylight. "Getting their money back won't be enough for the boys," I says. "They're liable to come hunting for you. Smart thing would be to get you a horse and leave now. You could be a long ways up the track before sunup, and I'd be a few days coming back if I was you."

That one-armed saloonkeeper seen it pretty much

the way I did and seconded all my advice. He said they was good people, them Texas cowboys, when they was on your side. But they was woolly boogers when they was against you. That gambler walked out of there with nothing much besides his silk hat and that swallowtail coat and whatever cards was still up his sleeve. I had all his money.

You couldn't say I lied to him, exactly. I didn't exactly tell him I *was* going to give the boys their money back. I just sort of let him believe that was the way it was going to be. But the way I seen it, it wouldn't be fair to give the money back to the rest of the boys if I didn't give it to Nettleton too. I didn't want to be dishonest about the thing, so I just kept all the money for myself.

I never told Arlee Thompson the whole truth. I told him I'd had me a set-to with the gambler after the rest of the boys got through, and that I had better luck than they did. I didn't let on to Arlee how much money I really had till we got back to South Texas. I had all my share of the cattle money, minus the little bit I had spent on whiskey and new clothes, and I had all the money off of that poker table. It was a pretty good road stake for them days.

I was a little afraid some of the boys would go back over there the next day and find out from that Yankee barkeep what had happened. Things could of got a little unpleasant. But none of them seemed like they wanted to ever see the place again. They didn't have the money to be going back there anyway, most of them. They'd had their plow cleaned.

We passed Jesse Ordway's trail herd heading north as we went south, going home. We had got out on the trail a long ways ahead of him and sold our cattle early in the season when the price was at about its

peak. First ones there generally lapped the cream, and
the late ones taken the skim milk. I know Ordway
wasn't none too pleased to see us. Them days it was
custom to invite passing strangers to stop for a meal
or two—even the night—at your wagon. But Ordway
didn't give us any invite. I didn't let it worry me. I
was already way ahead of him because some of the
mavericks I had branded had been his once upon a
time; he was so busy branding other people's that he
hadn't got around to all of his own. It was the quick
that won the marbles them days, and the slow just
wasn't in it at all.

Naturally we got home several weeks ahead of
Ordway, and I didn't let no grass grow under my feet.
I had done a lot of thinking about Millie Thompson.
I'd lay awake at night and imagine I could hear her
talking to me, laughing with me. She had a voice that
kind of lifted sometimes and broke and sounded like
a hundred little silver bells tinkling. It doesn't take
much of that to set a young man to making all kinds
of dreams and plans. I wanted to build her a home
and live in it with her for a thousand years.

I had kept that money a secret. When we got back
to South Texas I went to listening and looking, and
pretty soon through Felipe Rios I found out there was
three-four Mexican families wanting to sell out. Felipe was telling them they ought to stay and fight, but
he was just a bachelor, and they was family men. Jesse
Ordway had been pushing on them pretty hard, running off their cattle, burning their hay, scaring their
womenfolk. Not himself, understand, but people he
hired for that kind of thing. They knew when he got
back off of his trail drive that they was fixing to catch
hell. They couldn't look to the law for help. Them

lawmen wouldn't take two steps out of their way to help a Mexican.

Without acting too interested I managed to find out what Ordway had been offering them. When I figured out the places I wanted and could afford, I went and bought them. Them Mexicans thought I was one *crazy gringo*, but they was tickled to take my money and run. One of them told me Jesse Ordway would be shoveling dirt in my face before the first cold norther of the winter. But I reckon he figured it was better mine than his, because he was sure glad to take what I offered him.

I oughtn't to've been, but I was some surprised to find out that Millie Thompson wanted to marry me as much as I wanted to marry her. I had thought I might have to argue with her. You wouldn't think so to see me like I am now, an old man, but there was some folks—women anyway—who used to say I was handsome them days. I never was one to argue much with a woman.

We had us a church wedding with all the trimmings. Surprise you, preacher? Bet from all the things you heard about me, you thought I was never in church in my life. But I was, once or twice before that and at least once since that I can remember. There was a time long years ago when I climbed up into a church loft to get away from a bunch of angry old boys that was after me, but there wasn't no praying done that time, not that I recall.

We took us a short wedding trip to San Antonio . . . stayed in the best suite of rooms we could get in the Menger Hotel, just down the hall from where Captain Richard King himself was holding forth. The *King Ranch* King, you know. Looking at him, I even taken a notion that if I worked extra hard and played my cards right, I might get to be as big a man in the cattle business someday as he was.

You a married man? Then I suppose you know how sweet things was for me and Millie for a while. That picture I showed you in the back of my watch ... she had that made in San Antonio. You can see the sparkle in her eyes if you look close. Oh, that was a happy time.

I never completely put Jesse Ordway out of my mind, though. I kind of kept track of where I thought he would be, one day to the next. I had us a crew of carpenters camping out and building us a house before Ordway ever got home. Naturally he taken the Lord's name in vain when he found out what I had done. The places I picked was all on the river. The Mexicans had been doing a little irrigation, and there was a lot more good land that a man could have put into farms if he had the inclination and the strong back to do it. Ordway had figured on taking that land dirt cheap and growing a lot of feed on it so he could run even more cows than he already had. And I had come along and set myself square down in the middle of his road.

Couple days after he got home he came over to the place where I had the carpenters working. It was like he didn't even see that house, like all he could see was me, and he sure didn't appreciate the view. He told me I had as much as stolen the land from him, and I told him I had bought it free and clear from the previous rightful owners, and now I had all the papers to show that I was the present rightful owner, and he could go soak his head in a muddy tank.

He says to me, "You know what I mean. You'll have no luck here. You'd do a lot better to move far away and start over." He offered to buy the land from me at seventy-five cents on the dollar. The other twenty-five percent I could mark down on the books as a fee for education.

By this time he had hired him another gunhand, a beady-eyed *pistolero* named Sorrells. You probably never heard of him. He had a right smart of a local reputation, but that was a long time ago. This Sorrells sat on his horse alongside Ordway. Dun horse it was, best I can recollect; I remember thinking to myself that if anybody was to shoot Sorrells—which was more than likely—maybe I could buy that horse off of the sheriff. Sorrells didn't say nothing, just sat there and tried to look mean. I taken him to be of about the same caliber as Threadgill, the other one Ordway had sicced onto me, and I had salted him away without no sweat on my part.

I told Ordway I'd buy *him* out at fifty cents on the dollar, which would've been a good deal on his part because he didn't own half of what he claimed. I'd of had to steal the money someplace if he had taken me up, but I was satisfied I could do it. Ordway just stared at me, hard. Sorrells kept looking from me to Ordway and back to me again, waiting for Ordway to tell him to go ahead and kill me. He was awful anxious to earn his wages; I reckon he liked to see that a man got his money's worth. But Ordway had a pretty good memory, and maybe he thought I'd of shot him as well as Sorrells if he'd of given me the excuse. He was right; I sure as hell would.

Felipe Rios was there too, a few steps off to one side of me.

Ordway caved. He backed his horse up a little and told me I'd better chew on it and be awful careful of my luck. I could tell when they rode away that

Sorrells was disappointed. Some people just naturally enjoy their work more than others do.

Me and Millie had been sleeping in one of the old Mexican houses while we waited for our new one to be finished. Fresh married like we was, it didn't make a particle of difference where we slept. The days was way too long anyhow, seemed like, and the nights too short.

Well, that night turned out to be long enough. The Mexican house was maybe two hundred yards from where the new one was going up. Sometime about midnight I heard shooting. I jumped out of bed and grabbed my britches. The shooting stopped before I could get my pants and boots on and run outside. I could see the new house was afire. I could see people running around down there, and I could hear horses. I couldn't shoot because I was apt to hit the carpenters or Felipe; he was camped down there with them. I heard the horses loping away in the dark and men hollering in Mexican. But they wasn't Mexicans, I could tell. A man don't need much of an ear to tell when it's some *gringo* trying to *talk* Mexican.

There wasn't nothing we could do to save the house. It was plumb gone. So was one of the carpenters; they had put so much lead in him that it taken two extra pallbearers to carry him. Felipe wanted to chase after them, but Millie was scared for me to leave her alone.

Next day I called out the law. They said it was Mexican bandits. I knowed they knowed better, and I cussed them for a bunch of chicken-livered cowards. But they was local, and they was afraid of Jesse Ordway.

I thought once that I was going to get even. Ordway was married; had him a thin, shivery little woman he had found over in San Antonio teaching in a church school. Reminded me of a scared rabbit locked up in a cage. She was as afraid of Jesse Ordway as she would've been of a rattlesnake. They had a boy about seven or eight years old, and it seemed to me like he took after his mama more than his daddy. Didn't seem like there was any fight in her or in the boy either. His daddy would say something, and that boy would cringe like a pup that's had the whip put to him.

Anyhow, Ordway was on a kind of house-building spree of his own. His was going to be a lot bigger than mine would've been. For a while I had a notion of going over there and burning it down some night, but that wouldn't of paid me back anything. And after what he had done to me I knowed he would have it guarded like a vault full of gold bars. There was an easier way of getting him.

I found out he was having the lumber hauled down from San Antonio. Me and Felipe went out on the road one day and got the drop on them freighters and persuaded them to haul one whole shipment over to my place. I figured Ordway owed me that, and I also figured if he came to get it back it might give me a good excuse to kill him.

He didn't even try. He didn't have to, because that lumber never done me no good. I couldn't hire a carpenter anywhere in the country to start building that house back. The word had gotten around. I'd of built it myself, but a saw and a hammer just never did fit my hands. Millie had to keep living in that old Mexican house. She never once complained about it. That nice frame house had been my idea in the first place, not hers.

Things was quiet till into the fall of the year. I had

about decided Ordway had given up on me till one day he rode up with three or four hands, and the gunfighter Sorrells at his side. He taken a look at the pile of his lumber laying out there, but he didn't say anything about it. He taken a lot longer look at the rifle I had in my hands, pointed about six inches below his collarbutton. He told me that sure wasn't any polite way to treat company, and I told him I never treated *company* that way. He offered to buy me out for the money I had invested in my place. That was a twenty-five percent better offer than his first one, but I told him that wouldn't allow me any pay for the time and labor I had already put in.

He didn't seem inclined to raise the ante. He just told me what he had said the last time, that I'd better be careful of my luck.

I knowed he would have a hell of a time burning down the Mexican house because it was of adobe, and the roof had a covering of dried mud on it. He might *melt* it down, if he could make that much water, but he would never burn it down.

They hit us that same night. I can't say it was by surprise, because we sort of expected them. The surprise was that there was so many of them. I found out later that he didn't use his regular hands because he didn't want any of them talking when it was over. He went down to the border and hired him a bunch of renegades from the other side that he knowed wouldn't come back and incriminate him. So the ones that hit us that night was him and Sorrells and them renegades.

All I had was myself and Felipe and a couple of hands that I had hired to work cattle, not fight. They didn't do much fighting; they turned and ran. Felipe got shot in the leg in the first charge; he was sleeping out under an open arbor and couldn't get to the house in time. They swarmed over him and clubbed him and left him for dead. So then it was just me, with Millie loading my guns.

They tried first to set the place afire, but there wasn't much that would burn. Every time one of them would come charging up with a torch I would either hit him or come so close that he would drop the thing and run. They gave it up directly and set in to trying to cut the house to pieces. They shot out all the windows in the first few minutes—they was of wood, not glass—but them thick adobe walls stopped most of the bullets. Now and then one would bust through, but most of them either glanced off or stuck in the mud blocks.

There wasn't but one door to the place, and we had it barred. The only way they could come in was through that door or one of the front windows. They might've made it if they had had the nerve to gang up and all rush us at one time. But I reckon they knowed a bunch of them would die in the trying. They sat out there and potshotted at the windows, and I knowed we had them beat.

Then it happened. One of them slugs came right through the wall. The wall was of a double thickness of mud blocks, but I reckon there was a few places where the mud mortar on two blocks was on the same level. It was soft enough that the bullet came through.

Millie screamed. God, preacher, you never heard such a scream in your life. It hit her just under the heart. I had just time to catch her before she fell. All I could do was lay her out on the dirt floor and straighten her legs. She clutched at my shirt and cried out one more time; it must've hurt her something terrible. Then she was gone.

My Millie—my pretty Millie—was dead.

The shooting had stopped. They had all heard the scream. I heard a voice I knowed was Ordway's, telling them to rush the house. They just stayed put. Way I heard it later, that scream froze their blood, most of them, and the few others didn't want to try to swarm the house by theirselves. Ordway was out there in the dark, cussing a blue streak at them in Spanish and English both, because some was white and some was Mexican. Finally a couple of them made a run for the door. I dropped one of them six feet from the house; the other turned and ran. It was too dark to be sure, but I thought it was probably Sorrells.

After that I heard them pulling out. Ordway was telling them they wouldn't be paid a cent if they didn't go through with their bargain, but they rode off and left him. Directly everything out there got quiet. I sat myself down on the floor and taken Millie's hand and just held it for the longest time. I'm not ashamed to tell you, preacher, I cried like a baby. And when I was done crying, I sat there and talked to her like if she could of heard me, telling her what all plans I had had, and how much I loved her.

A long time after, I heard a noise and thought maybe they had come back. I got my rifle and eased the door open and waited, hoping they would try another rush so I could see just how many of them I could kill.

It was Felipe Rios crawling along, pulling himself a few inches at a time.

I helped him inside, and he saw Millie, and he crossed himself the way all them Catholics do, and he said something that sounded a little like Spanish but wasn't. I got him wrapped up the best I could in the dark; it was too risky to light a lamp. Then we waited for morning to come. It was one of the longest nights I ever spent in my life.

The two hands who had run away from us had done one decent thing, at least; they went to town and fetched the law. They didn't figure to find me alive, or they wouldn't of ever come back. I cussed them up one side and down the other and told them if I ever seen either one of them again I'd kill him like a dog. At the time, I meant it.

Word got to Arlee Thompson somehow, and he came over in a hard lope. He taken it pretty hard about Millie.

The law was no more help to me that time than they had been before. They declared the whole thing was the work of Mexican bandits who had surely gotten back across the river by now. I told them it was Ordway, that I'd heard his voice, but they told me I was mistaken. The last thing they wanted to do was to tangle up with Jesse Ordway. He could of stolen the county courthouse piece by piece and they'd of fetched him a wagon.

It taken me a while to figure out what to do about Ordway. What I really wanted was to go over there and just shoot him down. But I would never of been allowed to live that long.

We buried Millie on her old family homeplace. Arlee thought that was kind of strange, but I told him I wouldn't be keeping my land, and I wanted her to rest in her own ground where maybe there would be kin around through the times to come.

I sent word to Ordway that if he still wanted to buy me out, I'd sell to him on the terms of his last offer. I wanted cold hard cash because I figured on leaving the country. I didn't want no check, draft, or bank order. He sent me word what day to meet him in town at the bank with the deeds ready to sign over.

Felipe Rios was still weak. He had to have a crutch to walk, and he had to be helped onto a horse. But in the saddle he could handle himself pretty good. After all the help he had been, I hated to just leave him flat. I arranged with Arlee to give him a job. The morning I left for town I told Felipe to go to Arlee's. He wanted to go to town with me, but I told him he didn't have no business there, and he'd better do what I said. When I headed down the town road, I looked back once and seen him heading out in the direction of Arlee's.

I seen half a dozen O Bar horses tied at racks along the street. In front of the bank was a rig with Ordway's brand painted on it. Ordway's little boy sat up there all by himself. I figured he had been told to stay out of the bank, and he was way too young to wait in one of the saloons or Mexican *cantinas*. I rode straight up to the rack nearest to the bank door. I stopped and looked at the boy. He seemed to be a little afraid of me, because he kind of shrunk up on the seat of that rig. I asks him, "You a pretty good cowhand, son?"

He shook his head without saying anything, and I told him it was a thing a man could learn if he had to. I unfastened my saddlebags.

In the bank, Jesse Ordway was waiting for me. He had Sorrells there with him, maybe figuring I might come in shooting. But I didn't, and I could see in Sorrells's eyes that he was laughing at me. They had beaten me, and he was enjoying it. Maybe Ordway was enjoying it too, in his way, but he was more interested in business. With him it wasn't the principle of the thing; it was the money. He didn't try to shake hands with me; I wouldn't of done it noway. He says to me, "We have everything ready for you to sign. And I have the money all counted out for you. Sorry about your wife."

That was the order he ranked everything in. The money first.

I looked around the bank. Over to one side I seen Ordway's wife sitting near the bank president's desk. She was the same as every time I had ever seen her, scared. I had wondered a time or two how come she ever married such a man in the first place, because it was plain there wasn't no love lost for either one of them. I figured maybe she was too scared of him to say *no*. I wondered what she was in the bank for, and then I remembered that as the wife she was probably expected to sign papers.

Seeing her there kind of brought things back to me in a rush. Ordway's wife was alive, but mine was dead. And he had been responsible for killing her.

I tipped my hat to Mrs. Ordway and bowed a little, the way we was all taught to do, them days. I says, "Sorry my wife's not here to visit with you." I suppose I meant a little malice, because she must of known what her husband had done. She looked down and mumbled something I couldn't hear.

Ordway says, "Something's got to be done to stop those Mexican bandits."

I knowed he was a liar, and he knowed I knowed it. I seen a hard smile come across Sorrells's face.

Ordway says, "Too bad you didn't sell out earlier. All that misfortune would not have befallen you."

You know what hate tastes like? It's got a flavor all its own, not like salt, not like pepper, not like gall. It's not like anything else I know. I tasted it then like I've never tasted it another time in my life.

I laid out what papers I had, and he laid out some

legal agreements he had had a lawyer draw up. I never could figure out lawyer talk; I always suspected it was just a code they make up to rob the rest of us with. It didn't matter; the money stacked on that table did all the talking I needed to finish the deal. Ordway says, "It's all counted out."

I told him I'd count it myself, just to be sure. They had it in big denominations, twenty- and fifty-dollar bills. I doubted that this little cowtown bank had had all those bills on hand; they had probably had to send to San Antonio after them. It came out to about the same amount of money I had had when I first got home from that trail drive to Abilene, plus fifteen dollars a head for about two hundred cows I had mavericked or run a new brand on. There was probably more cattle than that, but the deal didn't call for a physical count, just range delivery.

I says, "This don't take into account the improvements." There hadn't been many, really. I had just fixed up some old pens and trap fences that was there to begin with but was run down some.

Ordway didn't seem too inclined to argue. He says, "All right, I'll add a thousand dollars."

It was too easy. I'd always found that when a man just up and gives you something, you'd better watch him because he's probably figuring to give you something *else* you didn't bargain on. I looked into Ordway's eyes, and I knew. It didn't matter what he paid me; he didn't intend to let me get out of this country alive. Once we finished this deal, I was as good as dead, and he would get most of his money back . . . maybe all of it.

I decided I had just as well take all I could get. I didn't really have any extra horses, but I didn't see where a little lie right there could hurt anything. I told him I had twenty head that hadn't been counted into the deal. He could have them for fifty dollars apiece or I would drive them to San Antonio and sell them. He motioned to the banker, and they counted me out another thousand dollars.

I put all the money into the saddlebags and then buckled the flaps down tight. I seen Ordway looking at them bags the way a hungry cat looks at a bird. I started to take them, and Ordway laid his hands across one of them. "The papers first," he says. "You got to sign the papers."

The deeds was all spread out there on the table. I wrote my name everywhere the banker told me, then blew on the ink to make it dry.

Ordway taken his hand off of the bag then. He had a look like a cat which had just got the bird in his mouth.

I says, "Jesse Ordway, you're a greedy man. Just what makes you want all this land so bad?"

He looked at his wife, then looked out the door toward where his son was still sitting in the rig. He says, "I got a family. I'm trying to build something worthwhile that I can leave to my son."

You ever notice that's what all them old land-hogs used to say? They was never building anything for theirselves, if you heard them tell it. They was always doing it for somebody else. The milk of human kindness was bubbling up and overflowing out of their hearts. Charity to the core. But they'd kill you for that charity if you got in their way.

I pushed my chair back away from the table and stood up. I says, "Ordway, I hope you're ready."

"Ready for what?" he asks me.

I says, "Ready to leave it to your son." I pulled my pistol out of my belt and shoved it up almost against his forehead. You never seen such a surprised look in a man's face. His mouth dropped open, and his eyes went as big as hen eggs. He made a reach for his gun, but he never touched it. I pulled the trigger. He fell back like he had been hit with a sledgehammer.

I had caught them all by surprise, but I could see Sorrells reaching for his gun. I swung around and caught him just as he cleared leather. I watched him fall on his face in the middle of the room.

The whole place was filled with powder smoke; it was hard to see across to the far wall. But nobody else in there was any threat to me. Surely not the banker, because he raised his hands like he thought it was a holdup. Mrs. Ordway had her mouth wide open like she wanted to scream, but nothing would come out.

I says to her, "You don't have to be scared anymore. You're shed of him. What's more, you're a rich woman."

I picked up the saddlebags, swung them across my shoulder and walked out the door.

From up the street came four of Jesse Ordway's hands, walking along like they had been sent for. I was the last person they expected to see come out after the shooting. Later, when I had time to think about it, I figured they was coming down to be Ordway's "eyewitnesses" after him and Sorrells killed me.

They pulled their guns and spread out. I was about to take a shot at one of them when somebody else done it for me. I seen one of them go down and grab his leg and scream like he had gone into a fire. The others stopped in their tracks, dropped their guns and raised their hands.

There was Felipe Rios across the street, sitting on

his horse. His gun was smoking like he had been burning greasewood.

I taken a look at Ordway's boy, who was trying to hold the team and keep it from running away. I says, "Boy, you better go in yonder. I think your mama needs you." Then I got on my horse, laid the saddle-bags across my lap and rode over to where Felipe was.

I couldn't decide whether to thank him or raise hell with him. I says, "Thought you was going to Arlee's."

"Later," he says. "I thought you might need help."

"You can't go to Arlee's now," I tells him. "I just killed Jesse Ordway and Sorrells. They'll figure you was part of it."

He nodded like it wasn't no surprise to him. He says, "It was in your face."

"I got to leave here now," I tells him. "You feel like you can keep up with me?"

"I don't see where I have any choice," he says. "These people will hang me if I stay."

Them days when a man got in trouble he went south. A day and a half of hard riding would take us to the Rio Grande. On the other side of the river they didn't care how many *gringos* you had killed; the more the better. Felipe wasn't in very good shape for a long ride like that, but I decided he would make it if I had to tie him in the saddle.

Good sense told me we ought to ride out of that town as fast as we could make those horses go. But that was Jesse Ordway's town, and I didn't want to run. I wanted us to take our time and let them all have a good long look at our backside. We rode slow and easy down the street, past them O Bar men. One of them was still holding onto his leg and trying to make the blood stop running. I says to him, says I, "You-all are working for a widow-lady now. You better go down to the bank and see what she wants you to do."

We just walked our horses till we got past the first bend in the road, to where the brush hid us from town. I says then, "Let's ride, Felipe."

And we rode.

2

I've come to many a fork in the road during my life, and a time or two I've took the wrong direction. One thing I've finally learned is that you never know what a woman is going to do. If I'd known more about Jesse Ordway's quiet, timid little wife, my life might of turned out a lot different. I naturally figured she would scream murder, and I didn't stay around to listen to her.

A long time later, way too late for it to do me any good, I found out she figured I'd done her a sizable favor. She told them I had killed her husband and Sorrells in self-defense. Naturally I can't exactly blame her for not telling me right then. I got away in kind of a hurry, and it taken her some time to get her thinking sorted out too, I expect. The banker, of course, told the story some different the first time, but he changed it later when he saw how the wind blew. He wasn't going to argue with a widow . . . not a *rich* widow.

Not knowing all this, and figuring they would keep

the telegraph wires hot all the way to the Rio Grande, me and Felipe kind of abused our horses in getting there. We didn't stop to rest till we was on the south side of the Bravo, drying the water out of our ears.

A man crossing the river for a day or a night's entertainment these days, he don't rightly appreciate how it was then. Going into Mexico wasn't something you done lightly or without good cause. Most of the *gringos* you found then was there because it was healthier than being someplace else, and not just because they chose it of their own free will. It was a nervous feeling to be in an alien country where they spoke a whole different language and where a man didn't know what the law was. You'll likely think that's funny, Joe Pepper worrying about obeying the law, but I always tried to. I never did hold with a man breaking the law without he had a good reason for it. I always had a good reason, or at least thought I did at the time. Once or twice, maybe, I might've erred a mite in my judgment. I was always in favor of the law as long as it didn't harm anybody.

I had a right smart of money in my saddlebags, and that was enough in itself to make a man nervous. You never know when you'll come across somebody dishonest. Some ways from the river we struck a road which Felipe said would lead us to a village ten or fifteen miles to the west. I got to thinking of all the things I'd heard about Mexican bandits and such, and of course I knowed there was many a Texas outlaw hanging out south of the Rio Grande. Them kind of people are apt to do a man harm for a lot less money than I had with me.

Along the way I kept looking around for landmarks that I would be able to remember. We came up finally to a place where the road made a bend around a motte of trees, and I thought I ought to be able to find it again. I rode on a little ways to where I didn't think Felipe would figure out the spot I had in mind, then I sent him on ahead while I doubled back. I paced out a spot due west of a certain forked tree and buried most of that money wrapped up in a slicker.

I didn't distrust Felipe, exactly, it was just that I didn't completely trust him, either. I never trusted *nobody* when it came to money, except maybe my mama and Millie Thompson. Probably that came from a time when I was a boy that my uncle gave me a silver dollar for helping him chop his cotton for four days, and my daddy taken and spent it on flour for the whole family. That was *my* dollar, not the family's.

I kept out a little traveling money so we wouldn't have no need to get lank or dry. After a while we came to this village Felipe knew about. I had a few minutes' worry as we met a bunch of soldiers guarding the road. They stopped us and asked questions about who we was and what we was doing there. Felipe answered for us—told the damnedest pack of lies you ever heard. He said later a man never wanted to tell the truth to a bunch of soldiers because they'll hold it against you.

It was a bigger town than I had expected from what Felipe had told me. It had growed a right smart since he had been there as a boy. The thing I noticed right off about it was the soldiers. You would of thought they was fixing to have a parade, they was so many. I never had paid any particular attention before to what was going on in Mexico. I didn't know they had their own war going on at the same time we was having that unpleasantness of ours between the states. It was a mixed-up deal. A bunch of Frenchmen had been in there muddying up the waters, but by this time they was out, and the Mexicans was fighting amongst theirselves over just who was supposed to be *in*. I never could get it straight in my mind just who was against who, because one time there would be a bunch who was friends, and the next time the same people was enemies and the people who had been their enemies was their friends, and ... well, you know how complicated life gets sometimes.

I tried not to get involved with it. I never did rightly understand what *our* war was about, so I sure didn't figure to mix into somebody else's. The longer I stayed there, though, the more I learned how hard it was to keep out of it. You couldn't stay on the fence. Somebody always had ahold of your leg, pulling to get you down.

People didn't seem to pay much attention to us when we rode in. They was used to *gringos* coming and going, and they didn't seem to get concerned about them as long as they brought money and didn't kill any of the local folks. During our War between the States there had been a good many Union sympathizers in Texas who found the climate kind of unhealthy at home and hightailed it across the river. After the war the traffic changed over ... there was Unionists going north and a lot of unreconstructed rebels going south, swapping places with one another. The ones that went south didn't know they was just leaving one war and wading up to their necks into another one.

And besides those that was in and out of Mexico on account of the war, there was always the plain-out fugitives, looking for a place where the long arm of the law was a little short in the reach. Some of them was outlaws and killers. Some was men like me ...

good men, you know, just a little down on their luck. For all I knew, every Ranger and sheriff and two-bit *pilón* constable in Texas was out hunting for me.

I had some little advantage in knowing the language. I had been around Mexicans a fair bit over the years and could understand the lingo if they didn't take to throwing any of that educated stuff at me. I could even talk back to them in pretty good fashion, enough that I wasn't going to starve to death because I didn't know how to say "beans." First thing a man learns in another language, if he's around the people that use it, is the cusswords. Give a man a fair vocabulary of cusswords and he'll get along.

We was tired and hungry and dry to the gizzard. We sure wasn't looking for no trouble. For once, trouble wasn't looking for us, either. We hitched in front of an adobe place where we could hear a guitar player and a fiddler, and some people laughing. We knowed we wasn't getting into no church, but it sounded friendly. We ordered us a bottle of *tequila* and some supper. Barman brought us the bottle; I had to ask him for glasses. Good thing you never seen what them glasses looked like, preacher, because you'd of never drank a drop. But them days I wasn't fussy, and besides, that Mexican *tequila* was strong enough to kill anything it touched that wasn't human. Anything human too, if taken in quantity.

We ordered up something to eat. I disremember exactly what it was; I just remember that they forgot to leave the fire at the stove. That Mexican cooking took a right smart of getting used to.

Afterwards, when we was working on the second bottle, I got to noticing how many *gringo* faces was coming in and going out. First thought I had was that some was probably spies for the Rangers and the other laws, but then I decided the hell with them, let them spy. As long as I didn't cross that river, I doubted they would come and get me. After I had studied on it a while, I decided most of the people was like me, they couldn't go back. Or wouldn't.

As Mexican towns went, it was a comfortable sort of a place. They didn't ask questions as long as you paid cash. Me and Felipe, we decided it was a good place to stay and rest awhile. His leg was still causing him a right smart of trouble. I hadn't made any plans as to what to do with myself. I had always thought I would enjoy just laying around someplace with nothing to do but play cards and drink whiskey and eat. I did, too, for the first few days. After that the days got to running forty-eight hours long. I was still young then. I hadn't learned patience.

In the back of my mind I had thought I would just sort of kill time there till I figured the law had put my case back in the warming oven, then I would dig up my money, cross the river and make my way west, maybe to Arizona or California. I sure didn't figure on setting down roots in Mexico. So we just laid around days, and nights we'd work our way from one *cantina* to another, trying to find one that had better liquor. None of them did, but the hunting gave us something to do.

I got to noticing how many gringos had taken up business of one sort or another, like *cantinas* and mercantile and that kind of thing. It began crossing my mind that maybe I ought to do the same. But I didn't know nothing about the mercantile trade, and all I knowed then about the saloon business was what I had learned from the front side of the bar, which is a damn bad place to learn anything.

Gradually I came to know that some of the boys

wasn't completely idle. One time there was half a dozen *gringos* whose acquaintance I had made that disappeared from sight for several days. They showed up again, finally, spending money like it was seawater and they was drunken sailors, scooping it out with both hands. Word filtered down about a big bank robbery in one of the Texas towns a ways up from the border. I played poker with some of them boys and won a fair part of their take and noticed a little bloodstain on some of the bills. Didn't seem to have no trouble cashing them at the bar, though. They was all negotiable.

I could've went with them boys on their little "trips" if I had of wanted to, but that wasn't my style of work. Being handy with the pasteboards, I could always get a good part of their money anyway without having to travel any farther than the gaming tables. That was safer than comparing marksmanship with some sharp-eyed Ranger, too.

By and by I got to feeling real restless, cooped up in town like I was, and sometimes I would take my good gray Tennessee horse and ride out over the country, just looking at it. Seemed to me like it ought to be good for ranching. There was some Mexican outfits, mostly owned by the big old rich *hacendados,* and some few that was owned by *gringos*. The way I was told, the best way for a *gringo* to operate was to take in some local Mexican as a partner. That made the deal set better with the other Mexicans, and they wasn't so apt to steal him blind. I had noticed a lot the same in regard to *gringos* who was in business in town. The most successful was the ones that had Mexican partners.

Looking at that land and the cattle on it made me start feeling a little homesick, which is a dangerous thing for a man on the dodge. It gets to giving him foolish notions about going back. I must of said something to somebody, when I was feeling the *tequila* a little, though I never could remember it afterwards. If I hadn't, that Orville Jackson never would of latched onto me.

Later on I figured it wasn't just chance that put Jackson into a poker game with me. But at the time it seemed like a natural thing that we sort of fell together. I figured from the first that he was on the up-and-up because his last name wasn't Smith, and his first name wasn't Bill or Jim. I figured nobody would just make up a name like Orville.

The way Jackson told it, he had been in business in Texas before the war, and his favor kind of stayed attached to the Union. After the war broke out, there was some people who felt so strong about it that they made it their business to roam around the countryside hanging Unionists, or people they thought might even have any inclinations toward the Union. Them same people are the kind that take prisoners out of the jail at night and lynch them but never have the guts to join a posse that goes out and catches them in the first place. They get real righteous, but they only kill when there ain't no danger in it.

Anyway, this Orville Jackson sold his property in something of a hurry and lit out for Mexico between two days.

Some of the Unionists who went to Mexico found ways to get to the North and fight us rebel boys, but Jackson didn't have that strong a feeling about the war. He looked around awhile and bought him some land in Mexico and built himself a ranch. He taken in a Mexican partner, naturally, and all in all he done right well for a *gringo*. But lately the partner had died

and there was a lot the partner's widow didn't understand about the ranch business. With the war long
since over, Jackson was kind of thinking he would
like to sell his ranch and go back to Texas. He figured
by now them old hanging parties was probably busy
licking the boots of the Yankee occupation soldiers
and selling them hay and oats and horses and whiskey and getting rich off of the Union. Which was correct, of course; that was exactly what they was doing.
Them kind of people was always changeable in their
politics.

Jackson didn't proposition me right off to buy the
place. I hadn't given him no reason that I remembered to think I had the money to buy it with. But he
had figured from looking at me that I knowed cows.
Once a man gets cow manure stuck to the bottom of
his boots, it don't ever all come off. We talked about
cattle a right smart, and I told him about me going up
the trail to Kansas. So he asked me if I would like to
go out and spend a few days at the ranch with him
and help him with the branding. He said he would
pay me for my time.

I figured I would make a lot more money at the
gaming tables, but I was hungry to get back out in
the country for a change. I told him I would go if
we could take Felipe with us. He didn't see nothing
wrong with that.

The morning we started out, things got a little excited in town for a while. We run into an agitated
bunch of the local citizens, running up toward the
local *calabozo*. They sort of swept us along. We got
there in time to see the soldiers bring out a bunch of
men—maybe seven or eight, including a couple that
couldn't of been more than just boys—and stand them
up against an adobe wall. The people was yelling and

cursing and begging, but the officer in charge seemed like a man who enjoyed his work. He lined up a firing squad and raised his sword and called off the signals.

Now, I've seen men die in battle more times than once, and I've seen them die other places. But I had never seen a firing squad before. Most everybody I had ever seen fall had a gun in his hand. Watching the soldiers stand them poor devils up there helpless and shoot them down like cattle at the slaughter . . . well, I tell you, my blood ran cold. It took half a bottle of *tequila* to burn the chill out of me.

Jackson didn't enjoy it either, but he said it was something a man had to pretend like he didn't see. Happened down there all the time, and a *gringo* just had to keep from taking sides or getting himself involved. Pretty soon he was talking about cattle again, but I kept seeing them people slammed back against that adobe wall with their blood leaking out.

We was half the day getting there. It wasn't nothing fancy, Jackson's place, just a kind of adobe headquarters and brush pens and the like. His wife that he had brought from Texas had died on him a good while back, and he was living with a good-looking Mexican woman. At this time he still hadn't made any move toward selling me the ranch, but I had already begun thinking about it. I got to wondering if he would throw that woman in on the deal if a man was to buy him out.

Don't look so shocked, preacher. My wife Millie had been dead for quite a while by that time. I had got to where I was watching them girls around the *cantinas* some, and they was looking better to me all the time. I don't suppose a man in your line of work ever gets them feelings, but a man in mine is subject to a lapse now and again, like the fever and the ague.

I've found that the best cure for temptation is generally to give in to it, get it over with, and then you can
turn your mind to other things. Long as you resist, it
keeps coming back at you and getting in the way of
your thinking.

As you get up toward the age where I'm at now, of
course, it don't bother you much. You get a lot more
of the fever and the ague.

Later on, remembering back, I come to realize that
Jackson must of sniffed it out somehow that I had
money, the same way he recognized that I knowed the
cow. He didn't really need no help from me for the
branding; he had more good Mexican *vaqueros*
than he needed. Mostly he just kept me with him and
showed me the good points about the place. He had
that good-looking woman bringing us something to
drink every time we was in the house. He didn't have
to be very smart to figure out that I enjoyed watching her go by.

I had been there three days before he throwed the
question at me. We was sitting in the house that night,
sipping at some good American whiskey. "What do
you think of it?" he asks me. The woman was walking away from us at the time. I told him I thought she
looked mighty good. He let me know he was talking
about the ranch, not about the woman. And he let
me know the whole deal was for sale. Including the
woman.

I remembered about his Mexican partner, and that
there was a widow. He said the partner was a partner on paper only, just for the satisfaction of local
politics, and that the widow didn't own but a token
share.

Not knowing the widow, I had my doubts. I was
afraid she might not be happy with the deal. She

could get me crossways with her countrymen and give me hell.

"But you *know* the widow," Jackson says, "and what's more, she likes you." He pointed with his chin toward the kitchen. "María there, she's my partner's widow."

After that he didn't have too hard a job selling me on the notion. His proposition sounded real good. Too good, in fact. I was suspicious of it at first. Nobody ever gives you anything in this life without they're trying to take something even bigger away from you. Bad as I wanted to, I couldn't see my way clear; the deal just sounded too good. But by and by I caught him lying about his calf crop. I had already seen enough of his tally books to know he couldn't have as many calves as he claimed.

Once I caught him trying to cheat me I felt better. If you can't find out where a man is trying to best you on a trade, you'd better steer clear of it.

The upshot was that we finally made a deal. I slipped off by myself, rode to where I had buried that money and dug it up.

I reckon I kind of expected Jackson to be a little sentimental about leaving the place after all of them years, but he must not of been. Or else it hurt him so much that he didn't want to stretch things out. We signed the papers in front of a magistrate in town, and he lit right out for the Rio Grande.

Felipe was my *majordomo,* sort of, though at first we had to leave things to the regular *vaqueros,* pretty much. They knowed the country, whereas me and Felipe had a lot to learn.

I hadn't been there more than two weeks before I learned why Orville Jackson had wanted to sell.

There was some four-legged wolves killing on the baby calves and some two-legged ones stealing on the grown cattle. A man could poison the four-legged ones, but the two-legged variety was a whole different proposition. I found out they was mainly of two varieties—the government soldiers on the one side and the local rebels on the other.

The one thing Orville Jackson had neglected to tell me was that he was serving as a sort of free commissary to both sides of the war.

In Texas there was always one quick and final remedy in a situation like this. If you caught a man stealing off of you, and you got the drop on him, you reformed him real quick. That way he didn't ever come back and trouble you again unless you was subject to bad dreams, which I never was. But this here was a lot more ticklish proposition. María pointed out to me that if I was to kill any soldiers they'd have me in front of that same adobe wall where I seen them citizens lined up. If I was to kill any of the citizens . . . well, all the adobe walls wasn't in town.

She said the best thing for me to do was to just accept that which couldn't be changed and go on the best I could. Keep the cows happy by putting out plenty of bulls on the range, she said, and hope they kept the calves coming faster than the thieves could steal them. I could pretty soon see it wasn't that easy. I was always a slow reader, but I'm apt with figures. I could tell without counting on my fingers that they was getting way ahead of me. Orville Jackson had left Mexico just in time.

Things really started closing in on me one day when I was up on the part of the ranch that fronted along the river. In a way that was my favorite part, and in another I hated it. I would go up to that river and look across and get to wanting so bad to go back to Texas that I couldn't hardly keep from spurring out into the water. But sometimes I could see people over there. I was satisfied in my own mind that they was all Rangers and sheriffs, camping over there waiting for me to do something foolish.

That particular day me and Felipe heard a sudden lot of shooting a mile or so upriver. Felipe's inclination was to head off in the opposite direction, which would of been smart, but I thought it was somebody killing my cattle. I told Felipe in a sharp way to come on and go with me. I didn't know exactly what I was going to do about it when I got there, but I figured it would come to me in due course. I generally found that when the time came, the idea came, too.

Felipe sure wasn't keen on it, which led me to wonder if maybe he didn't know more of what was going on than I did. We loped over a hill and seen a big clearing down there leading away from the river. There was maybe half a dozen men, dead and dying, scattered over that clearing, and some horses and packmules with them. We seen one man still laying down behind a packmule, firing a shot now and again at somebody over in the brush. By and by he ran out of ammunition. I seen some soldiers get up from that brush and walk out toward him. They was evidently hollering at each other, but me and Felipe was too far away to hear any of it. The man stood up with his hands in the air, and some more soldiers came out of the brush. There was one with them wearing a bright-colored uniform, and I knew right off he was an officer of some kind. He was giving orders. The soldiers scattered out, checking all the dead and wounded men and animals. The officer walked up to that prisoner, talked to him a minute, then pulled out a pistol and shot him in the head.

He hollered something at the soldiers, and they shot two more men that was only wounded, so that they wasn't just wounded anymore.

"Let's go," says Felipe. "It isn't healthy here."

Right about then they spotted us. I began to feel like Felipe was smarter than I used to give him credit for. I wished he had been a better persuader. The officer pointed in our direction, and I knowed it was too late to run. Some of the soldiers spurred up to us.

The only thing left for us to do was to stand our ground and try to talk ourselves out of trouble, seeing as it wasn't none of our business to start with. It wasn't none of mine, anyway, but I could tell right off that Felipe considered it his. While he waited he cussed the soldiers and called them a lot of things that didn't fit comfortable on the ear. I had taken great pains not to choose up sides, but being of the blood, I reckon Felipe couldn't help it. He might as easy of taken the other side, but he didn't.

I don't suppose you ever had occasion to look at the business end of a dozen rifles, preacher, I tell you, the muzzle looks as big around as a number-four washtub. Them soldiers invited us to go down with them for a conference with the *capitán,* and we accepted the invitation.

When we got down into the clearing I could tell real easy what the excitement was about. They had taken the packs off of them dead mules, and they was full of rifles and ammunition. Them citizens they had ambushed had just swum across the river from the Texas side with a bunch of U.S. Army goods for the rebels. Now, I'm sure the U.S. Army hadn't *given* them all that weaponry. There was a bunch of them unreconstructed

Confederates on the Texas side, though, that would cheerfully burglarize an armory and sell for gold to any and all comers.

I couldn't figure out at first why they had tried to cross the Rio Grande in the daylight instead of in the dark. Then I noticed one civilian amongst the soldiers and seen the *capitán* give him a handful of silver. It didn't take even a *gringo* long to figure out that these boys had been betrayed. The betrayer didn't wait around to count his money; he acted like he had a whole hive of bees in his britches.

I seen the way Felipe looked at him. I figured if we got out of this mess with our skin still on tight, and Felipe ever crossed trails with that Judas, there was going to be a little knifework done.

The *capitán* taken his slow, sweet time in getting around to us. He was like a cat playing with a mouse that ain't ever really going to go nowhere. He just gave Felipe a glance, but he stared at me a long time like a man who enjoys his work. "A *gringo*," he says, real pleased with himself. "I am Captain Tiburcio Santos. You would be, I believe, the Señor Peeler."

I told him he sure was right, that I was Joe Peeler. That was my real name, you remember.

He had a grin wider than the wave on a slop jar, only it wasn't at all funny. "And what reason, Señor Peeler, can you think of why we should not shoot you right here and leave you lying dead among your friends?"

Well, sir, I could think of a hundred good reasons, and ninety-nine of them was that I was too young to die. I didn't think that would impress him much, so I told him the other one. "Because these was no friends of mine. I never seen them in my whole life till just now."

He says, "I find that hard to believe. Convince me."

I didn't waste no time in the telling, how come me and Felipe to be here, how we had heard the shooting and had come to investigate because this was my ranch, and because I figured anything which happened on it was of more than just passing interest to me. I told him these citizens—whoever they was—was trespassers on private land.

Pretty soon I got to feeling like he knowed it all the time, that he was just playing with me because he liked to watch me sweat. And I was doing plenty of that. There was a sergeant sitting on his horse beside the captain, and he had his pistol pointed straight at me, and his finger was twitching. All he was waiting for was the word.

The captain said he thought it would be natural for me—being the owner of the land—to take a bribe or a *mordida* to let these louse-ridden, dirty rebels smuggle arms across it to fight against the freedom-loving, legally constituted authorities. I had to keep telling him that I wasn't in no way mixed up in their Mexican politics, that I was a peaceful, law-abiding man who had just bought this place and was trying in my own awkward way to make a decent living out of it.

It gradually soaked in on me that if I had really been part of the smuggling setup, he'd of known it through the Judas. He was just fishing around for a payoff. The *mordida* is a kind of a hidden tax that everybody pays. A little man pays a little *mordida* to a little official for little favors. A big man pays a big *mordida* to a big official for big favors. For me and Felipe to ride away from here without any surplus holes in us was going to be considered a big favor.

It never was in my nature to bow and scrape and

make myself little, not unless it was for a good cause. This was for a good cause.

I tells that captain, "I'm sorry if you or any of your men have come to any danger or harm on my land. And although I am in no way responsible for this, I would be glad to have you-all take a few steers back to town with you for the benefit of all your company."

The captain said he could take *all* the cattle and leave me and Felipe dead, if that was his inclination. I told him I realized he could but hoped he would see fit to take the gift as my guest . . . my *honored* guest. I damn near gagged.

The captain sprung his trap then. He says, "I had some conversations with the previous owner of this ranch and thought I had completed an arrangement with him. Now I must start over with you. It appears to me that what you need is a Mexican partner."

I told him I already had a Mexican partner.

"A woman." He kind of snickered. "I know all about that. What you need is a *strong* partner, one who has influence in the right places. One who has power at his command. One who someday will perhaps even be governor, *quién sabe?* In the right hands this property of yours could become a highway of commerce with those on the other side of the river."

I knowed what he meant by that. It would be a handy place to bring cattle stolen from the Texas side of the Rio Grande. That thought had already occurred to me.

I knowed then why he hadn't already shot me.

I says, "I'll have to think about it some." The longer he gave me to think about it, the longer my health would hold up.

He says, "You think, but be sure you think right. A partner in the right position could make you a wealthy man. An enemy in the right position could bring you ruin . . . and death. So think about it, Señor Peeler, until we meet each other again."

I couldn't decide right then who I was the maddest at, him or Orville Jackson. That was why Jackson had wanted to unload this place on me; he was fixing to get himself a new Mexican partner that wouldn't fit in his bed. Now Jackson was on the right side of the river, singing happy songs to himself and counting my money, and here I sat face to face with a brazen thief who was about to clean my plow.

The soldiers gathered up all the arms and ammunition including me and Felipe's guns. After they was out of earshot, Felipe commenced calling them bloody butchers and swine and such other endearments. I told him none of this was our fight and we'd better stay out of it. Didn't seem like he heard me, and anyway, we *was* mixed up in it already. I told him finally that it might be a cagy move on our part if we was to put the spurs to our horses and leave this locality. If any of them rebel citizens was to come along and find us here amongst their dead friends and kin, they might get the wrong idea and do us bodily harm.

Felipe understood those citizens pretty good. We left there in a lope, him taking the lead.

María was some upset when we told her that night. She seemed to be more sorely afflicted by the fact that the packtrain got ambushed than she was over me and Felipe having ourselves a narrow escape. By and by I found myself sitting at the table all alone. I got up and went to the kitchen for a cup of coffee and found María and Felipe in a real serious discussion. I pulled back so they wouldn't see me. My first thought was that Felipe was getting some partnership rights that I hadn't intended to give him. Directly I seen him and her go out together to one of the brush *jacales* where the *vaqueros* stayed. They talked to the *vaqueros* a while. Finally one of them went to the barn, saddled a horse and rode off in the night.

It gradually came to me that there was a lot more to María than Jackson had told me. Probably more than he knowed.

I can't say I ever entertained any real hopes of getting to be a big cowman in Mexico, but in my idle moments I sometimes let myself dream a little. It was the kind of dream some of them Mexican boys get from smoking that funny weed in their cigarettes. But it's a hard go being a cowman. Even when everything goes right, it's hard to make ends meet. And when you're trying to operate in a country where they're fighting a war across your land, and the only time they ever stop is to go fill up their bellies on your beef, well sir, you *have* got complications. They didn't just pick the big steers to butcher. Times I'd come across a calf bawling for milk and would find its mammy laying there with both of her hind quarters gone. A man can afford to lose the steers sometimes, but the cow is the factory.

I'd come in at night cussing about it, and María would always take the rebels' part.

"They are fighting for what is good and just," she would always say.

They probably thought they was. But I've watched them kinds of fights off and on for a good many years, and it always seems like somebody gets at the head of it sooner or later and turns everybody else's dying into a personal gain for himself. You show me a hero, preacher, and I'll show you a damn fool who is being used for somebody else's profit.

I would get so mad at María that I would almost

put her out of the house. But never quite. I had a notion that she would find all the sympathy she needed from Felipe.

I quit going to town unless I was forced to it, and then I would try to go in at night, do whatever I had to and get out. Sooner or later I knowed I was going to have to face that Captain Santos again, and I wanted to put it off as long as I could. If he made up his mind to declare himself in as my partner, I knowed I would have a hard time stopping him. He had the whole local military contingent to back him up, and all I had was a little bunch of *vaqueros* that didn't really owe me anything.

Of course I could do what I had done to Jesse Ordway; I could just shoot him. But I wouldn't live to see the sunrise.

I wasn't sure this Mexico ranch was worth dying for. Not *me* dying for, anyway.

Did you ever get yourself into a mess of fleas, to where you didn't know which spot to scratch first? Where you itched in a dozen places and had only two hands to scratch with?

That was the shape they had me in. I'd find out somebody was running off cattle on the south end of the place, and I'd ride down there as fast as I could go. While I was gone, some more would hit the north end. Sometimes it was the rebels, sometimes the soldiers from town. I can't say they was overgreedy; they just taken a few here and a few there. But you can finally empty a well with a teacup if you dip fast enough.

The whole thing come to a head one day just by pure luck ... *bad* luck, as it turned out. I heard some cows bawling and rode up on a bunch of them rebel citizens driving off twelve or fifteen head. They was taking the cows and trying to leave the calves behind so they could travel faster. If you know anything about cattle you know it ain't in an old cow's nature to go off and leave her calf behind without she puts up a devil of a struggle over it.

I don't know what I figured I could do about it, seeing as they had me pretty badly outnumbered, but I was so mad I rode down there anyway. I wasn't so mad as to be stupid, though. I didn't put my gun on them. A couple or three had their guns on *me*. There was seven or eight of them, a lot of people for such a small bunch of cattle.

I picked out the one I figured was the leader. I told him in the nicest way I knowed how that I considered him a lowdown sneak thief and a cross between a rattlesnake and a coyote. He was a fiery-eyed young gent of about Felipe's general size and age. I never thought about it then, but later I got to wondering if they might of been kin, seeing as Felipe had taken to such strong feelings about the rebels. That *hombre* just sat there and looked at me while I talked to him. His eyes crackled like dry brush on fire. When I had run down a little, he set in on me.

"These cattle are of Mexico," he says, "and you are a *gringo*. By what right do you claim cattle in Mexico?"

"By right of money," I says. "I bought these cattle and this ranch fair and square with good old American green-back money." I've never been noplace in my life where money didn't talk louder than the law, if there was enough of it.

"Stolen money, no doubt," says he. "Or money made from the sweat and blood of poor Mexicans you *Tejanos* have enslaved."

Me, I never had enslaved nobody, black, white or

brown, and I damn well told him so. But you ought to know how them fanatic types are, preacher, since the worst fanatics in the world are in the field of religion. They don't hear nothing except their own voices, and they think it's the voice of God.

He gave me a lecture on heaven and hell and the rights of the down-trodden and the greed of the rich, and all that. Later on, when I was in a better mood to ponder on it, I almost laughed. Why, he considered me *rich*. I reckon a man with a patched shirt looks rich to the one that's got no shirt atall.

Since he seen fit to bring religion into it, I tried to give him a lecture about that commandment which says "Thou shalt not steal." He acted like he thought I was trying to change the subject on him. He didn't see it as stealing to take something off of a rich *gringo,* especially when it was going to feed the poor and the rebellious.

It was pretty much of a standoff. I wasn't going to convince him, and it would've been suicidal to of tried to shoot him. I should of gone off and left them in possession, but that went against all my training. So I stayed and argued with them whilst they kept on driving my cattle away. I was just wasting my time. I wasn't any more to them than a gnat buzzing around a horse's rump.

Turned out that I stayed a little too long. All of a sudden there was the biggest bunch of shooting you ever heard, and bullets flying around and horses squealing and pitching. For a minute I thought maybe it was a bunch of my *vaqueros* come to my rescue, but I disabused myself of that notion when I seen the uniforms. It was the soldiers, ambushing this bunch of cowstealing rebels.

I can't say a lot for their marksmanship, because

most of the rebels got clean away. They rode like they was all married men, getting back to the bosom of their families. I decided it might be smart if I went home too. But I didn't get very far. One of them soldiers got off a lucky shot, and that was the end of my good old Tennessee gray horse that I had brought home from the big war I ate a bucketful of pure old Mexican dirt and had a little trouble getting my breath started again. Time I was able to get on my feet, there didn't seem to be much use in it. A bunch of them soldiers had me surrounded, and it was like it had been that day me and Felipe stumbled onto the ambush of the gunrunners.

Captain Santos wasn't with them this time, which I thought at first was some improvement. But his sergeant was there, the one with the itchy trigger finger. I figured I'd try to put the best face on a bad situation. I thanked him for rescuing me from that bunch of cattle thieves.

You know something? He didn't believe a bit of that.

One of the men tickled me in the ribs with the muzzle of his rifle. The sergeant motioned for me to get to my feet, *pronto*. I didn't see where it would help my situation to argue with him. They searched me and taken away the pistol I had on. That was the second time they had taken guns away from me. Seemed like they was determined not only to make me feed their army but to equip it with artillery. One of the men taken my pocketwatch, the one with Millie's picture in the back. I grabbed at it and got a gunbutt up beside my head. I ate another bucketful of dirt.

When my eyes cleared to where I could see, that sergeant had my watch open, listening to the little tune it played and looking at Millie's picture. He made some comment about her that I'd of been pleased to kill a man for if the circumstances had been more favorable. But I was at a considerable disadvantage at the time. I could feel the blood running down the side of my face, hot and sticky. I had a headache that would of set a mule on its haunches.

"This time," the sergeant says, "we have caught you redhanded, *gringo,* working with those damned rebels."

I had already argued myself out, trying to make that rebel see my side of it. I didn't have it left in me to argue with this sergeant. I expected them to shoot me right where I sat. I hurt so bad that it would of been merciful. But mercy didn't have no part in his thinking.

"*El capitán* will be most pleased to see you, *gringo,*" says he. "Especially when I tell him the company you keep."

I don't suppose you ever had your head cracked with a gunbutt? It makes it awful hard to concentrate. Just getting on the horse was a chore. Mine was dead, but they brought up one which a rebel wasn't going to need anymore. I couldn't tell what color it was, hardly. I fell off once. The sergeant tied a short piece of rope around my neck and the other end to the saddlehorn, and told me that the next time I fell off I would hang myself. That helped my concentration some.

It was way after dark when we finally got into town. The fiddles and the guitars was playing in the *cantinas,* but I didn't enjoy the music. They drug me through some big tall wooden doors into a *patio* of some kind, and across to a cell which had a wooden door that must of weighed five hundred pounds. They throwed me in there and locked the door and left.

I laid there a long time waiting for my head to quit hurting, but it never did. It was too dark to see anything, so I asked if there was anybody with me, and I found out I had the whole thing to myself. I felt around and found a goatskin, which was all the bed they provided. The way I felt right then, a feather tick wouldn't of helped. I can't say I slept much. My head hurt like thunder, and I found out I wasn't as alone in that cell as I thought I was. Little crawling and running things was in there with me. They must of liked the place because they didn't seem to be making any great effort to get out. They was just trying to be friendly, especially the lice.

There wasn't no window in the cell, but come morning I could see light start to seep around the edges of that heavy wooden door. The walls was of adobe. It appeared to me I could probably cut my way through them if I had plenty of time and something to scratch with. But that could turn into a lifetime proposition. Walls like that was often three feet thick. And when a man got through one, chances was he would find himself in another cell like the one he had crawled out of. I doubted they figured on keeping me around long enough for me to find out.

They didn't seem to figure I needed any breakfast; leastways they neglected to bring it. My head hurt me a lot worse than my stomach did, anyway. I'd been looking at the daylight around that door for a long time before finally I heard somebody thumping around out there, fiddling with the bolt. The light hurt my eyes when they swung the door in, but I got used to it in a minute. There stood that sergeant with a mean black whip in his hand, and right behind him was Captain Santos.

"Señor Peeler," Santos says, kind of smug and satisfied with himself, "I hope you slept well."

Now, that rankled me a little because I knowed he didn't care whether I'd got any sleep or not. I changed the subject considerable and tried to give him some idea what kind of a son of a bitch—pardon me, preacher—I thought he really was. The sergeant commenced a little persuasion with the whip.

It was the first time anybody had taken a whip to me in my life, if you don't count the times my daddy taken a quirt to my rosy little cheeks when I was a button. This wasn't no quirt, it was one of them old blacksnakes like they use down there to drive bulls into the ring. It had a bite like something out of hell. I rolled over to get away from it, bumped my sore head on the hard dirt floor and come near fainting.

I heard the captain say, "Enough, Sergeant. I think he understands you."

I understood *both* of them. I had very little hope right then that I would ever get out of that place alive.

The captain says, "So this time you were caught, Señor Peeler, helping those people drive away cattle to feed their accursed rebel camps."

I thought I ought to tell him once, whether he believed me or not, so I says, "I caught them taking my cattle. I was trying to stop them." I was wasting my breath, and there wasn't much of it to spare.

The captain says, "Why weren't they dead, then, some of them? And why aren't *you* dead? If you had really tried to stop them you would have killed some of them, and they would have killed you. You lie, *gringo*. Sergeant, show him what we think of *gringos* who lie to us."

There was nothing I could do but curl up in a ball

and take it, and try to think up all the slow and brutal ways I could kill them both, if ever I got the chance. With all due respect to your profession, preacher, these sky pilots that get up and preach against hate don't know what they're talking about. They don't know how good it can make a man feel to hate under the right circumstances. I've knowed times when hate was all that kept a man alive.

The sergeant finally quit whipping me. Santos says, "Are you ready to admit your guilt?"

I gave him some advice, which he didn't take, and the sergeant whipped me again. Then he left, and it was just me and the captain in there by ourselves. I figured up my chances of killing him before the rest of them could kill me. They wasn't much good. I was so weak I probably couldn't of made his nose bleed. He must of read my mind, because he reminded me that he had a whole squad of men just outside the door, and they would leave me looking like a milk strainer if I made one wrong move.

"I am sorry about this," says he. "I looked forward to being a partner with you."

"Go to hell," says I.

That didn't seem to bother him much this time. The shape he had me in, I can see why he was getting more tolerant. He says, "No, we can't be partners anymore. I am going to buy you out."

That sounded a little strange to me, him talking about *buying*. Looked to me like all he had to do was *take*.

I told him I wasn't selling, but he told me I would; it was just a question of *when*. He asked me if I was hungry. I told him I was. He said that sure was too bad, because I wouldn't get nothing to eat until I decided to sell out, or until there was snow three feet deep out there in the *patio*. And that wasn't no snow country.

The steel bolt sounded like a gunshot when they locked that door shut on me again and left me in there with the rats and the cockroaches and the lice. Off and on all day I could hear people shuffling around outside, but that door never opened again. Finally I watched the light fade from around it and knowed it was nighttime. That goatskin felt a little better; I slept a right smart. My head quit hurting, but my stomach got to raising Cain with me. I had done without anything to eat a good many times before, but I never had got to where I could get along without noticing it like some people seem to. I'd rather face up to a posse of deputy sheriffs than to put up with an empty stomach.

The light gradually come around the door again, so I knowed it was daytime. I got to listening for them to come, but they didn't. I drawed up my belt as tight as I could. People tell you that'll help, but I'm here to inform you otherwise. There's no substitute for a square meal.

I judged it was along about the middle of the day before finally I heard them working that bolt. I shut my eyes, because the light was going to hurt. The captain came in, him and the sergeant. The sergeant was carrying his old friend the blacksnake. My back was all sore and welted from the treatment he had already given me. I could feel my flesh crawl when I looked at that whip.

Santos had some papers in his hand. Says he, "I have been to a lawyer, and he has drawn up these papers for me." He handed me something all written out in a nice hand, and punched with a fancy seal.

It was all in Mexican. I could talk Mexican fair to middling and understand it when they talked, but I couldn't read their writing much. I handed it back to him and told him I didn't know what it was. He said it was a deed to the ranch. He reached in his shirt and pulled out a little leather bag with a puckerstring drawed up tight. He shook it so I could hear the rattle of coin.

"Gold," says he. "This gold and your freedom when you sign this deed."

For a minute I was sore tempted. I says, "And how about something to eat?"

"When you sign," says he.

I had no way to know how much gold he had in that sack. It probably wasn't nowhere near what I had paid Orville Jackson, but right then I was a whole lot more concerned with getting away than I was with the money. I was on the point of telling him yes when my thinking got to running a little straighter. All of a sudden it come to me that once he had my name on that paper, he could do anything he wanted to with me. He could kill me and take that gold back. If I was in his place, that's what I would of done.

If I signed that paper I was a dead man.

I never was one to beat around the bush, so I told him just the way my mind was running. It made him mad that I could see through him, I reckon, because he said something sharp to the sergeant and walked out. The sergeant went to work on me with that whip to where I quit worrying about my empty stomach.

That was the last I seen of them that day. Night come, and I sat there all huddled up on the goatskin doing a lot of thinking. Two whole days and a bit of another they had had me in there without a thing to eat. You can't imagine how one of them tight little cells gets to smelling, either, especially when nature calls and you got noplace else to go. I tell you, I was sure down in my thinking.

I didn't know how things went by Mexican law, but I knowed by American law I didn't have no legal right to sign away the whole ranch, just my own share in the partnership. Exactly how much of a share María owned had never been straight in my mind; it was maybe ten percent, or something like that—whatever her husband had to make it look right to the Mexicans. That was a technicality, and I never was no hand at technicalities.

One thing bothered me. If all they needed was my signature, why didn't they just forge it? Then they could shoot me and drag me off to the buzzards. I sure wasn't going to raise up from the dead and contest them. I wondered, but I had sense enough not to ask them; maybe they just hadn't thought of it.

Gradually I realized that in the end Santos was going to get my signature. But the longer I could hold it away from him the more chance I had to see another sunrise. When you're that close to the taw line, you realize that even living in a dark smelly cell is better than dying.

They didn't wait till noon the next time; they was there early, Santos and the sergeant, and a detail of men that stayed outside.

Under ordinary circumstances when you get into a negotiation in Mexico you'll find it takes a long time. They'll visit and talk about everything but the business at hand. When it finally comes into the conversation it's real casual, like something that just popped into their minds that minute and ain't important anyway.

Santos wasn't like that. Right off he says, "You ready to sign?"

I asks him, "How much gold you got in that sack?"

He says it don't matter, it's more than I deserve. I says, "I want more, a lot more." The sergeant moved up with his whip, but the captain says, "*Bueno*, you can have more."

Says I, "You fill that sack to where you can't cram no more into it and still draw the string tight."

The captain said all right, he would. No argument. Right then I knowed all my suspicions was right. He would pay me anything he had to because he was going to take it back off of my dead body anyway. Same as Jesse Ordway had figured. From his standpoint a man couldn't hardly beat a deal like that.

Santos waved the deed at me.

My hand was shaking, I was so weak from not having anything to eat. I told him I couldn't write my name in that kind of shape, that I was in bad need of nourishment. And I told him I couldn't eat it here in this place because it smelled so bad.

He thought he had me beat, so all of a sudden there wasn't nothing too good for me. He says to come on, he'll take me to his quarters and have some food brought to me. He led me out of that cell, and I made up my mind right then and there that I wasn't ever going back into it. I still held a few cards in my hand. I was going to play them out one at a time and as careful as I could.

Walking was a chore at first. I had been sitting or laying down in that cell for most of three days and hadn't gotten to exercise my legs.

I doubt that they fed their other condemned men as well as they fed me, but of course they wasn't trying to get as much from them. I had me some *tortillas* and some eggs and *cabrito* and black coffee, and I topped it all off with a long drink of *tequila,* which was of a pretty fair grade. He was a captain and could afford better than most of the *peons* and the convict soldiers. I had eaten till I had filled out every wrinkle in my belly and even hurt a little bit.

I always agreed with the Indians on one point: when you can eat, *eat!* You can't ever be sure when your next meal is coming.

A couple of good-looking young women cleared off the table. The captain pinched one of them twice, fore and aft. He was feeling pretty good about then. He had had a little snort of *tequila* himself. She slapped his hand, kind of gentle. I figured she was one woman whose work was never done.

The captain brought out the deed again, and he says, "Is your hand steady enough now to sign?"

I had played one card and got my belly filled. Now I played me another. I says, "In my own good time, Captain. You promised to fill up that sack with gold."

He walked over to the bed and got down on his knees and pulled out a strongbox. It had a Texas bank name on it, and I could well imagine how I come into possession. It had a padlock that could of been used for a leg iron. When he swung the lid open, he taken a big canvas bag out and opened it to get some more coins. Soon as I seen their gold color my natural ambition came to the front. I says, "That's all right, just let me have the whole bag."

He chided me some about the sin of greed, but I didn't figure he qualified as no preacher. Finally he brought that whole canvas bag over and laid it on the table. Oh, but it had a fine solid sound to it. The ring of gold and silver pieces was always my favorite kind of music.

"Now," he says, "sign."

I picked up the bags one at a time, the little leather

one first and then the big canvas sack. I had no way of knowing how much real money they held, but I sure liked the heft of them. The liking must of showed, and he thought he had set the hook for sure. He pushed the deed in my face.

Says I, "*Capitán,* it occurs to me that when I sign this deed you'll have all you want from me. You could take me out to that adobe wall and be shed of me good and proper. You'd have all this gold back and my ranch besides. I wouldn't be very smart to get into that shape."

The sergeant stepped up and volunteered to wear a little more shine off of that blacksnake. For a minute it looked like the captain was fixing to let him; his face went as dark as old shoe leather. Him and the sergeant went off in a corner and had theirselves a whispering conference. Directly the captain came back. He says in a hard voice, "Just what is it you want?"

I told him I wanted to go to the Rio Grande.

He drawed his pistol and cocked it and shoved it in my face. "*Gringo,*" says he, "I would not have to take you to the wall. I could shoot you right here and splatter your brains all over this floor. I could have your carcass dragged off to the brush like a mongrel dog."

He didn't have to tell me that; I already knowed it. Says I, "That's why I want to be safe at the river before I sign."

He cussed me for a double-crossing hound who had eaten his food and drunk his *tequila,* then refused to honor my word. I told him he still had my word. I would sign the deed. But I would do it when I was safe at the river. Signing it now, I says, I'd be dead in ten minutes.

Him and the sergeant had another conference over in the corner, a little louder this time. I could hear most of it. I heard the sergeant suggesting what I had already thought of, that they just shoot me and forge my name. But the captain said they had to handle this so that dog of a magistrate would accept it. The magistrate was a man with a gavel where his heart should be. He had no woman, and he slept with his lawbooks instead. He was a stickler for observing the last fine point of the law and was rich enough that he did not need to take the *mordida*. Worse, he was kin of the governor, so they didn't dare force him. Worst of all, he knowed my face and he knowed my signature. I had signed it in front of him when I bought the ranch.

The captain never would of made a poker player. I could read his face when he came back. He had decided to give me what I asked for. They probably figured they could still kill me at the river and get the gold back after I had signed the paper. But he had to try one more time.

He says, "*Gringo*, you ask for too much."

"It ain't much of a ride from here to the river," says I. "You want the ranch, and I want a sporting chance to live."

He gave in finally, like I knowed he would, though it killed his soul to bend so much for a lousy *gringo*. He sent the sergeant out, and in a little while he was back and said everything was ready. They had a detail of half a dozen men waiting outside of the office on horseback. They had throwed my saddle on a sorry plug that couldn't of outrun the rest of them if they had all had one leg broke.

I told the captain there was one more thing I wanted, my watch with Millie's picture in it. The sergeant had it, and it tore him plumb up to give it to me. He opened the case and let it play its little tune before he would turn it over. I reckon he was afraid it would get shot to pieces when they finished me off.

I didn't know exactly what I was going to do when I got to the river. I figured the only real chance I had was to make a wild sashay and jump into the water before they could stop me. Naturally they would shoot at me every time I came up for air, but I would just have to try not to breathe much. I had already seen that they wasn't very good shots.

It bothered me about the gold. I couldn't swim across with that big sack; it would take me under. But maybe that little bag wouldn't hurt. I says to the captain, "Been thinking I'd sure like to carry the gold."

He looks at me like I'm crazy and says, "You have not signed yet. You get the money when you sign."

"The little bag at least," I says. "Just let me enjoy the feel of it."

He handed it to me. Maybe he felt like it would keep my greed fired up and I wouldn't give him no more trouble about the deed. I kept feeling the gold, which I knowed was what he wanted me to do. The seat of my britches was all itchy from wanting to get this over with, from wanting to get away from them. But I did enjoy the smell of the good clean air. It was the first time I'd been out in the open in three days.

The captain made it a point for us to ride by the government house and to call out the magistrate so he could see me with his own eyes. He told him we was all on our way down to the office of the lawyer to sign some papers. I spoke up to invite the magistrate to go along with us, but the sergeant stuck a pistol in my back where the magistrate couldn't see it, and I had to give up on hospitality.

There wasn't no bridges over the river in them days, nowhere on the whole Rio Grande. There wasn't even a ferry at this point. There was just a place about fifty yards wide that you could swim a horse across. Wagons and carts and such had to go down the river a long ways to where there was a little cable-operated ferry.

Texas looked pretty good to me, laying over yonder across that little stream of muddy water. Sure, the law was hunting for me over there, or at least I thought they was. But looking across, I couldn't see a sign of anybody on the other side. I didn't hardly expect that there would be somebody come over and help me out of the predicament I was in.

The captain was getting awful impatient. He turns to me and says, "Here we are, just the way we promised you. Now, the deed . . ."

I had kept edging to the front, getting as near to the river as I could for my big break. But that sergeant outguessed me. He rode in close and taken the reins of that sorry plug I was on. If I ran for the river now I was going to have to do it afoot. I sort of measured the sergeant with my eye, figuring how to climb right over him.

I says to the captain, "Do I have your word that when I sign, I can cross the river and you won't shoot me in the back?"

You ever see a rattlesnake curl his lips back? That's the kind of smile the captain gave me. "You have my word. The word of an officer and a gentleman."

He was lying like a candidate. The soldiers began to back their horses away and form up a line. I knowed what was coming to me the minute I signed that paper. I had got to the river all right, but I was never going to cross it.

One word you never want to say is *never*. All of a sudden the whole thing was taken out of his hands.

There come, in the wink of an eye, a volley of guns like the Fourth of July. For a sorry old plug like he was, that horse of mine must of jumped four feet straight up. The sergeant fell off with his face all bloody and hit the sand and just laid there. His horse taken out in a panic and swam across the river. I finally got my spooked plug under control and looked around and seen half of them soldiers down just like the sergeant was. The rest of them was running off, all but the captain. He just sat there looking sort of foolish and drained out.

Down to the riverbank came a dozen or so ragged-looking Mexicans with guns smoking in their hands. I didn't know the faces, but I sure knowed the type. They was a bunch of them cattle-stealing rebels. Directly I seen a friendly face coming. At least, I thought it was friendly. Felipe Rios rode down to where me and the captain was. With him was that rebel leader that I'd had such a cuss fight with over them running my cattle off.

I was never more glad to see a Mexican in my life, hardly. I says, "Felipe, you sure have a way of turning up when a man needs you."

The captain just looked at them and swallowed. He still held the deed in his hand. I noticed that the hand was trembling a right smart. He says, "I was about to release this man." Which was true; he was about to release me from all worldly cares. Felipe reached up and jerked the deed away from him, looked at it and handed it to the leader. I remembered then that Felipe couldn't read. But that rebel could.

Now that I seen the two of them together, the resemblance was considerable. I would of bet they was first cousins, at least.

That rebel studied the paper and knowed in a minute what this whole thing was about. Says he, "*Gringo,* we thought they were simply going to take you out and kill you. But it appears there was more."

I ought to've knowed not to talk so much, but I was so glad to see them that I had no caution. I told them what Santos had figured on doing, and what I was planning to try to do.

He didn't look a bit pleased. He says, "You would have turned your property over to this butcher to save your own neck?"

I told him it was the only neck I had, and the property wouldn't of helped me much if I was dead.

He looked at the canvas sack on the captain's saddle. "You were going to sell it to him for money. That is like a *gringo.*"

Where I came from it was always customary to sell things for money. It was the best medium of exchange anybody had ever come up with. But I got a strong feeling that I wasn't in no position to argue details. I wasn't in no position to argue *anything.* The look in his eyes told me I'd better do a lot of listening.

He filled my ear with a lot of stuff about how they was fighting to stop oppression and bury the butchers like Santos and so forth, and about how hard it was for them to understand a *gringo* whose only interest was in money when there was people bleeding and dying all around.

The only ones I could see bleeding and dying right then was Santos's soldiers. They was in a bad way, the ones that hadn't gotten clear. I wouldn't of given a well-used chaw of tobacco for Santos's chances of leaving that riverbank alive, either. I think the only question they had about him was whether to slit his throat from the left or from the right. And he knowed it, too, because his face was drained from a nice brown down to about a *gringo* color.

The rebel shoved the deed back at me and says, "You were going to sign it for him. Sign it for me!"

I looked at Felipe. He wasn't going to be no help this time, I could tell. All his sympathy was with them others. We had come to the parting of the ways. I reached up and taken a lead pencil out of Santos's pocket, one he had brought for that purpose, only things hadn't turned in quite the direction he had intended. I signed the deed and handed it to the rebel. I asks, "Who gets the ranch?"

Felipe says, "María."

I couldn't argue much with that. It seemed proper, since she had been a partner in it anyway.

I says, "And who gets María?"

Felipe says, "I do."

I figured he already had, maybe even while Jackson was still there. Well, that meant he would get the ranch too, which was better than having it go to Santos. Or to that rebel leader, who didn't look much like a cowboy to me noway. He had that wild eye you see in people who are always going around over creation looking for something to raise hell about.

I reached to get the canvas bag of gold off of Santos's saddle. "That belongs to me," I says.

The rebel clamped his hand over mine. He says, "No! You have just given it to our cause. We have use for it."

He started telling me again about their great crusade, and about all the hungry and shirtless and barefoot ones, and I knowed damn well there wouldn't none of them ever see any of this money. It's always been my observation that the feller who hollers loudest about helping the downtrodden poor is usually counting himself at the head of the list. Soon as he gets his hands on some money of his own, the poor don't look near as hungry to him anymore.

I told him it didn't hardly seem right to leave me without a thing to show for all my trouble. I was giving up my ranch; I ought to have *something*.

They didn't know about that little bag of gold in my shirt.

"You have your life, *gringo*," he says. "It is not worth much, but it is more than Santos was going to give you. Now go, before we take that too!"

Everybody's eyes was on me right at that minute. Santos taken what little chance he had. He jabbed his spurs into that horse and jumped him off into the water as hard as he could run, taking gold and all. He caught them rebels by surprise. When they finally started shooting at him, he slid out of the saddle to make less of a target. Somewhere out there he got separated from the horse and had to try to swim by himself. I don't know if a bullet caught him, or if his clothes pulled him down, or if he just plain couldn't swim. In a minute or two there wasn't no sign of him anyplace. He was gone, under that muddy water. Next time he ever came up, he was going to be a long ways down the river, and deader than yesterday's fish.

His horse must of been boogered by the shooting. It went right on swimming across toward the Texas side.

I had shaken hands with Felipe and said good-bye to my ranch, so I started swimming that plug of mine across too. I kind of halfway expected them rebels to decide to send me along after Santos, but they didn't.

I got to the Texas bank without any holes in me that wasn't natural.

I had it in my head that luck was with me, and that I'd wind up with that canvas bag of gold and silver after all. I caught up to Santos's horse where it had stopped to rest itself on the Texas side. The sergeant's horse was standing there with it.

The bag was gone. It had slipped loose somewhere out there in the river.

Santos might float to the top, eventually, but that bag never would.

At least I still had the little sack of gold I had hidden in my shirt. And I had three horses, if the plug I was riding was to be counted as a horse. The captain's was a well-built black with an American brand. He had a pretty good Mexican-style saddle on him, and a carbine in a scabbard, so that I wasn't plumb unarmed. There was a saber on the saddle. I started to throw it away, till I decided maybe I could trade it later for supplies. Waste not, want not.

The shooting was liable to draw somebody curious. I didn't want to be there to explain things to them when they showed up, so I got on the captain's black horse and led the other two and taken out for the thickest brush I could see.

I was glad to be in Texas again. Hell, I was glad to be *alive*.

3

Of course I was still Joe Peeler then, and you the world know me now as Joe Pepper. You want to know how come me to get to be Joe Pepper? Well, I'll tell you if you'll be patient.

For a while there I was in an awful uncomfortable situation. There wasn't but two sides to the river, and I was in some demand on both of them. The best bet I had was to go west as far and as fast as I could without doing me or the horses any real hurt.

The Texas and Mexico border had a lot of variety in them days, same as it does now. Down on the very lowest part, toward Brownsville, there was getting to be a certain amount of farming on both sides of the river, and the country was settling up. It was a good fertile land where cold weather didn't bite very hard or very long, and just about anything you wanted to plant would grow. Go up the river a hundred or so miles, though, and you start to get into a desert type of country where a man trying to farm had better have himself some awful big buckets to carry water out to his crops. You'd find that the farmers, especially over on the Mexico side, would dig irrigation ditches to carry water to fields about three times the size of a postage stamp. Back away from the river it was mostly just ranchland. Good ranchland, everything considered, only you had to give your cattle lots of room and not let them see too much of each other or they would soon be overstocked.

It was a big old wide-open country where you could go for a long time and never run across a lawman, or where you might—if your luck ran sour—turn a corner in a wagon road and run into a whole covey of Texas Rangers.

There was a good many people in that section them days that wasn't very popular where they had come from and couldn't go back home without some risk of winding up as guests of the state. But down in the border country they might go for years—maybe forever—and not have to answer any embarrassing questions. As long as they didn't raise any undue hell, people didn't worry overly much about where they had come from or what the homefolks might of thought about them.

If I had been in trouble in some other state, or even up in East Texas, I might of stayed in that lower border country and never had to worry about old times. But I had shot Jesse Ordway in South Texas, not far from the Rio Grande. I felt like the risk was too much for me to put up with. Sooner or later, the way people had of drifting west, I'd come face to face with somebody who knowed who I was and knowed about Jesse Ordway. It stood to reason that Mrs. Ordway had posted a reward on me. She was rich enough to've made it a big one.

A lot of people are good about minding their own

business as long as it don't cost them nothing, but you put money into the situation and they come down with a bad case of public responsibility.

I had three horses on my hands, and a saddle for each of them. A man leading two saddled horses just naturally attracts attention. People get to wondering who used to fill the saddles, and they think maybe he knows something he ain't telling. A few miles from where I had crossed the river I came upon a young Mexican boy herding a bunch of spotted goats on a paint pony, bareback. I gave him the sergeant's saddle. He was a little dubious about it till I told him it had come to me in a vision that I was supposed to give it to the first boy I came across herding goats on a paint pony. He was a religious boy, evidently, because he taken it.

I was kind of tempted to keep the captain's saddle because it was made of good leather and had some fancy silver on it. But a man that ain't used to them big-horned Mexico saddles generally has trouble with them at first. They'll pinch right where it grabs you the worst. I came onto a Mexican pack-train loaded down with contraband Mexican liquor heading north to San Antonio. I traded that saddle to them smugglers for a sackful of *tamales* that they had packed in lard to eat along the way, and a goat-skin full of raw *pulque*. I tell you, a man that drinks a little old-time *pulque* every day ought not to ever have to worry about a tapeworm. There ain't nothing could live bottled up amidst that stuff. It taken a right smart of it to burn the stench of that cell out of my nose. There I was with a little leather pouch full of gold coins, and all them tamales and that *pulque*, plus two good horses and one plug. I was rich, when you figure the times.

But a man can get tired of *tamales* pretty quick when they're all he has to eat. It was mostly Mexicans living along the border then, whichever side of it you happened to be on. One evening I reined in to a place and found a young Mexican woman there all by herself without so much as a pony to ride if she had to go anyplace. She said she was married, and her husband was off someplace on business. By the conversation I got a pretty good notion what kind of business it was; there was people on the Texas side that used to raid the ranches there and sell stolen cattle and horses and mules down in Mexico, and people on the Mexican side would drive up stolen stock from Mexico to sell in Texas. Sometimes the same horse might change ownership three-four times and wind up back where he started from. It made for a lot of business, anyway. Like I was saying, the woman had been by herself a good spell, and I found her mighty lonesome, same as I was. She never said it in so many words, but I figured she had already made up her mind that her husband was dead. Oftentimes when them outlaws got shot, whichever side of the river it was on, the people who killed them just left them laying where they was, and nobody ever heard from them again. It wasn't no easy life.

I stayed there with that woman three, maybe four days, resting up the horses, filling up on her cooking, comforting her in her loneliness. When I left there I just taken two of the horses with me. I left her that plug.

Past Laredo, and especially beyond Eagle Pass, things got pretty thin on the border. It started to getting into Indian country, and things tended sometimes to be a little wild for a man of genteel tastes. The government had a military post on upriver that they called

Fort Clark, and the troops there was kept busy most of the time running after Indians and renegades that had learned how to use the border to their advantage. There was Lipan Apaches and Kickapoos and the like down there, all of them kind of having it in for the *gringo*. Folks told me the Kickapoos had been friendly Indians one time, never gave nobody any trouble till a bunch of Confederate soldiers—this was during the war, you know—mistaken them for a bunch of hostiles and plowed into them on one of the creeks that run into the Concho. It came as a surprise to the Indians, first, then a big surprise to the soldiers because them Indians turned around and whipped the britches off of them. After that, they was enemy Indians like all the others.

I'd never fought no Indians up to that time, and hadn't lost any, but I figured it would be about as unhealthy for me to run into a bunch of soldiers as a bunch of Indians, so I tried to skirt around all the posts and towns and such. I was on one of them wide sashays when I got the name of Joe Pepper.

I hadn't seen any Indian sign that I could recognize. Up to this time I'd never even seen or been around Indians anyhow, except them few on the cattle trail to Kansas, and they wasn't really wild. Maybe I didn't know what to look for. But to play it safe I would stop early of an evening and build me a little campfire while it was still light, cook me some supper, kill the fire and move on a ways till it got dark, then make a cold camp. I didn't want Indians finding me at night by seeing my campfire or by smelling the smoke from it.

So one evening a while before sundown I was cooking up some *tortillas* out of ground corn I'd got from the woman, and boiling coffee in a can, when I seen a feller come riding in from the east. I could tell right off that he wasn't no Indian, and I had a feeling by the looks of him that he wasn't a lawman. You get a sixth sense about lawmen if you spend long enough avoiding them. So I hailed him to come on in and invited him to share what vittles I had. He was a tallish sort of a gent, with stubbly whiskers—rusty-colored—that hadn't felt a razor in quite a spell. I could tell by the way he wolfed down them *tamales*-cold lard and all—that he hadn't eaten a good square meal in a while. You never seen a man more needful than he was, or so grateful for what he was given. It kind of gave me a glow inside to know how much good I was doing for a needy and grateful stranger.

Now, if you've ever heard anybody cock a hammer back on a pistol, and that pistol is pointed at you, it's a sound you'll never forget the rest of your life. It's like a rattle-snake's rattle—you can hear it a hundred yards away. I whirled around and tried to grab my rifle. But I was too late.

That grateful stranger shot me.

I can't swear that I heard it. I seen a flash, but I can't even swear it was from the gun. It might of been from the pain when that thing hit me in the ribs. I remember feeling like I'd been kicked by a Missouri mule—a big one at that—and I went down like I had been sledged. I remember fighting for breath and not getting any. I remember that grateful stranger feeling around over me, finding that little bag of gold in my shirt and stripping me to the waist to see if I had any more money. And I remember the warm feel of the blood running down my hide.

It's bad enough having somebody shoot you. It's that much worse when he makes you feel like six kinds of a fool for letting him. I remember laying there trying to get a breath so I could cuss him, and cuss myself for letting him into my camp.

Better it had been the Indians. They wasn't in the habit of repaying a kindness by killing you. Of course, there wasn't many people them days bent over backwards to be kind to Indians.

For a long time I figured I was dead, and I wondered how it was that I could be laying there thinking about it. I couldn't move . . . couldn't even breathe, hardly. I couldn't see enough to tell, but I was satisfied he had run off with everything I had.

It was getting on dark when somebody came along and found me. Things was so hazy by then that I couldn't tell much. I knowed they lifted me up onto a big wagon or something, and I could tell it hurt like thunder. They probed around my gizzard with a knife. By this time, of course, I knowed I wasn't dead—yet. I figured they would kill me off, though, the way they was doing. The pain got so bad that I passed out. Next thing I remembered, I was riding on my back in something that felt like a wagon, and every time it hit a bump it was like somebody had jabbed me in the ribs with a crowbar. It was an awful bumpy road.

I got clear enough in my head to know they was talking Mexican, not *gringo*. It didn't make much difference at the time. Way after dark they stopped and lifted me down. They laid me on a blanket and gave me a big drink of some kind of liquor and covered me up.

Come daylight I could see that I was amongst some Mexican freighters. They had a bunch of oxen and them old big high-wheeled carts that you still see now and again down in the border country. They asked me if I felt like having any breakfast. I didn't, but I wanted another drink. Turned out it was *tequila*. You probably wouldn't know about this, preacher, but *tequila* ain't half bad when you're in need of it.

I gradually sat up and began to take stock. My ribs was sore as the devil, but I wasn't near as bad off as I had a right to be, getting shot in the side that way. I asked them what they had done to me. They said they had dug out a bullet that was laying in beneath the skin, up against the ribs. One of the Mexicans—a boy of fifteen or sixteen, I'd judge—brought it to show to me. It was flattened out, like if you'd laid it on a rail and let a train run over it the way kids will do sometimes with a coin, when they don't know the value of money. I knowed old Joe Peeler was tough, but I didn't see how I could of taken a slug and flattened it out that much and lived to look at it.

Then I realized that grateful stranger had shot me in the gold pouch. I had that leather bag under my shirt, and as I wheeled around his bullet had caught it. The gold coins taken up most of the force so that it was nearly spent by the time it got through to me. I had bled like a stuck hog, though. He must of figured I was near dead or he'd of seen to it.

Every move I made brought a little jab that made me use the Lord's name in vain. I always figured that was one of the lesser Commandments, and since I had already broke so many of the bigger ones, I didn't see what harm could come of it. It helps a man feel better sometimes to cuss a little, like you'd stick a knife into a bloated steer to let the gas out and relieve the pressure on him.

Them Mexicans was good to me. I felt bad that I didn't have a thing I could pay them with. The stranger had taken the gold, my horses, my rifle, my *tamales,* my *pulque* . . . everything but my boots. My feet must not of been his size.

I've always had a kindly feeling toward Mexicans since that time. Them freighters was God's people because they could just as well of left me laying where they found me. They sure didn't owe me nothing, a *gringo* stranger like I was, and trouble to boot. They wasn't of your church, preacher; maybe they didn't go to no church. But they was God's people.

I laid on top of the load on one of them big carts and rode all day. Along toward night we come to a settlement named Catclaw. It had some older Mexican name, but the *gringos* had come along and changed it. It was still Mexican, mostly. But I could tell by the names on the stores that it had a share of *gringos* in it. It was a county seat, too, because it had a frame courthouse up on the town square. It takes a *gringo* to want to build something frame when the lumber's got to be hauled three hundred miles, and when they've got all the material within a mile that they need to build out of adobe or rock. Next to the courthouse, almost as big and a lot stronger built, was a rock jail with walls that must of been a foot and a half thick. Looking at it even from a distance, I could almost smell that Mexican cell again. It always made me a little sick to my stomach if I thought about it much. You never know what freedom is really worth till you've done without.

I hadn't made any plans. I was broke, afoot, and for all I knowed had a price on my head. I had it in my mind that I would wait till way up in the night, then steal me a horse and cross back over the river into Mexico again. I was far enough west that I doubted my troubles from downriver would find me.

It never occurred to me that them freighters would

take matters out of my hands. I was sitting around
the fire with them at supper, eating a bite and trying
to figure out exactly what I was going to do, when
somebody came up from behind me. I thought it was
one of the freighters till he spoke out in *gringo*. He
says, "I understand you've had some trouble."

I turned around right quick, and there stood a man
with a badge on his shirt. That badge looked as big
as the lid on a five-gallon bucket. I let my hand drop
down to my belt where my six-shooter would of
been, if I'd had one. I figured he had me.

I says, "No, I ain't had no trouble to speak of."

The sheriff says, "They tell me somebody shot you
and robbed you and left you to die. If that ain't trouble, I'd hate to see what trouble is." He acted kind of
out of patience.

I told him I had no earthly idea who the grateful stranger was, or where he had gone to, so there
wasn't much either me or the law could do. I thanked
him kindly and told him I was sorry he had bothered
himself.

By then he was getting suspicious, because most
people in my shape would of been hollering for the
law to drop everything else and help them. He says,
"What's your name, friend?"

Him being a sheriff and all, I sure didn't figure he
had much cause to be calling me friend. And I sure
wasn't going to tell him my name was Joe Peeler. I
looked across the fire and saw one of the Mexicans
pop a hot *chiltipiquin* pepper into his mouth. Right
quick I said my name was Pepper . . . Joe Pepper.

If I'd said my name was Smith, like so many of
them do, he'd of knowed I was lying. But I suppose
Pepper sounded natural enough, because he taken it

for the gospel truth. He says, "Well, Joe Pepper, how would you like to come down to the office with me?"

I can tell you, I didn't like the idea atall. I figured he had a nice little cell waiting for me, and there wasn't a blessed thing I could do to protect myself. I says, "Any particular reason?" Seemed like a foolish question at the time.

He says, "I've got a stack of flyers over there with descriptions of various and sundry fugitives. Maybe you'll find your man on one of them. It would help, at least, if we know who we're hunting for."

I could think of twenty-seven places I had rather of gone than to a sheriff's office, but he had a gun in his belt, and that gave him a right smart advantage.

I figured at the time that he knowed who I really was and intended to slam the door shut on me soon as he got me inside. But he didn't. His office was a little box of a room in the front end of the jail. He motioned for me to sit down. He went to rifling through a drawer of a big roll-top desk and brought out a stack of papers. He says, "I'm taking it for granted you can read."

Lots of people couldn't, you know. But I told him sure, I'd been reading since I was ten-eleven years old. Slow about it, sometimes, but I could read. He handed me the papers and told me to go through them. While I was reading he would go rustle us some coffee.

By then I decided he didn't suspicion who I was. And all of a sudden I figured it would be an advantage for me to go through the flyers. I could find the one on me, stick it in my pocket when he wasn't looking, and he would never miss it. Soon as he left the room I went through the papers right fast, looking for one on me. When I got to the last one in the stack, I hadn't found anything. I went back through them again, a little slower. But it wasn't there.

At that time I still had no idea that Mrs. Ordway never had pressed any charges against me. I figured maybe the mail was slow; it wasn't fast and efficient like it is now. They even lost stuff, sometimes. Well, I thought, if I could stay out ahead of the reward notices, maybe I would be all right till I got out of Texas. New Mexico and Arizona was big places, and California was even bigger. A man could lose himself.

I went back through the notices a third time, taking it slow and reading each one. When I got through, I had pulled out three that sort of fit the grateful stranger. The sheriff came in with a pot of coffee he had made or had had made for him someplace else. He looked at the three and wadded up one of them. "I ought to've pulled this one," he says. "I got word he was killed in Laredo. Killed by a wagon. A hundred law officers after him and he got run over by a beer wagon." He studied the other two. Especially one of them.

"Owen Rainwater," he says. "He could sure be the one; he's ornery enough. He's got a brother that lives up north of here. Owen's bad. Harvey's a lot worse."

I figured that wherever I could find Harvey Rainwater, I could probably find Owen Rainwater too. And my horses. And maybe my gold, if he hadn't already spent it. I says, "How do I get to Harvey Rainwater's?"

"You ain't going," he says. "Whatever he stole, it ain't worth the trip."

I told him I had already made a fair trip; a little extra wouldn't hurt me. But he says, "It'd be the longest short trip you ever made. If you need money, Pepper, I can probably find you enough work around here to

get you a little road stake. You don't want to be mess-
ing around with them Rainwaters."

I told him I didn't intend to mess around with
them; I just intended to get back what belonged to
me. He told me to forget about it; I was probably
still running a fever from that wound and I would get
over it in a few days.

The Mexican freighters moved on next morning,
soon as it was daylight. I thanked them all very kindly
for what they had done for me, and they wished me
all the best of luck and went with them big carts. You
could hear the wooden wheels squeaking for a mile.

The sheriff had it fixed up for me to sleep in a wagonyard and help fork hay to the horses and such in
return for three meals a day till I was feeling better
and could either move on or get me a better job. It
wasn't much, but I decided to stick with it a few days
till my side quit hurting and I felt like I could handle
a long ride. I was still figuring on borrowing me a
good horse some dark night.

I didn't have to go. The second day, I was raking
spilled hay up off of the ground and putting it back
into a wooden rack when my eye was caught by a
man riding one horse and leading another down the
street. At the distance I couldn't tell much about him
except that he was tall. But I knowed the horses; they
was the Santos black and the bay I had inherited
from the late sergeant.

I dropped the rake and went into the barn. I had
already noticed that the feller who owned the wagonyard kept a big rifle in there on a rack. It was some
kind of handmade rifle, manufactured for the Confederacy by a homegrown armory over in East Texas.
He just stared at me when I taken that rifle down
and asked him for the loan of two-three cartridges.

Naturally he wanted to know what I was going to do with the gun, and I told him I thought I had seen a coyote.

He went on to tell me the rifle wasn't none too accurate at long range . . . it was one of them hurry-up war jobs. I told him I figured I'd stalk this coyote and get up close. He gave me half a dozen cartridges. I figured I wouldn't use more than one, if I used any atall; I never was wasteful with high-priced ammunition.

The two horses was tied in front of an adobe saloon, which was to be expected. I would've found it funny if that grateful stranger had tied them at the church. The stable man followed me out and watched me start down the street. I don't suppose he had ever seen a coyote shot in town.

I stopped and looked at the horses. They wasn't any the worse for wear as far as I could tell. They looked the same as when I had lost them. The black had my saddle on him. I didn't see no sense in waiting; that stranger was in the saloon spending my money. I cocked the hammer back and stepped through the door.

I don't suppose you ever watched a man look at a ghost. That was my rusty-bearded friend, all right; I knowed it the second I laid eyes on him. He sat there staring at me like he couldn't believe what he seen. He dropped a glass that was half full of whiskey and let it spill all over the little square table he was sitting at. There was another man sitting with him. He couldn't figure out what the trouble was.

I says to the stranger, "You borrowed some things that belong to me. I come to get them back."

Along about then he decided I wasn't no ghost, and I wasn't dead. He didn't have anything to say for himself. He just reached down for the pistol at his hip.

That "wanted" notice in the sheriff's office had

said something about Owen Rainwater being dangerous with a gun, and I suppose he was when he stood
behind a man, like he had done with me. But face to
face he just wasn't much. He never did get his pistol
clean out of the holster.

One thing about it, when you shot a man with one
of them big old rifles close up, they didn't have to
hold an autopsy over him to find out if he was dead.
He just laid there on his back on the dirt floor with
one leg all tangled up in his chair.

I always figured the reason people like Owen Rainwater shot men in the back was because they knowed
their limitations.

That friend of his at the table with him was considerable agitated. I reloaded the rifle real fast in case
I might have to reason with him. But he wasn't much
on this face-to-face business. He ran mostly to talk.

He hollers, "You know what you done? You killed
Owen Rainwater!"

I says, "That was sure my intention."

He goes on hollering about what a big man Owen
Rainwater was, and what a big man his brother Harvey was, and how bad Harvey was going to feel about
this. I told him I was sorry if I had caused anybody
any undue inconvenience; I had just come to get back
what was mine.

I felt of Rainwater's pockets, and sure enough he
had my sack of gold. I had to take it out kind of careful to keep from spilling coins. The sack had a big
hole in it. It also had a dark stain that I knowed was
from my blood. It didn't make me feel atall sorry for
what I had done. I held the sack up for the bartender
and a couple of the customers to see.

Says I, "I'm just taking back what's mine. He stole
this from me."

They didn't seem disposed to argue about it. They was as agreeable a bunch as you could ask for. That friend of Rainwater's, he seemed to decide he wasn't thirsty anymore, because when I looked around he was gone. I taken Rainwater's pistols . . . figured they was fitting interest for the use of my horses and gold.

You've probably noticed how a gunshot or two tends to draw a crowd. In two or three minutes that little saloon was jammed so full of people that it was hard to draw a breath. There wasn't anything left in there that I was interested in. I went out front to see after my horses. Pretty soon the sheriff came trotting up, puffing pretty good. He was carrying some extra weight for what frame he had. He says, "What's going on in there?"

I told him nothing was going on in there now; it was all over with. I told him I had just got my property back. Seemed like he pretty well pictured the rest of it, because he said for me to stay right where I was at, and he went inside. In a minute he was back outside with me, awful flustered.

He says, "Do you know you just killed Owen Rainwater?"

I told him I'd already had that pointed out to me. I told him I was reclaiming my horses and hoped I wasn't going to have to argue with anybody over it, because I was getting awful tired. He said if they was my horses I was welcome to take them.

Then he said something that I ought to have remembered for myself but had somehow forgot. It was a thing that kind of set the pattern of Joe Pepper's life for a long time afterwards.

He says, "You know, there's a reward for Owen Rainwater."

He had gotten me interested. I says, "How much?"

He scratched his head and wrinkled up his face like it hurt him to think so hard. He says, "About five hundred dollars, best I recall. Maybe it was a little more. I'd have to go look at the flyer." Then he twisted up his face even worse. "But it'd take several days to get it cleared and paid to you. You'll need to be moving on. That's too bad, because I'll bet you could of used that money."

You know how it feels to have somebody wave money at you and then take it away? Sort of grates at you, it does. I says, "I ain't in no hurry."

"You ought to be," he tells me. "When Harvey Rainwater finds out about this he'll come looking for you. He ain't no man you'll want to fool with."

"I wasn't fooling with his brother Owen," says I. "Is there a reward on Harvey too?"

The sheriff's jaw dropped down to about the second button. "You don't think you're going to take him *too?*"

"Well, sir," says I, "as long as I got to wait around anyway, I'd just as well turn my hand to a little paying labor."

He stared at me like he couldn't figure out what breed of horse I was. Finally he says, "You know what I ought to do? I ought to deputize you so whatever you do'll be legal."

I would of had to study on that some; the idea of me carrying a badge didn't set real good with me right then. But in a minute he taken it all back anyhow. He says, "I can't afford to do that. Harvey'd kill you, and then he'd be mad at me because I had pinned a badge on you. I don't think I favor getting him mad at me."

I says, "If he's such a wanted man, why ain't you been out there hunting for him yourself?"

"Three reasons," says Sheriff Smathers. "First place,

he's in another county. Second place, he's never caused us no trouble here, up to now. Third place, he'd shoot hell out of me."

I questioned the sheriff pretty sharp on whether he really thought Rainwater would be coming into town looking for me. He said he would bet his life on it. Seemed more like he was betting *my* life. I could think of lots of things I'd rather do than sit around there waiting for somebody to come in and kill me on his own terms.

One reason I had gotten Owen so easy was that I had taken him by surprise. That gave me a little advantage. I figured maybe the smart thing to do was surprise Harvey Rainwater, too.

I asked the sheriff where to find him. For a lawman talking about an outlaw he was supposed to go out and get for himself, he sure seemed to know a lot of details.

He told me about every wagon track, every cowtrail and rat's nest between town and the adobe *rancho* where Rainwater was holed up.

I asked him how I would know Harvey when I seen him. He says, "Just remember what his brother looked like. Add ten or fifteen pounds of flesh and thirty pounds of meanness. That'll be Harvey."

I bought me a few traveling supplies and some fresh cartridges. I told the sheriff to get things moving on the rewards for both of the Rainwater boys, because I would be back to collect.

He seemed to doubt me.

The way I figured it—and the sheriff had agreed with me—the friend who had been in the saloon sipping whiskey with Owen had probably lit a shuck to tell Harvey. Brotherly love being what it was—it always seemed to me that the worst of kinfolks stuck together better than respectable kinfolks—Harvey Rainwater would probably not waste no time heading for town to hunt for me. He would figure it was a cinch I'd leave, so he would move at a good clip. From the sheriff's description it was going to take that friend till way up in the night to get to Harvey. More than likely Harvey would start for town as soon as it was daylight.

I rode till a while before dark, then stopped and fixed me a bite of supper over a small fire that wouldn't put out much smoke. Folks said there wasn't much to worry about from Indians in that part of the country, but there was worse things than Indians. I put the fire out and rode a ways more into the dark, like had become my habit. I knowed where I was going. The sheriff said the wagon trail led up to within a few miles of where Harvey was staying. All I had to do was keep on the trail.

I had me a good night's sleep with that gold sack in my shirt. Odd, how much comfort a man gets out of a handful of coin, especially when it's got that yellow color. I've had pretty women sing good night to me, and their songs wasn't half as sweet as the clinking of them gold coins, one against another.

Next morning I had me some coffee and bacon and started up the trail. Outside of cattle, I didn't see much till upwards of dinnertime. Then I seen half a dozen horseback riders way off in the distance. I watched them till I decided they was sure-enough coming my way. I knowed within reason who they'd be—one of them, anyhow. I slipped Santos's carbine out of the scabbard and pulled off into some brush and settled myself down to wait.

You'll find lots of people who like pistols, and I always carried one, but if you want something to really

display your authority, show them the front end of a
rifle or a carbine. That'll get their attention every time.
I just sat there amidst the greenery of the mesquite
and catclaw and let them ride on past me. They didn't
see me, of course, because people don't generally
see me when I don't want them to. I didn't have no
trouble recognizing Harvey Rainwater. He was Owen
Rainwater all over again, and about two collar sizes
bigger around the neck. He had a look on his face
like some of them old vigilantes must of had a long
time ago when they was getting ready to break in a
new rope.

I pulled my horse out into the trail, stepped down
behind him so I didn't show too much of myself, and
I hollers, "Harvey Rainwater!"

My voice always carried good. He turned his horse
around real quick. I don't know which he seen first,
me or my carbine. He didn't know me, of course, but
a shooting iron has a way of introducing itself.

He couldn't see me very well, which is the way I
wanted it. I never was one to take undue advantage,
just enough so I'd be sure to win. He says, "Who are
you?"

Says I, "My name is Joe Pepper. I believe you're
hunting for me. I come out to save you a long trip."

The tall feller was riding alongside him, the one
who had been with Owen Rainwater in the saloon.
He recognized me right off. I heard him say, "That's
him, Harvey. That's the gink that done it."

I says, "Owen taken what was mine, and I taken
it back. He shot me once when I wasn't looking. He
was looking straight at me when I shot *him*. Now, I
ain't asking for trouble with you, Harvey, but if you
want me I'm at your convenience."

He just looked at me like he couldn't believe none

of it. A lot of them old boys earned a reputation for being quick on the trigger and dangerous, but most often that was only when they had everything going for them the way they planned it. Catch them on their left foot and they're uncertain which way to turn.

I says, "You other boys, if you ain't relatives of his, I'd advise you to stay out. I don't like hurting a man when it ain't necessary."

He said something to the men that was with him, and they all pulled off to one side except the tall one. Harvey reached for his pistol. I let him get a grip on it and start bringing it up before I squeezed the trigger. I didn't want it said afterwards that I killed a man whose gun was still in the holster. That bullet taken him about six inches under his chin. His pistol went off and grazed his horse's right forefoot. That horse broke to pitching and sent him sailing out there like a big old floppy bird.

I doubt as Harvey Rainwater ever knowed it.

My own horse was cutting up, too. He didn't like the way I had used the seat of my saddle for a gun-rest. I levered another cartridge into the chamber and brought it back up to my shoulder because I didn't know what the rest of Rainwater's crew was apt to do. All of them just sat there looking dumb except the tall one. He drawed a gun and was bringing it down on me when I let him have what was in the carbine. It sure seemed to come as a surprise to him. His horse made a couple of jumps, and the tall man wound up laying on top of Harvey Rainwater.

I watched the other four real close, afraid one of them might take a notion to do something rash. But they was all well-behaved.

I says to them, "I've had about enough of this. Any more kinfolks amongst you?"

They was quick to let me know they wasn't kin, just friends. And friendship has its limits. One of them pointed to the tall man. "Slim yonder, he was the only one that was kin. He was a cousin to Harvey and Owen. They wasn't too bright on his side of the family."

I didn't say so, but it seemed to me like the whole Rainwater tribe had been shorted some on brains. I says, "Well, if you boys are sure you ain't got no further quarrel with me, I'd be much obliged if you'd all drop your guns right where you're at." They seemed agreeable to that. It didn't take but a minute. I says, "Nobody's going to disturb them guns. You-all can come back here in an hour or two and get them. But right now I'd like to see how far you can get in the shortest possible time, right back the direction you came from."

They done pretty good, I thought.

When they was a fair distance and still going, I commenced catching up the Rainwater horses and petting them and talking to them gentle to calm them down. You can talk to a horse a right smart easier than you can talk to some people. They was a little skittish about me putting the Rainwaters back up onto them. They was used to a man riding head up instead of head down. My side was still hurting me a little, too, from where Owen Rainwater's bullet had hit me in the ribs. But directly I got the two tied into place. I looked back once to be sure where the other four was at and found they had understood me real well. They was still riding off.

I've always had a suspicion that Sheriff Smathers turned in for the reward on Owen Rainwater and figured to keep it himself. The last thing he expected was to see me come riding back down that street with two more Rainwaters tied across their saddles. I pulled up in front of his office at the jail and hollered for him to come out. He just stood there leaning against the doorjamb like he thought he might fall, otherwise. He finally came down the steps and walked around and pulled up the two Rainwaters' heads to take a good look at the faces.

He kept saying over and over again, "I'll be damned! I'll be damned!"

Says I, "I got one more here than I figured on. They called him Slim. You know him?"

He just nodded. "Slim Rainwater. A cousin."

Says I, "He got a reward on him too?"

The sheriff shook his head. "Not that I know of. Just Owen and Harvey. Slim never done anything much but tag along and drink bad whiskey."

I told the sheriff I was sorry to hear that. I hated to kill a man when there was no reason for it.

That seemed to strike him odd. He says, "If there'd been a reward, would you of felt better about killing him?"

I told him I would. A reward made a pretty good reason.

In such a case as that, when nobody knowed of any more family, it was customary to sell the horses and guns and saddles and such, and whatever was left over from the expenses of the burial was divided up by the sheriff amongst them he felt was entitled to it. In this case it was a fifty-fifty split between him and me. I never did see that he really had it coming to him, but it wasn't no big lot of money, and I had to depend on him to get me the reward for the Rainwater boys. I didn't feel like quibbling. Most of the sheriffs and marshals them days didn't draw much salary for the kind of job they did. A little extra money was always appreciated.

It taken me about ten or twelve days to get the reward because there wasn't no telegraph there, and the mail service wasn't none too peart. Meantime I just hung around town and played me some poker and taken a drink or two when I wanted it. I didn't sleep in the wagonyard no more, or fork hay. People came from a long ways to see Joe Pepper, the man who killed the Rainwater boys, and funny as it seems, I found this was good for business. They all seemed like they felt honored to get to play a hand of poker with Joe Pepper. I can't say as I favored their reasons much, but the main thing was the money. Taking them as a whole, they was a pretty miserable bunch of poker players. By the time the reward came in, I had cleaned up around there pretty good.

The sheriff came one day and says, "I got the authorization in today's mail. If you'll walk down to the bank with me, I'll see that you get paid."

It was a nice, refreshing walk. I enjoyed it a lot. I had already met the head man of the bank, a friendly old German by the name of Dietert. I had met his number-two man, too, a sour-faced, sour-tongued gink by the name of Clopton. Lord knows what *his* pedigree was.

I preferred old man Dietert myself. He had come out west from San Antonio a few years earlier and had established this bank and a mercantile and lumber and wool-buying and hide-buying business, and no telling what else that might turn him a dollar. He had sat in with me on a couple of games of poker at one of the saloons. He was good at handling money, all right, but he didn't have much knack for cards.

I had thinned him a little. Them old Germans, they wouldn't play long enough to let you trim them to the quick. Some folks thought because they talked a little funny that they wasn't very smart, and that's how they generally bested you in business. They was thinking in two languages and out ahead of you in both of them.

Of course old man Dietert knowed what the letter was about; he had knowed it would be coming. But he read it over and looked at the draft real careful to be sure everything was in proper order. Them Dutchmen was always particular about proper order. He might make mistakes at the poker table, but he didn't make none at the bank. He says, "Vell, Mister Pepper, by the looks of this you're fifteen hundred dollars richer."

I told him that was the way I figured it, too.

He went on to tell me about the bank and how stable and safe it was and how fast the country was growing and how much bigger the bank was going to be in another five years. He suggested maybe I'd like to put my money there on interest and watch it grow with the bank. I told him I hadn't made plans to stay that long myself, and that I'd rather just get the cash money and go.

He said he was right sorry to hear that. He thought a man of my talents might find it profitable to stay around awhile and help out the sheriff. There was still some desperate sorts in the country who needed to meet up with Joe Pepper, and whose apprehension or demise was likely to be worth money to somebody, someplace.

The way he put it, I couldn't help but get to thinking. I wasn't going noplace special. Since the sheriff didn't already have my real name and description on a flyer, maybe he never would have; maybe they wasn't being mailed this far west. And even if one *did* come, there was a good chance I'd be the first to see it. It would be real easy to fold it up and shove it into the stove.

The banker's remark kind of taken the sheriff by surprise. I says, "What do you think about it, Sheriff?" I could already tell by the look on his face that he wasn't real keen on the notion. But the banker was a man of influence, because he taken on like he thought it was the best idea to come along since bourbon whiskey.

And that's how come Joe Pepper to wear a deputy sheriff's badge.

4

It didn't take me long to learn some things about the sheriffing business, things that ain't wrote down in the statutes. Sheriff Smathers taken pains not to antagonize me about it, but he just the same let me know sort of kindly that the idea of me being a deputy was the banker's, not his. He had as soon I hadn't stayed because a feller like me tended to draw lightning, and he was getting to be an old man. He wasn't sure he could dodge fast enough when it struck. Another thing, since I was working out of his office and had his official stamp on me, so to speak, he said it was clear to him that any rewards I came up with ought to be divided with him, share and share alike. I didn't see his case quite as clear as he did, but I told him we would talk about it when the time came. His part of any split, I told him, ought to be calculated according to how much effort he put into the job, the chances that was taken, and such like. I've always been one that believed a man works best when he's got a proper incentive. Give him the same whether he

works or sits down, and he'll wear out the seat of his
britches before he wears out the knees.

There was some other things about sheriffing that
came as a little of a surprise to me. There was some
places around town that didn't operate strictly according to the statutes. There was laws that said it
was illegal to gamble. There was laws about a saloon
being open till way late at night or on a Sunday. And
there was laws about them fancy houses down on
Red Lantern Row. Most of them laws, I found out,
was honored mainly in the breach. About once a
week the sheriff made him a little round of all them
places, and when he came back his pockets was fuller
than when he left. You know as well as I do, that ain't
the normal order of things with most folks that pa-
tronize them kinds of businesses.

If I'd of wanted to put the boot on the other foot
I could of asked him to share that with me, same as
he wanted me to share rewards. But at the time the
thought of taking a percentage off of them poor un-
fortunate girls went against my grain. Being partial to
the cards myself, I thought I could see the gamblers'
side of it, too. Later on I learned better; I learned that
the smart one takes what he can while the rest ponder Scripture. But wisdom ain't born in you; you got
to cultivate it.

Catclaw was an agreeable kind of a town, once I
got used to it. There was a little farming along close
to the creek, but not enough of it to be any real set-
back to the community. People had a way of tending
to their own affairs and not crowding in too much
on other folks'. Big part of the town was Mexican,
of course, and the sheriff being white, he didn't mess
around much in the south part of town as long as the
trouble there didn't spill over. The way he seen it them

people had been keeping their own laws since long before the rest of us came. If a man was wronged, he taken it on himself to set things right. If a man was killed, his kin taken it on themselves to balance the books and take an eye for an eye. It wasn't anybody else's business, sure not the government's.

I used to wonder if that wouldn't be a good policy for us *gringos,* too. It would sure starve a lot of lawyers to death.

There wasn't much money to be made over in the Mexican section, which is another reason why Smathers didn't care to go over there. What little real money there was, it accumulated in the Anglo section. Texas was still dirt-poor. Main thing it had was land and cattle, and neither one of them worth real specie. They was hard times for us honest men, and none too easy for all them other folks. About the only actual money that had come into the state had been brought back by cattlemen taking their herds north, and by the carpetbaggers who had come in to steal everything that wasn't bolted down tight. No matter how hard they tried, they couldn't keep some of their money from getting into circulation.

The town had a fair to middling trade territory, selling goods to the ranchers and farmers and whatnot on down to the Rio Grande on the south, way out into the edge of Apache country on the west, and north up to where there was nothing but Comanches. A couple of big general stores did business to the outlying country, and seven or eight saloons did business without having to go anywhere. Them days, no matter how hard the times, the last man to starve out was the saloonkeeper. When *he* left, you could take down the town sign.

There wasn't too many ways for people to move

west without going through this town or some other
one like it. Most of the people from San Antonio or
points south had to come through unless they made it
a point to leave the main road and go around. It was
them roundance people I mostly kept a lookout for.
I memorized all the "wanted" flyers, pretty near, and
kept notes in a tally-book in my shirt pocket, the way
I've seen Texas Rangers do. One of them Rangers ever
come upon a suspicious-looking bunch of strangers,
he would take out his notebook and flip through it
and check descriptions. If any looked like they might
fit, he invited them to go with him. They hauled in a
lot of the innocent along with the guilty, but one of
them Ranger invitations was hard to refuse.

I made me a regular patrol north and south of
town, cutting sign on people that taken the long way
around. As scattered and few as the towns was, any
man that taken pains to go around instead of coming through was naturally suspect. Biggest part of
the time it was for nothing. Either I never would find
them, or they would turn out to be Mexican cowboys
looking for stock, or like once happened, some black
troopers out of Fort Clark hunting for a couple of de-
serters. The Army was always asking us to help find
these runaway boys, but I didn't feel like it was my
place; them damnyankees could hunt for their own. I
felt like any soldier that had gumption enough to run
was beginning to display some good sense.

Besides that, the Army didn't usually offer any reward.

Once in a while I would strike paydirt and catch
me somebody that was on the dodge. Generally they
would come peacefully enough, once I showed them
the seriousness of my intentions. Getting them to
town was only the first part of the trouble, like as

not. Them upstanding citizens that put up reward money was always looking for some excuse not to pay it, once you done your part of the job. They would claim that the time had run out or that the reward wasn't meant for no regularly paid officer, or some such dodge, trying to rob an honest lawman of his due.

I remember one time I caught an old gotch-eared boy that had robbed a carpetbag bank in one of them settlements over east of San Antonio. They had put up a thousand dollars on him. It wasn't just that he had robbed the bank which bothered them so much. He didn't really get off with much money. But afterwards he had taken the head banker for a hostage. He taken him along with him for maybe twenty miles, then made him strip off naked so he wouldn't be in no hurry to run to somebody's house for help. It's bad enough to lose your money, and even worse to lose your dignity on top of it.

Of course I didn't know the whole story when I went after him. All I knowed was what he looked like, and that part about the thousand dollars. The rest was just unnecessary details. I found him hiding out in the same general part of the country where Harvey Rainwater had been. I knowed him on sight; a man with a gotch ear just don't hardly melt into a crowd. I figured right off that he was a likable sort because he hadn't been there more than a couple of days, and he already had made friends that was willing to risk getting punctuated with my gun to protect him. But friendly don't count for much against a thousand dollars. I persuaded him, you might say, that he ought to come and go with me and not cause them new friends of his any undue grief. He came around to my point of view after I put a bullet through the fleshy part of his leg. I was kind of sorry about that later, seeing the way them people there made a fuss over him and patched him up so neat and fixed him a lunch to eat on the way to the jail. They didn't fix *me* nothing.

After he had time to get over the pain in that leg, and after the fever had run out, I could tell what the people seen in him. He had a grin wider than a pasture gate, and he could tell the biggest and funniest lies. If lies get a man sent to hell, I reckon he wouldn't have a chance. But they was healthy lies, the kind that make you laugh and don't hurt nobody. He asked for a guitar, and we brought him one. Worst guitar player you ever heard in your life.

Naturally I sent word back where he had come from that we had him in jail, awaiting their pleasure. Well sir, they didn't lose much time getting theirselves over there . . . the county sheriff, a deputy, and the banker himself, a fat, whining kind of a Yankee. I knowed from what Gotch had told me that he was one of them carpetbaggers who had come down on us like a plague of locusts after the war, working in cahoots with their reconstruction laws to freeze people off of their land and then buy it up cheap for the delinquent taxes. He had cleaned out Gotch's family that way, which was why Gotch picked on him so. Gotch had told me all about walking that banker home, barefoot plumb to his chin, and I don't know which of us had laughed the hardest at the story.

The sheriff wasn't a bad sort, as them scalawag officeholders went, but that banker was one of them dollar-nursing kind that wouldn't spend two bits to watch a bumblebee whip a bald eagle. Soon as he seen we had his bank robber safely behind the bars, he crawfished on the reward. Said it had been for Gotch's capture within a month, and this had been two-going-on-three. I looked real close at that flyer. It didn't say a word about no time limit. He said it was supposed to have, and it was the printer's mistake, not his. If I wanted my thousand dollars, I would just have to take it up with the printer. I've seen enough printers in my time to know they're always broke.

On top of that, he had the nerve to ask us for the borrow of a horse that they could take Gotch home on.

I've been shot at in my life, and I've been cheated, and I believe I was always maddest at being cheated. I used the Lord's name in a shameful manner. It didn't change nothing. They still had the legal papers to take my prisoner, and they wasn't going to pay me a dime.

On top of that, I had come to like old Gotch. The truth wasn't in him, but neither was there any real harm.

They was going to leave at daylight the next morning. The banker had a hotel room. The sheriff and the deputy slept in the hay at the wagonyard because their county wasn't allowing them much in the way of expenses, and the banker sure wasn't paying. I sat in the front office, stewing over the situation and listening to Gotch abusing that Mexican guitar. All of a sudden it come to me. Gotch hadn't tried to shoot me when I taken him; he had just refused to go with me. I went in there and says, "Gotch, you ever shot a man in your life? You ever tried to?"

He said he hadn't. I says, "If somebody was to slip you a loaded pistol through that window, would you shoot that fat banker to get yourself free?"

He says, "No, I'd maybe try to scare him to death, but not shoot him."

There was maybe twenty pistols in a drawer that had been taken off of one man or another and never given back. I didn't get Gotch's because that would be a dead giveaway, and his wasn't much account anyway. If you're going out of your way to give a man something, you ought to give him something good. I picked me one and taken several cartridges and loaded it, then got to thinking. Now and again I'd been fooled about people. Maybe I oughtn't to take any undue chances. I taken the cartridges back out and pulled the lead from them, poured the powder into a spittoon and fitted the lead back in place. Then I reloaded the pistol with them, walked around back of the jail and rapped on the bars with the barrel. I seen a hand reach out, and I put the gun in it.

In a little while I heard Gotch playing on that guitar again.

I didn't go next morning to unlock the cell for that visiting sheriff and his deputy and the banker. I just gave them the key and told them I was going down the street to have me some breakfast. I seen that they had their horses, plus one they had had to buy at the wagonyard for Gotch to ride. The liveryman owed me a split on that.

I walked down the street a ways, then ducked behind a corner where I could look back. Sure enough, I seen them three come out in single file with their hands up, and old Gotch bringing it up behind them with that pistol in his hand, grinning like a dog licking clabber. They rode out of town, heading west instead of east.

I went on and did what I had said I would . . . had me a thousand-dollar breakfast. It was one of the best meals I ever ate. Old Sheriff Smathers came around later in the morning, and I never let on to him.

Way after dark that night, the three of them came a-limping back into town sorefooted, all of them as naked as the day they first come into the world. And a whole lot smarter. They hadn't only lost their prisoner, but they had lost four head of horses and their guns and whatever cash and truck they had brought with them.

I think that banker suspicioned what had happened, because he tried awful hard to get me fired. But old Smathers wasn't keen on it, seeing as he would of shared the reward with me if there had been one. The banker finally offered to put up the reward again, a thousand dollars alive, two thousand dollars dead. But by then his welcome had plumb worn out. I told him it was a little like trapping coyotes. If you ever catch one in a trap and he gets loose, he's trapwise from then on and ten times harder to catch. I wanted to hunt easier game.

That banker had to float a loan from old man Dietert at the Catclaw bank to buy them some clothes and horses.

I always had a hunch Smathers smelled a rat about Gotch, but he never said nothing. The only thing he ever wondered about was what happened to his spittoon. He pitched a smoked-down cigar butt in it and damn near caught his britches afire.

By and by I had added five or six rewards to my bank account, probably two or three thousand dollars in all. I still had it in my head that I wanted to be a rancher, even though all my attempts at it had come to considerable grief. That wasn't the part of the country I especially wanted to do it in, though. For one thing it was a heap dryer than the land I was used to, back home. It was really a lot better than it looked, I know now, but it always appeared to be in the midst of a drouth if you was from a greener part of the country. Another thing, I still figured they was looking for me back yonder, and sooner or later somebody might come straying through who knew me. I'd already had to leave a ranch in South Texas and another in Mexico. I didn't aim to leave one here.

Time came when one office seemed a little close for me and Sheriff Smathers. We come to something of a disagreement over a five-hundred-dollar reward on a feller that had shot a woman back in East Texas. Now, you're probably wondering how me, on the dodge myself, could go out and bring in other people on the dodge and keep my conscience clear. Truth is, I didn't. Like with old Gotch there; if I'd of turned him over to that fat banker and his laws, I'd of lost some sleep over it. I always hurt a little over most of them, and I couldn't of done it if money hadn't been such a cool balm for a troubled conscience.

One like that woman-killer, of course, didn't trouble me a bit except that he hadn't given me any excuse for shooting him. I always figured the best cure for a man like that is a deep burying. The reward was the same dead or alive.

Anyway, I had to catch him all by myself. I didn't get three cents' worth of help from old Smathers or anybody else. So when the reward came through, naturally I was inclined to figure I ought to keep it myself. Old Smathers seen it different. He wasn't overly strong at sharing danger, but he was real apt with pencil and paper when it come to sharing money.

Things didn't improve a bit when some old boy breezed into town one day and robbed our old Dutch banker in broad daylight. I was off at the time, looking for suspicious tracks on the trails south of town. First I heard of it was along late in the day when I was heading back toward town, tired and in bad need of a drink. I ran smack into a wild-eyed citizen posse, carrying more guns than Lee had at Gettysburg. You take the majority of them posses, they're more danger to each other than to the people they're hunting.

Feller in charge was that sour-faced loudmouth, Clopton, from the bank. I always figured he had a grand notion that one day he was going to be the high muck-a-muck in charge of all the money, when the old man died. He wasn't ever very civil, and that day none atall. He asked me if I didn't know the bank had been robbed, and of course that was a silly question because he knowed I'd been out of town.

He gave me a lecture about how a peace officer was supposed to be on hand when he was needed instead of out pleasure-riding around over the country, and I told him I was hot and thirsty and tired, and it had sure been no pleasure. Besides, bank robbers wasn't in the habit of making an appointment before they favored us with a visit.

I had been told that this Clopton was an officer in the Confederate Army, which didn't overly surprise me. It helped explain his extra airs, and some of the reason why we lost. He had been in the bank when the robber came in. Of course he didn't tell me all of it, but I found it out later when I finally got back into town. The robber was a youngish sort, no different from a hundred or two others you'd of met on the ranches and in the army and on the freight wagons. What Clopton didn't tell me was that the old banker Dietert stayed cool and just about had the robber bluffed into thinking the bank had sent nearly all of its cash out in a payroll. But Clopton was scared for his life, and he opened up the safe. The robber got off with maybe a thousand dollars in paper money; the silver was heavy, and he must not've wanted to get his horse loaded down. Clopton was afraid the boy would kill all of them when he got through, so as to leave no witnesses. When he left without doing anybody any harm, Clopton went and shut the safe—a little late to be doing that—and then went into a crying jag.

By the time I met him on the trail he was over it, and he was talking and acting tough. He was probably trying to make up for the show he had put on earlier.

The robber had come south; they generally did them days, because it wasn't far to Mexico. Clopton said if I'd had my eyes open I was bound to've seen him. But I hadn't seen anybody all day except a couple of Mexican oxcart men and a little detail of them black soldiers out of Fort Clark with a consumptive-looking white lieutenant who probably *needed* to rob a bank.

There wasn't nothing I could do but turn around with that posse and help them hunt. It was a big rolling country of mesquite and catclaw and *guajillo* and all that other half-desert kind of growth that could swallow a man up with you looking straight at him. We cut for signs but didn't find any. Sheriff Smathers had gone out with another posse, in a little different direction. I found out that the boy had managed to cover his trail just a little ways out of town, and nobody could tell where he went to.

We hunted till full dark. By then I was glad it was a town posse, because they was all ready to turn around and go home. One of them *serious* posses, now, they'd of stayed out two or three days without a bite to eat. I wasn't ready to do that, not for an amateur robber who hadn't gotten off with but a thousand dollars and hadn't shot anybody.

I changed my tune when I found out what else got taken. I went down to the bank early next morning to see if old man Dietert could give me a better description than that idiot Clopton. I found the old Dutchman busy trying to convince several people that their money was still safe, that he would stand good for any loss out of his own personal pocket. But for me he had to make an exception.

"I'm sorry to tell you this," he says, "but you vill remember that leather pouch you vanted me to keep in the safe? It is gone."

Well sir, I couldn't help cussing a little. I had almost got myself killed getting hold of that gold in the first place. And I had had to take it away from a thief and kill him. I swear, it began to look like the good Lord didn't intend for me to have it.

The cash money I had on deposit was all right, but it sure made me sick to lose that gold pouch again after all the trouble I had been to.

I didn't wait around for anybody to form up a fresh posse. I set out by myself. But it was too late to pick up that old boy's trail. There had been so many people riding around over that country looking for him that it was hopeless. I rode on south, all the way to the river, hoping to pick up some kind of a clue. I found lots of tracks, but there was no way of knowing which one of them might be his, or if any of them was. I brewed it over in my mind for a long time before I finally got up nerve to cross that river into Mexico. I had thought once that I'd seen enough of Mexico to do me for a lifetime. But I decided to take the risk. This was so far upriver that they had probably never heard of Santos, much less of Joe Peeler.

I hunted around down there for several days, looking over all the suspicious characters. Just about every *gringo* I seen that was past seventeen looked suspicious, the frame of mind I was in. About all I had to go on was the description of the horse, a smallish mustang-type bay with a little streak on his nose. I must of found a hundred like that, but no *gringo* riding any of them. I finally gave it up and went back across the river where I belonged, tired out and feeling low. I wasn't ready for the griping of old Sheriff Smathers. He was saying I must be turning lazy, that I ought to've stayed down there till I found the robber because by this time the bank had put up a five-hundred-dollar reward on him.

He sure hated it, not getting a cut of that reward. But he didn't hate it half as bad as I did, because he hadn't lost a sack of gold coin that he had become attached to.

He kept grousing, and it was a pleasure to get out of town again. I kept on for awhile working that country between town and the river, not getting nothing for it but a saddlesore.

That old boy was gone, and there was nothing to do but accept it. The hell of it was, I was the biggest loser of anybody in town.

5

One thing about me, I could always tell when the gravy was running thin. I knew my time in Cat-claw was about up. It was getting so every time old Smathers opened his mouth, I had to open mine too. The strain between us got considerable. He would of loved to've sat in the office and watched me bring in the feller who taken the bank, so he could share in the reward. But some games are meant to be won and some are meant to be lost. That time we had a busted flush.

It was a good thing for me, I guess, that Samantha Ridgway came along when she did.

Actually she came the second time before I chanced to see her. I was off on one of them wild goose chases when she first came through with one of them little emigrant wagon trains that seemed to pass there about as regular as a man washed his socks. It wasn't a big one like you read about, the kind with a hundred wagons. There wasn't ever as many of that kind as folks seem to think, at least not down in our part of the country. Most of the time they was more like five or six, maybe eight or ten wagons. Those was the easiest managed. The folks in the front wagon could always look back and see the hindmost, and vice versa. The last ones didn't eat near as much dust as on a big train. An outrider could see the fore and aft wagons all at the same time and knowed right away when anything went wrong.

Oft as not when you came onto one of them little wagon trains, you found a lot of people was kinfolks. I always had a fondness for families myself, growing up in a big one the way I did.

Like I say, I missed Samantha the first time. If it hadn't been for some Apaches off out to the west, she would of never left any footprints on my life. The wagons camped at the edge of town one night while the folks picked up some supplies, then headed west toward old Fort Davis, way off out across the Pecos River country.

This, you got to understand, was before Mackenzie made his big cavalry raid out of Fort Clark and tore up the worst nest of them border-jumping Indians in northern Mexico. These Indians would stay in Mexico most of the time because the Mexicans was too busy with problems of their own to bother them much. Now and again they would cross the river, hit somebody with some devilment, then not let their breechclouts touch them till they was safe south of the Rio Grande. Mexico didn't care much, seeing a bunch of *Tejanos* get bloodied up.

Well sir, this emigrant train never made it to the Pecos. Them Indians came skinning out from behind one of the flat-topped mountains you find in that desert country, and before the folks could get the wagons circled the red devils was amongst them. Things got fiercesome for a few minutes till the Apaches took what they mainly wanted, the loose horses and mules. They would always kill a few people if it came handy, but the stock was the main thing.

When the dust cleared, the emigrants had three men to bury out on that greasewood flat. Before they could get back to town they had to stop and bury another one.

I was west of Catclaw a few miles, scouting around for suspicious sign, when I met a feller pushing his horse pretty hard, heading east. He asked me how much farther it was to Catclaw, and I told him. "Thank God," he says, and points back over his shoulder. "There's a wagon train behind me needing help. There any doctors in the town?"

I told him there was two, one *gringo* and one Mexican. Told him to get the Mexican because he didn't drink much. He allowed as they would need them both.

He went on toward town, and I followed the mail road west till I came finally to the wagons. A more desperate, hard-whipped bunch I never seen. Not only did they lose their loose stock, but the Indians killed some more in the traces. That was the way with the Indian when he went to war: kill what he couldn't steal, and leave the white man afoot if he couldn't leave him dead. So these people had to double up with what stock they had left. They even doubled some of their wagons in tandem, one behind the other like freight wagons. The wagon canvas was shot full of holes, and a couple was partly burned. They was a confused and staggered lot of people, I'll tell you. Some people went west them days that shouldn't of ever left hearth and home.

It was Samantha that caught my eye, sitting up

on a wagonseat, driving the wagon all by herself. She wasn't a lot to look at just at the time, I'll grant you, but somehow she sort of grabbed me. Her face was smudged with dirt and ashes. There was streaks down her cheeks where the tears had run. Her hair was all blowed out and wild-looking. But with all of that, she taken my breath.

I says to her, "You're kind of small to be driving that team all by yourself. You need some help?"

She says, "My mother's the one that needs help. You a doctor?"

I told her I wasn't. I stood up in the stirrups and looked into the wagon. A woman was lying in there on a pile of blankets, white and pale as if death was knocking on her door. And it was. A big middle-aged woman was sitting in there with her, holding onto her hand.

As things unfolded, I found out that her husband had been more or less the captain of the wagon train, a family leader and all that. He had been out front trying to get the wagons circled when the Indians hit, and he was the first one to get killed. The old lady—Samantha's mama—went running out to try and help him. She grabbed up his rifle and tried to fire it, but it was empty. She swung it like a club till one of them put a bullet in her.

They was a strong, loyal bunch of women them days, preacher, not like them little bicycle-riding, croquet-playing dolls you see around nowadays. Why, just a little while back I even seen a woman smoking a cigarette . . . a *cigarette*, mind you . . . and she was supposed to be a lady, not a saloon girl. Some people these days don't know the first thing about morals.

But that's got nothing to do with what I'm telling you. I rode back to the lead wagon. A big, stocky farmer was sitting there on it, looking grim as death. And he had plenty to be grim about. I found out his name was Zebulon Wentworth. They was great on Bible names in them days. Of course the ones that knowed him called him Zeb, which kind of took the Bible back out of it. Zebulon was for Sunday, like the Bible generally is.

Old Zeb's wife was a sister to Samantha's mother, and now people looked to him to head up the wagon train. He was one of them tough East Texas farmers that had spent so long behind a plow that his hands was shaped to fit the handles. Big hands, like a ham hanging up in a smokehouse. He could knock a man rolling if he was of a mind to, though generally him and his kind had no such inclinations.

He asked me if I had met his man on the road. Then he told me they had had some trouble, which I could plainly see for myself. But I reckon he needed somebody new to talk to, because he commenced telling me all about the Indian raid. I found out that the big woman sitting with the wounded lady back in that other wagon was his wife Addie. Zeb was sore afraid he was fixing to lose his sister-in-law. He was telling me how hard that was going to be on his niece Samantha, both of her folks getting killed and leaving her to shift for herself, a young and innocent girl of nineteen, facing the cruel world. My heart kind of weakened as I listened to him.

By and by I could see a bunch of horses coming. Old Zeb tensed up like he thought it might be Indians again, but I told him it was likely a bunch from town, coming to meet them. And that's what it turned out to be. That Mexican doctor was in the lead with a black bag tied on behind his saddle. The *gringo* doctor couldn't come, somebody said, but he would be waiting when the wagons got to town. I'd seen a good bit of him since I had been in Catclaw, and I figured somebody was getting him sobered up.

They stopped the wagons so the *medico* could look at the wounded. He started with Samantha's mother. She was fevered and talking out of her head. I had seen enough wounded men in the war to know that she didn't stand much chance. The doctor must of knowed it too, but he didn't tell the folks so. He looked at her pretty good, then went to the other wagons. There was two men wounded, and one little boy that got a broken arm by falling out of a wagon while the fight was going on. They wasn't in any big danger of dying unless it was from embarrassment because of so many of them people from town, crowding around looking at them.

The doctor went back to Samantha's wagon. He told Samantha and her aunt Addie and Zeb that old lady Ridgway was in a bad fix, and that the bullet needed to come out of her right away. He hated to do it there, but he was afraid to wait till they could get to town. So we spread some blankets on the ground in the shade under the wagon, and unhitched the team so they couldn't spook and accidentally run the wheels over her. I helped a couple of men lift her down from the wagon and put her on the blankets. Then the doctor shooed all the extra folks away so there wouldn't be a bunch of people watching when he opened up her dress. He kept me and Zeb there to help him, and of course three or four of the women. He didn't have anything to put her to sleep, so he gave her all the laudanum he thought was safe. Then he commenced.

I watched that girl while the operation was going on. She stood back out of the way. The tears ran down through the dust on her face, but she didn't let out a whimper or break down and get to be a problem like lots of women would've done. She had her head down some, praying. I thought to myself how lucky that woman was to have such a daughter.

I see people nowadays who get more loyalty out of a yellow dog than out of their kids, but there I go talking about things that have nothing to do with the story.

We had to hold Mrs. Ridgway tight because it hurt her. That bullet was in there solid. The worst part was that it had already been in too long. By and by the doctor finally brought it out. Old Zeb gave a sigh of relief, and his big wife Addie said, "Thank God," but I knowed from the look in that Mexican doctor's face that it had all been for nothing.

The poor woman had fainted from the pain, and I personally had some doubt that she would ever come to. The doctor got the blood stopped and the wound taken care of the best he could. We put the lady back into the wagon, and the train started moving again toward Catclaw.

A big lot of people had gathered to watch the wagons come in. I pointed Zeb toward a big open piece of camping ground next to the wagonyard.

There was one thing about people in them days: They might quarrel and raise hell amongst theirselves, but when trouble came most of them was there to help each other. Being summer, the schoolhouse was empty. A bunch of people had already rushed over and fixed the place up to make a kind of hospital out of it. The woman teacher normally stayed in a little room in the back, where there was a stove and a bed and dresser and such. The women in town had already fixed this up for Mrs. Ridgway to give her some privacy. Cots had been brought in and set up for the wounded men and the boy in the main schoolroom. The benches and tables was shoved back against the wall.

They had the *gringo* doctor sobered up pretty good, but his hands was still shaking. I was glad the Mexican had already done the operation on Mrs. Ridgway because folks would of naturally chosen the *gringo* doctor over him. That would of been a bad mistake.

Like I said, people was good to pitch in and help where they could. The liveryman over at the wagonyard had all the people's stock brought into one of his corrals, and he put out hay for them. Said he wouldn't let the people pay him for it. Later on I figured out that he already sensed he was going to get to sell these folks a bunch of horses and mules to make up for the ones that the Indians had killed or got off with. That would make a little hay look cheap. But maybe what he done was all out of the kindness of his heart; it ain't for me to say it wasn't.

The wagon people made camp but didn't have to cook supper. People from the town kept coming out, bringing them stuff. I circulated amongst the wagon folks, talking to the ones that felt like talking. I found out that most of them was kin. They had come out of the old colonies of deep East Texas. The carpetbaggers had taxed them out of most of what they owned, and they was going west for a new start. They had heard farming land could be had cheap along the Rio Grande west of El Paso. They had elected Samantha's pa to head up the bunch. He had never done no Indian-fighting, but he had stood up against his share of Yankees in the war. He knowed a man's duty.

After he was killed, folks naturally looked to old Zeb Wentworth to lead them. He hadn't been off to war, but he had been in the home guards. He was there when the Yankees tried to invade Texas by way of Sabine Pass and got the pants shot off of them. I watched him there at the wagon, going around to the folks to be sure they all got camped all right, seeing that the stock was all cared for. I knowed he would of rather been down at the schoolhouse with his wife, seeing after his sister-in-law and his niece.

There might of been a lot he didn't know about westering, but he had the nerve to give it a good try. He had the look of a mild and gentle man, and mainly that's what he was. But one of the wagon people told me something that made me study him closer. Seems like the carpetbaggers and scalawags wasn't content to just take the land away from these people, but they tried to stop the wagon train and take away what little else they still had, claiming it was due on back taxes. One carpetbagger made a bad mistake, though. He laid his hands on a woman, trying to make her open a big wooden trunk so he could see if there was any money in it. In just the time it taken him to fall, he was laying on his back with a big hole between his eyes, and old Zeb was standing there with a rifle smoking. The rest of them thieves ran as fast as they could, back to the county seat.

That's the kind of people them farmers was. They minded their own business and was no worry to anybody except those that tried to mess with them.

It stood to reason there was probaby a reward out for Zeb back where he came from. But *I* wasn't tempted to do anything about it, not a particle.

I went up to Zeb finally and asked him if there wasn't something more I could do to help. He said if I wasn't a minister and wasn't a doctor, he guessed not. I had helped patch up a few wounded in my time, but I sure wasn't no minister.

I says to him, "What'll you-all do now? You're too crippled to go on."

He looked at me like he didn't understand what I said. He says, "We're crippled, but we ain't all dead. Sure we'll go on. We ain't finished what we set out to do."

That was their way; if there had just been one of them left alive, he would of gone on for the rest of them, or died making the try.

I rode down to the schoolhouse with him, partly because I knowed I'd see that girl and partly because something about this old man and his tribe had sort of got to me. I noticed that the first thing Zeb done when he walked in the door was to take his hat off, like it was a church or somebody's house, instead of just an empty school. His eye was on the door to the room where his own closest family was, but first he went to the wounded men and the boy and inquired after their health.

Samantha heard his voice and came out the door. She shut it behind her, kind of a sign that it was closed to the public in there. Real gentle, old Zeb asked her how her mother was. She didn't say anything; she just kind of answered him with her eyes.

All that time I had been trying to figure what it was about her that had hit me so hard. All of a sudden I knew. She reminded me of my Millie, my lost Millie. She was just about Millie's size and build, and with her face all smudged up like it was with dirt and grime and soot, the differences didn't show. Even her eyes was like Millie's.

She was, right at first, like Millie come back to me alive.

By the time I finally seen her with her face clean, and could tell she was a whole different woman, it didn't matter anymore. I was hooked tighter than a catfish on a trotline.

The old man hugged her, which I would of loved to of done, but of course that was unthinkable. I'd of wound up like that carpetbagger, trying to see out through a third eye. And I'd of had it coming to me.

Sometime during the night Samantha's old mother just drifted away in her sleep. Looking for her husband, I reckon. She never came back. Next afternoon they buried her in the town cemetery, over on the side with the "good" folks, away from all the hardnoses who had died wearing their boots. I'd have to say for the credit of the town that just about everybody turned out. Even the saloons closed. Not a soul there had knowed her, but they all done her honor. They went up on the hill after the hearse and sang about amazing grace and the blood of the lamb, and a few of the womenfolks cried like she was an old friend. They done right by her.

Samantha wished her mother could of been buried with her pa, but that wasn't practical. Old lady Addie told her they would find each other in Heaven; it didn't make much difference where they laid the clay.

Well sir, I kind of appointed myself an unofficial guardian and assistant to Zeb Wentworth. I made out like I figured it was my duty as a law officer. Mainly what it done was to give me a chance to see a right smart of that girl.

One thing was clear to me: These folks couldn't start out again the way they was, weakened so much. They had lost four men and a woman. It was going to be a few days before the two wounded men ought to have to suffer the hardship of the trip. Besides, they needed to heal up some so they could help if things came to another bad pinch. I told Zeb if he

would wait a few days maybe there'd be some more
emigrant wagons come along to reinforce them. A
man might make twenty trips across that desert and
not see an Indian. Then, on the twenty-first trip, one
would raise up from behind a little greasewood bush
and take his hair. It was all a matter of chance. The
Indians came and went like the weather, and didn't
leave many tracks.

All this time Sheriff Smathers was plaguing me
about that bank robber. Even if I caught him and got
the reward, after I split with old Smathers I wouldn't
have but two-fifty for my trouble. By then I was interested in something worth a lot more than any two-
fifty. I wanted that girl. So I spent most of my time
with the wagon people.

I didn't intrude myself on her or nothing, you understand; I just made it a point to always be around, so
that if she needed anything she didn't have to call on
nobody else.

The waiting was bad for me in one way, though,
because it gave the town women time to get acquainted with the train women and swap gossip. You
know how women will talk. Some of their opinions
of me wasn't near as good as the opinion I had of
myself. Well, that's natural. People sometimes need a
hard man to do their fighting for them, and take the
worst of the risks for them, but he don't fit in with
parlor society, or even front-porch society. He stands
outside someplace, needed too much to turn loose of
but not enough to bring him into the family. It's like
they're never quite sure of him, afraid maybe he'll go
bad on them one day. It's happened, plenty of times.

You'll often find that the man doing the hunting is
more like the man he's after than like the people that
pay him to do the job.

The wagon people wasn't loaded down with specie, but they had enough cash for the absolute necessaries. Main thing they needed was some extra draft animals to take the place of the ones they had lost. The people in town was friendly enough and sympathetic, but they was like most folks . . . when it comes to business, friendship don't cross over.

During the time I had been at Catclaw, traveling around looking out for the snorty breed, I'd got to know a lot of the ranchers. I thought I knowed some who might have horses and mules they would sell cheaper than the wagonyard operator and the folks in town was asking. A couple of the wagon folks needed oxen, and I had gotten acquainted with enough Mexicans to know where some such could be had. So I went wih Zeb Wentworth and a couple of others, trying to help them spend where the dollar was biggest.

Naturally that left some of the townfolks thinking sour thoughts about me, and speaking sour words. The keeper of the wagonyard had seemed like a pretty good friend of mine, but he cooled off after I done him out of the sale of twelve horses and mules. I figured he wasn't hurt none. There would be plenty of wagon folks coming through after these was gone, needing stock to replace some that went lame or died along the way. I wouldn't care if he stuck *them,* but these was *my* wagon people.

Doing this little chore gave me a chance to get these wagon folks on my good side—the men, anyway—and maybe offset what some of the town people might be telling them. Of course the people in Catclaw didn't know nothing about me except what I had done while I was there. They didn't even know Joe Pepper wasn't my real name. But some of the women told Addie Wentworth that I was now and again seen down on Red Lantern Row in broad daylight, where a respectable man wouldn't go except in the dark of the night. They told her I was a man who went out and hunted people down for money, like a wolfer killing varmints for the bounty, as if that was a bad thing. The men I went after was always somebody they wanted to get rid of anyway.

Each family on the wagon train done its own cooking. Since Samantha was alone now, Zeb and Addie taken her under their wing. They was her closest kin, so it was the Christian thing to do. The old lady always seemed like she went out of her way to keep Samantha busy when I came around. She said it helped keep the girl's mind off of her grief. I figured it was to keep her mind off of *me*, if she had been thataway inclined.

I didn't try to press her. I just always tried to be somewhere close in case she needed somebody to talk to. I never tried putting my arm around her or kissing her when she wasn't expecting it, or stuff like that. I had a notion that would scare her off. I had intentions toward that girl, and they was all honorable.

I started dropping suggestions to Zeb that it looked like they was going to need some extra men to go with them. I didn't volunteer, exactly; I thought it would look better if he asked me instead of it being the other way around. And I figured that if I played the cards careful and easy, he would do it. Old Zeb and Samantha was alike in some ways. I could tell they both liked me.

But not Addie Wentworth. A more suspicious old woman you'd never find. She could see through me like a pane of window glass. Every time me and Samantha was about to strike up a conversation, the old woman thought of some chore that wouldn't wait, and she'd put Samantha on it. Then she would give me a look that would turn sweet milk into clabber. I tried to take it kindly and tell myself she was just interested in Samantha's welfare, same as I was, but I couldn't help wishing sometimes it had been *her* that got in the way of the Indians.

She was a hefty sort of a woman. Two or three times when I watched her climbing into her wagon, I almost let the devil talk me into pushing her just to see how hard she would fall. Of course I never actually done it, but thinking about it was pleasuresome.

She kind of taken me by surprise one day. Another time I might of told her off, but Samantha was there and I couldn't afford to say anything she might take bad. The old lady bored a pair of holes through me with her eyes. She says, "People tell me you're a gunfighter who kills for money."

She caught me on my left foot, so to speak. All I could do for a minute was stammer. Finally I says, "I never shot no man that wasn't looking at me, and never one that didn't need it."

She didn't let up. She says, "I suppose you always considered that you did the world a favor."

I hadn't thought of it in quite that way. Any time I ever done a thing like that, the notion of doing the world a favor was a long ways from my thinking. I says, "I never been one to brag. But yes, I expect the world is better off without the ones I've put away."

I taken a long look at Samantha. I couldn't tell that I'd hurt myself in her sight. But I sure hadn't helped myself with old Addie.

It was pretty soon decided that the wounded was in shape to travel. And along about that time there come two more sets of wagons. One was some emigrant wagons with white folks. The other was a bunch of them old big-wheeled Mexican carts, traders headed out for El Paso with goods come all the way from ships that unloaded at the mouth of the Rio Grande. Naturally when the settlers on that mover train heard what the first wagon train had run into, they wasn't hard to talk into all joining together for the trip across the Pecos River country and out into the Davis Mountains, and then on to El Paso. There was a little discussion about maybe they could get along without the Mexicans. Some of the emigrants didn't know nothing about Mexicans except that they remembered the Alamo. But old Zeb asked me and I told him they wasn't *marrying* the Mexicans, they was just traveling with them. That kind of tickled the old man; he always loved a joke.

I suppose I had planted enough seed so that the idea seemed to sprout in Zeb's head all by itself. He comes up to me after having a powwow with men from the other wagons, and he says, "Anything keeping you here, Joe?"

I acted like I didn't know what he was getting at. He told me flat out that he'd be pleasured if I was to come and go along with them. He had a notion I could be of help to them in that wild country. I told him I never had been out that way very far, and I didn't know the trail. I had played enough good poker that I figured my eyes wouldn't show how much I really wanted to go. I wanted them folks to figure it was all their own doing, so they would feel grateful to me instead of it having to be the other way around.

Zeb told me they had some maps that was supposed to be reliable, and he figured the trail had been beaten out so well that we wasn't apt to get lost. Main thing he wanted me for was as a guard, to help be sure they didn't get slipped up on again.

I told him I sure did feel bad about having to leave Sheriff Smathers, him depending on me so much. That was all a poker bluff, of course. Far as I was concerned old Smathers could go soak his head in a trough till he quit bubbling. He had about wore out his welcome with me.

I told Zeb I didn't have a wagon. He said it was better that way. They wanted me to be an outrider, a scout. A wagon would be in my way. "We can't afford to pay you," he says, "but you can take your meals at my wagon with me and Addie and Samantha. Addie'll be right tickled."

I figured Addie would only be tickled to feed me some ground-up glass. But the idea of sharing a campfire with Samantha made the whole thing sound fine.

Zeb still thought he was the fisherman. I didn't intend to let him suspicion that he was the fish. He says, "When we get out yonder to the valley, I expect there'll be farmland enough that you can get a share for yourself. We'll be pleased to have you for a neighbor."

I could still remember my boyhood pretty good. One thing I didn't share with these emigrants was their feeling for the plow. But I had begun to picture me having a ranch out there, with cattle running all over the hills, and a little ranchhouse with Samantha in it, fixing my supper every night. So I told Zeb if they really felt like they needed me, I'd make the sacrifice and settle up my affairs in town.

Old Smathers had already sensed that I wasn't long for that place. He didn't act very pleased when I laid the badge on his desk, but he didn't seem surprised none either. He says, "Throwing in with them farmers, are you? Anybody can tell by looking at you that you ain't no farmer. Maybe you figure you can get ahold of their money somehow."

That was about what I had expected of him. He always thought of everything in terms of money. I didn't tell him about Samantha because she wasn't none of his business, and he wouldn't of understood anyhow. He was long past the point where a good-looking woman stirred him up much.

I went over to the bank to draw my money. Old man Dietert seemed like he was sorry to see me go, especially since I was pulling a right smart of cash out of his safe. He told me how risky it was to carry all that cash around and offered to write me a draft on a bank out in El Paso. I told him no thanks. I knowed what to do about a man that tried to rob me with a gun, but it wasn't so easy to keep a man from robbing you with pen and ink. I was looking at Clopton when I said it, just being sure he got the message clear. The old man was all right, but one of these days he was going to die of his infirmities, and this town would be at the mercy of Clopton.

I got me a moneybelt and put all that money in it where it belonged, just under my heart.

The next morning at daylight we pointed them wagons west. There I was, way out yonder with a whole train of farmers, standing in some danger of contamination. You know what a wagon scout is, don't you? He's a fool who rides way out in front of everybody and says to the Indians, "Here I am, come get me." Of course he hopes there ain't none of them around to take up the invitation.

Well, there wasn't, not for a while. The wagon people was pretty tense for the first two or three days, till we got to where the battle had taken place. They sure didn't let the wagons stretch out much; they had the lead horses or mules of every team sticking their noses over the tailgate of the next wagon. Zeb hadn't figured to stop at the battle site, but it was late in the day, and everybody just naturally quit. There was fresh graves out there, and they wanted to pray over them one more time, since it wasn't likely any of these people would ever pass this way again. I think Zeb was more worried over the state of mind this would put them in than over the time they might be losing.

It was an awful quiet supper. Afterwards Samantha got up and started walking real slow out to where her father was buried. I went to follow her, but old Addie stepped in front of me. "She'll want to be alone," she warns me, meaning that *Addie* wanted her to be alone.

"I won't bother her," I says. "I'll just go out there and make sure no Indian slips up and joins her."

I just stood back and watched her. I could see her shoulders shake a little and knowed she was crying, and I wanted to go up and take her and hold her so bad I couldn't hardly stand it. But I knowed old Addie was watching from over by the wagons, and she would be out there like a hornet. Finally Samantha says, "You'd of liked him, Joe."

I told her I knowed I would've, which was likely true. I liked Zeb, and from what I could hear, Samantha's father had been cut out of the same timber.

She says, "It scares me, going on out yonder alone."

If she had any doubt before how I felt about her, I didn't leave her any. I says, "You ain't alone. If I have anything to do about it, you ain't ever going to be."

I don't know what I expected her to say to that. Maybe I thought she would come and fall into my arms. She didn't. She just turned and looked at me, and I couldn't read what was in her eyes. She smiled, just a touch, and she says, "I know that, Joe." And then she walked back toward the wagon.

As far as I was concerned, I had asked her to marry

me. She hadn't said *no*, but she sure hadn't said yes, either.

We went on and never seen so much as a moccasin print. We had a little scare one day when a bunch of horsemen showed up in the distance, and we got all the wagons and carts circled in a hurry. The riders, though, turned out to be a patrol of black troopers with a white lieutenant working out of Fort Clark. They was on their way in after a hundred-mile scout, and they hadn't seen a thing.

People began to get so relaxed and confident that a few even quit being nice to the Mexican freighters. Decided, I reckon, that they wasn't going to need them after all.

Nighttimes, when I could talk to Samantha after supper where her old aunt couldn't hear us, I'd point out to her that a young woman all by herself that way couldn't take up a farm. It was by way of trying to get her to say she would step into double harness with me. But she would always say the Lord would show her the way when the time came; she figured He had plans for her.

I sure had plans for her.

I never did get to talk to her very long at a time. That old Addie seemed like she had twelve eyes, and half of them in the back of her head. She wouldn't give the two of us much chance for any real serious conversation.

Once when the old lady was busy digging through a trunk in her wagon and wasn't watching us, I got Samantha out and we started for a walk around the wagon circle in the moonlight. We hadn't got fifty yards before I heard somebody come trotting up behind us. I had my pistol out before I had time even to think about it. When I spun around I seen the old lady catching up to us. She didn't pay any more attention to that pistol than if it had been a matchstick. She says to Samantha, "You better get back to the wagon, sugar. It's dangerous out here."

Samantha says, "There ain't any Indians."

The old lady tried her best to kill me with a look from them two hard eyes. She says, "All the danger ain't from Indians."

Samantha done as she was told and started for her own wagon. The old lady hung back. When Samantha was out of hearing she turned on me like a mad cow hooking a wolf away from her calf. She says, "The rest of them don't see through you, Joe Pepper, but *I* do. You're trying to turn the head of a poor little orphan girl."

I pointed out to her that Samantha wasn't a little girl.

"She ain't old enough yet to know her own mind," Addie says. "Till she is, I'll help do her thinking for her. And *you* have no place in my thinking."

I didn't have anything but the best of motives in mind for that girl. I wasn't going to do a thing till the words had been properly read to us out of the Book. But I knowed there wasn't no use trying to convince Addie of that fact. I figured I would just keep working on Samantha, kind of slow and easy, and maybe by the time we got to El Paso I'd have her in a frame of mind to run off and look for a preacher with me. *That* would fix the old woman.

I t was the next day, or the day after that, when Pete Ogden showed up.

I was way out in front of the wagons, kind of edging over toward some flat-topped mountains. We kept the wagons as far back from the mountains as we could because it was a favorite stunt of the Indians to hide till the wagons got to the closest point, then come charging and catch the wagons strung out. I worked over fairly close, but not so close that they wouldn't have theirselves one dandy horserace trying to catch me.

That's when I seen the Indians, coming at me through the greasewood, running hard. One looked like he was a good ways out in front.

First thing I done was fire my pistol into the air three times to let them wagon folks know they was fixing to have a visitation. Then I put spurs to that Santos black and figured to see just how fast he could really run. He was even better than I figured. He had seen them other horses coming at us, and I reckon he sensed that I was some excited. Horses have got a way of knowing. If it had been a matched race on some country track, we could of taken the whole pot.

The farmers didn't waste no time. When I got to the wagons they had already circled up and put all the loose stock inside. They had left a little gap for me to ride through, was all. The second I loped in, they pushed the wagons up tight.

I had left them Indians like they was caught in the quicksand. But the odd thing was that one man was still way out in front of the others. It finally struck me that he wasn't with them; they was chasing him. And he was coming for the wagons as fast as he could travel.

Old Zeb hollers, "That's a white man!"

Sure enough, I could tell now that he was wearing a hat, something the Indians hadn't commenced doing at the time. And under that hat was a wad of hair he was fixing to lose. His horse was giving out under him.

Samantha all of a sudden got to remembering seeing her father shot down in front of her eyes. She started hollering, "Somebody save him!"

I tried to tell her that anybody who went out there might not come back. I didn't feel like going out and risking my life to save a fool. It was damned obvious that the man was a fool or he wouldn't of been out there by himself in the first place. But she wasn't listening to that kind of argument. She was hollering for somebody to do something, and then she grabbed a rifle and started out there herself.

Way I seen it, that man could take care of himself or take what was coming to him, but I wasn't just about to let that girl get herself killed for some stranger. I ran out and grabbed her. I turned her around and pushed her back toward the wagon. Then I dropped to one knee and started shooting past the man, into that bunch of Indians. At the distance I couldn't do them any great damage, but maybe I was looking good to Samantha. In a minute several other men came out afoot and joined me, and we all started walking to meet the rider, shooting our rifles as we went.

The Indians kind of wavered at all that fire. I don't think we was hitting any of them, but we had sure got their attention. The rider was in a pretty fair way to make it, then, but his horse went down. He was still out there a hundred yards or so past us, afoot. That gave the Indians a last chance, and it looked for a minute like they was going to get him. Old Zeb got up and started running out to meet him. I couldn't do no less with that girl watching, so I jumped up and followed after him. A couple of the Mexicans was right up beside me, and one or two of the farmers. I suppose I'd of looked better to Samantha if I'd been out in the lead. But I'd always believed that the Lord helps them that help theirselves, and I couldn't see where I was helping myself much out there so far from the wagons. Not with a dozen or fifteen Indians out there looking mad.

That feller was coming in to meet us even faster than we was going out to meet him. The Indians had stopped out there a ways and was taking potshots. Only three or four had rifles, and it was way too far to send an arrow. One of them got lucky and put a bullet in that feller's leg. He went down like he had been hit with an ax. He got up again, cussing like a politician who has just lost the election. You'd of thought, after the narrow escape he had, that he would of been more considerate of the Lord's feelings. He kind of hopped on his good leg and went down again.

Zeb hollered for him to lay still, that we was coming. But he kept right on crawling and scrambling toward us on his hands and knees, still looking back over his shoulder. A man don't rightly respect fear, I suppose, till he's had a bunch of Indians breathing on the back of his neck.

He was in a right smart of a panic when we got to him. I thought he was going to fight us right at first, like he couldn't tell for sure if we was Indians. I told him if he didn't behave himself I was going to stomp him a little. I grabbed him under one arm and a Mexican grabbed him under another. We lit out with him toward the wagons. Zeb and the others followed along behind us, walking and running backwards, keeping their eyes on the Indians. I was too busy to look, but I was satisfied they kept edging on in toward us till we got them up to good rifle range of the wagons. Then they stopped.

As we got to the wagons I turned for a quick look. I seen one of them Indians a hundred yards away. I didn't know much about sign language, but I got the gist of what he was telling us. The wagon people started shooting at him, and he decided to leave.

We laid the feller down in the shade of a wagon. He was groaning and cussing a little and wasn't feeling too good. That leg was bleeding. It wasn't flopping, though, so I felt like the bone hadn't been busted. All in all it wasn't much of a wound. I've been gouged near as deep by a cactus thorn.

There was more than enough people around to do the doctoring, so I didn't make no effort to help out. I had already done a right smart more than I figured was my duty to a damn fool. I stood in front of the wagon and kept my eyes peeled on the Indians. I didn't figure they was likely to make a charge at the wagons, knowing how they was outmanned, but I also knowed that Indians would sometimes do the opposite of what you expected. It never hurt to be ready.

Well sir, first thing I knowed Samantha was there with a pan of water and a towel, and she was washing that feller's face and talking soft to him while Zeb and a couple of the men was pouring whiskey into the wound and holding him down. He used language that ought to never fall on a good woman's ears, but I suppose he wasn't thinking along them lines at the time. Pretty soon Zeb had the bleeding stopped and the wound tied up and was telling everybody the damage was nothing very serious. I could of told them that from the start. The feller had calmed down considerable. Samantha was still putting that wet cloth to his face and trying to make him feel better.

It didn't make *me* feel any better, I'll tell you.

Now that I had time and the inclination for a closer look, I could see that he was young, a good deal younger than me. He had several days' growth of whiskers, but there wasn't no tracks around the corners of his eyes yet. When he finally managed to tear his eyes away from Samantha he looked at me. He says, "You're the one that dragged me in here, ain't you?"

I already felt like that could of been a mistake, and I didn't want to claim all the credit. I says, "One of them. Soledad Martinez was the other one."

He thanks us both and says, "That was sure a tight spot you-all got me out of."

I was about half mad, thinking how easy it would of been for some of us to have gotten ourselves killed. If it hadn't been for Zeb and Samantha, I'd of let him take his chances out there with them Indians.

I was about to walk off and leave him, but I decided to ask him, "What the hell was you doin' off out yonder by yourself, anyway? Didn't anybody ever tell you that Indians are dangerous?"

He says, "There's other things just as dangerous."

I seen the way Samantha was looking at him, with enough pity in her eyes to drown a gray mule, and I thought, *There sure is.* I walked out between the wagons and looked toward the mountains. The Indians was still out there, riding away but taking their time about it, kind of tempting the foolhardy to go chasing after them. There wasn't no fools with our wagons, though, unless you count that stranger.

When the Indians was clean gone I caught up my black and rode out to the stranger's horse. It was a little bay, still alive but too badly wounded to live. I pulled the saddle off of him, then put a bullet in his brain. I carried the saddle back to the wagon circle. A saddle ain't ever a cheap and easy thing to come by. I figured this stranger would need his to ride out of here as soon as he was able, which I hoped would be *real* soon.

Well sir, if you think you already begin to see the turn of things, you're plumb right. Just about the time I was beginning to have some dreams about buying me a ranch out west and settling down in a nest with Samantha, she gets a patient to worry about and motherhen over. I've never understood it, but I've seldom seen it fail. Watch a nurse, and nine times out of ten she'll marry one of her patients. You can be as big as a mountain, stout as a bull, brave as a bear, rich as old Croesus, and chances are you won't get no more than a passing glance from a woman. But get yourself sick or hurt to where she can wait on you and play nurse to you, and you've got her in the palm of your hand.

I got to wishing it had been *me* with a wound in my leg. Then maybe I'd of got some attention. Way it was, I hardly even got a thank-you-sir.

There wasn't nothing to do but camp right where we was till we could tell about them Indians. We figured there was some risk they might go for some of their friends. If the subject was to be pursued any further, this was as good a place as any to do it. They had to come at us over a big open greasewood flat where they made a lot better target than we did.

Time I got all the necessaries took care of and went back to the Wentworth wagon, Samantha already knowed a great deal more about the stranger than I was interested in finding out. His name was Pete

Ogden, she told me, and he had come from over around San Antonio someplace. He was on his way west to seek his fortune when he had run into the Indians, who had a little different plan worked out for him.

"You know something else?" she says. "He's a farmer."

Well, so had I been once, but I sure didn't brag about it.

She says, "If we try we might talk him into staying with us and locating in the same part of the country that we do."

I could tell by the way he kept looking at her that it wouldn't take any talking to convince him. It might take talking to keep him from it.

That old lady Addie was tickled to death over the way things turned out. She grinned at me like the jasper that's about to kick the stool out from under a man with the noose around his neck. I could've choked the old woman if there hadn't been so many witnesses.

Well sir, me and Soledad taken us a long ride early the next morning, swinging over to them hills to look for sign the Indians might be getting ready to come at us again. The country was as clean as a hound's tooth. We decided there wasn't anything to keep us from proceeding ahead except timidity.

Soledad was kind of the *caporal* over the Mexican part of the wagon train. Seemed like a decent sort, a man we could depend on. After that little set-to which gained us a new passenger, he got to acting as an outrider. I'd scout out front. He'd trail along behind the wagons, and far out toward the hills, making sure the train didn't get sneaked up on from behind. About all we ever seen out there was jackrabbits and *javalina* hogs.

You'd be surprised how fast Pete Ogden's leg started healing up. Of course he had him a good nurse that seen after his welfare every spare minute she had; he *ought* to've done good. Pretty soon he was getting around on a cane, then limping about without it. Looked to me like he was fit enough to start making some real use of himself around the wagons. But Samantha said he oughtn't to rush nature.

Nature was rushing along pretty good, it seemed to me. Nights, him and her would take out and walk around the edge of the wagon circle, the way I'd tried to do with her. Old Addie never would let us out of her sight when it was *me,* but she didn't seem to worry about Pete Ogden. Matter of fact, she would kind of stick the knife in me and give it a twist every time she seen the chance. She'd say, "Ain't they a handsome couple?" or such as that.

I'd remember the old Bible story about how the Lord handled all them sinners at the Tower of Babel by making them speak different languages so they couldn't understand each other, and I'd wonder how come he hadn't fixed it so men and women couldn't talk to one another. It would of saved a lot of grief in this old world, preacher. I'm surprised the Lord hasn't thought of it.

My eyes have always been pretty good. I could see by the look that came into Samantha's every time Pete Ogden passed in front of her that I could forget all them pretty little dreams I had been building up about her and me.

After awhile Pete got tired of riding in a wagon all day and volunteered to help out however he could. I mentioned the loose stock, thinking how it wouldn't hurt to let him eat dust at the tail end of the wagon train, bringing up the extra cattle and horses. He got the borrow of a horse and fell in back there and went to work. I watched him a right smart, and I'll have to admit he made a hand.

I was some disappointed about that. I had hoped he would show up as one of them slough-off types, and old Zeb would run him off from the train first time we came to a settlement. But he showed himself to be a willing worker and acted like he understood stock. There's nothing leaves a man as frustrated as wanting to dislike somebody and not finding anything solid to dislike him about.

It's even worse when you wind up owing him a debt. And one day pretty soon I found myself owing Pete Ogden.

We was way off out in that old dry country west of the Pecos River, where the Davis Mountains come down and cut across the desert, and you either have to climb over them or go way around or hunt a pass through. All the old wagon and stagecoach trails led through the passes, which is fine except when the Indians come looking for horses and hair. A nice narrow pass is just made to order for an Indian, like buffalo hump and eagle feathers. We came up to one, and there wasn't nothing else to do except me ride in there and see if there was anything waiting for us that we might not want to meet.

There was.

Did you ever accidentally strike a hornet's nest and watch them hornets pour out after you? I doubt that you did much watching because you was too busy running. That's the way it was with me. These stories you read about the Indian always knowing everything that goes on within a hundred miles of him are just so much imagination on the part of some Eastern writer that never heard an arrow sing by his left ear.

I think I surprised them Apaches about as much as they surprised me, or I wouldn't of had a chance for any kind of head start.

I've known a few old men in my time that had a reputation as Indian fighters. They always told me that one secret of getting to be an *old* Indian fighter was to know when to run, and always ride a fast horse just in case you come to one of them times unexpected. I was riding that Santos black and doing real good. I could see the wagons going into a circle ahead of me. Way out behind, Soledad was spurring like hell to catch up to the train.

I was making a dandy gain on them Indians. I was maybe three hundred yards from the train and at least a couple of hundred ahead of them Apaches when I seen somebody come spurring out to meet me from the wagons, firing a pistol as he came. Now, talk about useless . . . somebody shooting a pistol at Indians five hundred yards away is just plain wasteful.

Another old story you hear sometimes is that Indians couldn't shoot a gun straight. That's about as truthful as a lot of the other Indian yams. I was looking back over my shoulder and seen one of those Indians stop his horse, jump off, drop to one knee and fire. I seen the smoke, and a second or two later that horse of mine turned a flip.

I hit the ground like some giant had picked me up and throwed me as hard as he could. All the breath was knocked out of me, and that horse's rump came down and pounded on both of my legs. I reckon it was imagination, but I thought I could already hear them Indians singing over my hair. I tried to get up and run, but I didn't have the breath in me, and my legs was both too numb. I sort of halfway pushed myself to my feet. My eyes was so blurry I couldn't see which was the way to the wagon train, and which to the Indians.

I heard a horse come running at me, and tried to shoot my pistol at it, but it was all jammed with dirt and wouldn't fire. I throwed my hands up to try and protect my head, because I figured I was about to get a stone ax right over my ear.

Somebody hollered. "Grab on! Let's get out of here!"

It was Pete Ogden. He leaned over and reached out his arm, and all of a sudden my legs didn't hurt me a bit. I grabbed onto him. He socked the spurs to that horse and held me as tight as he could up against the saddle. My legs was both hanging off on one side, dragging through the low brush. I could hear them Indians hollering behind us. I could hear that horse straining with the double load, and I could hear Pete Ogden promising him all kinds of good things if he wouldn't let the Indians catch us.

You never tried to hang onto a running horse when all the breath's been knocked out of you, I suppose. Under any ordinary circumstances it would be hard to do. But knowing what was back there to catch me if I fell off, I didn't have much trouble at it.

I heard the wagon people shooting, trying to drive the Indians back, but I couldn't see anything. The saddlehorn kept punching me in the ribs and knocking the breath back out of me every time I could get a little air in. We made it to the wagons. Pete Ogden jumped his horse over a wagontongue and dropped me on the ground like I was a sack of oats. I was still in a daze when people picked me up and started hunting over me for wounds. By the time I could get enough breath back to tell them I was all right, there wasn't a secret birthmark about my body that half the wagon train didn't know. My clothes was pretty well torn off of me, first by the fall when my horse went down, and then by the brush Pete drug me through.

Directly I was laying under the shade of a wagon and looking up at Pete Ogden the same way he had looked at me the time before. Except that I didn't have any wounds for Samantha to fuss over, and get her all moon-eyed.

Saying "thank you" never was hard for me like it is for some people, but this time it was like pulling my own teeth out to get it said. I almost gagged over it. I finally told Pete I was right obliged to him for his little favor, and what the hell was he shooting up all that ammunition for? He said he was hoping he might scare the Indians away, which showed how little he knowed about Indians. I hoped he knowed more about farming.

You might think what Pete done just squared up a debt he owed me, but I knowed deep inside that it was more. The only reason I had gone out to rescue him was because Samantha shamed me into it, and I knowed the others was going out anyway. But Pete Ogden came after me all by himself, and without anybody shaming him. This young farmer was a *man*, and I resented him for it!

Talk about things turning out backwards . . . this time it was *me* that was laid up and needing help, and all Samantha could do was hug Pete Ogden's neck and tell him how brave he was, how scared she was that something might of happened to him. Nary a word about what might of happened to me.

A man who tells it around that he understands women is just letting everybody know how big a fool he really is.

I got my breath back awhile later. Zeb asked me

what I thought we ought to do about getting through that pass. I told him it seemed to me that if them Indians wanted it so much, the neighborly thing was to let them have it and work on north. Maybe we could find us another one that wasn't being used. Soledad rode out and got my saddle back for me when the Indians was gone, the way I had done for Pete Ogden. The Indians had carried off my carbine. I sure hated to leave that black horse. He was as fast a one as ever I rode, excepting maybe my Tennessee gray. But they don't make horses that can outrun a bullet.

That was the last of the Indian trouble for us, though Pete Ogden didn't take Samantha outside the wagon circle for any more night walking. They just stayed at the wagon and spooned in front of everybody. Odd thing happened, too. Pete Ogden had always seemed grateful to me for helping drag him away from the Indians, and after he done the same thing for me he got downright friendly, like we was old partners or something. I didn't encourage him. Even if he didn't know it, I owed him a right smart more than he owed me, and owing a man a debt don't endear him to you.

It got to be common knowledge amongst the wagon folks that when they got to El Paso him and Samantha was going to hunt up a preacher. There wasn't nobody prouder over it than Addie Wentworth. She had finally got to where she would even treat me like a white man, knowing I wasn't no danger to her niece any longer.

But I could tell something was bothering Pete. I'd catch him sometimes watching her when she wasn't looking, and there was a worry in his eyes that got to worrying *me* a little. I got to suspicioning that maybe he already had him a wife back wherever he came from, and things had gone so far that he was afraid to tell anybody. I got to thinking maybe there was hope for me yet.

One night Pete tapped me on the arm and gave me a nod of his head. He motioned for me to walk out with him a ways, past the wagons. By this time we had got amongst some Mexican settlements along the Rio Grande, and we wasn't much concerned about Indians anymore. It wasn't far to El Paso.

Pete says to me, "Joe, I got something to tell you. If I don't do it now, I'm going to bust."

I figured he was going to confess to me about the wife he had went off and left behind him. I was going to hear him out and then do the manly thing: knock him halfway to El Paso.

He says, "You figured me for a stranger when I joined this train, but I wasn't, not quite. You never seen *me* before, but I seen *you*, Joe. I knowed who you was from the start."

That throwed me a little. I just looked at him and tried to think back to when I could of ever crossed his trail before. I was afraid he knowed I was Joe Peeler instead of Joe Pepper.

He says, "I rode into Catclaw one night, and I spotted you with your badge on. I made it a point to stay out of your sight. I needed me a stake to go on west; I was flat busted. I waited till you was out of town, and I taken it."

He didn't have to tell me any more. I guessed the rest of it. I says, "You're the bank robber I hunted all over hell and half of Texas for."

He just nodded at me. He says, "I was hungry, and it seemed like a smart thing to do. Now that I've throwed in with these good folks, and you and Samantha, I'm ashamed of myself. I can see that I really ain't good enough for her. I ain't worth much, Joe."

That wasn't exactly the truth. He was worth five hundred dollars to me, right there the way he stood. That is, when I delivered him in at El Paso and notified the bank at Catclaw.

I was a little put out at him. I says, "Have you got an idea how many miles I rode hunting for you? I wore saddle-blisters on my butt and went hungry so much that I had to punch a new hole in my belt."

He tells me, "I'm sorry, Joe. I didn't know you at the time, and I thought it would be funny to have people hunting for me and not finding me. It was the first time in my life anybody paid any real attention to me."

"If they'd of caught you they'd of paid you more attention than you really wanted."

Pete says, "I still got nearly all the money, Joe. I just spent a little dab in Mexico, is all. I'd like to get you to send it back to them for me." He reached inside his shirt and brought out a little canvas pouch. I ran my hands into it. I could tell it wasn't no big lot of money.

He says, "There's a shade over nine hundred dollars. I never spent more than twenty-thirty of it."

I thought about my little leather bag of gold. I wasn't in the pouch. I says, "There's something else, Pete. You got something that belongs to me personal."

He didn't act like he understood, so I told him. He just blinked at me. He says, "I didn't see nothing like that. All I taken was the currency."

Something about the way he looked at me, I knowed he was telling me the truth. Which meant that somebody else had lied to me.

Clopton! Old man Dietert's number-one helper had been the one who opened the safe for Pete, and the one who shut it afterwards. *That* crooked coyote had got off with my gold and blamed it on Pete Ogden.

I cussed a blue streak. Pete thought it was against him. He says kind of sorrowful, "I don't blame you for being mad at me. I got it coming. You want to turn me in to the law at El Paso, I'll stand ready to take my medicine."

There it was, the opportunity to get Pete Ogden out of the way, to maybe have a new chance at Samantha. To rub old lady Addie's nose in the truth. The chance I'd been waiting for, and I spoiled it.

I got to feeling noble and generous, which is a feeling I never had but a few times, and generally always lived to regret. I says to Pete, "You really love that girl? You really mean to try and make her happy the rest of her life?"

"I would if I could. But she won't want me when she finds out what I am. I ain't worthy of her."

"She don't have to know about it. I'll turn in the money for you. I'll send a letter back to Catclaw and tell them I found you and had to kill you. As far as they'll be concerned you're dead and buried, and the case is closed. Nobody ever has to know except me and you."

I don't reckon Pete had expected that. I do believe he was about to break down and cry. He says, "I'll owe you for the rest of my life, Joe."

Better *him* owing *me* than the other way around. What he didn't know wouldn't hurt him. I wasn't really all that noble. I knowed if I was to turn Pete in to the law, Samantha would blame me more than she blamed him. Chances was she wouldn't of spoken to me again, ever. All I would've got out of it would've been the reward. I figured to get the reward anyway.

Well sir, we got in to El Paso, and they had theirselves a wedding, and Pete Ogden moved right into
Samantha's wagon. Old lady Addie grinned at me,
so much as to say she was glad Samantha had got
herself an honest, hardworking young farmer boy instead of a crooked, whiskey-drinking, gambling gunfighter. And I grinned back at her because I knowed a
lot more about it than she did.

The wagon train pulled out for the valley where the
farmers figured to sink their plows into new ground.
I stayed in El Paso because it would of hurt too much
to see Samantha and Pete Ogden together.

I really did intend to turn that money in at first.
Then I got to thinking. They owed me a five-hundred-
dollar reward for finding the bank robber in the first
place. On top of that, they owed me for that bag of
gold Clopton had got away with. I figured the money
Pete had given me didn't quite cover all I had coming
to me. But I was still in a generous mood and willing
to accept my loss. I just kept what I had.

I did write old man Dietert a letter, though. Best I
remember, I told him something like this:

Deer Mr Dietert,
Just a line to let you know I come across that
bank robber and we had a fight and I am sorry
to relate that I was obliged to kill him. Before he
died he told me he had went and spent all the
money so there aint none to send to you. I saved
his ear to mail you as proof but it spoiled on me
and I dont think you want it. He also told me he
didnt get as much as was supposed to have been
lost and that he suspected somebody in the bank
must have helped himself and blamed him for it.
I was thinkin maybe it might be smart if you and

Sheriff Smathers was to surprise Clopton with a serch of his house, you might be surprised at what you come up with. He always looked kind of shifty eyed to me.

Best regards and yours truely.

Joe Pepper

I would of liked to have been there if they found my gold sack on him. I never did hear one way or the other, but years later I run across somebody from Catclaw and asked if they knowed old man Dietert or his helper Clopton. They said the old man had finally died of a heart seizure, and Clopton had long ago run off to Mexico. Seemed there was trouble of some kind, and he got away with nothing much more than his britches.

6

I'm ashamed to tell you, preacher, but for a little while I tried to drown my sorrows in bad whiskey and sinful surroundings. Old El Paso was a good place for a man who wanted to do that kind of a thing. They had people there who was experts at helping you. I consorted with women of bad character and men who was worse. Pretty soon that fat money belt had shrunk to a little of nothing. One morning I come face to face with myself at the mirror and done some pretty stern talking. I had to get myself into some productive kind of labor.

So I went back to gambling. I know you don't approve of it, but the way I done it, there wasn't a lot of gamble in it. I cheated. Not all the time, mind you; just when I had to. Nine out of ten of them people didn't have to be cheated; they would just naturally beat themselves. Pretty soon I had built me up a first-rate stake again. Not as much as I had come to town with, but enough to set me up in a game where I stood a chance to come away with some real important money.

I had given up on my dream of a home with Samantha, of course, but the idea of another ranch hadn't altogether left me yet. I had a notion that if I could clean up good in El Paso I'd drift on out to Arizona and maybe buy me a ranch and live the rest of my life in peace.

At one place in town they had a high-stakes game in a back room almost every night. Big cow men and big mine people would come there and try their hand against the best gamblers in town. Their luck wasn't usually any too good, but they would keep coming back, most of them, hoping the next time Lady Luck would turn her face on them instead of her back. That's what kept them high-stakes games going, was the hope that when a man lost big, he might go back and win big. Now and again one would, just enough to keep the others hoping. Meanwhile them gamblers skimmed the cream off of a lot of the cow business and the mining without ever getting cow manure on their boots or picking up a shovel.

The place was a saloon known as the Rio Bravo, which was the name a lot of the Mexicans had for the Rio Grande. Owner was a man named Frank Feller. He was a fair-to-middling poker player and sometimes sat in on the games, but mostly he was a shill for the real gambler of the outfit, a tall, spidery kind of a gent named Arthur Phelps. Folks around town called him "Slick" Phelps, but not to his face. He was said to be a good shot. He had long hands that had never known a callus, and tapering fingers that could make a deck of cards do almost anything except sing a hymn. Feller provided the place and bankrolled

Phelps's games and got a percentage of the take, though they always pretended the game was Phelps's own, and Feller appeared to lose a right smart to him. That was just to bring the suckers in.

I had got a little rusty at the game, since them people in Catclaw hadn't been much of a challenge, but I polished it up in El Paso and bided my time till I thought I was ready to match up with Slick Phelps. Finally, after I had been there two months, I sat in on the game one night, figuring I was ready. Now, I considered myself a right smooth hand, but I could tell right off that I wasn't a match for Phelps. I lost a thousand dollars in one night and knowed he was cheating me more than I was cheating him, but I never once caught him at it.

So I went back to lower-stakes games in other places to practice up some more. I practiced cheating other people, then I would turn around and cheat myself on purpose so they wouldn't catch on to what I was doing. I wasn't after these small fry anyway, except for the practice they gave me. I had my sights set on cleaning out Slick Phelps. Finally I went back and sat in with him again. I thought I had improved to where I could give him a contest. It didn't take me but two hours and another thousand dollars to figure out I wasn't good enough to wipe the dust off of his boots.

I noticed a couple of things about Slick Phelps. One thing, he never drank. The only thing he ever taken was a cup of coffee, which seemed to sharpen him up. Whiskey was for idiots when it came to high-stakes gambling. It just slowed the hands and dulled the eyes. Then Slick Phelps would come down his web and grab you like a fly. Another thing he always done was to excuse himself every couple of hours. He would walk outside and take a little air, and he would ease his kidneys. Little as you might think about it, the strain on a man's kidneys in a long game can be just the edge that a smoother player needs on him. Slick Phelps didn't give nobody any edge.

When Phelps was out, Feller would take over the game. He was no cowboy playing for matches on a saddle blanket, of course, but he wasn't a pimple on Phelps's backside when it come to the pinch. Often as not he would lose more than he taken in, and when Phelps came back it was up to him to recover the house losses. Some of them high-stakes players always kind of waited for Phelps to take his constitutional, then they would bet big against Feller, trying to get back what they could.

I knowed if I stayed in El Paso till I had a beard to my belly, I would never beat Slick Phelps. Not in any ordinary way, that is. But Joe Pepper didn't get his reputation doing everything the ordinary way.

They had an outhouse behind the saloon, up against the alley. I set myself out there one night in the shadows across the other side and watched Phelps. He done everything by habit. He would come out the back door and stand on the stoop two or three minutes, looking up at the stars. I figured he was probably looking for sign of rain, which was a waste of time at El Paso. Next thing he would do was to roll himself a cigarette and stand there and smoke it about half up. He never smoked inside, at the game. Cigarettes was a distraction, and he didn't allow himself no distractions.

Finally he would throw the cigarette away, walk to the outhouse, take care of nature's call, then stop at the washstand, wash and dry his hands, and go back in to the game. I watched him all that night, and never once did he vary from the routine.

I had sort of worked up an idea in my head. The sheriff was an agreeable sort of feller, considering the things he had to put up with, and he generally rode around town in a buggy. One night there was a disturbance in one of the fancy houses down toward the river, and he went trotting his horses down there to see about it. I trailed along behind him in the dark. While he was inside I fished in the back of that buggy and found a set of handcuffs. I didn't steal them, exactly, I just took the borrow of them awhile. I didn't have a key to them, but I kept pestering them a couple of days, off and on, till I learned how to open them up with a piece of wire.

The night I brought off my plan, I taken all the money I had been able to work up and shoved it into my shirt. I taken the handcuffs and a fair piece of rawhide rope, and I set myself up in the dark behind the Rio Bravo. I let Slick Phelps go the first time he came out. The second time I watched him smoke his cigarette, and watched him go to the house out back. When he went to the washstand and poured a pan of water out of the bucket, I stepped up behind him and gave him what people used to call a cowpuncher shampoo. That is, I fetched him a lick up beside the head with the barrel of my six-shooter. You never seen a tall man fold up so limber.

I had found where there was an old empty corral a piece off down the street. I drug him down there in the dark while he was still enjoying the benefit of the shampoo. I laid him on the ground, handcuffed him to the bottom of the fencepost and tied his feet with the rawhide rope. I stuffed a handkerchief into his mouth and tied another one around it to where he couldn't holler. Time he come to he was trussed up like a hog on a spit.

I dusted myself off, walked in the front door of the Rio Bravo and marched back to that high-stakes game in the rear room. I bought me a stack of chips and set in to see how much I could win from Frank Feller.

He didn't seem bothered right at first when I started beating him. He would glance over towards the door once in a while, figuring Phelps would walk in any minute and polish me off in short order. My stack of chips started growing right peart. Before long Feller was spending a lot of time looking at that door. Every time he did I taken the occasion to improve my hand a little. Sweat started running down into his eyes, and he would rub a sleeve over them, and I would see him pull a new card out of that sleeve. That didn't bother me much; as long as I could see what he was doing, I could do him one better.

He got to talking about how something must of happened to Phelps, and maybe we ought to wait up the game for him. I told him it didn't matter to me whether Phelps was in the game or not, that if Feller was able to play for the house there wasn't no reason why the game shouldn't go on. One by one the other players dropped out. By and by Feller had dropped so much money to me that he couldn't afford to quit. He kept thinking, I guess, that Phelps would finally show up and bail him out of trouble.

But Phelps didn't show up. I had picked me a good place to put him, where nobody was apt to come across him till daylight. By daylight I figured to have myself that ranch in Arizona.

What I *did* get was something different. By the time the sun came up and hit Feller in the eyes through the glass panes of the east window, he didn't own that window anymore. *I* did. The Rio Bravo was mine.

The story told around town was that somebody figured Phelps would have money in his pockets when he stepped outside that night. They waylaid him to rob him, then handcuffed him to give theirselves plenty of time to get away. Most people agreed it was probably Mexicans from over in Paso del Norte, across the river. It was the custom if you couldn't find out who had done something to just blame it on the Mexicans.

Most people accepted that theory, but Frank Feller never did. I think he had it figured out from the time they found Phelps where I had left him. He came to me at the Rio Bravo, where I was figuring what color I wanted to paint the front. He was loud and threatening; most people hadn't heard much about Joe Pepper at the time. He left there in a lot worse shape than he came, one eye shut and the other hard to see out of. He went then to Slick Phelps and convinced him it was me who had done him to a turn.

I wished he hadn't done that, because I figured on making Phelps a proposition to stay on and play for me the same way he had played for Feller. That loudmouth ruined it.

Phelps sent word he was coming to have satisfaction. I sent him back a note telling him I was already satisfied and didn't want no trouble. People around the saloon told me he was a man to watch out for; he had helped several undertakers across the country to get on their feet and pay their bills. I decided if that was the way it had to be, I didn't want anybody saying I wasn't ready.

I taken me a rifle and walked across the street to a little barbershop. I sat down where I could watch the front of the place through the window while the barber cut my hair. By and by Slick Phelps came walking down the street on them long, spindly legs. Just before he got there he shucked his swallowtail coat and laid it across a hitching rack where it wouldn't get dirty and wouldn't be in his way. He had a six-shooter on his hip.

Up to then I had entertained some notion I might still be able to talk to him. After seeing him I decided that talk was the last thing he had come for. He stopped in front of the Rio Bravo. He hollers in, "Pepper, you coming out here?" He drawed his pistol and held it.

Them fellers that drawed before they faced you was hard to beat.

I didn't say anything. I taken the barber's cloth from around my neck and got up from the chair.

Phelps waited a minute and hollered again. Then he walked inside. I reckon he didn't find me in there, because in a minute or two he was back. Meantime I had stepped down into the street, into the sunshine. It just so happened that this was late in the afternoon, and my saloon faced west toward the sun. Afterwards, some people accused me of working it all out this way. I never did admit to that.

He had been inside long enough that his eyes was accustomed to the dark instead of the light. I says, "Slick, how about me and you working out a deal? We'd make good partners."

He hadn't come there to talk business. He raised up his pistol, but the afternoon sun hit him in the eyes. I leveled my rifle and taken a good clean sight while he started to shoot wild. You can imagine, preacher, it wasn't no contest.

I sure did wish I hadn't had to shoot Phelps. Him and me could of made us a right smart of money together if he hadn't listened to Frank Feller so much. If

I had had my choices I would rather of laid out Frank Feller.

Well sir, that's how come Joe Pepper to start making a reputation in and around El Paso. Folks figured I must be something special to have beaten Slick Phelps, but I didn't take no credit and still don't. I'd still rather bring a man around to my persuasion than to kill him.

Them days they had a custom in El Paso. Somebody had nailed a big board to a tree in the middle of town, and it was kind of a bulletin board for everybody to see and use. Somebody had something he wanted to sell, he tacked a note on the board. Somebody wanted to call a man a thief or a liar in public, he wrote it out and tacked it up on the board. A friend told me there was a note on the board that I ought to go see. Frank Feller had wrote it. He called me twelve kinds of a cheat and a black-hearted killer. I looked all over town for him. I had it in mind to take him over to the board and persuade him to eat that note, with witnesses. But folks told me he had remembered some business in Mexico.

That Rio Bravo turned out to be quite a place. I'd never had me a saloon and gambling house before. Pretty soon I gave up any notions I'd had about a ranch. The cow business never was half what people sometimes made it out to be. A man can starve himself into a little bitty shadow trying to nurse along a bunch of money-losing cows. A man who has a good saloon is always popular, especially in a thirsty place like El Paso was. Any direction you came from, when you got to El Paso you was dry to the bone.

I taken over the run of the games. I handpicked me a couple of good house gamblers, bankrolled them and taken a split of the proceeds. Once in a while one of them would get to putting aside too much money for himself and start to feeling independent, and then I'd have to get into a game with him myself and teach him a little humility, and also take enough money from him that he appreciated working for me again.

There's an art to handling employees. Some people never learn it.

Things was running my way for a change. I won't try to tell you we run a hundred-percent honest house because you wouldn't believe me, and I don't see no point in telling a lie if there's no profit in it. But I will say we tried to give everybody as even a shake as they could get anywhere in town, and better than most. We had the odds with the house anyway because I didn't keep men around working for me that wasn't almost as good a hand with the pasteboards as I was. And we tried never to clean a man out of his last dime; we always quit in time to leave him a taw. That way maybe he would come back for another game. Take a man's taw away from him and you've lost a customer for good.

About the only worry I had was politics. I never seen a town so mean on politics as El Paso was. The Democrats and the Republicans was at each other's throats. And there was factions within both of them groups that was fighting each other almost as hard as they fought the opposite party. Me being an old Confederate veteran naturally leaned me a little toward the Democrats, but I tried never to worry about a man's politics when I played him. I taken money gladly from Democrat and Republican alike.

It was during that time that I first run onto Burney Northcutt. Folks told me he was a big rancher from west of the Pecos. He wasn't an old man then, the way *you've* knowed him in late years. He was just sloping over the hill into middle age. He had a pinch of gray in his hair and a dab in his mustache, but his eyes was pure fire. He had built a big spread by having the guts to take what he wanted and the iron will to hang onto it. He had fought Yankees and Apaches and bandits and drouth. He had a natural taste for combat; it was like fresh air and sunshine to him. When things ran quiet for too long he would take an itchy notion to come into El Paso, ream out his innards with strong whiskey, and see if his luck at the tables was as good as his luck on the range.

It never was. Folks told me he had always lost to Slick Phelps. Nothing changed when I taken over the Rio Bravo. He lost to me every time we ever played.

He would cuss like a muleskinner and threaten to shoot me, but as long as he kept his hand away from his pistol I didn't pay him much mind. I wasn't one of them people who rankled at every insult and called on a man to apologize or draw his gun, not if I knowed he still had some gambling money left in his pockets. Anger is bad for the digestion, and none too good for business, either.

Half a dozen times I could of shot Burney Northcutt, and not six people in El Paso would of criticized me for it. Maybe if I'd done it then, I wouldn't be in the fix you find me in here tonight.

But of course that's spilt milk, and there's no use rolling in it.

I found me a nice-looking girl down on the row. She had corn-silk hair and big blue eyes that seemed to touch a chord in me someway. I taken her out of circulation and kept her in my own private stock, so to speak. I got to where I didn't waste much time fretting over Samantha. She was just another game I had played and lost. If a man's going to be any kind of a gambler, he's got to get so he don't cry over his losses.

I had me some good times there in El Paso. Things rocked along pretty smooth for a long spell. That's not to say there wasn't little difficulties once in a while over a game, and once I had to kill a holdup man who tried to bulldoze the place and take all the money. But I went for a whole year once without ever having to draw a gun on anybody. Joe Pepper's reputation went a long ways toward holding down trouble.

One day that girl of mine told me she heard a rumor that Frank Feller had been seen in town. He was talking about getting even, some of the girls had said. I had got kind of careless in my good fortune, but I taken to sitting with my back to the wall and watching the doors and windows. I didn't figure him for a face-out shooter, not after what happened to Slick Phelps.

After a while I decided the reports must of been false, because I never did see or hear anything of him. Then all of a sudden I had something a lot more than Frank Feller to worry about. A new face showed up in the high-stakes games.

This feller didn't look a bit like Slick Phelps or I'd of taken him for his brother. He had Phelps's same techniques with the cards. He had the same kind of long, tapering fingers, the same quick and easy shuffle that left you convinced you had missed seeing something but never could tell exactly what. And every time he sat down at the table, the stack of chips in front of him growed while everybody else's got smaller and smaller. The gamblers that worked with me played him first, till he cleaned them out. I gave them a good talking-to about paying attention to business, but that didn't do no good. They was simply outclassed. So finally I sat in on the game with him myself.

It would of been better if the doctor and sheriff had come along and quarantined the place for smallpox. He taken me the way Grant taken Richmond. He got me in the same shape that I had got Frank Feller, in so deep that I couldn't afford to keep on but couldn't afford to quit, either. When it was all over, he had the Rio Bravo, and I had had me *some* experience. He left me with a hundred dollars—said he never liked to leave a man without a taw.

That's when I first seen the fine hand of Frank Feller at work. He showed up looking like a cat that's stole the cream and left the family nothing but the skim milk. He announced to all and sundry that he had gone all the way to California hunting a gambler good enough to take me to the poorhouse.

For a little while I studied on killing him, and I expect I would of done it if I could of decided on a way. No way I could think of seemed like it was quite bloody enough. Then after awhile I began to see that he hadn't done nothing more to me than I had done to him. The more I thought about it, the more it got to looking funny, except I couldn't get myself to laugh much.

Sooner or later, I figured, somebody else would take him. He wouldn't die rich. I would live to see him flat on his butt again.

But while I was waiting for that, I couldn't just sit around. I had got in the habit of eating regular. That hundred dollars wouldn't take me far. In fact, I sat in on a low-ante poker game and lost most of it in about the same time as I would of spent eating a good meal.

Lady Luck had turned her back on me. I don't know what I done to sour the old girl on me, but whatever it was, it must of been something big. Got to where I couldn't hardly beat a bunch of cowboys playing on a saddleblanket.

My girl with the corn-silk hair was spending her nights with other people. I was eating *chili* and sleeping on a bedroll down by the river when somebody came to me with a story that Don Luis Terrazas was hiring guards on the big ranch he was building down in Chihuahua. He was paying good money to *gringo pistoleros*. I borrowed a few dollars from some friends and bought me a few days' supplies and struck off across that sandy desert south of El Paso.

I didn't have no trouble getting the job. My only trouble was getting to like it. I never did. Terrazas had been a soldier under Juarez, people told me, and he grabbed up a big chunk of Chihuahua state after they run the Frenchmen out. I reckon that was his reward. Naturally there were already some natives there who didn't want to give up what they figured was theirs. He needed people who could use a gun and convince them they was wrong.

It was some of the easiest money I ever made, away from a gaming table, but the job always had a sour taste to it. Every time I brought back a runaway *peon* on a rope, or somebody they had classed as a *bandido,* I'd get a whiff of the cells they throwed them in, and I'd remember the one Captain Santos had used for me. They all had the same smell to them. It's a stench that, once it gets in your nostrils, it never quite leaves you the rest of your life. It marks you someway, like the smallpox.

I got sick of it. So one night I drawed my pay and slipped down to the cells. I gave the two guards there a cowpuncher shampoo. Then I taken the keys and opened all the doors I could get to and let the prisoners out. Some of them taken to running the way I expected them to. Others just sat there, afraid to try to get away. They had been *peons* all their lives to one *patrón* or another, and the idea of freedom was beyond their thinking. I didn't have time to stay around and give them any Fourth of July lecture. I figured Don Luis would probably have some of his gunfighters on my tail by daylight, and it was a long ways from the mountains of Chihuahua back up to the Rio Grande. I taken my horse, and a couple of Don Luis's that seemed like they wanted to follow me. When I looked behind me after sunup, I didn't see nothing back there but desert.

I tried the cards again in El Paso, but Lady Luck still had me on the list. I had to sell the Terrazas horses to be able to eat. I thought about going back to the kind of work I done at Catclaw, but the sheriff wasn't hiring. He didn't care much for retired gambling-house owners, or for men that had carried a pistol for Terrazas. Kind of a narrow-minded sort, he was.

I thought maybe I'd go bring in fugitives for the reward, but that turned out not to be worth all the wear and tear, either. I guess it taken an awful crime out in that part of the country to make them offer much of a reward, they was used to so much devilment anyway. Most people who had the law after them would run off down into Mexico, and I couldn't afford to cross the river. Don Luis and his *pistoleros* had a long memory for faces.

Like I've said before, one thing I always had was the sense to know when the gravy was going thin, and it was time to change. It was bully for me that I'd built up a right smart reputation. The word had passed around the country that Joe Pepper was a good hand with a gun. An outfit over in New Mexico was mining silver, and they had been having trouble getting their stuff out. A bunch of bold and brassy *hombres* kept riding in and taking it away from them. The law wasn't doing them much good, seemed like. Everybody knowed to their own satisfaction who was taking the silver, but they didn't have proof. Without proof the law couldn't do much—or wouldn't—so the mine owners came and asked if I could help them. I told them if they paid enough, there wasn't no practical limit to what I could do.

They was, I thought, kind of generous.

One thing people always use around a mining camp is dynamite. I taken me a bundle of it, rode back up into the mountains where the robbers stayed, and located their cabin. There wasn't much to it; they didn't expect no trouble with the law, and they didn't hardly even have a guard out. All I had to do was to tap the one lone sentry over the head kind of businesslike. The rest of them was inside, playing poker with the take from the last robbery. I planted that dynamite up beside the house, lit the fuse and moved out a little ways to watch.

You never seen a poker game break up quite as sudden. That cabin was poorly built anyhow. When the smoke cleared I only seen two of them come out of it, and I picked them off with my rifle.

After that the boys over in that district sort of lost interest in stealing other people's silver shipments. The local law was a little put out about it and said I had denied them boys the protection of a trial by jury. But the mine owners was happy, and they was the ones that paid me, so I just made a couple of suggestions to the local law, none of which they took.

I stayed on the payroll a good while, till the mine owners was sure their trouble was over. They knowed some people having similar difficulties up in the northern part of the state and sent me up there with a letter of recommendation. I was hired on the spot and told that anything I wanted to do, they would back me up. "Due process of law" in that country just meant that every man taken care of himself. After I had laid out three of them boys on a board, the rest decided the high altitude wasn't good for their health, and they moved out to a warmer climate.

There again I came in for a certain amount of slander. There was some folks who said I didn't give them boys a sporting chance, but I did. I sent them word before I came that they'd be a right smart healthier if they left the country before I got there. They didn't take my advice.

One thing, preacher, there never has been one of my bullets ever found in a man's back, except a couple of times when they was trying to run away to escape arrest. I always got a man from the front side, even if that exposed me to a little danger myself.

Naturally I had work in that part of the country as long as any of the wild bunch was still around. I done pretty good for some years, drifting from one mining section to another across New Mexico and Arizona, and for a time clear over into California. There was times when I didn't have to do anything except show up. The sticky-fingered crowd would hear Joe Pepper was in the vicinity, and they would just naturally go hunting for a different place to ply their trade. Couple of times the mining people decided I hadn't done anything to earn the money they promised me, and I had to use some persuasion to bring them around to my way of thinking. Last I knowed, there was still a "wanted" flyer out for me in California, charging me with robbery. But it wasn't me that done the robbery, it was *them*. They backed off from what they duly owed me, and I had to collect the bill the best way I could. I tell you, preacher, I found out a long time ago that all the people who go to rob you don't do it with a gun. There's some big-business men that needed planting about as much as the people they sent me after.

I read in one of them penny-dreadfuls where I was supposed to have been in the Lincoln County war, and ridden with Billy the Kid and such as that. A lie, every word of it. I had no part in that war atall.

Truth of the matter is, I figured there was money to be made out of that Lincoln County mess and went over there to see if I could hire on. Either side, it didn't matter. Way I figured it, both sides was a little shady, but their money would spend good.

It was a wasted trip. Each side figured I was a spy for the other, and I was damn lucky to escape from there with my life.

I never stayed in one place long enough to ever get elected as a sheriff. Once in a while a sheriff would hire me for a deputy, but seemed like there was always somebody against me. They would hear or read some wild story like them lies in the newspapers and the penny-dreadfuls, and some righteous citizen would raise up in indignation and want me run out of the country. Times, it got awful hard to make an honest dollar.

Such as that would occasionally lead me to have to take jobs that I would as soon of left alone. Like that Johnson County war in Wyoming. Now, *there* was a fiasco. You've probably heard of it.

There was a bunch of big cattlemen up yonder that claimed a considerable part of Wyoming as their range. And there was a bunch of homesteaders and nesters and little cattle raisers and so forth that sort of figured they also had a right to some of the land. A thing like that naturally leads to a certain amount of unpleasantness. It also leads to jobs for people like me.

I was sure needing work at the time. I'd been back in El Paso, finding out to my own dissatisfaction that Lady Luck still hadn't eased up on me for whatever it was I done that offended her. Every once in a while I would hope to catch her looking the other way, and I'd sit in on a high-stakes poker game. But she always looked around and seen me before my stack of chips got too high.

I had a visit from an old friend who had put me onto a job or two before. If I would take the train to Paris, over in East Texas, he said, and meet a man there by the name of Tom Smith, I was a cinch for work. The pay was to be good. I just barely had me enough money left for a train ticket and a few days' eating, so I went. This Smith had rounded up a bunch of other people, same as me, all of them supposed to be men of nerve and good with a gun. He didn't tell us what we was to do except that we was supposed to serve warrants on some bad characters and to draw five dollars a day and expenses. On top of that we would get a bonus of fifty dollars for any man we had to kill. Them days, five dollars wasn't bad, especially when your axle was dragging on the ground.

He told us to be quiet and say nothing to anybody. We went up to Denver and then on to Cheyenne with a cattleman named Wolcott. He was one of them that had decided to hire us for the job. I taken a disliking to him right off, because I could tell he didn't like *us*. He let us know that we wasn't nothing but hired gunfighters, and not in the class with the "gentlemen" who was paying us to take care of the work they was too clean-handed to do by themselves. He was an old man by then, which I reckon lots of people would of said *I* was, too. He had been an officer for the Union during the Civil War. That might of been another reason I couldn't take to him much. There had been a whole new generation growed up since that war; they had never smelled powder. I think maybe they put too much faith in him because he *had*. The truth is, he was probably too old to lead an expedition like ours.

They fixed us up with horses and ammunition in Cheyenne, and we pulled out for Casper on a special train with all the blinds down so people wouldn't notice us. We got to Casper in the cold dark of the morning, caught our horses from the stock car and headed out so we wouldn't be seen by the townspeople after the sun came up. The whole thing was a bad go, right from the start. A bunch of the horses got away. It had been raining, so the wagons kept sticking in the mud, and it was cold enough to bite a Texas man to the bone, especially if he was running to gray hair the way I was.

It wasn't till about this time that they ever really told us just what we was expected to do. Seemed like the cattlemen had been having lots of trouble with thieves. What we was supposed to do was make a roundup of these thieves and arrest them. If they resisted arrest we was supposed to shoot them. Seemed like the cattlemen hoped they would *all* resist arrest. It would of been a lot simpler that way.

You've probably read since that a lot of the men they was after wasn't really thieves at all, but just people who was resisting them and laying claim to lands that the cattlemen had been using. We didn't know nothing about that at the time. Way I looked at it, I was working for the man who paid me. If he said a man was a thief, that man was a thief. If I thought different, I asked for the wages I had already earned, and I rode off.

I'd never been to Wyoming in my life. I had no reason to think these cattlemen might be lying to us. For five dollars a day, which I needed pretty bad, I didn't question their word.

There was a regular little army of us—fifty or so, best I remember—moving out from Casper toward the town of Buffalo. It was supposed to be a secret, and everybody we come upon was made prisoners to be sure they didn't leak to anybody.

First night's camp, I would of pulled my freight if I hadn't been so broke, and so far from home. The leaders of the army was all drinking and arguing with one another over what to do next. Some of them wanted to go to Buffalo like the plan called for. Some others wanted to go off on a tangent and hit a bunch of rustlers at the cabin of a man by the name of Nate Champion. They figured him for one of the biggest rustlers. They taken a vote, finally, amongst theirselves. We didn't get a vote; we was just the hired hands. A man's reputation back home didn't count for nothing up there. The vote was that we go to Champion's cabin. We had to pack up and leave in the middle of the night.

I was getting to the point in my life where I needed my rest. I sure hadn't had much of it on this trip, and it looked like I wasn't going to get any for a while. I got to thinking to myself that five dollars a day wasn't much. Many's the night I've bet fifty times that much on one hand of cards. If I hadn't been so far from Texas I'd of told them what they could do with all of Wyoming, and I'd of gone south to a warmer climate.

It was a miserable ride, a regular blizzard blowing

against us all the way. We stopped to build some fires and thaw out a little then went on to Champion's cabin. We surrounded the layout.

Somebody had made a mistake, not the only one made on that deal by a long shot. There was supposed to be a dozen or more rustlers staying at the place. There wasn't but two, the way it turned out, plus a couple of trappers that had dropped in to get out of the storm. When the trappers came out at daylight, they was made prisoners. They told us there was just two men left inside, Nate Champion and a friend of his called Nick Ray. We had orders to get them dead or alive, best way dead.

Ray came out and looked around, hunting for the trappers, I suppose. Somebody gave an order to fire on him, and a bunch of them did. My hands was so numb from the cold that I couldn't handle my rifle. Ray crawled to the door, and Champion reached out and pulled him in. No telling how many bullets was chipping at the wood all around him, but he didn't let his friend die out there alone.

There wasn't nothing to do but wait. We figured it would be worth a man's life to try to rush that cabin because you would have to cross too much open ground. For five dollars a day they could have it. That feller Champion, somebody said, was an old Texas cowboy. You don't monkey around with that kind until you find out whether they can shoot or not.

By and by somebody came along, one on a horse and one in a wagon. One of the ranchers hollered that the man on the horse was one of those we was supposed to arrest. A lot of shooting broke out, but none of it was any good because both of them got clean away. Everybody's hands was too cold, I reckon; I know mine was.

The wagon had been left behind. We piled it high with wood, set it afire, and some of the boys run it up against the cabin. Pretty soon the place was burning. We didn't know it then, but Ray was dead. Champion was the only one left alive in there. All of a sudden he busted out running with a rifle in his hands and tried for a ravine. He nearly made it. A couple of the boys was posted back there and brought him down.

I felt kind of low about the whole thing, especially after hearing he was a Texas man. Seemed to me like anybody that game deserved a little more of a show.

But like I say, I was working for wages, and when a man pays me I don't ask a lot of fool questions. I do what he asks me to, or I draw my time.

Seemed to me like we never did stop riding, and the leaders of the crew never stopped bickering and arguing amongst theirselves. That one thing alone was enough to tell me we was in for a hard time. Them two that got away from us was our downfall. They had rode on ahead and given the alarm. We got word that a big gang of rustlers was coming to meet us and would wipe us out like them Indians had done Custer, not too far north of where we was. There was another big argument over whether we ought to go on or back up.

The backer-uppers won. We retreated back to the JA Ranch.

You talk about mad! The cattlemen wasn't half as mad as them rustlers or settlers or whatever they was. They come in on us like a swarm of bees. Before they was through they must of numbered three or four hundred men, which meant there was six or eight of them to every one of us. We forted up at the ranch-house, and they set up a siege.

We had a good place to make a stand. The house

had been built solid, back when people still wasn't sure of the Indians, I reckon, and the logs was thick and square. We found a lot of big timbers and built us up an extra fort outside. We thought we could stand just about anything. But we couldn't. They waited us out, shooting every time they seen something to shoot at, and lots of times when they didn't. We done the same.

Finally we was about out of ammunition and plumb out of anything to eat. A man can stand up to almost any kind of a fight when his belly's full, but let him get hungry and he falls down on you. Seemed to me about then that the damnfools had taken over, because it was ordered that we would all make a break at the same time and try to shoot our way out of the trap.

I never was one to consider suicide. I've never shot a man I didn't think needed shooting, and I never was that mad at myself. Running out in front of that mob would've been about the same thing as killing yourself, because we'd of lasted about as long as a snowball in a firebox.

Just about the time we was fixing to send ourselves to hell, the army showed up. The cattlemen had friends in high places, but they hadn't come more than five minutes too soon. Any later and they'd of slapped dirt in our faces with a shovel.

Two of the Texas men died of gunshot wounds. I got this bad scar on my cheek from a big splinter, when one of their bullets grazed a log I was behind. We was a pretty hard-used bunch, all in all. They hauled us off to jail. Us Texas boys was moved around from one jail to another and finally even to the state pen while they waited to put us on trial. We hadn't even knowed what the whole thing was about.

The cattlemen that hired us was all out on bail, walking around free and talking big.

The shooting had been in April. We was turned loose on bail finally in August and put on a train for Fort Worth, Texas. We was supposed to go back later for the trial, but I don't suppose any of the boys ever did.

I sure as hell didn't.

7

How did I finally come to get into *this* fix? Well, preacher, I'll tell you.

I've had some mighty lean years since that Johnson County episode. I got awful tired of them gun-carrying jobs, but what else could I do? I never did seem to have any more luck with the cards, especially after the years taken to putting arthritis in my joints. Look at them swelled knuckles! Sometimes it's all I can do to even hold a deck, much less to deal with any kind of grace. Old age has its dignity, I reckon, but it's damned inconvenient.

I tried cowboying, but who's going to hire an old man whose joints creak on him when he gets on and off of a horse? And you take most of these cow outfits, they think it's a sin for a hired man to ride anything except a raw bronc. Truth is, they're so tight, most of them, they don't want to buy a horse that costs them over twenty-thirty dollars. Soon as one gets to where he knows something and won't pitch anymore, they sell him to a farmer. Claim they don't want their cowboys getting lazy. I'm way past the bronc-riding stage, as you can plainly see.

I tried a little more freelance manhunting, but the day is over. I even hunted for Butch Cassidy and his Wild Bunch once, till they crossed over into Wyoming. I knowed my name was still on the list there, so I tipped my hat and turned back, hungry.

I done some wolfing for a spell, too. Now *there's* a dirty job for you, wolfing. But when you look at it, killing wolves for a bounty ain't much different from doing it to men, except wolves don't shoot back at you. Cattlemen had trouble with them big lobo wolves pulling down their calves. And *sheepmen* . . . there just wasn't no way a sheepman could operate in the same part of the country with them wolves. They would get all the lambs first and then take in after the mamas.

A lot of people looked down on the wolfer as a sort of scavenger, like the men that gathered buffalo bones. But it was a living. Hard times, a man can't be choicy.

I done a little bartending, one time and another. It's no life for a man who's known better things. You have to deal with such a low class of people. Nothing I hate worse than wrestling with a drunk. The only time I could ever tolerate a bunch of drunks was when I was drunk myself. In late years I ain't been that way much. My stomach's gone to the bad, and it gets real put out with me when I eat anything or drink anything that it don't approve of.

So, when you come down to it, there ain't been much else for me except *pistolero* jobs of one kind or another. Sometimes I'd get on as a guard for a mine or a bank or an express company, or for some bigshot who thought somebody might want to shoot him. Jobs like that don't have much dignity to them, and you have to swallow a right smart of dirt.

An old man gets used to a certain amount of dirt, but not *that* much. I've walked off of jobs and told them where they could go with it, when I didn't even know where supper was going to come from.

But that gets expensive. Now and again I got so hungry I just had to take a job that I wouldn't otherwise of touched. Like once I was guard to a fat politician from back East who was taking him a long vacation in a big *hacienda* down the river from El Paso. The voters back home was paying his expenses and was being told he was on a long trip out West examining the prison systems. What he was really doing was bathing himself in whiskey and having the women brought to him two at a time, white and Mexican both. It was my job to keep any outsiders from finding him. But one sneaked in anyhow, one of them nosy newspaper reporters. He taken a picture of old Big-Gut with one of the pretty *señoritas* on his lap, and neither one of them wearing anything much except a surprised expression. It run in one of the El Paso papers, and then got back to that politician's home state.

I lost my job, of course. That's another reason I never was partial to them newspaper reporters, always poking around where they ain't got no business.

Them kind of jobs would gag a gut-wagon dog. But when you're in my shape you got to take them or go hungry.

That's why when I got word awhile back that Burney Northcutt wanted to see me at his ranch, I came down here as quick as my little Mexican pony could travel. I remembered how I used to play poker with him in El Paso, back when Lady Luck still approved of me. I remembered how he would cuss and stomp and swear to have me killed, but next time he came to town he'd try to best me again. We wasn't ever what you'd call friendly. In fact, I never did particularly like him. I reckon he felt the same about me. But we had a respect of sorts, one for the other. We was both pretty good at what we done.

I remembered he was a big operator. He came out into this West Texas country right behind the Indians. He fought old Mother Nature when she was at her meanest, and taken from her when she was at her best. He had carved himself an almighty big country. It wasn't the finest grazing land in Texas; fact is, it's probably some of the sorriest. But it'll do the job if you have enough of it to give your cows plenty of room.

I had heard stories about how he had throwed people off of country he wanted, how he had bought up the law in some counties to where nobody jumped till they heard him holler "frog." But I never gave it much thought because it didn't pertain to me.

But you know, preacher, about Texas and its four-section law? A big part of this land out here belonged to the state, and they passed a law that said a man could homestead four sections of it, and if he could stay there three years without starving to death he could buy it dirt cheap. Well sir, the biggest part of the land that old man Northcutt had, he got on a cheap lease off of the state. When the new law came in, he found people claiming four sections here and four sections there, generally out of the best parts of his ranch. They was four-sectioning him to death. Now, he'd of been right pleased to have bought the whole thing from the state if they'd of let him, but they said he couldn't buy no more than anybody else, which was four sections. Hell, the old man probably had *that* much in corrals.

I got down to the ranch and went to see him. It had been a good many years since we'd laid eyes on each other, and I expect we was both a little surprised. He looked at me real sour-like and says, "By God, Joe Pepper, you've turned into an old man. If I'd of knowed how old you was, I wouldn't of sent for you."

I told him he wasn't apt to turn no schoolgirl's head either.

For a little while I thought I had wasted a long trip. He scowled at me like he was thinking about throwing me off of the ranch. I bristled up a little, just thinking about it. I doubted he had anybody young enough or tough enough to do that to me; I could tell by looking at him that *he* couldn't.

We glared at each other till it seemed like both of our faces would break and fall off. Finally he says, "Well, you ain't likely to scare them with your looks anymore, but maybe you can scare them with your name."

"Who am I supposed to scare?" I asks him.

I didn't know how much raw hate that old man really had in him until he told me about the four-sectioners. I'm glad you wasn't there to hear him, preacher; that language would of shamed you. And the look in his eyes . . . well, I'm not one to scare, but that look made a cold chill run down between these hunched old shoulders. I do believe if he'd of had one of them there in front of us, he would of choked him to death with his hands, or tried to.

I says, "You're hiring me to scare the four-sectioners?"

He cut his eyes at me, and they stabbed like the

point of a Bowie knife. "I want you to *kill* one. That'll scare the others."

It had been a good many years since I had killed anybody, though I'd scared a few within an inch of killing themselves. I wasn't sure I needed his money quite that bad. I decided to test him out and see just how serious he was. I says, "You know I'll protect myself if one of them comes at me."

He says, "I want you to make sure one of them *does* come at you. I want you to crowd him till he loses his head, and then you kill him."

I can't say the idea was a new one. But I'd always used it against somebody I figured the world wasn't going to miss, somebody who had it coming to him. I'd never used it against somebody who had done nothing but steal land away from an old thief. Of course I had seldom ever been quite as hungry before as I was right then.

I says, "We ain't talked price yet."

He says, "I ain't got time to horsetrade or quibble with you. It's worth a lot to me to get rid of them nesters, and get rid of them fast." He walked over to his safe. I noticed he didn't move any too quick, and he was dragging his right leg just a touch. The years hadn't been kind to him. If this trouble had come on him twenty years earlier he wouldn't of hired anybody like me to take care of it; he'd of done it for himself.

I could hear his knee joint crack as he eased himself down to work the dial. He gave me a hard look back over his shoulder like he was afraid I'd watch and see the combination. The idea *had* occurred to me, just in case he was a little reluctant afterwards to pay me what he agreed to. I looked off out the window till I heard the door squeal on its hinges. He got out a little tin box and thumped it down on the table. He opened it and taken out a bundle of the prettiest green bills you ever seen. He pitched them across the table at me. "Five hundred dollars now," he says, "and five hundred more when the job is done."

I hadn't seen that much money in one pile in years. My poor old hands began to tremble, just wanting to get in there and feel of the bills, the way when I was younger my hands used to tremble every time they got close to silk. But pardon me, preacher, you wouldn't know about them things.

I wanted to be sure we understood each other. I says, "How will we know when the job is done?"

"When they've buried the nester you shot," he tells me, "and when the rest of them have loaded their wagons and left the country."

I told him I hadn't seen his four-sectioners, but it might be that killing one man wouldn't put them all to flight. I might have to kill more than one. I figured that ought to call for more money.

He cussed a little and told me I was a black-hearted holdup man. I told him that was my natural upbringing, and if I hadn't been that way he wouldn't of wanted to hire me. So he upped the ante. That thousand was to cover the job if it went as easy as he expected it to. He'd put up another five hundred apiece for any extra four-sectioners I had to kill.

Five hundred dollars was probably more than some of them ever got in one bundle in all their lives. Here they was, bringing that much dead.

"All right, done," I tells him. "You got any special man picked out, or do you just want me to shoot one at random?"

That hate came back to him the way I've seldom seen it in a man. He let the breath out between his teeth real slow, and then he says. "There's one. His name is Clayton Massey. You kill *him* and I'll give you a two-fifty bonus."

I drawed old man Northcutt out about this Massey that he seemed to have such a special hate for. Seemed like this was a young fellow from back over in the Concho country. Not only did he have the nerve to come out and file a claim on some of the old man's best water, but he had the extra nerve to bring *sheep* with him. Now, you got to understand that Burney Northcutt was one of them old-time cattlemen who thought all a sheep had to do to ruin a country for fifty years was to walk across it. Sheep outfits trailing west had learned to go forty miles around his place if they wanted to get where they was going without leaving a hundred dead sheep for every mile. The old man had taken a bunch of his cowboys over to throw Massey off of his place, and Massey met them with a gun and a set of state papers out of Austin that said the four sections was his, and he could run anything he wanted to on them . . . even giraffes, if he had any. The old man tried to ride over Massey, and Massey shot the horse out from under him.

The old man owned the sheriff of the county. He had Massey arrested for killing the horse and for trespassing. But the case got transferred out of the county, and the court held that Massey acted in self-defense, and that the old man was lucky it hadn't been him that got shot instead of the horse.

I knowed then why he hated the four-sectioners so bad, especially Massey. What made it even worse was that some of Massey's friends and kinfolks came too, out of the Concho country, and some of them brought sheep as well as cattle. First thing the old man knowed he had him half a dozen little sheepmen sitting on land he thought was going to be his for five hundred years. And it wasn't the nature of them people to homestead the worst land; they always picked the good places, where the water was.

He gives me a description of this young Massey, and how to get to his place, and he tells me, "The quicker you go on over there and kill him, the quicker you can get your extra money and be gone."

I asked him if it would be all right with him if I waited till in the morning. It had been a long ride, and my horse was tired. I was a little weary myself. One thing I didn't want to do was to come up against somebody when I was tired, especially if he had the advantage of being young.

Caution is what makes *old* gunfighters.

I had me a good supper at Burney's expense, a good night's sleep in his bunkhouse, and a good breakfast the next morning. When you get to my age you'll realize how important such small compensations can be. Next morning I set out to Massey's place.

Now, you know this ain't the best ranching country in the world, but I couldn't help thinking as I rode that if my life had taken a different turn in the beginning, I might have had a big spread like Burney Northcutt to pleasure me in my declining years. I wouldn't be riding around all over the country selling my gun to people I didn't particularly like. I'd look at Northcutt's cattle—all colors of the rainbow, half leg and half horn—and think how all this could of been mine. I could understand how he would hate to see it cut up and given to people he didn't think was good enough to shine his boots.

I got to thinking back through all them bygone years. I got to thinking of the time just after the war, and me and Arlee Thompson and our first start, mavericking cattle, making them our own. I thought of me and Millie and our place, of things that hadn't crossed my mind in years and years. A feeling came over me that I'd forgot I ever had, a feeling of being young and having somebody and someplace that belonged to me, something I was a part of, something where I wasn't just an outsider looking in. For a while there it was like I was back in South Texas, and all this was mine, and I wasn't just a lone and lonely old man.

It was a big country, so big that it taken me all morning at a pretty good trot to get to Massey's place. I came to a creek that was the way Northcutt had described it and knowed I was either on the place or close to it. I followed it upstream to the spring where Massey had built him a house. I kept watching all the way for sign of the four-sectioner and his sheep, but I didn't see them. First thing I came to, outside of a scattering of improved Durham cattle, was the house and pens.

You couldn't call it much of a house; there wasn't two wagonloads of lumber in the whole thing. It was one of them little box-and-strip outfits that says "hard times" the minute you look at it. It wasn't more than maybe fifteen feet square, sitting up on sawed-off cedar posts to keep it off of the ground. An old dog came out from under the porch and barked at me. I seen a woman come to the door and stand there, shading her eyes with her hand.

I almost fell out of the saddle.

I tell you, preacher, you couldn't of hit me harder with a tow-sack full of red bricks.

That woman was my Millie, that I had buried nigh forty years ago.

Now, I know you're going to laugh at that, and say it was just an old man's bad eyesight failing on him, and maybe a little of the heat, too. You're going to remind me that I thought the same thing the first time ever I seen Samantha Ridgway. But say what you want to, it happened. There she was, the spitting image.

I rode on up to the house. She spoke to me, but I couldn't hear what she said, and I couldn't say anything back. My tongue was all stuck to the roof of my mouth. She spoke to me two or three times, and finally it got through my thick head that she was telling me to get down and have myself a drink of cool water, because it looked like I was suffering from the heat.

I finally managed to say, "You're Millie!"

She looked kind of surprised. She says, "No, I'm Jill. Jill Massey. I'm afraid you've found the wrong house."

I was still confused. I says, "But you're Millie. Don't you know me?" The whole thing had hit me so sudden that I had a hard time remembering Millie would've been near sixty years old by now, if she had lived. This woman wasn't much over twenty.

I think I must of scared her a little, and that kind of brought me up. I finally got it through my head what she was saying, and that this couldn't be Millie.

I *did* notice then that my head was swimming a little, and that the sweat was running down my face like I'd been caught in a rain. Maybe the heat *had* got me. I eased down from the saddle and leaned against my horse for a minute. I asked her where I could water him, but she told me to go sit in the shade on the step and rest a little. *She* would water him for me.

But first she brought me a dipper of good cool water out of a barrel. I sat down there like she said, and I watched her lead the pony down to the creek and loosen the girth and let him drink. She made him take it slow, which showed she knowed something about horses. Sometimes when they're dry and hot they'll drink enough water to give themselves a bellyache. Same way a man does. I watched her all the time, and I'd swear—if my mind hadn't cleared some—that she was my Millie, born again.

Directly she led the pony up to a corral and pulled the saddle off of him. She turned him loose where he could roll in the dust. She hung the bridle on a post and came back to the house. She says, "You're staying for dinner."

That hadn't been my intention, but I was still too numb to argue. She says, "Clayton'll be in after awhile to eat. He's ranging the sheep over to the east. They won't stray much during the heat of the day."

I'd never made any big study of herding sheep. I didn't care to learn any more about them than I already knowed, which wasn't much. I says, "Where'd you come from, Jill Massey?"

"Over in Concho County," she tells me. "Close to Paint Rock."

I knowed Paint Rock was on the Concho River east of San Angelo, but that didn't answer my question. I says, "I mean, where did you come from originally? Where was you a girl at?"

"Right there," she says. "Where I grew up, you could see the cupola on the Concho County courthouse."

I got to questioning her about her forebears, whether any of them had ever come out of South Texas. I kept thinking maybe she was blood kin of Millie, but as far as I could ever tell, she wasn't. Seems like her folks had come over out of Tennessee before she was born, but after the time of Millie Thompson.

While she was cooking up some red beans and mutton for dinner, I taken my watch out to see what time it was, figuring probably her husband would come riding along pretty soon. All of a sudden I remembered that I carried Millie's picture in the back of the watch. Lord knows how long it had been since I had last looked at it—twenty years, probably. Time does get away from a man. I opened the back. It had been shut so long that I had to prize it with a knifeblade.

There she was, my Millie, just the way I remembered her. Now that I looked at her picture, and compared it to Jill Massey, I could see where this girl didn't look all that much like her after all. Time was playing tricks on me again. When you get old, your mind's eye starts failing on you, same as the ones on the outside.

I got to wondering about myself. I decided I had got to letting my mind wander when I was on the way over from Northcutt's. I had got to thinking about the old days, and I guess without me realizing it, Millie had taken to haunting me again, trying to come to the surface in a way I hadn't let her do in many and many a year. The minute I seen this young woman, I also seen Millie. They wasn't the same atall; they just seemed to be to an old man whose eyes and mind was getting confused.

But I sat and listened to her talk, and it was like it had been the time I found Samantha; the years just rolled away. It was like I was sitting in my own house with Millie again, most of forty years ago. It was like I was a young man, just starting out on the road of life instead of coming up on the end of the trail. For a little while there I think my arthritis quit bothering me, and my shoulders squared up. It was a good feeling.

Her husband came along directly. He seen the

strange pony in the corral, and he came rushing to the house to make sure his wife was all right. He seen me sitting there at the table, drinking coffee, and he was sure relieved. I might of been feeling like a young man right then, but all he could see was a harmless coot too old to be a danger to anybody. He shook hands with me and told me he was Clayton Massey, and he hoped I was staying for dinner.

Naturally I was, or my horse wouldn't of been unsaddled. I didn't tell him my name; I wanted to size things up first. He would find out soon enough who I was.

I watched him kiss his wife, kind of gentle and self-conscious. I had the notion he would of done it some different if I hadn't been there. That taken me back a long ways, remembering when it had been the same with me. I figured him for a man of maybe thirty, young enough to have all the energy in the world and old enough to know how to use it.

Jill Massey got dinner finished and put it on the table. She had baked bread in the oven, Mexican style, flat in the bottom of the pan. Clayton Massey says to me, "It ain't much, but you're welcome to what there is. The whole place ain't much yet, but it'll be a lot more someday when I've had time enough to work on it."

I got to thinking how he sounded a lot like I had when I was his age, when I had a pretty woman to work for, the way he did. By and by I asked him why he had come way out here instead of staying in Concho County where he started. He said there wasn't room anymore. His daddy had settled in that country when it was still young. Now the son had to move out to a country that was still young and do like his daddy did. I pointed out to him that when his daddy went to Concho County there probably wasn't nobody else claiming the land he settled up, except maybe the Indians. But out here, there wasn't an acre that somebody hadn't already claimed before him.

He said that was the truth, but the law had decided it wasn't enough anymore to have all this big open country in the hands of just a few men. It wanted to have people settle and towns grow; the frontier was gone and wasn't coming back. He said the country had already more than paid the first people here for their pains, and it was in its legal rights to ask them to move over and make room. I suppose that made sense to an ambitious young man, but I could also see how it would seem hard to an old mossback like Burney Northcutt who had dripped sweat and sometimes blood all over this land.

I mentioned Northcutt and how I had heard he wasn't too partial to the things that was going on around here, that he felt like they was taking away what belonged to him.

Massey told me a little history that Northcutt had neglected to mention to me. He told me that in the early days there was Mexican settlers—squatters, of course—all up and down these creeks, and Northcutt had come along and run them off. He had even killed a couple or three in the process to show his intentions was serious. He told them their day was over, and it was time for a new deal all around.

Massey says to me, "Now it's *his* day that's over, and it's *us* that have the new deal. You watch, we'll make this country support fifty people for every one that it used to have. This country is meant to grow, not to stand still."

Somehow time kept running backwards for me. I kept thinking about the old times in South Texas, and of the trouble I had with Jesse Ordway over the piece of land that I had and he wanted. I got to trying to see Jesse Ordway in my mind, but it had been so long that I couldn't hardly remember anymore what he looked like. I kept putting Burney Northcutt into the picture in his place.

Massey says, "He's tried a lot of things to get us out of here. He's tried to buy me out, and run me out. He's tried to stampede my sheep, but sheep don't stampede very good. He's tried shooting into them, but he's found I shoot back. He's even had his cowboys ride in here at night and shoot into the house."

I taken a sudden chill. It all came back to me in a rush. I remembered the night they had killed my Millie. It was forty years ago, but it seemed like it had been yesterday. I closed my eyes and I could hear them riding around the house, shooting into it. In my mind I heard Millie scream. I got to shaking and couldn't quit.

Clayton Massey grabbed hold of me. He says, real worried, "What's the matter, old-timer? Jill, get that bottle of whiskey, quick!"

He handed me the bottle, and I tipped it up and taken a couple of long, hard slugs of it. Gradually I got to feeling warm again, and I quit shaking. He says, "Better take another, old-timer." I told him I had had enough. I tried to get to my feet, but my old knees just couldn't do it. I sat back down and tried to take a grip on myself. I tried to get the old times and the new times separated from one another, so I could think. It was hard, because they was all so mixed up.

Directly I had a grip on myself. The two of them was sitting across the table, looking like I had scared them half to death. With an old man, you never know when he's going to kick over and leave you.

I says, "I'm all right now."

"It's the heat," he tells me. "Man your age has got to watch himself and not overdo it. You better stay with us a day or two and rest. Then you can go on about your business."

I figured it was time to tell him. "I came *here* on business. I came here to kill you."

His mouth dropped open, and his eyes got like a saucer. He shook his head like he didn't believe none of it. "You better go lay down, old-timer. You're sick."

I says, "You ever hear of Joe Pepper, son?"

He nodded his head. "Sure, everybody has. He used to be a gunfighter, long years ago."

"He's *still* a gunfighter," I says. "I'm Joe Pepper."

You know how it is, I reckon, when you have a raving old man on your hands; you try to humor him. The Masseys didn't believe a word of it. I could tell they figured the heat had got me.

Massey says, "Joe Pepper died years ago. He *must* have."

"Not unless I'm a ghost," I tell him.

Gradually he began to come around. I guess there is still a little of the old-time Joe Pepper in my face, if you look hard enough. Finally he gets kind of nervous and says, "Jill, I believe him."

I could tell she did too. All of a sudden I seen fear laying way back deep behind her eyes. Massey taken a quick look toward the corner, where his rifle was propped. He wasn't wearing any pistol; I had taken note of that when he first came into the house. I says, "I wouldn't do what you're thinking, boy. I'd just sit real still."

He didn't look like one who would try to run away. Grab for the rifle, maybe, but not run away. Either choice wouldn't of done him any good if I'd decided to shoot him. He says, "You figuring on killing me right here?"

I says, "That's what I was sent here to do."

"What about Jill?" he says. "Whatever you do to me, don't hurt her, please."

The thought had never entered my mind, but it laid heavy on his. He says, "She's carrying, mister. For God's sake, don't hurt her."

Millie had been carrying, too. I remembered now. Lord, I hadn't even thought of it in years.

The tears commenced to well up in Jill Massey's eyes. She started to plead with me to let her husband be. She said they would move; they would turn this country back to Burney Northcutt if he wanted it so bad.

But Clayton Massey stood up and pushed his chair back. He says to her, "Hush, Jill. Don't you tell him that. The only way Northcutt gets this place is to kill me. I'll never give it to him." He taken a couple of steps backward, and I knowed he was about to make a try for that rifle.

I had real quietly pulled my pistol out of my belt. I brought it up where he could see it real good, and I pushed to my feet. I was afraid my old knees would betray me, but they stood me in good stead. When the pressure comes, I ain't as old as I look. I told Clayton Massey to stand where he was and not do anything that him and me would both be sorry about. I stepped around him, went over to the corner and picked up his rifle. I taken it and pitched it out the door as far as I could.

"Just removing temptation," I tells him. "Thing like that can get a man killed."

By this time I reckon he was convinced that he was as good as dead. He looked at his wife, and back at me, and he says, "If you've got to do it, at least don't do it here in front of *her*. Let's go outside where she doesn't have to see it."

I wasn't going to do it, not there or anywheres else.

I says as harsh as I can, "Now you sit back down at the table and listen to me, boy." He was a little slow about it, so I nudged him with the muzzle of my pistol. "Sit *down*!"

He did. I could see the girl's knuckles as white as flour, gripping her chair. Her face didn't have much more color than that, either.

I says, "Now listen to me, both of you. I said I came here to kill you. But I'm an old man, and an old man's mind is always changing."

"You said Burney Northcutt hired you."

I patted my pocket. "I got the money right here, five hundred dollars."

He says, "You mean you're going to take his money and *not* kill me?"

I shook my head. "No, I'm a professional man. I don't take money on false pretenses. That would ruin my reputation. I'm going to take his money back to him and tell him I've thought it over and changed my mind."

"He won't like it," says Massey. "He's set in his ways."

"He don't *have* to like it. I'll tell him that times have changed for *me*, and they'll just have to change for *him*. I don't like what's happened to me, but I've learned to live with it. He can too."

Jill Massey says, "If he wants my husband dead so bad that he hired you, he'll just go and hire somebody else."

I says, "Not if they know Joe Pepper is here. My name still stands for something in the trade."

Massey says, "What do you mean, if Joe Pepper is here?"

I told him I kind of liked their place, and I was about to be out of a job, and if he could use an old man's help I would hire on real cheap.

He argued that he couldn't pay me much, and I told him an old man didn't need much. A little to eat, a little to drink . . . a lot of time to sit in the sun.

They never did understand what had made me change my mind, and I couldn't tell them because I didn't altogether understand it myself. All I knowed was that them two young people was me and Millie, given another chance to start over. I wasn't going to let Jesse Ordway . . . I mean Burney Northcutt . . . do them out of that chance.

It was a little before dark when I rode up to Northcutt's big frame house. He was sitting on the gallery, taking his evening rest and his pipe. He was some surprised to see me back so quick. He taken his pipe out of his mouth and stared at me. He says, "You always had the reputation of being a fast worker, Joe Pepper. But damn if that ain't the fastest five hundred dollars I ever spent. I reckon you've come for the rest?"

I reached in my pocket and taken out the roll of greenbacks that had felt so good in my hands. I pitched it over into his lap. I says, "No, I come to give your money back to you. I don't take pay if I don't do a job."

I reckon it was typical of him that he thought the worst. "Taken a look at it and got cold feet, did you? I ought to've knowed better than to hire a man that's got so old the nerve has gone out of him. Time the word gets around about this, there won't nobody hire you to slop hogs."

I shrugs my shoulders and tells him, "Don't matter, I already got work."

"Doing what?" he says real nasty. "Washing out spittoons in a bar?"

"Herding sheep," I tells him.

He stood up, and when he did I seen the pistol in his boottop. An old badger like Burney Northcutt wasn't going to get caught without a six-shooter, not even on his own front gallery. He says, "You sold out. I've heard of you doing lots of things, Joe Pepper, but I never heard of you double-crossing anybody before."

I says, "I never needed to before, Jesse."

It occurred to me that I had called him by the wrong name, but somehow it didn't matter. Standing there like he was, he looked to me like Jesse Ordway of almost forty years ago. All of a sudden the front gallery of that old ranchhouse was the bank where I had met Jesse. I was a young man again, and full of grief and anger because I had just buried a young wife that I had loved, and Jesse Ordway was the man who had been the cause of it.

Burney Northcutt reached down for the pistol, but it wasn't Burney Northcutt I shot . . . it was Jesse Ordway. I shot him once and seen him fall back against the wall, and all the grief and the anger and the pain came rushing up from forty years' burying, and I shot him again, and again and again. I kept shooting till the pistol was empty.

I could hear men hollering around me. I was still in that South Texas town, running for my horse. I got on him and started down the street, only it wasn't really a street atall, it was just a ranch yard. I managed to get some cartridges back into the gun and shoot at Jesse Ordway's men who was shooting at *me*. I looked around for Felipe Rios, but he wasn't there. I couldn't understand why he wasn't; he was *supposed* to be.

They came after me, but I was still ahead of them when dark came.

I wasn't familiar with the country. I rode way into the night, trying to tell myself I wasn't lost but knowing I was. Finally these weary bones had all they could stand, and I had to get down and stretch out on the ground and rest.

I remember dreaming a lot through the night. There was a woman . . . she was Millie awhile, and then she was Samantha, and then she was Jill Massey, but always the same woman. And there was me and Clayton Massey, all mixed up with one another so that I never did know for sure which one of us was which.

Finally I felt something touch me. I opened my eyes to the sunlight, and there was a man leaning over me. He had just lifted the pistol out of my belt. He had a badge on his shirt. It looked as big as a washtub. So did the muzzle of the rifle he held down to my nose. I seen then that he had a bunch of men with him, all of them pointing guns at me.

Well sir, that's how come me to be where I am now. They hauled me here and throwed me in this jail. Ordinarily there wouldn't of been a term of court for two months, but because old man Northcutt was a power in this country, and because Joe Pepper had a name for himself too, they rushed things a mite. They brought in a district judge that Northcutt had helped get elected, and picked them a jury of Northcutt cowboys.

It didn't make no difference to them that the Northcutt power died when he did. Without him, the old ranch of his won't be long in breaking up. The people who talk so bitter about me killing him won't let him get cold in the grave till they start filing on his lands to grab what they can of the leavings.

Clayton Massey came in and testified about Northcutt hiring me to kill him, and me changing my mind. That didn't change the jury's mind, though. They'll all be out of work pretty soon on account of me. They'll have to be drifting off and hunting jobs somewhere else, unless they decide to file on four sections of Northcutt land themselves.

That's about all there is to the story, preacher. I don't know if I've told you what you wanted to find out.

They've finally quit hammering on that scaffold out on the square. I reckon they got it finished.

I feel kind of sorry for them boys, having to work on it most of the night. They'll be disappointed when they come down here in the morning and find out they won't get to use it after all.

That noise out yonder? Just some friends of mine, come to get me a change of venue. Friends of yours, too, I expect, so if you recognize any of them I'd be obliged if you keep quiet about it. I wouldn't want to get them four-section people in trouble.

Better stand back here against the door, preacher, away from the outside wall. They're fixing to pull the window bars out with that team of mules, and I'd hate to have a stone fall on your foot and cripple you.

There it goes. Mind giving me a lift up through that hole?

Well, been nice talking with you, preacher, but I got to be hurrying along. Tell the boys I'm real sorry about their jail. Next time they ought to build it stronger. This one won't even hold an *old* man!

MANY A
RIVER

For Ross McSwain, friend, fellow writer,
keeper of our history

1

North Texas, 1855

Jeffrey Barfield wondered how much farther Papa would continue to travel before he found a settle-down place that suited him. The family had left Arkansas by wagon two months ago and slowly picked their way across the eastern part of Texas, looking for land Papa would consider to be just right. Mama had seen a dozen sites she would be happy with, but Papa invariably said, "There's bound to be better a little farther west."

Eight-going-on-nine, Jeffrey was beginning to fear the family would still be wandering when he celebrated his next birthday. They had passed through Fort Worth, then moved on westward, stopping hopefully here a day, there a day, and going on. Now they had camped on a pleasant, clear-running creek miles beyond Weatherford. Papa walked in a slow circle, kicking up soil with his boot, then reaching down with calloused farmer hands to scoop up a bit of it.

He sniffed at it and let it slowly spill out between his fingers.

Watching from afar, Jeffrey said, "Reckon this is it, Mama? Reckon he'll decide this is the place?"

Mama touched his shoulder gently. She looked tired. "I don't know, son. I've wished so many times . . ." She turned toward her campfire. "You'd better fetch me a little more dry wood."

Jeffrey heard a boyish shout and glanced about for his younger brother. Todd was romping with a brown dog that had accompanied the family as the wagon bumped its way through Arkansas. With a fleeting impatience, Jeffrey shouted, "Hush up, Todd. You'll run off any game that's within hearin' of you."

Todd quieted down for a minute or two but quickly forgot Jeffrey's admonition. He began playing fetch-the-stick with the dog. Jeffrey shrugged. Remaining quiet seemed too much to ask of an energetic five-year-old boy.

He gathered a few small branches from dead brush and broke them across his knee, carrying them back to the fire. Papa had strayed three hundred yards from the wagon. Mama raised her hand to her slat bonnet to shade her eyes from the noonday sun. She said, "Better go fetch him, son. Dinner'll be ready when you-all get back."

"Yes, ma'am. Papa loses all track of time."

He met Todd walking in from his game. Not seeing the dog, he asked, "Where's Brownie?"

"He got tired of chasin' a stick. He took off after a rabbit."

"You better get back to the wagon and wash your face and hands. It'll soon be time to eat."

Todd quickened his pace. He liked to play, but eating pleased him even more.

Jeffrey gave Papa the message. Papa sounded disappointed. "All right, I'm done here. Soon as we've finished eatin' dinner, we'll break camp and move on."

Jeffrey tried not to frown. Mama always said Papa knew best, even when she didn't believe it herself. "This isn't the place?"

"Maybe a little farther on."

They had not seen a soul since they left Weatherford. Jeffrey asked, "Ain't we gotten out pretty far past everybody else?"

"That's the way I like it. We get first pick."

At the wagon, Papa broke the news that they were moving on. Mama took it without comment, but Todd protested, "Brownie ain't come back. We can't just leave him."

Papa said, "If he don't find his way to us, we'll have to go without him."

Todd puckered up. Papa said sternly, "You're too big to start cryin'."

Todd said, "I don't ever cry."

Jeffrey saw the hurt in his brother's eyes. He said, "I'll go hunt for him. He may not have sense enough to follow us."

Papa warned, "Don't waste much time. We'll be startin' pretty soon."

The noonday sun bore heavily on Jeffrey's thin shoulders and sent sweat trickling down his freckled face. He never cussed in front of Papa or Mama, but he was a mile or more from them now. He stated his opinion of the wayward dog in terms he had heard his father use in addressing a team of mules. Papa often relied on profanity for its ability to relieve stress.

"You can stay out here and starve to death for all I care," Jeffrey shouted at the absent animal.

Well, no big loss. Brownie rarely played with him,

preferring to rip around with Todd. Jeffrey turned and started back, his feet dragging, his steps shorter than when he had begun. He had not gone far before he heard the dog barking off to his left. He saw a moving cloud of dust and heard the drumming of hooves. Someone was pushing a band of horses in a slow lope. As wind shifted the dust, he counted a dozen or more riders.

He froze in midstride. They were Indians, and they were riding headlong toward the wagon camp.

The shock gave Jeffrey fresh strength. He broke into a run, shouting a warning. His was a boy's voice, high-pitched and too weak to carry far. Remembering terrible tales he had heard about Indian raids, he began crying. He heard a shot and recognized the sound of the rifle. Papa was serving notice that he intended to defend himself and his family.

Several Indians left the horse herd and circled the wagon. Papa's rifle fired once more, then a shotgun blasted. That would be Mama, pitching in. Jeffrey was close enough now to see Papa go down and to hear Mama scream before a warrior crushed her head with a club.

He realized that the Indians could see him if they looked in his direction. He dropped to his stomach and hid himself in the tall grass. Instinct cried out for him to rush to the wagon and try to help, but fear paralyzed him. An inner voice told him it was already too late, that he would only get himself killed.

He heard Todd cry out as an Indian lifted him onto his horse. The boy futilely beat the warrior with his fists. The man swung the hard handle of a rawhide quirt and struck Todd a sharp blow to the side of his head. Todd went limp. Jeffrey then lost sight of his brother and the Indian in the stirring of dust as warriors circled the wagon. He heard them shouting in celebration while they looted it of blankets and foodstuffs. They gathered up the mule team Papa had staked on grass near camp and tried to set fire to the wagon. They succeeded only in burning much of the canvas cover before wind snuffed out the blaze. They rode away, adding the mules to their band of loose horses.

Jeffrey lay on the ground for several minutes, trembling, fearing that some Indians might lag behind and see him. Finally, choking with fear, he forced himself to his feet and trudged to the wagon. He knew what he would surely find, but he denied it to himself. Mama and Papa must somehow have survived. They had to.

But they had not. Mama lay twisted on the ground, eyes open but not seeing. Her head was bloody, her scalp torn away. Wind tugged at her long skirt. Papa lay across a hot cast-iron dutch oven that sat atop live coals. His clothing smoldered, and Jeffrey smelled burning flesh. Papa too had been scalped.

Todd was not there.

Jeffrey dragged his father away from the heat and used his bare hands to beat out the slow flames that had burned holes in shirt and trousers. He dropped to his knees and let the tears flow. Body quaking, he shouted out in grief and fear and rage.

He lost all sense of time, crying until he was exhausted. Eventually he forced himself to his feet and began to look around, to take stock of the situation into which he had so suddenly been thrust. Mama and Papa were dead. Todd was gone, probably dead too, or he would be when the Indians grew tired of him. Of what use could a five-year-old boy be to them?

Flies had already found his parents' wounds. Mama had been wearing an apron. Jeffrey spread it to cover her head. He found Papa's fallen hat and laid it across his father's still face.

He knew there was no need to look for the rifle or the shotgun. The Indians would have taken those as prizes of the raid. He thought of the dog. It had barked at the horses, probably alerting the Indians to the wagon camp even before they saw it. Jeffrey ventured out, calling again for Brownie.

He found the dog a hundred yards away, dead, with two large wounds in its side. A third wound still had part of an arrow shaft in it. Evidently the Indians had tried to retrieve their arrows but had broken one off.

"Damn you, Brownie," Jeffrey said, "you had it comin' to you."

He realized then that his own life had been spared because the dog had wandered off. Otherwise he would have been in camp when the Indians struck. He moderated his tone. "I hope you caught your rabbit."

The family milk cow had been staked near the wagon. She lay dead, a hind leg cut off and carried away. It had been one of Jeffrey's chores to milk her twice a day. She was mean about kicking, so he did not mourn her.

Jeffrey could not bear to see Mama and Papa lying there on the ground. They needed to be buried. He found the shovel where it was supposed to be, strapped to the side of the wagon. The Indians had seen no need for it. He was practiced in use of the shovel. He had dug fire pits and unearthed old stumps to serve as firewood for his mother as they had moved west from Arkansas. He chose a piece of ground above the creek's high-water mark and began to dig a hole wide enough that he could bury Papa and Mama side by side, the way they had been as far back as he could remember.

The grave was waist deep when he heard horses. Fear fell over him again like a smothering blanket. He dropped to his stomach in the hole, certain more Indians were coming. He heard the horses stop at the camp. As men raised their voices in excitement, he recognized familiar words. These riders were not Indians. Climbing out of the hole, he waved his hat over his head, afraid the men might ride on without seeing him. He began running, stumbling toward the wagon, trying to shout but not finding his voice.

A couple of men raised rifles, startled by the boy's unexpected appearance. They lowered them quickly. One rider moved out to meet him, dismounting and kneeling, anxiously studying Jeffrey at his own eye level. The man was two hundred pounds of muscle and bone. His bearing indicated that he was the kind who would automatically take charge without waiting for someone else. Touching a huge hand to Jeffrey's shoulder, he demanded, "Anybody here besides you?"

"No, sir," Jeffrey managed, his voice breaking. "The Indians didn't see me." Guilt burned deeply as he admitted, "I hid."

"A good thing you did. I suppose that's your mother and father we found back yonder?"

Jeffrey sobbed once, then forced a measure of control. "Yes, sir. And they carried off my little brother." He felt a moment of hope. "Maybe you can catch them and make them give Todd back."

The big man's heavy eyebrows came together in a dark frown. "We're tryin' to catch them, but I doubt it'll do your brother any good. The minute we close with them, they generally kill any prisoners. Best we can hope for is to make them bleed for what they've done. And maybe we can get back the horses they stole on this raid."

Hope collapsed as quickly as it had risen. "You can't save Todd?"

"I'm sorry to put it to you so strong, but if they haven't already killed him, they will."

Jeffrey lost control and wept again. In a kindly voice the bearded man said, "You've got to face it like a man. He's gone, like your mama and daddy are gone."

The other men gathered around, some voicing sympathy, others demanding angrily that they keep riding. They had raiders to catch and kill. The bearded man said, "Adam, how about you and Matthew Temple stayin' here with this boy? The rest of us will see if we can get us some Indians."

Jeffrey said, "I want to go with you. I want to find my brother."

"You'd best put aside any notion of seein' your brother again. It'd just lead to fresh disappointment. You've got hurt enough already."

The grim-faced group of fifteen or so volunteers set off in a long trot, following the plain trail beaten out by the warriors and their stolen horses and mules. Jeffrey turned to the two men left behind. Matthew Temple had a ragged beard that once had been black but now was spotted with gray. He looked like most of the farmers Jeffrey had known back home, men used to hard work. His hips were broad but his stomach flat. He said, "Fletcher's probably right to leave us, Adam. My horse is about worn out, and yours looks little better."

Adam was younger, his beard short and brown,

covering much of a face dark and weathered. He said, "I'd just like to be there for the fight. I lost two horses to them damned Comanches."

"We don't know for sure they're Comanches."

"I don't see that it makes any difference. They're Indians, and they'll all kill you if they get the chance. Like they done this boy's folks, and some others back yonder."

Matthew took a wrinkled handkerchief from a hip pocket and wiped the tears from Jeffrey's dusty face. "Son, we can't just leave your mama and daddy layin' there. We'd best be gettin' them under."

Jeffrey pointed to the higher ground. "I'd done started diggin' before you-all came."

"How were you goin' to get them all the way up there?"

"I'm pretty strong."

Matthew's expression showed he was dubious. "How old are you?"

"Eight, and some past."

"About the age my boy Henry was." With a sad look in his eyes, Matthew shook his head. "You're too young to shoulder a man's load. You ought to be playin' schoolboy games and learnin' to read and cipher. But sometimes the Lord in his wisdom throws a thunderbolt at us. Are you a God-fearin' lad?"

"My folks are churchgoin' people. My grandpa used to preach."

"Looks like we'll have to send you back to him. Where's he live?"

"He don't, not since last summer. Mama and Papa are all the kin I got, and Todd." The tears burned again. He fought them back. "I ain't even got *them* anymore."

Matthew's voice was soft. "Well, you've got friends.

Between me and Adam, and all them other fellers, we'll do what we can. The rest is up to the good Lord."

The two men took turns digging while Jeffrey stood and watched, numb. Matthew wiped a sweaty forehead and leaned on the shovel. He asked, "How come you-all to travel this far west by yourselves? Didn't anybody tell your daddy the Indians still think they own this part of the country?"

"We stopped in a place called Weatherford. Somebody said it had been a while since there'd been any trouble. Papa had a notion that by comin' out farther than most other folks, he'd have his choice of places. He wanted to start us a good farm."

"I wish he'd asked me. The farther west you go, the less it rains and the poorer the land is for the plow."

Adam took over the shovel. He argued, "Ain't nothin' wrong with the land. Once it's settled up with farms and towns, we'll get more rain. There's an old sayin' that rain follows the plow."

Matthew snorted. "That old sayin' has sent many a broke farmer draggin' back to his wife's family."

When the two decided the hole was deep enough, Matthew said, "Son, you stay here. Me and Adam will bring your folks up."

They carried Jeffrey's parents to the site one at a time. They had bundled Mama in a hand-sewn quilt the Indians had left undisturbed in the bottom of a trunk. Papa was wrapped in the singed remnant of the wagon sheet. The two men lowered them into the grave. Matthew said, "We've faced them east so they'll be lookin' into the sunrise on resurrection mornin'. You'll see them again on that glad day."

Jeffrey would much rather have seen them now, the way they had been this morning, Papa full of hope about the land they would find, Mama just fretting about getting dinner fixed. The land had been Papa's concern. Making a home had been Mama's. "As long as we can have a decent place to raise these boys, I'm happy," she had said.

A bleak thought brought Jeffrey almost back to tears. This lonely grave was all the land they were ever going to have.

Adam said, "Matthew, you're the preacher. Hadn't you ought to say some words?"

Matthew considered for a moment. "If I had my Bible I could do it proper, but I believe the Lord pays more attention to what's in the heart than what's in the words." He bowed his head. "These are two poor pilgrims, Lord, lookin' for your mercy. I don't know why you took them before their rightful time. I don't know why you chose to let this good land be plagued with savages, no more than why you give us arthritis and chilblains, but I suppose we'll understand it all someday. In the meantime I hope you'll fix it so we can deliver your word to these heathens from the muzzle of a rifle. Amen."

He turned to Jeffrey. "Why don't you go back down to the wagon and sit while Adam and me fill the grave?"

Jeffrey did not want to watch dirt shoveled over Mama and Papa. He wandered disconsolately down the gentle grade, wondering if maybe they ought to bury the dog, too.

As for the cow, the two men skinned her out, Matthew saying there was no need in letting good meat go to waste. Later he sat on the ground, whittling letters into the wagon's end gate. "I'm fixin' a head board, such as it is. What were your folks' names, son?"

"Barfield. Papa's Bible name was Alexander. Everybody just called him Alex."

"I'll make it Alex. Alexander is too long for the board. And your mama?"

"Cynthia. I don't know how to spell it."

"I don't either. I'll just carve a C."

Jeffrey wondered if anyone would ever see it anyway. To him, this had suddenly become a bleak and lonely land, unlikely ever to attract many people. He could not understand why his father had thought he would find a good place around here to begin a farm and a new life. All this land had brought was death.

He wished they had never left Arkansas, where the grass seemed always green, the trees tall and shady, the corn growing higher than his head. But the farm had belonged to someone else. Papa was just working it on shares. After falling out with the owner, Papa had little of his own except the wagon and team, the milk cow, a moldboard plow, and a set of hand tools in whose use he was proficient. Texas had advertised cheap land and promised to allow many years for the payout.

Jeffrey saw nothing cheap about it. It had cost his family all there was.

He realized he was hungry. The Indians had carried away or destroyed most of the food. They had taken off a sack of sugar but had emptied a barrel of flour onto the ground. They had also spilled a bag of coffee beans. Jeffrey scooped these up by hand, shaking out as much sand as he could. Matthew carried them to the creek to wash them. Jeffrey tried to salvage some of the flour, but it contained too much dirt. The two men fried strips of beef and boiled a can of coffee.

At dusk, Matthew stared in the direction the Indians and their pursuers had gone. "Don't look like the boys'll be back tonight. Son, you can have my saddle blanket to lay on. You'd better get some sleep."

A little of the afternoon's fear still lingered. Jeffrey said, "What if more Indians come?"

"Ain't likely. Anyway, me and Adam will take turns standin' watch. We'll need to keep the fire goin' so the boys can find their way here."

Jeffrey thought it might help Indians find their way, too. He slept fitfully, reliving the terror over and over. He grabbed at the forlorn hope that when he awakened he would find it had just been a bad dream. Daylight brought no such gratification. He quickly saw that the rest of the men had not returned during the night.

Matthew claimed not to be concerned. He said, "They likely had to chase them red devils further than they expected. I bet you they'll be back today." But Jeffrey saw concern in his eyes.

The Indians had not disturbed the harness, which Papa had hung on the wagon. Adam inventoried all that was still useful after the raiders had finished. "I don't find a choppin' ax," he said. "Found a hammer and a box of nails, though. The Indians ain't fixin' to build any houses. And the plow's still there. They sure don't aim to do any farmin'."

Matthew told Jeffrey, "I've seen many a boy makin' his own way and not much older than you. At least you can start with a wagon and a good set of tools. Even a plow. You could set in to farmin' right here where you're at if you had another two or three years of size and muscle on you. Your daddy would probably like that."

Jeffrey gritted his teeth. "If I had another two or three years on me, I'd get a gun and go to killin' Indians."

"Right now you'd best just think about livin'. You

can't make it by yourself, not for a while yet. We've got to find you somebody to stay with till you're big enough to stand alone."

Jeffrey's initial response was rejection. "Ain't no-body can take the place of Mama and Papa."

"I know. But you'll have to let them make their own place till you're ready to quit the nest and fly on your own."

The two men sat sipping coffee and talking about people who might be prospective guardians. Adam said, "There's Old Man Spears. His son up and went to California. The old man hasn't got any help."

"No," Matthew countered, "he'd work this boy down to a nub. That's what made his son leave. The old man drove him till he was tired to the bone."

"There's the widow Nelson."

"She never did grieve enough to suit me, and she's got too many callers now. Some of them come after dark. Wouldn't be a fit influence."

"But she's a good cook."

Matthew raised an eyebrow. "How do you know?"

Adam hesitated. "A feller told me."

Matthew smiled.

Adam said, "What about you? You and Sarah have got a nice little farm. It'd be a good place for a boy."

Matthew seemed surprised at the thought. He con-sidered, then said, "I'd do it in a minute, but I don't know how Sarah would take it."

Jeffrey wearied of their conversation and walked up to visit the graves. He studied the headboard Mat-thew had carved and thought it was mighty little to show for two lives. His throat was so tight that he could barely swallow, but he did not cry again. He rubbed his sleeve across his eyes, which seemed to have gotten a little sand in them. Turning, he saw a rising of dust like he had seen when the Indians came yesterday, except from the opposite direction. His heart leaped, and he set off running down the slope so fast he almost fell. "Indians!" he shouted. "They're comin' back!"

Matthew and Adam fetched their rifles, but they did not seem as concerned as Jeffrey thought they should be. Matthew squinted. "It's the boys, thank the Lord. Looks like they got back a bunch of horses."

Adam said, "I hope they got mine. I paid forty dollars for one of them."

"Where did you ever get forty dollars?"

"I still owe twenty."

There seemed to be as many riders as when they had left here yesterday in the wake of the Indians. One was bent over in the saddle. Jeffrey had never seen a wounded man, but he sensed that this one was hurt. One pants leg was stained by blood. The big fellow who was their leader rode up to the wagon while most of the others brought the loose horses to a stop. Jeffrey thought there might be more horses now than yesterday.

Matthew walked out to meet the black-bearded one. "Looks like you found your Indians, Fletcher."

"They got careless. Didn't even post a guard. We hit their camp at first light."

"I hope you reformed a bunch of them."

"Four or five. They scattered like quail. We think we got back most of the horses they took in the raid. Some extras besides. Got one man wounded, is all."

Jeffrey asked anxiously, "Did you see my brother?"

Fletcher dismounted, knelt before Jeffrey, and gripped his arms. Grimly he looked him in the eye. "This'll be hard, son, but you've got to know. We found a boy on the trail. They'd killed him."

Jeffrey swayed, trying hard not to cry.

Fletcher said, "We've brought him back to be buried beside your folks."

Jeffrey said, "I want to see him."

Fletcher shook his head. "No, you don't. You'll want to remember him the way he was, not the way they left him."

While three men watched the horses to keep them from straying, the rest gathered around the wagon. They made short work of what remained of the milk cow, frying the meat in one of Mama's dutch ovens. They were so hungry that most ate it half raw. Matthew and Adam went back up the slope and set in to digging a grave beside the one where Papa and Mama lay. A small body was bundled in a blanket Jeffrey recognized as having been taken by the Indians. He burned to open it and see his brother, but he took Fletcher's advice to heart. He would always remember how Papa and Mama had looked after the Indians were done with them. He did not want to remember Todd that way.

His brother had often been a bother with his childish play, but he had also been an eager student when Jeffrey sought to teach him serious stuff like mumblety-peg and knocking over a rabbit with a stone. One winter evening Todd had moved too near the fireplace and had fallen against the grate. Jeffrey had pulled him back and ripped off the smoldering shirt. The red-hot iron grate had left a permanent scar on the inside of Todd's left arm, just below the elbow.

Papa's mules had been recovered along with the horses. Fletcher told Jeffrey, "We'll need for our wounded man to ride in the wagon. We'll hitch up the mules and take you and him back to Weatherford."

Jeffrey felt anxious. "What'll you do with me when we get there?"

"We'll find somebody to take you in. It won't be like charity. A boy with a wagon and team has got somethin' to offer."

Jeffrey turned his head and looked back as they pulled away from the family's last campsite. He kept watching the stark grave marker until it was lost in the dust that followed the wagon. He felt guilty that he had survived while the others had not. Maybe there was something he could have done. . . .

Never in his short life had he been alone before. Though he had all these sympathetic strangers nearby for company, he felt alone and desolate.

2

Two Bulls held protectively to the *teibo* boy captive, aware that some of the others preferred to kill him. They had just killed another, taken two days ago from a burning farmhouse. Wearying of his whining, three had beaten his brains out with their clubs. Two Bulls had forcibly kept this boy quiet by clapping his hand over the youngster's mouth at the first sign of complaint.

He thought he should be able to ransom his captive for something of value, perhaps even a rifle, when they went down on the Las Lenguas to meet the Comanchero traders. Compassion was a weakness of these Mexican merchants who ventured out onto the plains from the west. Or perhaps they had ways of obtaining an even higher ransom than the Comanches could.

The boy stirred restlessly in Two Bulls's arms. Obviously frightened, after an initial resistance he had settled down and accepted the treatment, rough though it was. Two Bulls reasoned that he had taken an object lesson from watching the other boy's violent death.

Seeing no sign that they were being followed, the raiders became complacent as they moved nearer to their accustomed hunting grounds. Only occasionally did the Texans organize effective pursuit and inflict meaningful punishment upon invaders. Usually they followed for a day or so until they used up whatever provisions they had brought or wore out their horses. They seemed unable to hold to their purpose once they were far from home. A truly wicked group known as Rangers stuck to the trail like hunting dogs, but most others were aroused farmers whose homing instincts were stronger than their commitment to revenge.

Two Bulls was contemptuous of Texans. They were a greedy people who lusted after the Indians' lands and scarred Mother Earth with their plows. They were easily killed, however. It had long been his conviction that if all the Comanches and their Kiowa allies would join together in a single determined band, they could drive the *teibos* into the big water and watch them drown. But it went against the People's independent nature to organize so efficiently. Too many wanted to be chiefs, or answer to no chief at all.

The Texans' daybreak attack caught the raiders by surprise. Off-balance and unable to throw together an effective defense against the relentless gunfire, they scattered in several directions, abandoning the horse herd they had accumulated during their foray into the settlements. That pained Two Bulls, for he had claimed first right to a couple of the likeliest-looking. He felt fortunate to have escaped on his best war horse, which he had staked next to his blanket on the ground. And he had grabbed up the bewildered boy before any of the others could kill him to prevent his falling back into the Texans' hands.

He had anticipated a celebratory return to the band's encampment, but that was spoiled now. The warriors had been shamed by losing the fruits of their raid, and Two Bulls had seen at least two of them fall to the Texans' guns. There had probably been more.

He and two other warriors, separated from the rest in the initial rout, left a crooked trail for any Texans who might have the courage to follow. The party, or what remained of it, would reunite at a hidden spring more than half a day's ride toward the plains. Two Bulls knew it would be an unpleasant reunion, rife with recriminations, but he was adept at putting the blame on others in the event of a failure.

At least, with the boy, he still had something to trade. And he had two fresh *teibo* scalps to show for the effort.

It was customary to travel light on these raids. Warriors carried only enough food to sustain strength, consisting mainly of dried strips of buffalo meat, or pemmican, made by pounding the meat into a pulp and mixing it with nuts, berries, or whatever came to hand, even dried mesquite beans. The boy must be hungry. Two Bulls gave him a piece of dried meat, tough enough to crack teeth, and motioned for him to eat. The youngster eyed it with distrust, then gingerly tasted it. A deep frown showed he did not like it, but he was hungry enough to eat anything.

It would be unwise to fatten him up, not that this sparse diet could do so. He should have a lean and desperate look to make the Mexicans feel sorry for him and offer a better ransom.

Sometimes Comanches kept likely Texan and Mexican boys and, after a suitable testing period, adopted them into the tribe. It was a way of offsetting the heavy loss of young men to accidents of the hunt and to deaths suffered in the People's constant wars with the enemies who surrounded them. Two Bulls had no such thought in this case. The boy was simply property, much less valuable than a horse, an object to be traded for something of more practical use.

He knew his plan would receive opposition from his sits-by-me wife. Doe Eyes would want to keep the boy to help relieve her grief over their own son, trampled in his first buffalo hunt. Two Bulls would not compromise, however. He believed that a woman's duty was to cook, take care of the children and the tepee, and perform other types of manual labor that went into moving, camping, and everyday life. It was not for her to offer advice to her husband on matters of importance.

She usually tried, nevertheless.

He and his two companions were the first to reach the spring. They drank their fill and watered their horses, then sat down to chew on dried buffalo meat while they waited. A limping warrior named Bent Leg kept eyeing the boy in a way that made Two Bulls uneasy. Bent Leg had not taken a scalp, and he showed a strong interest in the boy's light-colored hair. He said, "You do not need to go to the Comancheros for a trade. I would give you a horse for that boy."

"I think the Mexicans will give me better than that."

"But it is a long way, and many things can happen."

"I know what would happen if I sold you the boy."

"What difference would it make to you? You would have your trade. It is of little matter what happens to a Texan boy. We have killed many, and yet there are many more of them."

"But I have this one."

"The spirits punish the selfish."

"I have no dread of the spirits. My medicine is strong."

Bent Leg had acquired his name from an injury suffered when a horse fell on him. It was unthinkable for one Comanche to kill another, but Two Bulls would not hesitate to cripple him further if he made a move toward the captive. Bent Leg sensed it, for he quit pressing.

A second party, four this time, arrived to join the first group at the spring. Two Bulls said, "Are you sure the Texans did not follow you?"

One of the party said, "We circled back on our trail. They were satisfied to regain their horses."

The last group came at dusk. Two Bulls counted. They had lost four men. It was not a good day. He said accusingly, "Someone spoiled our medicine."

Comparing notes, they decided the fault lay with a green young warrior named Bad Water. He had inadvertently frightened an owl from its perch on a tree limb, and it had flown over the party. Owls were bad medicine. It was fitting that he had been one of the four who went down before the Texans' guns. That absolved the others of blame.

The boy watched with alert eyes, understanding none of the conversation and probably assuming most of it was about him. He seemed less frightened and more accepting than at first. Not bad for a *teibo*, Two Bulls thought. He wished they could talk with each other, but Texan words were as meaningless as the chatter of birds. He did no better with the Comanchero traders' Spanish, but at least the Mexicans had learned the rudiments of sign language well enough that both sides could reach an understanding. Not many of the People learned anyone else's language. It was their conviction that anyone who wanted to talk to them should speak Comanche.

Instead of the preferred triumphal entry into the encampment, the raiders simply rode in quietly and unadorned. Those who had stayed behind did not have to ask questions. They understood from the riders' solemn attitude that the event had turned out badly. Each man broke off and rode to his own tepee. There would be no dancing tonight.

Doe Eyes waited outside the lodge, her due as first wife. Two Bulls's second wife, her younger sister, stood behind her, accepting the lesser place. Doe Eyes did not rush forward as some of the younger wives did, greeting their husbands. They had been together long enough that such a demonstration was neither expected nor particularly wanted. She stared at the boy sitting in front of Two Bulls, then reached up to help him down from the horse.

She said, "He is not large enough to do heavy work. But he will grow."

Two Bulls warned, "Do not let yourself become attached to him. I intend to trade him to the Mexicans."

Her eyebrows lifted in criticism. "To the Mexicans? But they may make a slave of him. They have enslaved many of the Pueblo and the Navajo. We can raise him as our own. He would be of help in our old age."

"Old age is a long time away."

"Horses are easy to trade to the Mexicans. You took none on this raid?"

"We did, but the Texans stole them."

The downward curve of her mouth indicated a low opinion of the group's fighting ability. "I am taking him inside," she said. "He looks hungry."

Two Bulls was hungry, too, but her sympathy seemed to be only for the boy.

Women! Two Bulls wished it were not necessary to have them.

At first hesitant, then eager, the boy dug into a bowl of stew she gave him. She said, "He has to have a name. We cannot just call him *Boy.*"

Two Bulls had to get his own stew. "He needs no name. He will not be with us long."

Ignoring him, she pondered. "I will call him Little Colt. He can make a better name for himself when he is older."

Two Bulls suspected Doe Eyes was losing her hearing.

The boy seemed caught in the middle of a terrible nightmare, events swirling around him in a bewildering blur. The deaths of his mother and father had come so quickly and without warning that they seemed unreal. The murder of the other boy captive and the dawn attack by the Texans had been more than his young mind could absorb. Only now was he coming to grips with the fact that Indians had carried him away from everything and everybody he had known, to a world of unimaginable strangeness.

He sensed that the two Indian women were trying to be kind to him, especially the older one. Her words were gentle, though they were foreign to him. He stared blankly at her, trying to comprehend. Now and then he understood her gestures, as when she bade him eat or lie down to sleep. Her husband, on the other hand, was mostly indifferent, occasionally impatient when he issued commands that left them both frustrated by their inability to communicate.

Todd tried in vain to decipher his captor's name. He thought of him simply as The Man.

As the trauma began to wear away, he wondered what was ahead for him. He did not understand why the other boy had been killed and he had not, except perhaps that it had to do with the youngster's constant crying. Todd made it a point not to cry. He sensed a great deal of hostility from the other Indian families. Boys near his own age felt free to beat him with sticks and pelt him with rocks. His male captor made no move to stop them until they began to draw blood. The older woman, however, would chase them away with strong words. She made comforting sounds and treated his cuts and abrasions with a pungent-smelling grease.

The younger woman rarely had much to say. She appeared subservient to both The Man and the older woman. Todd noticed, however, that The Man spent much more time in the blankets with her than with the older woman.

After a time he had difficulty visualizing his mother's and father's faces, or that of his brother, Jeffrey. He comprehended that they were gone forever. He began to accept this captive existence as a new reality. Memories of life before the attack were becoming as elusive as last night's dream. Fear was still with him but less intense than at first. He began to take interest in what went on around him, the comings and goings of horsemen, the everyday chores of the women. He began to recognize a few words, such as *erth-pa* for "sleep," and *mah-ri-ich-cut* for "eat." From the other boys he learned *na-ba-dah-kah,* "to fight." He found that when his anger flared he could give as good as he got, unless they were simply too big for him.

He began paying attention to his surroundings

inside the tepee, so much different from the house back home. He noted the way the belongings were distributed around the perimeter. He was fascinated by the open fireplace in the center and the way smoke escaped through an opening in the top without need for a chimney. He took it upon himself to bring in wood, for The Man seemed to regard it as woman's work, beneath his dignity. He frowned upon Todd's doing it.

He saw other men teaching their boys the use of small bows and arrows and how to mount and ride a horse. He began to wish he received such attention, too. He felt that he could do it as well as anyone else.

At least The Man had stopped tying him up at night. Evidently he had become confident that Todd would not run away. Where would he run to? This country was wild and unfamiliar, a long way from where he had spent the first few years of his life. The old home had been surrounded by forests. This was open grassland, timber scarce except along creeks and draws. It was as if he had been carried off to another world.

A day came when The Man and the older woman had an angry argument that threatened for a time to come to violence. Todd could tell that it was about him. He hoped the woman would win, but she didn't. She sulked about the tepee, turning waspish looks upon her husband and treating Todd with extra kindness. The younger woman kept her gaze turned away from him, but he saw sadness in her eyes.

Early one morning, Todd sensed unusual activity in the camp. Many men were catching up their horses. Women were preparing travois, piling them high with buffalo robes and dried meat. The Man approached the tepee, riding one horse and leading two others.

The younger woman mounted one of them. The Man pointed to Todd, then to the third mount. He and the older woman argued angrily until she began to cry. She hugged Todd, then lifted him up onto the bare-back horse.

In the past, Todd had occasionally ridden his father's plow horse home from the field where Papa had been working, but not often enough to gain much profi-ciency. He had to hold on to the long mane to keep from sliding off. The woman shouted harsh words as the man led the horse away from the tepee, joining fifteen or twenty others. Todd had no idea where they were going, but he surmised that it was not to be a raid. Several women were accompanying their men.

Back home, his father had taught him to tell direc-tions by the position of the sun. In early morning they were riding almost into it, and a little to the south. He looked back toward the tepees strung out in two irregular lines adjacent to a tree-lined creek. He saw the older woman still standing, watching. He had just begun to adjust to life in the encampment, and now he was leaving it. Uneasy, he wished he knew where he was being taken, and to what. It would do no good to ask The Man. They could not understand each other. He asked the young woman, for she seemed at times to comprehend what he said. She glanced fearfully at The Man and made no attempt to answer. Her atti-tude compounded Todd's uneasiness.

The procession was impressive to Todd's young eyes. Ahead, several men drove a band of horses. Be-hind these, moving slower, men and boys pushed a herd of cattle. He had never seen the likes of it. The wonder of this new experience soon eclipsed his ap-prehension. He wished his brother, Jeffrey, could see it. Then he remembered something he had almost managed to erase from memory because it was too terrible to contemplate. Jeffrey was dead. Todd had not seen him die, as he had seen their parents die, but surely he must have or the Indians would have brought him along.

He realized anew that he had no one now except these Indians. Most remained unfriendly to him except the two women, and perhaps The Man. Of him, Todd was unsure. For the most part he was brusque and demanding. Yet he showed solicitude, as when the horse made a misstep and Todd fell off. The Man dismounted quickly and looked him over with concern before scolding him and roughly putting him back on the horse. With motions of his hands he indicated that Todd should grip with his knees and not fall off again, or he could expect a beating.

They came to a place where the open plains crumbled off into rough canyons, dark and eerie at first sight from above. Erosion had chiseled the high walls into all manner of shapes, many standing like tall monuments to some past race of giants. They were marbled with layers of rust red and brown, with seams of chalky white. Todd felt awed, and more than a little frightened.

The Indians worked their way down a well-beaten trail to gentler ground, then on to a clear-water creek that snaked its way among heavy trees. Their shade was welcoming, deep and cool. Todd felt little of the wind that had seemed constant on the higher ground above the canyon walls. His horse almost caused him to slide off down its neck when it lowered its head into the green and abundant grass.

The Man seldom smiled, except occasionally when he put his arms around the younger woman. He smiled now, seeming to exult in the luxury of this val-

ley. He had much to say to the woman, though Todd
recognized only one word. It sounded like *Mexican*.

Todd had seen very few Mexicans. He remembered
little about them except that their skin was darker
than his. His father had said something disparaging
about them, but Papa had said something disparaging about a lot of people, and a lot of things. A share-
cropper, he had spoken harsh words about a man he
called the landlord, who lived in a big house on a hill
overlooking the farm. It came back to Todd that he
had run away frightened when the two men fell into
a fistfight. That was shortly before the family loaded
the wagon and left home.

Home. He rarely thought of it. Already it had begun to seem unreal against the stark reality of this
broad land, this new life so alien to everything he had
known.

He wished Jeffrey were with him. Jeffrey was older
and knew much more. Perhaps he could explain the
many things Todd could not understand. He might
even be able to talk to these Comanches. There was
much Todd wished he could ask them.

Like several others who had accompanied the men,
the young woman raised a tepee. It was smaller than
the one back in the larger encampment, using fewer
buffalo skins. This was more like the tents Todd had
seen along the way as the family had trailed westward. He surmised that the stay here was not to be
a long one. He sensed also that the Indians were
waiting for something. The Man periodically looked
toward the trail down which they had come since descending into the valley. He showed no anxiety, so
whoever or whatever was coming must be friendly.

They camped two nights before anything happened. Fresh meat was plentiful, for hunters brought

down deer and a couple of buffalo, which they freely shared. In Todd's estimation, however, the younger wife was not as good a cook as the older one. He wondered why The Man seemed more attentive to her than to the other.

A ripple of excitement spread through the camp on the third day. Ox-drawn carts came lumbering along the trail, each with two solid wooden wheels that looked to be considerably higher than Todd's head. He heard the wheels squeal as dry wood rubbed against dry wood. Papa would have greased them long before they reached that condition.

Three men on horseback preceded the carts, riding into camp with no evident fear. These must be the Mexicans whom The Man had spoken of, Todd thought. Their faces were dark, much like those of the Comanches. However, most wore mustaches, and some had dark beards, unlike the Indians. He stared at them with a curiosity that outweighed any sense of fear. Nothing about them suggested they were here for any unfriendly purpose. One of the three gave him a look of surprise, then quickly cut his gaze away.

As the carts entered camp, he saw that they were piled high with various kinds of goods: blankets, cooking utensils, and everyday implements such as axes and hatchets. There were also some kegs which he guessed held gunpowder. He imagined all this was for sale, but he had seen no sign of money among the Comanches. He wondered how the Indians could buy anything without money. His father never could.

A delegation of Indians moved forward to welcome the newcomers. Todd realized that most of the Mexicans had the same difficulty as he in trying to communicate. The newcomers' language sounded different from that of the Comanches, though it was

just as alien to him. Both groups did most of their
talking with their hands. Todd had begun to pick up
a limited understanding of the Indians' sign language,
but he understood few of their spoken words.

The Mexicans set up a separate camp near that of
the Indians. They made no effort to unload their carts
at first. Instead, they sat with most of the Indian men
as if in some sort of council, smoking together, making sign talk. One passed a jug among the Indians.
They quickly finished it and made it clear that they
would appreciate more, but no second round was offered.

Todd had seen many jugs back home and knew
what they contained. He had never seen his mother
drink from one, but Papa had favored them. When
Todd had expressed an interest, he was told that it
would stunt his growth and he had to wait a few
years. He wondered that the Mexicans did not offer
more to the Comanches, inasmuch as they had finished growing.

He had learned back home that children were not
supposed to intrude upon adults, and he noticed The
Man giving him a threatening frown when he moved
too close to the gathering. He retreated and watched
from a safe distance.

In camp that night, one of the Mexicans played
a guitar and another a fiddle. Others sang in tones
that Todd found melancholy. He was unfamiliar with
the music—he had never heard much music of any
kind before. After a time, the Indians brought out a
leather-covered drum and began to sing in a manner
that fell harshly on Todd's ears, more like a wail than
like music. Several danced in circles to a steady drum-
beat that after a time became hypnotic. The Mexicans gave up their own music to watch.

He noticed a burly man observing him with quiet curiosity. He looked somehow different from most of the other newcomers. Certainly he appeared to be larger than most of them. Todd returned the man's stare for a little while, until sleepiness overtook him. The music and dancing went on as he retreated to the little tepee. The young woman gave him a sad look that he wondered about until he drifted into sleep.

After sunup, the Mexicans busied themselves unloading the carts, spreading their goods on the grass for display. It became obvious that they were not chance travelers but had come for a purpose. Todd began to understand why the Indians had brought the cattle and extra horses along with buffalo robes and dried meat. They had no need for money. They were here to barter for goods they could not provide for themselves.

It occurred to him that the horses and cattle had been stolen, but that seemed of no concern to either the Indians or the Mexicans. They must never have heard an Arkansas preacher expound in terms of fire and brimstone about the wages of sin.

The haggling and bargaining seemed to go on for hours without much changing hands. Then, when both sides had compromised as far as they would go, blankets and implements were exchanged for buffalo robes and dried meat. The powder kegs also went over to the Indians, but Todd saw no firearms change hands.

Suddenly The Man loomed over him, grabbing his arm and dragging him out to where the trading was being done. Todd felt a surge of fear as he realized he was being shown off like the other trade goods. He was for sale, like a horse or a cow. The Man talked in loud tones with a busy working of his hands. The

Mexicans looked at one another, shaking their heads. The Man's talk became louder and more insistent. Still, the Mexicans showed no interest.

With a quick moment of his hand, The Man whipped out a sharp knife and placed it against Todd's throat. Todd felt the sting of the blade and a trickle of blood on his neck. Panic made him want to break away and run, but The Man held him too firmly. He begged for his life, not considering that no one could understand him.

The Man made another pass of the blade along Todd's throat. It burned as if he had touched fire to it.

One of the onlookers shouted, "Now, hold on there, damn you." Todd had noticed him last night. He was a bear of a man with long reddish hair and a tangled beard. He gestured rapidly with his hands, moving toward Todd and the Indian. He made sign talk and spoke in a deep voice that sounded like the croaking of a bullfrog. "Ain't no use killin' that boy, you gut-eatin' heathen. Don't you know he's worth money?"

For the first time in days, Todd understood what someone was saying.

The Man lowered the knife. Todd's stomach turned at the sight of blood on the edge of the blade. He raised a hand to his throat and felt stickiness. The Man had not cut deeply enough to endanger life, but he had forcefully made his point.

The protester went to one of the carts and brought back a muzzle-loading rifle. He handed it to The Man. "This is worth a lot more than a dead boy." He followed the sharp words with hand talk.

A scar-faced trader protested, "Don't you do it, January. You'll just encourage them to steal more young'uns."

January paid no attention. He haggled with The Man at length before returning to the cart for a small keg of gunpowder and a bag of shot. The Man seemed satisfied. He pushed Todd toward the trader with a few gruff words.

Thoroughly frightened, Todd had difficulty speaking. Trembling, he clung to the big man's arm and blurted, "Thanks. He was fixin' to kill me."

January said, "He was, if he couldn't force somebody's hand. You wasn't worth nothin' to him if he couldn't swap you off."

Todd swallowed hard, imagining how it would have felt to have his throat cut. He knew now what his life was worth: one rifle.

A black-bearded, scar-faced man approached January with accusation in his eyes. Todd realized that, like January, he was not Mexican. Angrily the man said, "Better you'd let him kill the kid. Next time we come here they'll have a dozen young'uns to sell. It'll play hell with serious tradin'."

January said, "Torrence, that old gun don't shoot true, but he'll never know the difference. With an arrow an Indian can knock a mosquito's left eye out, but with a rifle he can't hit a buffalo at six feet."

"Now that you've got this kid, what're you goin' to do with him?"

"Turn him over to somebody willin' to pay me a nice reward for savin' him from gettin' his throat cut."

Torrence declared, "It's *your* throat that needs cuttin'."

"You tried that once, remember?"

For a moment Todd feared the men were about to fight, but Torrence said, "This ain't the time or place," and turned away.

The traders began gathering up the results of their bargaining. As they prepared to leave, January and the Mexicans gave the Indians several jugs of firewater. January said, "That'll keep them too drunk to follow after us. Sometimes they get to wantin' their goods back."

In addition to Todd, January had acquired the pony that Todd had ridden here. He put a makeshift rawhide hackamore over the animal's head and handed the reins to Todd. He spoke to a young Mexican cart man in the driver's language. He watched as the carts began moving toward the trail that would take them up on top, then beckoned for Todd to follow.

Todd puzzled over him. Now that he had time to study his rescuer, he could see that January's eyes were a washed-out blue instead of the Mexicans' dark brown. His shaggy hair and scraggly beard were of a rust color, the whiskers stained by tobacco juice. His arms looked as big as most men's legs.

Todd's parents had taught him to say *sir* to grown men and *ma'am* to women. He asked, "Who are you, sir?"

Gruffly the man said, "It ain't polite out here to ask a lot of questions. You better learn that before somebody takes a strap to your britches."

"I didn't mean nothin'."

"If you've got to call me somethin', call me January. Everybody else does."

"That don't sound like a real name."

"I like it. Made it up myself after I used up my real one. What's *your* name, anyway?"

"Todd."

"Sounds like a drink of whiskey. I think I'll just call you Dogie."

Todd knew that a dogie was an orphaned calf. He

guessed the nickname was a fit. January could call him anything he wanted so long as he took him away from here.

As they set off on the trail toward the canyon walls, he looked back down at the Indian camp. It appeared that, as January had said, the Comanches were working at emptying the jugs.

January saw what Todd was looking at. He said, "That'll be one sick bunch after a while. The Mexicans make that stuff to sell, not to drink."

"You're not a Mexican. Neither is that feller Torrence. How come you're with them?"

"Life don't always take you where you'd figured on goin'."

"I sure hadn't figured on comin' here."

"I was raised to be a farmer, but me and some of my neighbors never did gee-haw. A time came when I had to leave home or lose my health. I drifted west into the Spanish country around Taos and Santa Fe. Learned how to trap varmints for their skins. And fight off varmints like Torrence."

"You're a trapper, then."

"In the wintertime, when the skins are prime. Summertime, I trade with the Indians, run whiskey, catch horses, whatever comes to hand. A man can make a livin' almost anywhere if he's fast enough on his feet."

Todd had to screw up his courage before he asked, "What you figurin' on doin' with me?"

"Let somebody have you for more than I paid. Buy low, sell high, that's how I do business."

"You're goin' to sell me? Who to?"

"I expect your mama and daddy would be glad to pay me for bringin' you back."

"But Indians killed my mama and daddy. My brother, too."

He saw disappointment in January's squinted eyes. "That's a bad turn of luck for me. But you must have family someplace. What's the rest of your name, boy?"

"Just Todd."

"Todd what?"

Todd strained, trying to remember. The trauma of recent events had left him in something of a daze. He was not sure what was real and what was a nightmare.

January's patience began to thin. "What was your daddy's name?"

"Papa."

"Just Papa? Nothin' else?"

"Grown-up folks called him Alex, but I wasn't supposed to. I was supposed to call him Papa."

"Don't you even know his last name?"

"I'm tryin' to remember, but my mind is all muddied up. Everybody just said Alex."

January became more insistent. "Where'd you come from?"

"They called it Arkansas."

"What town?"

"There wasn't no town."

January cursed. "Hell of a note. This is what I get, feelin' sorry for somebody. Nobody ever felt sorry for me."

Todd wanted to cry, but he held his feelings in check. He asked, "What're you goin' to do with me now?"

"Looks like I'm stuck till I find somebody to unload you on."

"I could be a right smart of help."

"Doin' what? You're just a little dogie. You wouldn't make a meal for a half-growed catamount."

"I'll get bigger."

"And expect me to feed you till you do? You ain't lookin' at no do-good preacher, boy. I'm sorry I swapped that rifle for you, poor as it was. I could've got more for it." January grunted. "Maybe when we get to Anton Chico I can trade you for tortillas and beans."

Todd knew about beans. He had no idea what kind of bird or animal a tortilla was.

3

January lighted a black, smelly pipe and grimaced at the bitterness of the first draw. He said, "We ought to be crossin' the New Mexico line about now."

Todd looked around, trying to find it. "I don't see no line."

"It ain't a line you can see on the ground. It's just on maps."

"What good does it do if you can't see it?"

"Damned if I know, but it ain't been long since there was a war fought over it. The Mexican government lost, so New Mexico belongs to the United States now, same as Texas."

Todd knew nothing of geography. He had heard the word *Texas* a lot before and during their wagon trip, but he had never heard of New Mexico. It sounded strange, like everything else he had encountered since the Indians had taken him. "Do people there talk to where I can understand them?"

"English? No, you'll have to learn Mexican unless

I find somebody white who'll pay my price. Damned if I intend to take a loss on this deal."

"You said that old rifle wasn't worth much."

"Never mind. It's the principle of the thing."

Todd was apprehensive over the prospect of changing ownership again, though it might be for the better. It had already happened twice. He had taken comfort in being able to understand what January said to him, even if he did not understand the man himself. He had been listening to the Mexican cart men's conversation and doubted he could ever learn to talk as they did. After all, they were grown men and had had years to learn. He was only five-going-on-six, or so Mama had told him.

Thoughts about Mama brought sadness. She had been trying to teach him his letters, but studying had come hard. He doubted that being able to read was worth so much effort. Lots of people didn't know how, yet they appeared to get along all right. At least January seemed unlikely to give him any reading lessons. He suspected that the man couldn't tell if a book was right side up or upside down.

He noticed that most of the cart men took a stand-offish attitude toward January. They seemed to regard him as an outsider.

Todd remarked, "They don't act very friendly."

January said, "They're Mexicans. They took this country away from the Indians a hundred years or so ago. They don't feel kindly toward Americanos who come in and stake a claim on any of it."

"How do they make a livin'?"

"Most of them have got a little farmland. They keep sheep and cattle. These here trade with the Indians, too. That's why they're called Comancheros.

They ain't thieves, but they buy goods that the Indians stole from somebody else."

"Like you bought me?"

"That's different. I saved your scrawny little neck. If I can show a profit out of doin' good, I don't see nothin' wrong with it."

The flat plains continued well beyond the place January had said was the state line, but stunted cedar trees gradually became more numerous. Mountains began to rise in the west, and the carts labored over increasingly rough ground, down into narrow valleys and back up timbered hillsides. The pines reminded Todd of the homeplace the family had left so many weeks ago, but there was wildness in this land. He saw deer dart out of the clearings and back into the cover of trees as the groaning carts approached. Twice he saw what January told him were black bears. He had never seen a bear before, but he had heard Papa say they used to be thick when he was growing up in Arkansas. He had warned that they liked to eat naughty little boys, so each sighting now gave Todd a chill.

January said, "That'd be a prime skin if I could get it this fall before he goes into hibernation. A good bearskin will fetch a smart price."

Despite his dread, Todd felt a little sorry for the bear. "Seems like a pity to kill it just for the skin."

"Preachers say the Maker gave man dominion over the animals. He put bears here so we can skin them and make some money. Of what other use are they?"

They crossed a river that January said was the upper Pecos, then followed it until they came to a wide, green valley stretching out of sight to both north and south. A village lay scattered along its bottom. Todd sensed from January's pleased manner that they were approaching their destination. January said, "Pretty soon now I'll be gettin' a fit and proper dinner, cooked by a woman."

Todd had not heard him mention a woman before. "Mrs. January?"

"Not *missus*. I just said I got a woman. Name's Yolanda."

"I never heard a name like that before."

"I've had others, Indian women. I wish Yolanda was better-lookin', but she knows what to do with a pot and a skillet." He almost smiled. "She was a widder woman with a boy to raise, and had this little farm to take care of. I figured she needed a man, and I needed a place to stay when I wasn't on the go, so I moved in with her. Out of the goodness of my heart."

Todd had not seen a lot of goodness in January, from the heart or anywhere else, but Mama used to say there was some goodness in everybody. With certain people you just had to look hard to find it.

The houses he saw were mostly square-sided and had flat rooftops. They did not look like the log and lumber houses he had known.

"They're made of adobe bricks," January said. "Dried mud. They don't cost much. They're mostly poor folks around here, so the cheaper the better. A man don't need much anyway, just a roof to shade him from the summer sun and keep the rain and snow off of him. Folks back in the old states always want more than they can afford. Keeps them broke. All a man really needs is a warm fireplace, a jug, and a woman to cook and fetch for him."

The carts began splitting up, each taking its own direction. Soon January's was the only one still following the two riders, carrying the results of his trade with the Indians. Its driver was a young Mexican who lived on a nearby farm and hired out his labor. Like the others, he kept an invisible wall between himself and January, speaking to him only when spoken to.

January pointed to an adobe house at the far side of a small field where green cornstalks stood waist high. "That yonder is mine."

A few white-and-brown spotted goats trotted away as the riders approached. Two dogs of questionable bloodlines ran to meet them, barking until January shouted a threat. They retreated with tails tucked under. "Damned dogs are useless," he said. "I'd shoot them both, but I'd probably have to shoot Yolanda, too."

A woman stepped out the front door, shading her eyes with one hand. She was short in height but more than ample in width. Her brown skin would have told Todd that she was Mexican if he had not already known. She offered no visible or verbal greeting but wiped her hands on a dark apron and watched solemnly as January and Todd rode in. The cart followed fifty yards behind them.

January's only greeting was a brusque *"Comida."* Todd had already learned that meant it was time to eat. He sensed that this was a partnership of mutual convenience, not of love like his parents' had been.

The place was a menagerie. Chickens pecked around the door. A turkey strutted up to give the newcomers a quick appraisal, then turned away when it saw that nobody was going to offer feed. Ducks floated on the surface of a small dirt pond out by the garden. In a crude stake pen, a sick sheep stood with head drooped, mucus sagging from its nose.

January unsaddled his horse. Todd had ridden bareback all the way from the Indian encampment, so all he had to do was to slip the hackamore from the horse's head. The cart pulled up near the house. January said, "We'll unload it in the cool of the evenin'." He spoke to the driver in Spanish. The man led the oxen to a pen and removed the heavy wooden yoke.

January said, "I told Manuel he could go home. If he hung around here, I'd have to feed him dinner."

Yolanda gave Todd a long study without asking any questions. January spoke in Spanish, evidently telling her why the boy was here. She shook her head sympathetically and said, "*Pobrecito*." Todd took that as a favorable sign.

Then January told her something more, and her eyes narrowed in disapproval. Her voice was sharp. Todd hoped she was arguing against January's plan to sell him. If so, the try was futile, for January stood his ground. She turned away, beaten but unbowed, and stirred up coals in the open fireplace. She added small chunks of wood to rekindle the fire.

Todd said, "You told me she's got a boy."

"Name's Felipe. He's out herdin' sheep. Won't come in till it's time to pen them for the night. It's a caution how wolves and coyotes love mutton." January sat in a handmade wooden chair and looked Todd over critically, as if he were a horse up for sale. "Got to take you out to the creek this evenin' and see that you get a good scrubbin'. In the mornin', I'm goin' to show you to some folks and see if any of them want to take you off of my hands."

Apprehensive, Todd said, "You're still figurin' on sellin' me?"

"It's business, like trappin' and tradin' and raisin' them snot-nosed sheep. I already got Yolanda and her young'un leanin' on me for support. That's all I can handle."

"Maybe I could learn to herd sheep."

"Felipe don't need no help. He barely earns his keep as it is."

Soon, Yolanda placed a meal on the table. Todd did not know what the mixture was, but he was hungry enough to eat almost anything. One bite told him there were things here that contained fire without showing flame.

January said, "You'd better get used to it if some Mexican family decides to take you. They raise lots of chili peppers around here."

Todd had seen several strings hanging from the rafters outside, drying in the sun.

Late in the afternoon, after a long nap, Todd helped unload the cart. January had acquired several buffalo robes and a substantial quantity of dried meat. He said, "I'll be takin' this stuff to Santa Fe to sell. May have to take you, too, if nobody here wants you."

January walked with him to the creek and had him remove his clothes. Todd had been wearing the same ones since before the Indians had taken him. They were caked with dirt, horse sweat, and other vestiges of a long trail. January pitched him a rough bar of lye soap. "Scrub yourself till it feels like the hide is comin' off. You'll want to make a good impression."

When the bath was finished, January handed him some clean clothes. "These belong to Felipe, but you can roll up the sleeves and the legs. They'll do till Yolanda gets these others washed and mended."

Yolanda was milking a brindle cow beneath the low cover of a picket shed. The roof was dry brush stacked atop several long tree branches that served as rafters. Almost every structure here seemed to have come up out of the earth.

Hopefully, Todd said, "I could do the milkin', I think."

January shook his head. "Forget it. Your hands are too small. *You're* too small. It'll be two or three years yet before you're big enough to be of much help to anybody. I doubt I'll live that long."

"How come?"

"There's folks around here that would be pleased to gut me like a catfish. And there's Indians out yonder that'd wade waist-deep into hell for a try at my scalp."

"Why didn't they do it at the tradin' place?"

"They keep a truce there because they don't want to stop the traders from comin'. But once you leave, you're fair game. That's why the Mexicans sold them whiskey, to keep them busy till we got plumb away."

Todd heard the bleating of sheep as a boy herded them into a pen and closed the gate. "That's Felipe," January said. "I've raised him from a pup, almost. A fair worker, but he eats too much."

Thin as a post, Felipe appeared to be a few years older than Todd, perhaps Jeffrey's age or a little more. He gave Todd a moment's notice and did not seem pleased by what he saw.

January said, "Felipe, this boy is Dogie. He'll be with us a day or two. Maybe a little longer."

To Todd's surprise, the brown-skinned Felipe spoke in words he could understand. "How come? We don't need no gringo boy."

January's reply was curt. "That's for me to say. You just do your work and don't give me no sass." He walked back to the house and left the two boys standing there, staring at each other.

Todd asked, "Why don't you like me?"

"You're Americano. Americanos take but never give. Like January."

"He feeds you, don't he? He gives you a home."

"The farm is my mother's. He thinks it is his. We do the work, me and her. He takes the money."

"He's fixin' to sell me."

Felipe's eyebrows went up. "Sell you? Like a burro or a goat?"

"He bought me. I guess he can sell me."

Felipe frowned, thinking about it. "He don't like me much, but he ain't ever sold me."

"Maybe your mama wouldn't let him."

"She would kill him. Or maybe I would kill him myself. But then the gringo government would hang me. We don't like them, and they don't like us."

Todd said, "Seems like a lot of people don't like one another around here."

"Maybe someday we have another war, and this time we win. Then *adiós*, Americanos."

Supper was tortillas and beans and some kind of roast. Todd supposed it was goat, because he had seen part of a goat carcass hanging outside. Whatever it was, he stuffed himself despite the burning peppers. January watched with silent disapproval, probably thinking about the cost of food. After the meal, he told the two boys to help Yolanda clean up. He went out onto the narrow, brush-roofed veranda, sat in a rawhide-bottomed chair, and took additional nourishment from a jug.

"It's mighty hard work," he said, "earnin' enough to keep up a household like this one."

Felipe said quietly, "It is hard work, but it is not January who does it."

Yolanda's son was the only person other than January who had spoken English to Todd since he had been stolen. Todd asked, "Where did you learn to talk like that?"

"From January. And at school. Had a gringo teacher till people in the valley run him off."

"You called me a gringo. Is that bad?"

"Sure you're a gringo. Got skin like a fish's belly. People here don't like gringos much."

"Then how come they let January stay?"

"Afraid, most of them. One time, one of Mama's brothers come to run him off. Got shot in the leg. Now everybody waits. They hope the Indians kill him, or some other Americano."

"What do *you* hope?"

Felipe shrugged. "What is to happen is in the hands of God. The Americanos take everything. Soon I will be grown, and I will go down to Chihuahua, where the grandfathers came from. No gringos, no Indians. Just us Spanish."

Breakfast came early, soon after the sun rose over the mountains to the east and spilled first light down into the valley. January said, "Today's Sunday. That's lucky for both of us, boy. I'm takin' you to church."

Todd had not figured January to be a churchgoing man, but he realized this was the trader's chance to show him off to the largest number of people at one time.

Todd rode double with January, sitting behind the saddle. The church bell was ringing, and people were coming from all directions. January said, "The padre is from Ireland. He talks a pretty good Spanish, though, so folks here like him. They don't even call him a gringo."

The priest's look of surprise told Todd that he had guessed right. January's presence in church came as something of a shock to everybody who saw him. January explained in English the purpose of his visit, that he was trying to find a decent home for a hard-luck kid orphaned by the Indians.

The robed cleric saw through him. "You will expect payment, of course?"

"I been out some expense. I figure it's right and proper to at least get back what I've got invested."

"How much?"

"Say, a hundred dollars."

"So, along with your other sins, you would now traffic in human beings? I forbid you to use this church as a marketplace. Begone from here, January."

"But, Padre . . ."

"I'll tell all in this parish to beware of you and your devilish scheme. Now go, before the Lord decides to strike you down with a lightning bolt, here in this holy place."

January took Todd's arm and roughly led the boy outside. He grumbled, "Some people that preach about God's mercy don't have much of it theirselves."

A rough voice spoke from behind. Todd turned. He saw the man called Torrence, whose piercing gray eyes suggested bottled-up violence. A scar started at the corner of a dense eyebrow and lost itself in a bristling black beard. Torrence demanded, "Ain't you afraid of the Lord's vengeance, January, gettin' this close to a church house?"

January said, "There's one thing I *ain't* afraid of, Torrence, and that's you."

"I'm givin' the Lord time, but if he waits too long, I'll see to the job myself."

The man's threatening manner made Todd's heart beat faster, but it seemed to have no effect upon January except to make him moodier than he already was. As Torrence walked away, Todd asked, "What's the matter with him?"

"Him and me had a little disagreement once over some peltry. He tried to carve out my liver, but I got ahold of his knife and done a little carvin' of my own. Thought about earmarkin' him while I was at it, but he had cut my belly open. I decided I'd better stop and sew myself up before things got serious."

"You sewed yourself?"

"Wasn't nobody else around to do it. I wasn't goin' to trust the needle to Torrence. He'd've stuck it in my eye."

January took Todd to several of the more prosperous people in the valley. They expressed sympathy for the boy's situation, but none was willing to pay what January asked for the right to adopt him. In a couple of cases, Todd regretted that. He thought he could be contented with the people, though he would have to learn Spanish to talk to them. In other cases, however, he was glad they rejected him. He did not like their looks. He feared they might be inclined to mistreat him because he was gringo, and were interested only in the work they might get out of him as he grew older and stronger. One man even felt of his arm, testing Todd's muscles.

Yolanda fed him well, always urging him to eat more. Felipe seemed to mellow toward him, teaching him Spanish words that might prove useful, and some not to be used in polite company. When January was not showing him to prospective foster parents, Todd hoed weeds from the garden and became acquainted with the farm's considerable variety of domestic animals and birds. He decided that, all in all, he preferred to stay with January despite his shortcomings. At least he knew what to expect, and what not to. He could not be certain about the other people.

January became increasingly frustrated by his in-

ability to place Todd at an advantage to himself. One
night at supper he declared, "Dogie, there ain't nobody around here has got enough charity about them
to take you in."

For a moment Todd felt relieved. January quickly
took that away from him by adding, "Come mornin'
we're goin' to load them robes and dried meat on
pack mules and head out. I'll bet there's somebody in
Santa Fe that'll want to do their Christian duty."

Yolanda protested, to no avail. Felipe waited until
January went out onto the veranda with his jug before
he said, "Maybe it is not so bad. There's rich people
in Santa Fe. Maybe they'll feel sorry and adopt you.
I would not mind livin' in a big house, with servants
fetchin' and carryin'."

"What if they make a servant out of *me*?"

"You are not big enough. But you can steal a horse
and come back here. Me and you, we will go to Chihuahua." He grinned at the thought. "We would laugh
big, seein' people make January give their money back.
He would bust a gut."

Todd tried to visualize how January would look
with a busted gut. The image was not altogether dis-
tasteful.

He said a melancholy goodbye to Felipe as the
boy prepared to take the sheep out to graze. Yolanda
handed him a sack of food to get him started on the
trip. From the smell he knew it was a generous supply
of roast goat and a stack of tortillas. Somewhere in
there would also be a few sugary *dulces*. He hugged
her, his eyes burning. He said his goodbyes in a mix
of Spanish and English, adding a plaintive *adiós*.

Impatiently January said, "Come on, we got to be
movin'. It's a long ways."

January put him on an old saddle with a huge horn,

the wooden tree only partially covered by leather. Todd knew it was going to rub him raw. The stirrups were too long, but January did not take the trouble to adjust them.

He said, "I got this saddle pretty cheap. I'll sell it in Santa Fe."

Along with me, Todd thought. He felt some of the same sense of loss that had come over him after Mama and Papa were killed.

The way was crooked but plain, for a hundred years and more of hooves and wheels had worn deep ruts in the trail. January explained that the first settlers had been Spanish, migrating north from Chihuahua. They intended to move as far from the authorities as they could get.

"They was Spanish for a long time. Then they fought and won their independence from Spain. For a while they was Mexicans. A few years ago there come another war, and they belonged to the United States. It ain't any wonder half of them don't know for sure who they are, or what."

Todd had only a vague idea of what he was talking about. "What does that make us?"

"We're Americans, boy. No matter who winds up gettin' you and where you go to live, don't ever forget that you're an American. Be proud of it."

Todd guessed he would be, when he figured out just what the difference was.

Their last night out from Santa Fe, they camped at the base of a red hill where they found a hole of water left by a recent rain. January considered it too muddy for him and Todd to drink, but the horses and pack mules showed no prejudice against it. Todd worried a little about Indians. January assured him there was no danger. "The ones around here ain't apt to cause trouble. They'd rather sell us somethin'."

Todd was tired. He slept the night through and awoke to see the first light of dawn breaking over the cedar-dotted hills. Turning, he saw that January was still covered by a blanket. Then he was startled to see that they were not alone.

The man called Torrence stood at January's feet, a pistol in his hand. He looked twelve feet tall from Todd's position on the ground. Torrence kicked January's foot and said, "Wake up. I'm lettin' you load your goods for me."

January peered sleepy-eyed over the edge of his blanket. "Torrence? What the hell you doin'?"

"Collectin' on an old debt, and payin' one I owe. I'm takin' your animals and your goods. Thanks for bringin' them this far for me."

"Better think again. Every time you've tried to rob me you've come out poorer than you was before."

"This time'll be different. I'm fixin' to blow your light out."

"What about the boy?"

"Can't have him tellin' lies about me all over the country."

The cold hand of fear clutched Todd's throat. He realized Torrence intended to kill both of them.

January had not thrown off the blanket. "There's no use in hurtin' the boy. Nobody's goin' to believe a dogie kid. Just tell them he's got a wild imagination."

"Sounds to me like you've got attached to him. That ain't like the January I used to know."

"I just don't like to see a kid killed. That's why I bought him, to keep that damned Comanche from cuttin' his throat. See here, Torrence, I'll make you a deal."

"What you got?"

"This." Flame burst through January's blanket, and a shot echoed against the hills. Torrence's eyes seemed to bug out of their sockets as he took a ball in his right leg and went down on his knees. The pistol dropped from his hand.

January said, "Pick it up, boy, but don't touch the trigger." He laid the blanket aside, revealing a smoking pistol. He stood up and accepted Torrence's pistol from Todd's trembling hands. "Boy, the blanket's afire. Stomp on it."

Todd stepped on the smoldering area that ringed a new hole.

January said to Torrence, "See what comes of bein' greedy?"

Torrence gripped his bleeding leg and whined. "Damn you, January."

January said, "Fetch him his horse, boy. He needs to go find him a doctor someplace, or a *curandero*. Else he's liable to bleed to death."

The horse had run off at the sound of the shot but stepped on the reins and stopped. Todd caught it and led it back. Torrence muttered and moaned as he struggled to crawl up onto the horse. January offered him no assistance, and Todd was too small to help. Still wailing, the wounded man rode off westward, hunched over in the saddle.

Todd marveled at how coolly January had met Torrence's challenge. January said, "I always sleep with a loaded gun. You never know when somebody'll show up that needs shootin'. But it bothers me that I just got him in one leg. I aimed at where the legs come together."

"He's liable to try again, ain't he?"

"I wouldn't be surprised, but I don't like to kill a man if I can keep from it. Always causes more trouble than I want to put up with."

"Two times now you've saved me."

"I was savin' myself this time. You just happened to be here."

Santa Fe was a haphazard collection of mostly flat-topped adobe buildings scattered among red clay hills. Todd thought it might be larger than Weatherford, the last town of any size he had seen, but it looked vastly different. He followed January and the pack mules down to an open plaza, fronted by rows of stores and a large church.

January said, "This is where most of the tradin' gets done. We'll lay down our packs here."

Todd helped where he could, though January had to do most of the lifting and carrying. He studied the people and found them a mix of Mexicans, Americans, and Indians. A number of uniformed soldiers watched him and January with interest. He was pleased to hear them speaking English. Maybe here he could understand what folks were talking about.

Soon, several people were examining January's trade goods and haggling with him over prices. Todd found it interesting how easily January shifted from one language to another. After a while the trader and a merchant came to terms over the buffalo robes, though January did not seem happy with the price. "You're robbin' me," he told the buyer.

"Not half as bad as you robbed the Indians you got these from," the buyer said.

January then called Todd to his side and placed a

hand on the boy's thin shoulder. He said, "I rescued this lad from the Indians, and I'm huntin' for somebody to give him a good home."

The buyer stroked his muttonchop whiskers and gave Todd a severe study. "He's too young to do much work."

"But he'll grow. He'll be a lot of help to you when he gets a couple more years on him, and he'll be a comfort to you in your old age."

"I've already got five kids of my own. Taking care of them is making an old man of me before my time. I sure don't need another." He thought for a moment. "It's the army's job to take care of rescued captives and get them back to where they belong. Why don't you go see the colonel?"

January nodded. "I might just do that."

He offered Todd to almost everyone who came by if they looked as if they had any money. The few who initially showed an interest backed away when he mentioned that he needed a hundred dollars to recoup what he had spent on the boy. He managed to unload the dried buffalo meat on another merchant. "Now," he told Todd, "I've gotten rid of everything except you. Looks like there's nobody left but the army."

For a while Todd thought they never would get to see the colonel, but finally an orderly ushered them into the office. The colonel appeared to dislike January on sight, or perhaps he already knew him.

January quickly got down to business. "Colonel, I got this orphan boy here. Rescued him from a Comanche that was fixin' to cut his throat. I'd see that he gets home, but he's so young he can't tell me where that is. Maybe the army can find out, or at least settle him someplace."

The colonel wanted to know all the circumstances. He asked Todd the same questions as January had.

"What's your name, son?"

"Todd."

"What else besides Todd?"

"I don't know. Sometimes they called me Son."

January said, "It's like I told you, that's about all I got out of him, except the Indians killed his mama and daddy and his brother."

Todd was able to say that his family had left a farm in a place called Arkansas and were moving west. He had no idea where in Arkansas.

The colonel said, "That doesn't give us much to go on. I doubt that we can ever find any family."

January said, "Maybe you got a school or an orphans' home or someplace where you send young'uns like this."

"I would have to make some inquiry."

"Then I'm turnin' him over to you. All I'm askin' is a hundred dollars for my trouble and expenses."

The colonel's eyes narrowed in sudden anger. "In other words, you bought him, and now you want to sell him."

"It's only fair that I get a little somethin' out of it. After all, I saved his life. Wasn't for me, he'd be dead now."

The officer's anger grew. "You saved him because you thought you could get a profit out of him. Isn't that right?"

"That's a raw way to put it."

"Raw or not, I won't buy him from you. Trafficking in human beings may be legal in Texas, but slavery is forbidden in New Mexico. I could bring charges against you for trying to sell this boy. In fact, I think I will."

January was becoming agitated. He grabbed Todd's arm and pulled him to the door. "Come on, Dogie, before we both wind up in the army hoosegow."

The colonel shouted after them as they hurried through the office door, "January, you bring that boy back here."

"To hell with you." January quickly mounted his horse and pulled Todd up behind him. They left the post at a gallop. January kept looking back as if expecting pursuit, but there was none. He slowed the horse to a walk, cursing beneath his breath. As they reached the plaza, he drew rein and looked across at the church.

He said, "I ought to've left you with the army, but the colonel made me so damned mad that I couldn't think straight. Looks like you're a dead loss to me, boy."

"Are you takin' me home with you?"

"What use would I have for you? You've already eaten more than you're worth. Time you got big enough to be of real help, you'd probably run away anyhow. That colonel may send a patrol out lookin' for me. I'll have to leave you here."

Todd felt fear like he had experienced when the Comanche held a knife to his throat and when Torrence spoke of killing him. "By myself?"

January pointed to the church. "See that feller in the robe yonder? He's a padre. You go over to that church and talk to one of the padres. They'll see that you're took care of and maybe find you a new home. They have to, because they're holy men and that's what the Bible tells them to do. They set a lot of store in the Bible."

Todd choked, trying not to cry. "I'd rather go back to Yolanda and Felipe."

"Like I said, I've already took enough loss on you. It's somebody else's turn now. Slide off onto the ground and go over to the church like I told you."

Todd held to the saddle strings until he felt his feet touch the ground. Without saying more, January turned away and set the horse into a long trot, traveling eastward. Todd watched him through tears until he disappeared. He seated himself on a knife-scarred wooden bench and tried to recoup his battered courage. The padre walked back into the church. Todd knew that sooner or later he would have to follow, but he wanted to put it off as long as he could. He knew what life was like at January's place. It had its good points, and it had its bad. At least he knew what they were. He had no idea what might lie ahead with the padres.

He sat until dusk, watching wagons and carts, mule and burro trains moving along the outer edges of the plaza. He watched the people who walked past him, white, Mexican, Indian, black, some he could not identify. He was not used to seeing such a wide variety of human beings. He began to notice an increasing number of young people, walking in slow circles around the plaza, men in one direction, women in the other. From time to time they stopped to talk, then paired up and walked together.

He began feeling hungry. January had left him nothing to eat and no money with which to buy anything. He began thinking it was time he went over to the church and turned himself in to the padres. He felt empty and alone and desperate, trapped in a strange land of strange people, nothing about any of it resembling the home from which he had come. He closed his eyes and wept.

He felt a presence and looked up, blinking to clear the tears. There stood January, holding two horses.

January said, "I know a lot of people call me a son of a bitch, and I reckon I am. But I ain't no *goddamned* son of a bitch. Come on, boy, I'll take you home."

4

As the wagon lumbered along, picking its way around the gentle hills and the scrub oaks, Jeffrey recognized a few landmarks he had seen while traveling west with Papa and Mama and Todd. Now he was returning east with the men who had rescued him. Matthew Temple sat beside him, driving the wagon. His horse was tied on behind. The band of horses taken from the Indians trotted ahead, following a homing instinct that drew them eastward. Most of the volunteers were strung out between the loose animals and the slower wagon.

Matthew said, "Too bad your folks didn't decide to stay and settle around Weatherford. There's still good farmin' land to be took up, and the Indians don't raid that far east anymore."

"They don't?"

"Well, not much. What we need is more settlers, so they won't come at all."

"You been here a long time, Mr. Matthew?"

"Me and my wife and our baby boy, we came seven

years ago from Ohio. We had it in mind to go farther west, but folks warned us about the Indians. We decided to take up land over by Weatherford. Glad now that we did."

Jeffrey said, "I wish they'd warned us." In truth, several had, but Papa had wanted land so badly that he had shrugged off their admonitions. Looking back, he could see how he might be angry at Papa, but it was not in him to be critical of his father. He had been brought up to accept that adults were always right. Usually, anyway.

Matthew was a comforting presence, but not enough to relieve Jeffrey's loneliness and the dull ache of loss. The future was a dark void he regarded with dread. There had been uncertainty about the family's move westward, too, but at least he had been with Mama and Papa. Papa had always had a contagious confidence. This time, it had taken him and the family over the precipice.

Matthew said, "I won't tell you everything will be all right. It won't, not for a time. I know what you're feelin' because I felt it when typhoid took our boy Henry. At least now I've got to where I can think about him without wantin' to crawl off somewhere and die. My poor wife, though, she hasn't got over it. I wonder sometimes if she ever will."

"I heard them say you're a preacher."

"Not for a livin'. I've been a farmer all my life, but I heard a call to spread the gospel. I do that as much as I can."

"I wisht you'd tell me how come the Lord lets things like this happen. He could've stopped those Indians, and he could've cured your boy."

"Some say he tests us in this life to see if we're fit for the next one."

"My folks wasn't through with this one yet."

"There's so much meanness goin' on in the world, the Lord can't be everywhere at once. He leaves most of the fixin' to us."

They stopped at a small lake. Jeffrey felt thirsty, but the horses had already been there, wading in and stirring the mud until the water was a marbled brown. Matthew said, "Wait. We'll be comin' to a nice little stream after a while. They can't muddy it all."

When they reached the creek, Matthew pulled the wagon farther upstream than the horses had been. Jeffrey took a cup from the wagon and drank his fill.

Matthew said, "You need to learn how to lay on your belly and drink out of your hand. You won't always have a cup."

Jeffrey knew how, but Mama had admonished him to use a cup when he could. It showed he was civilized.

The stream looked somehow familiar. It resembled one back home where he had sometimes gone fishing with Todd. The thought of his little brother brought the sadness rushing back. He had been trying to teach Todd about the important things in life, like fishing. The boy had been a more eager student on subjects of that type than on learning his letters.

Matthew asked, "How much did your daddy teach you about plantin' and cultivatin' and such?"

"I can handle a plow if the ground ain't too hard. Papa said I need some more weight to do a man's work, though."

"You'll grow into it. What about book learnin'? Had any schoolin'?"

"Mama taught me my letters, and we had an old-maid schoolteacher for a while. I can read parts of the Bible where the words ain't too big."

"There ain't a better book to learn by."

"There's some words in it that I can't figure out. Looks like they ought've written it plain enough to where everybody could understand it."

Matthew nodded. "There's things that throw me, too. But I guess that's the way people talked a long time ago."

"They must've had a hard time understandin' one another."

Most of the men went ahead with the recovered horses. Adam remained with the wagon, as did the pursuit leader, Fletcher. Jeffrey had felt the big man's speculative gaze touching him at times throughout the day.

Trying to decide what to do with me, he thought.

He asked Matthew, "Who's Fletcher? A sheriff or somethin'?"

Matthew made a tentative smile. "No, Fletcher Knight's not a sheriff. He's a blacksmith. But when he talks, sheriffs listen."

As the sun went down behind them, Fletcher said, "We won't reach Weatherford tonight. We'd best make camp on the next water."

Jeffrey was uneasy about Indians. He wished more of the men had stayed with the wagon. Fletcher tried to reassure him. He said, "We gave that bunch a sound whippin'. They won't be back for a while."

"But there's other Indians besides them, ain't there?"

Matthew said, "We'll put the fire out before dark. They can't hurt us if they can't see us."

Adam rode out looking for a deer but came back empty-handed. He said, "I shot at one, but he outran the bullet."

Supper was black coffee and some bacon the Indians had missed. Fletcher said, "We'll eat better when we get to Weatherford."

Jeffrey was apprehensive about reaching town. There, he feared, someone he didn't know would make the decision about his future. He would probably have little or no say.

Sipping his coffee, Matthew said, "Fletcher, I been studyin' about Jeffrey. It'd be a disgrace in the eyes of the Lord to send him to one of them workhouses back east."

Jeffrey had heard tell about such places, where orphans were placed until they were old enough to go forth on their own. Such a prospect made him feel cold.

Fletcher said, "That notion doesn't set well with me, either. We need to do better by him."

"What would you say to me takin' him, me and Sarah? We're a long way from bein' rich, but we've got the farm and we've got an extra room in the house. He wouldn't lack for nothin' that he really needs."

Fletcher frowned. "Hadn't you ought to find out first how Sarah would feel about it? It hit her awful hard, losin' her son."

"That's why I think it'd be good for her, havin' another boy to take care of. She wouldn't have as much time to grieve about Henry."

"No other boy will ever take the place of her own."

"I wouldn't expect him to. But maybe he'd give her somethin' else to think about, somebody else to do for."

Fletcher's eyes indicated reservations. "It's your decision to make, not mine. I hope it works out."

"It has to. The way she's goin' now, she'll grieve herself to death, and I'll have to bury her alongside Henry."

They passed several farms before reaching Weatherford. On one, the house had been burned, a pile of blackened rubble remaining to show where it had been. Matthew said, "Same Indians did that. The family managed to slip away in the dark."

Jeffrey asked, "What'll they do now?"

"This is their land. They'll build back in the same place."

"I'd think they'd be too scared."

"Faith, son. Faith and determination built this country. You don't give up. You lick your wounds and get back in the fight. In the long run, you'll win."

"Or get killed."

Weatherford was an outpost village west of Fort Worth, considered to be on the edge of the Indian frontier. There and to the east, settlers regarded themselves as relatively safe, though Comanches and Kiowas occasionally still made incursions like the one that had orphaned Jeffrey. To the west, the thinness of settlement made outlying farms and ranches easy prey for raiders who struck like lightning and were quickly gone.

Matthew said, "Maybe some of this is our own fault, takin' the huntin' grounds away from them."

Fletcher was riding close to the wagon. He said, "It wasn't always theirs. They came in and took it away from somebody else. We're just doin' what they did, and bringin' civilization with us."

Matthew winked at Jeffrey. "Depends on what you call civilization. Adam, yonder, I ain't sure you'd call him civilized."

Fletcher said, "From the time of the pilgrims, every generation has pushed the frontier back twenty or thirty or forty miles at a time. The boldest go first. The timid ones follow and fill in the gaps. You'll see a time when there won't be a frontier anymore."

Matthew said, "Maybe Jeffrey will live that long. I imagine the Lord has got other plans for me and you. And especially Adam."

More than a dozen horses stirred in a large pen near the edge of town. Matthew said with satisfaction, "I see the boys got in all right. Looks like they've already sent a lot of the horses back to whoever they belong to."

Adam said, "There's supposed to be two of mine in that bunch. I hope nobody carried them away."

Matthew chuckled. "Yours'd be the last ones anybody'd want to steal. I'm surprised the Indians took them."

Adam feigned insult. "What would an old broken-down Yankee preacher know about horses? You never had a good one in your life."

Jeffrey had taken the two men's banter seriously at first, until he realized they were joking with each other. He sensed a strong bond between them, a bond that included Fletcher. He supposed shared experiences, especially shared danger, tended to cultivate close friendship. He had had that kind of relationship with Todd, except that Todd didn't always know when he was joking and would occasionally come at him with his tiny fists clenched.

He wondered if he would ever be that close to anyone again.

While they were paused at the pen, studying the as-yet-unclaimed horses, a burly farmer with a belligerent countenance rode up on a quick-stepping sorrel. A black man followed on a mule, keeping a respectful distance between slave and master.

Matthew muttered, "Here comes the devil's disciple himself."

The farmer declared, "It's about time you got in, Fletcher. You didn't recover all my horses."

It was evident that Fletcher disliked this man. He made no effort to hide it. "Be thankful for the ones you got back, Nash Wickham. We caught all that were runnin' loose. Like as not, some of the Indians that got away were ridin' your horses."

"If I'd been with you, none of them would've gotten away."

"Why weren't you? We called for every man that could ride."

"I had property to see after."

"So did the rest of us, but we went anyway."

Matthew's shoulders had squared as Wickham rode up. His voice sounded testy. "You're like the man that lost a sheep but gave no thanks for the ninety-and-nine that didn't stray."

Wickham gave Matthew a look of resentment. Jeffrey wondered if he liked anybody.

Wickham said, "I lost more horses than any of you."

"Because you had more to start with. You can afford it."

Red-faced, Wickham turned his attention to Jeffrey. "Is this the boy they were tellin' me about?"

Matthew said, "This is him."

"Too bad his daddy didn't have any better sense than to take his family out into Indian country. I know for a fact that he was warned, because I warned him myself."

Jeffrey bristled at the insult to Papa. He was about to offer a retort when Matthew gently pinched his leg. "No need to torment the lad. There wasn't nothin' he could've done."

Wickham nodded. "No, he did the smart thing. At least he took care of himself, hidin' out while those savages slaughtered his family." He turned away with a final shot at the blacksmith. "If you-all hadn't caught those Comanches asleep, you wouldn't have had the guts to go amongst them. I'll go with you next time and show you how to fight Indians."

Dryly, Fletcher said, "We'll let you ride point."

Wickham rode out of hearing. He was followed by the black man, who had listened without saying a word. Matthew told Jeffrey, "Don't pay any attention to Wickham. The first time he saw a feather he'd run like a scalded dog. The big talkers generally do."

Jeffrey said, "I don't think I'm goin' to like him."

"That puts you in the majority. But he's about the wealthiest man around here, so he swings a big club."

Two of the horses recovered from the Indians were Matthew's. He said, "Reckon you can handle the wagon the rest of the way?"

Jeffrey said, "I drove for Papa sometimes."

Adam was pleased about retrieving his two lost horses. He tied them head to tail and waved as he led them away. Matthew said, "Just follow me, Jeffrey. It ain't all that far." He pushed his two horses ahead of him.

Fletcher lingered for a few words with Jeffrey. "I'm glad you're goin' with Matthew. You won't find a better man. I don't know what reaction you'll get from Sarah, though. Just bear in mind that she's a good woman at heart. Have patience with her. She's been through one of the most awful experiences a woman can have, losin' a child."

"I reckon I understand." Mama had experienced a similar loss, a daughter born between Jeffrey and Todd.

"If things don't work out, let me know. Maybe I can do something."

"Much obliged." Jeffrey watched Fletcher as long as he was in sight. Despite his liking for Matthew, he half wished he were going with Fletcher instead. He had initially been put off by the man's stern air of authority. Now he realized the blacksmith had assumed that authority because he was the most capable of using it wisely. Other men were instinctively drawn to follow him.

Perhaps Papa would have paid more attention if Fletcher had been the one who warned him, not Wickham.

Matthew's horses set a fast pace the wagon could not match. Jeffrey feared they might move out of his sight and get him lost. The horses cut across country, while the wagon had to remain on a rutted trail that meandered as if it had been staked on a Sunday morning after a Saturday-night drunk. Matthew came back to finish guiding Jeffrey, letting the loose horses go the final distance on their own.

Matthew's grin showed he was eager to get home. "Just a little ways now," he said.

Climbing a small hill, Jeffrey saw a green field spread out before him, the cornstalks immature but tall enough to bend with the wind. Beyond them, a frame house looked much like the one he remembered from home, except that it had a coat of white paint. The old house in Arkansas had never felt a brush.

Matthew said with pride, "Had the lumber hauled

in from the East Texas piney woods. I could've spent that money for more acres instead, but I figured Sarah and the boy deserved somethin' better than a picket house."

"It looks mighty fine."

Matthew said, "I hope you like workin' in the garden. Henry did. He'd eat tomatoes off of the vine till he made himself sick."

Jeffrey was neutral about gardens. Papa had handed him a hoe when he was no more than four years old. Though he had appreciated the produce, he had been in a constant race against the weeds. As soon as he'd finished the last row, he had to start over. It was a race that never ended until frost.

A dog came to meet them. It seemed to Jeffrey that every farm he had ever seen had a dog, or half a dozen of them. This one wagged its tail so vigorously that its hind quarters threatened to twist permanently out of shape. It reminded him a little of Brownie, especially when it became distracted by a rabbit and barreled away in pursuit.

Matthew said, "He still searches for Henry from time to time. I think he'll take to you right off."

Jeffrey was not concerned about the dog. He was more concerned about how Sarah Temple would take to him. He had read some reservation in what Fletcher had said about her.

She stood waiting on the shady porch, her arms folded. She was a slender woman—some would call her skinny—with graying hair rolled into a bun on the back of her head. She wore a plain gray housedress much like the ones Mama had, the skirt almost sweeping the floor. She showed a momentary pleasure as Matthew rode forward and stepped down to hug her. She said, "I saw the horses come in by themselves, so

I knew you wouldn't be far behind." Her faint smile faded as her gaze went to the wagon, and to Jeffrey. "Who's this?"

Matthew said, "His name's Jeffrey. The Indians killed his folks."

"That's too bad," she said. "But what's he doin' here?"

"He's got nobody to look after him. He's goin' to stay with us for a while."

Her brow furrowed. "Why us?"

"Why not us? We've got room, and he could be of help to both of us. Besides, it's been kind of lonesome around here—" He broke off without finishing the sentence.

She finished it for him. "Since Henry died? Do you think anybody can take Henry's place?"

Matthew tried to argue. "That's not what I'm thinkin' at all. I know we'll always miss him. Nothin' can change that. But this boy needs somebody."

"There's lots of other families around here. Take him to somebody else." She turned quickly and retreated into the house.

Matthew stared after her in disappointment. Turning back to Jeffrey, he said, "You'd just as well climb down from the wagon. Get you a drink of water out of the well yonder while I go in and talk to her."

Jeffrey's face burned. Stunned by her rejection, he wanted to jump down and run. But where to? The country was strange, and the people were strangers. He felt trapped. He made his way to the stone-encased well and turned the windlass to bring up a bucket of water. Though thirsty, he gave up before the bucket reached the top. He slumped down with his back to the stone wall, wanting to cry. But he had been through too much. No tears were left.

He could hear voices from within the house, especially Sarah's. She said, "I know you mean for that boy to take my mind off of Henry, but I don't *want* to forget. Nobody can take his place, not for a minute."

Matthew's voice was softer. "It's on account of Henry that I thought you'd understand this boy. He's lost his mother and father and the only brother he had. I don't know anybody who should understand him better than us . . . better than you."

"Every time I looked at him, I'd think about our own boy. You're asking too much of me."

"I know. I'm askin' a lot of myself, too. But this is a call. If we deep down believe what we say about Christian duty, we'll answer it. You know what the Book says about takin' in the stranger. We might entertain an angel and not know it."

After a long pause Sarah said, "You're not fair. Every time we disagree about something, you bring the Bible in on your side."

"I may be wrong once in a while, but the Book never is."

"Very well, tell him to come on into the house. He may be hungry. But don't expect me to act like he was our own son. He'll never be Henry."

Matthew came outside. He said, "Sarah had a little bit of a shock, seein' you. She's over it now. She says come in and she'll fix you somethin' to eat."

Jeffrey knew it was not so simple, for he had heard what they said. He was nervous about going into the house. But he was hungry. He arose and started toward the porch with Matthew. He said, "Maybe I'd better not stay here. Reckon I could go stay with Fletcher?"

"Of course you'll stay here. Fletcher wouldn't know what to do with you. He's lived a bachelor's life since his wife died. You need a whole family around you."

Jeffrey wondered what kind of family he could ever have here when the woman of the house resented him.

5

As soon as Matthew finished ax-trimming the small side limbs from a dead oak branch, Jeffrey picked it up and dragged it to the wagon. With a hard grunt, he pitched it up on top of the wood already there. He said, "Looks like we've got a load."

Matthew said, "I'll finish this one and we'll call it a day." The ground was littered with fallen branches. Matthew had told him they were broken off by a severe ice storm back in January. By next winter they would be cured enough to burn easily.

Matthew placed the final branch and checked the load to be sure the wood was secure enough not to fall from the wagon. He motioned for Jeffrey to climb up on the seat, then followed him. As he flipped the reins to set the mules into motion he said, "Wood warms you three times: once when you gather it, once when you cut it up for the fireplace, and once more when you burn it."

Jeffrey would agree that it had warmed him, for sweat rolled down from beneath his hat and burned his eyes. Yet, he enjoyed this little break from the more monotonous chores of hoeing weeds and pitching hay to the livestock. It brought up memories of times in Arkansas when he and Papa had taken the wagon out to gather wood. Todd had gone along but had been of little help, romping around with the dog Brownie. In the weeks since the Indian attack, Jeffrey's grief had diminished enough that he could think of his family without breaking down.

He had accustomed himself to the routine of the Temple farm in most ways. It was much the same as back home. One striking difference was that Matthew never ventured far from his rifle. He carried it with him to the field, and it lay against a wagon wheel on this wood-gathering mission. Most of the neighbors Jeffrey had met were similarly cautious. Though no one talked much about Indians, Jeffrey realized the subject was never far from people's minds. Certainly it was never far from his.

Matthew pulled the wagon up next to a woodpile back of the house. "I'll unload it," he said. "You go tell Sarah we're home so she can start fixin' supper."

Jeffrey had a cold feeling about approaching Sarah. She was civil enough, but her coolness toward him had not improved. He found her in the kitchen. "We're back," he said.

She nodded. "So I see." She seldom looked directly at him. She seemed purposely to avert her gaze and avoid eye contact. "Tell Matthew I'll have supper ready by the time he gets the wood unloaded and the team put away."

"Yes, ma'am."

Her back turned, she said, "I hope you were of some help to him."

"I tried to be."

"Henry always was. He worked the hardest of any boy I ever saw."

Jeffrey tried to think of an adequate response. He had already told her several times that he was sorry about Henry. It probably would do no more good now than at the other times. Saying no more, he walked back outside and told Matthew what Sarah had said about supper.

The unexpected appearance of a rider never failed to startle him, though all he had seen since that terrible day had been harmless. He watched the approaching horseman and said, "Somebody's comin'."

Matthew looked in the direction Jeffrey pointed. He shrugged. "Don't worry. It's Fletcher." Grinning in anticipation, he took off his hat and wiped sweat from his face.

Jeffrey was in awe of the tall man with the dark beard and compelling eyes. He had seen how other men gravitated toward Fletcher for leadership. Even Matthew, who seemed more than self-sufficient.

Matthew spoke first. "Git down, Fletcher. I've just finished unloadin' this wood. We'll be havin' supper directly."

Fletcher said, "Much obliged, but that's not what I came for."

"You'll stay anyway. I've done enough bachin' to know how lank you can get on bachelor cookin'."

Jeffrey saw a troubled look in Fletcher's eyes. Fletcher said, "I want to talk to you out here. I wouldn't want to trouble Sarah if we don't have to."

Matthew's smile vanished. "What's wrong?"

"Just want to alert you. Nash Wickham says he's missin' a couple of horses."

"Nash is always missin' somethin'. He thinks everybody but him is a thief."

"But I'm short one, too. So are a couple of other people."

Matthew glanced toward his rifle. "Indians?"

"Maybe. Or white horse thieves. Whichever it is, it'll pay everybody to keep a close watch on their stock, and on their families as well."

"I always do." Matthew gave Jeffrey a moment's sober study. "Looks like we'd better start pennin' our horses and mules every night, boy." He turned back to Fletcher. "You're stayin' for supper, aren't you?"

"I'd better be gettin' home."

Sarah stepped out onto the small back porch, shading her eyes from the lowering sun. She smiled when she recognized the visitor. "Fletcher! Don't you even think about leaving until you've had supper with us."

Fletcher seemed torn. Matthew said, "You won't get out of it now. Sarah's got a determined mind when she makes it up."

Fletcher said, "I'll be in after I've tied my horse. You go ahead." He watched until Matthew joined Sarah and the two entered the house. Jeffrey thought he saw a wish in Fletcher's eyes. He remembered that the man was a widower.

Jeffrey hung back to be near him. He recalled Matthew's telling him, "It's always a comfort to know Fletcher's somewhere around. If you ever need help and I'm not handy, go to Fletcher. He knows what to do, and he's man enough to get it done."

Tying the horse to a corral post, Fletcher asked Jeffrey, "How are you doin', son? Is Matthew treatin' you right?"

"Yes, sir," Jeffrey said. "He treats me fine."

"And Sarah?"

Jeffrey tried to answer in the same cheerful tone. "Just fine, too." He sensed that it sounded hollow.

He had an uneasy feeling that Fletcher could read the truth in his voice.

Fletcher bore out his suspicion. He said, "I was afraid that was how it would be. Sarah doesn't mean to hurt you, but she's carryin' a lot of pain. Your bein' here stirs up some hard memories. Do you understand?"

"I guess I do." Jeffrey had pain of his own. He broached a subject that had been on his mind: "Mr. Fletcher, I could be a lot of help if I was to go live with you."

Fletcher seemed startled. "With me? But I live by myself. There'd be no woman to cook for you and scrub your clothes and help you with your learnin'."

"I could do all that as soon as you showed me how."

"A boy needs a woman around to keep him pointed in the right direction. Otherwise he'll grow up with an old bachelor's ways, all rough edges and ill temper. You're a lot better off here with Matthew and Sarah."

"Most days I dread walkin' into the house."

"Don't give up yet. She's a fine woman. Have patience with her."

Jeffrey saw that he had lost this time. But there would be other days. "Yes, sir. I'll try."

They washed their faces and hands in a pan on the back porch. Jeffrey said, "She won't let me eat till I've cleaned up. Mama was like that, too. I didn't see where it made much difference as long as I wasn't real dirty. The food tasted the same either way."

Fletcher seemed about to ask him about his mother but stopped himself in midsentence. He said, "It's for our own good. The womenfolks teach us healthy habits and see that we stick with them."

"I guess. It's just that sometimes . . ." Jeffrey did

not know how to finish what he started to say. Sarah was stricter with him than his own mother had been. When Mama criticized him, it had been comforting to know that she did not love him any less. When Sarah did it, he feared that it was out of resentment.

There was little talk around the table at first. Jeffrey noticed that Fletcher kept stealing glances at Sarah, looking away when she turned her gaze in his direction. He wondered if Matthew noticed. If so, he gave no sign. Instead, he talked about crop conditions. The subject turned to the growing tension between North and South over slavery. Matthew said, "I don't see where we've got any part in that squabble. The only slaves around here are Nash Wickham's field hand and his kitchen cook."

Fletcher said, "There's a lot more to it than that."

Sarah said, "It's a long way from us, so let's not talk about it."

Jeffrey had been brooding over something a lot closer to home. He forgot what Fletcher had said about not worrying Sarah. He asked, "What about those missin' horses and mules? Who do you think has gotten off with them?"

Matthew frowned at him. Fletcher looked at Sarah. She demanded, "What's this about horses and mules?"

Reluctantly, Fletcher repeated what he had said outside. He said, "It could be Indians, but I lean toward the notion of white men. Nobody's reported any Indian sign for a while."

Matthew said, "I can't believe it'd be any of our neighbors. We know them all. And they couldn't afford to keep stolen stock anywhere around here. Somebody would find them out."

Fletcher said, "My guess is that it's outsiders. They

steal what they can get easy and take them back to East Texas to sell."

Jeffrey had listened with growing anxiety. "But what if it *is* Indians?" The thought gave him a chill.

Fletcher said, "We'll do what we've always done. We'll be watchful and ready to fight to protect what belongs to us."

Supper finished, Fletcher stood up and pushed his chair back against the table. "I'm sorry if I've caused you any worry, Sarah. I hadn't intended to talk about it."

Sarah spoke more softly to Fletcher than she usually did to Jeffrey. "What goes on around here concerns us women as much as the men. We have a stake, too."

Matthew and Jeffrey followed Fletcher out to retrieve his horse. Mounting, Fletcher said, "Keep a good watch, Matthew. And, Jeffrey, you help him."

"Yes, sir, I will."

When Fletcher rode away, Matthew told Jeffrey, "You'd better hop on one of those mules and bring the horses in."

Jeffrey had often ridden one or another of his two mules, usually to or from the field. He rode out bareback and found Matthew's three horses grazing by the creek. He brought them in and threw them into the pen. He turned his mule loose to join them.

He told Matthew, "Because we put them in a pen doesn't mean somebody couldn't sneak in here and steal them, but this does make it harder."

Matthew closed the gate. "The dog would probably tell us. Anything that moves, he barks at it."

Jeffrey had grown fond of the dog for its company, but he considered it next to useless when it came to being of help. He had seen it bark at a ground squirrel, yet slink away when a stranger rode up to the house or barn. Old Brownie, even with his faults, had served better than that. This dog was a free boarder.

Matthew sat in a rocking chair on the front porch, smoking his pipe in silence as the sounds of night began to rise and the stars came into full brightness. Jeffrey sat on the edge, wondering if Matthew was angry at him. He said, "I didn't mean to get her upset. I oughtn't to've said anything about the missin' horses."

"It's just as well. I was probably wrong, tryin' to keep things from her."

"Just the same, it wasn't my place."

At length Matthew said, "You're a big boy, Jeffrey. You notice things."

"Like what?"

"I know you saw the way Fletcher kept lookin' at Sarah. Don't make too much of it, son. He means no harm. He had a fine wife, and he lost her. He's just lonely."

"I reckon."

"He's too much of a man to take advantage, and Sarah's too good a woman to give him any cause. He'll find somebody."

Then maybe I could go live with him, Jeffrey thought.

Sarah came to the door. "It's about time you get to bed, Jeffrey. You, too, Matthew, when you've finished that pipe."

Matthew arose and knocked the pipe against a porch post to free the ash. He said, "Don't you worry about them thieves, Jeffrey. I'm a light sleeper, and I'm settin' my shotgun just inside the door."

Jeffrey tried to sleep but could not. When he heard

snoring from the other bedroom he wondered how light a sleeper Matthew really was. He was haunted by the thought of someone making off with his two mules. They, and the wagon, were almost the only tangible connections he still had with Papa and Mama. He arose, finally, and put on his clothes. He did not bother with shoes because he was used to going barefoot in the summer. He felt the wooden floor creak beneath his weight and paused to listen for any change in Matthew's snoring. He detected no interruption.

At the front door he picked up the shotgun. Outside, he checked to be certain it was loaded, though he knew Matthew usually kept it that way. He had heard Matthew say once that an empty gun was more dangerous than a loaded one in the event of a sudden need. He walked out to the barn, where the dog met him, wagging its tail in a frenzy of friendliness.

He was relieved to see that the horses and mules were in the corral, the two mules lying down, the horses sleeping on their feet. He sat on the step in front of the open barn door. The moon was rising. He felt sure he could see anything that moved within twenty-five or thirty yards.

He did not feel sleepy, so he was confident he could remain awake. His good intentions gradually faded, however, lulled by the gentleness of the night. He found himself sitting on a creekbank, tending his line and Todd's as well while his brother played fetch-the-stick with Brownie. He was, for a time, back in a simpler, gentler life where his only worry was whether the fish would bite.

He was jarred to reality as one of the horses snorted and a mule jumped to its feet. In a moment of panic he thought he saw the dark figure of a man climbing over a fence. Without time for thought, he swung the shotgun muzzle in that direction and fired. The recoil flung him backward, through the open barn door. The dog set in to barking. The horses and mules raced excitedly around the pen. Gunpowder smoke burned his eyes and nose, and his shoulder felt broken.

He heard Matthew shout. Before Jeffrey could summon the voice to answer him, Matthew was there, carrying the rifle he kept on hooks above the fireplace. He shouted, "Jeffrey, what happened?"

Jeffrey regained enough of his wits to explain in a broken voice, "I saw a man climbin' the fence yonder." He pointed.

Crouching, Matthew made his way cautiously among the excited animals and reached the fence. He looked between the log rails, then climbed up partway for a better view. After a long couple of minutes he returned. "There's nobody out there. Somethin' woke you up all of a sudden, and you pulled the trigger."

"I wasn't asleep," Jeffrey said, then realized he had been. "I was certain I saw somebody."

"Indian or white man?"

He heard the doubt in Matthew's voice. "I couldn't tell. I saw him, though."

Sarah arrived, a wrap of some kind covering her sleeping gown. "What in the world?" she exclaimed.

Matthew explained, "Jeffrey saw a ghost."

"It wasn't no ghost," he argued, then saw the futility of it. They were not going to believe him. He was beginning not to believe it himself. On reflection he realized Matthew was probably right. He had gone to sleep like some dumb kid and had been frightened awake by a figment of his imagination.

Sarah demanded, "What were you doing out here

anyway, in the middle of the night? And with Matthew's shotgun?"

"I didn't want anybody to get my mules."

Matthew said, "It's a wonder you didn't shoot one of them."

Jeffrey was beginning to consider himself twelve kinds of a fool. "I'm sorry."

Severely Sarah said, "Now you get yourself back to the house and into bed where you belong." She turned and took the lead. Head down, Jeffrey followed along with Matthew. His shoulder ached, and he reached up with his left hand to grip it.

Matthew said, "That old shotgun kicks like one of your mules, don't it? You've got to hold it firm, or it'll knock you flat on your back."

"It did."

Matthew's voice softened. "You had good intentions, boy. But you've got to learn good judgment, too. You've got time. You're only eight."

"Goin' on nine," Jeffrey said.

He awakened the next morning to hear boots tromp across the floor and out onto the porch. Matthew was not one to be in bed when sunrise brightened his window. It was his custom to milk the cow while Sarah fixed breakfast. Jeffrey yawned, still tired, and put his feet on the floor. He fumbled with his clothes, buttoning his shirt wrong and having to start over.

Matthew was back sooner than usual, and without the milk bucket. His expression was apologetic as he faced Jeffrey. He said, "Looks like we wronged you last night. Somebody was here. I found tracks out by the corral fence."

Sarah's eyes widened. "Moccasin tracks?"

Matthew shook his head. "No, boots. And there

was a spot of blood where the buckshot hit the top of the fence. Somewhere this mornin' a no-good horse thief is diggin' pellets out of his hide and probably cryin' like a baby."

Sarah's hands went to her mouth. "He could've killed Jeffrey."

"I doubt he even thought about it. Tracks show that when he came down off of that fence he was runnin' like a jackrabbit. From now on I'll chain that gate shut every night."

Sarah asked, "Will that stop them?"

"The only way they'll get a horse or mule out of there will be to tear the fence down. But they may not try here again. A load of buckshot is hard to forget." He smiled at Jeffrey. "How's the shoulder this mornin'?"

It ached, deeply bruised by the shotgun's recoil.

Matthew said, "I'm goin' to town to report what happened last night. Maybe the sheriff can follow the tracks."

Jeffrey asked, "Want me to go with you?"

"No. Stay close in case that thief comes back. If he does, you get in the house with Sarah and bolt the doors."

"What if he tries to take our stock?"

"Let him. A boy your size has got no business tanglin' with a horse thief. He'll hurt you." Turning to Sarah, Matthew said, "I reloaded the shotgun and set it beside the door."

Jeffrey could see reservation in her eyes. She said, "Don't tarry longer than you have to."

When Matthew left, she picked up the shotgun and checked to be sure it was loaded. "Sometimes he forgets things," she said.

Matthew's instructions did not allow for Jeffrey to

take the hoe out into the field for the constant war against weeds. On the other hand, he did not relish the idea of being cooped up in the house with Sarah. He said, "I'll go out and start choppin' up the wood me and Matthew brought in."

Her voice was stern. "You heard what he said. Don't stray far from the house, and keep your eyes open."

The long branches had to be cut into shorter lengths to fit the fireplace. The more he cut now, the less would have to be done later in winter's cold. He sharpened the ax, then went to work. He found the exertion eased the frustrations of his uneasy relationship with Sarah. He worked up a sweat and enjoyed the way the breeze worked through his shirt to cool him.

Absorbed in chopping wood, he did not notice an approaching horseman until one of Matthew's mares preceded him through the corral's open gate. The stranger dismounted stiffly and began awkwardly unsaddling his horse, mostly using his left hand. He slipped the bridle from its head and hid it behind his back as he turned toward the gentle mare. She offered no resistance.

Jeffrey's heart pounded hard. He had not done anything when Mama and Papa and Todd were being killed. Now he intended to do something. Forgetting Matthew's admonition, he shouted, "Stop! That mare don't belong to you." He ran toward the corral, pausing to pick up rocks and chunk them at the intruder.

The bewhiskered thief gave him a quick glance and reached down for the saddle he had dropped on the ground. "Stay back, kid. I don't want to hurt you."

Burning with indignation, Jeffrey grabbed at the saddle to prevent the stranger from putting it on the mare. He saw dried blood on the man's shirt, and some small holes. Buckshot, he realized. His buckshot. This was last night's horse thief, come back.

The man said, "Stay away from me, kid. I said I don't want to hurt you."

The thief did not waste time with a blanket. He struggled to lift the saddle onto the mare's back. The buckshot wounds hindered him. Jeffrey grabbed the girth and tried to pull the saddle off. The thief gripped his arm and twisted it so hard that Jeffrey thought he had broken it. He gave Jeffrey a hard push that thrust him backward against the fence.

"Dammit, kid, I ain't got time to fool with you. There's some fellers back yonder awful anxious to catch up with me."

Jeffrey heard Sarah shout. She was halfway between the house and the corral, running toward him. "Jeffrey! For God's sake, come here to me."

The thief said, "Better go, kid, or I'll have to hurt you."

Jeffrey had acted by instinct, without considering the risk. He realized now that confronting this man had been foolhardy. Limping from his fall against the fence, he ran to Sarah. She grabbed him by the arm and rushed him into the house. Slamming the door behind her, she said, "He could've killed you."

Then you wouldn't have to put up with me no more, he thought.

She demanded, "What did you think you were doing?"

He could not tell her about the guilt that still lay heavy on his conscience, guilt for not dying with Mama and Papa and Todd. "I wanted to stop him from takin' Matthew's mare."

"Better to lose the mare than to lose you."

He was not surprised that the first thing she did was to scold him. He *was* surprised when the next thing she did was to hug him and cry. "Jeffrey, you gave me the fright of my life." She clung so tightly that he could hardly breathe. "I could see it happening all over again, like it was with Henry."

He heard heavy boots hit the porch. The back door flew open. The thief stood there, his eyes wide and desperate, his tattered shirt shining with fresh blood. Exertion had reopened the buckshot wounds. He shouted, "I need money."

Though fearful, Sarah placed herself protectively in front of Jeffrey. "We have no money."

"This is too good a house not to have money hidden away. Bring it."

When she did not move, he struck her with the back of his hand. "Hurry up, woman. I ain't got much time."

Jeffrey broke free of Sarah's weak grip and ran for the shotgun in the corner. It was in his hands before the thief had time to react.

"Git!" he ordered. "Git, or I'll shoot you again."

The outlaw turned angry eyes on him. "I'll bet you're the one done this to me last night."

"I'll do it again if you don't git."

"Damn you all to hell!" the man shouted and ran out through the open door. Jeffrey heard hoofbeats as the mare galloped away.

He hurried to Sarah. He could see a trickle of blood and a large red splotch rising on her cheek. He said, "He hurt you. I wish I'd killed him."

"No, you don't. You're too young to carry a burden like that."

They walked out together to watch the horse thief's

rapid retreat. Jeffrey said, "If I was stealin' horses, I'd have picked somethin' better than that old mare. She's blind in one eye and stumbles a lot."

Sarah turned to look in the other direction. "I doubt he'll get far. Those men coming yonder look like they mean business."

Several horsemen raced toward them. Jeffrey recognized Nash Wickham in the lead. As they reached Jeffrey and Sarah, she pointed in the direction the thief had taken. He was still in sight. They rushed on, spurring hard. Jeffrey watched them through the dust.

He saw the mare stumble, throwing the thief to the ground. She recovered and ran away from him, leaving him afoot. He tried to catch her, but she stayed ahead of him, the reins trailing as if to tantalize him. In a minute the posse surrounded the fugitive. With a gesture of helplessness, he raised his hands.

Sarah said, "It's a wonder they didn't shoot him on the spot. Nash Wickham is not a forgiving man."

A rider caught the mare and led her back to the thief. He mounted with difficulty. Jeffrey guessed that the fall might have aggravated the buckshot wounds. Riding back to the house, guarded by five well-armed men, the thief slumped in the saddle. His head was down in an attitude of defeat.

Wickham touched the tips of his fingers to his hat as he approached Sarah and Jeffrey. He stared grimly at the blood on her face. "It appears that this man harmed you, Mrs. Temple."

"Nothing that won't heal. He roughed up the boy a little. Jeffrey tried to stop him."

"Courageous, but unwise." Wickham's expression remained severe. He said, "We found this man and a companion where they had hidden a dozen stolen horses. The companion foolishly decided to stand and fight. This one chose to run." He started to turn away. "We need the use of the mare a little longer. We'll return her when we're done." He pointed toward a stand of timber. "Let's go, gentlemen."

The prisoner began to wail.

Sarah appeared suddenly alarmed. "Mr. Wickham, this man should be tried in a proper court."

She could as well have shouted into the wind, for Wickham gave no sign that he heard. He rode off with his companions and the pleading thief. They stopped a couple of hundred yards away. Jeffrey saw someone pitch a rope over a tree limb. A desperate cry reached him on the wind.

Sarah caught his arm and led him quickly into the house. "This isn't for a boy your age to see."

Jeffrey thought he knew, but he asked anyway. "They fixin' to hang him?"

"This is still a rough country. Sometimes justice doesn't wait for judge and jury."

She closed the door behind them, then sank into a chair beside the kitchen table. She was trembling. Jeffrey asked, "Are you all right?"

"No, I'm not, but I'll get over it." She took him into her arms and held him. He felt the wetness of a tear on her cheek. It left him confused.

He said, "He had no business hurtin' you."

She looked at him through tears. "He didn't hurt me as much as I hurt myself."

"What do you mean?"

"All of a sudden I realized how badly I've treated you. I didn't intend to, but I couldn't get past the notion that you were trying to take Henry's place. I didn't want anybody to do that."

Matthew arrived a couple of hours later with

Fletcher and the sheriff. It was obvious they had seen the thief dangling from the tree limb, for all three looked deeply shocked. Matthew immediately saw the bruise on Sarah's face and took her into his arms. Fletcher could only stare in anger.

The sheriff asked, "What happened here?"

Jeffrey waited for Sarah to answer, but she was sobbing against Matthew's shoulder. He said, "That horse thief came back. Mr. Wickham and some others caught up with him."

"So what we found out yonder was Nash Wickham's work?"

"Yes, sir." He repeated what Wickham had said.

The sheriff mumbled something under his breath.

Fletcher said, "This country isn't civilized yet. It won't be until people learn there is a legal and proper way to address their grievances."

The big words went over Jeffrey's head. "What's that mean?"

"When there's trouble, they should let the law handle it. But so far we don't have enough law to do the job. Someday things will be different."

Jeffrey mused. "I don't see how I could ever take somebody out and hang him off of a tree limb." He saw that Sarah's bruise was darkening. He added, "Bad as he might need it."

6

New Mexico, 1861

Todd had helped January apply hog grease to the cart's wheels, but the hubs squealed anyway. A case of rifles, a bundle of blankets, and a dozen jugs of snakehead whiskey put a heavy load on the axles. A hired Mexican named Manuel drove the oxen. Todd rode a horse named Beaver at some distance behind the cart, remaining in the rear so January could not hear his conversation with Felipe. There were parts of it he would not like.

Felipe said, "Are you not nervous, to let January take you amongst the Indians again? He might trade you back to them if they made a good offer."

Todd could remember only fragments of his experience with the Comanches six years earlier. "He wouldn't do that to me, no more than he'd do it to you."

"He would do it to me if not for my mother. She's the only thing in the world he's scared of. He'd trade his own mother for the right price. Except I wonder if he ever *had* a mother. I think he just crawled out of a badger hole."

"He's never made me go hungry. Not real hungry."

"Only because he has been able to get a lot of work out of you. It is the same as with me. That is why he takes you this time. He needs me and you to drive the cattle or horses he trades from the Indians."

No matter the reason, Todd was glad for a chance to get away from the confines of the valley, out onto the open plains where the horizon seemed endless and flat, the grass bending with the wind, a greenish carpet as far as he could see. He tried to remember landmarks from his last time out there, but it had been too long. Landmarks were few anyway. The terrain appeared the same in every direction, and had for much of the way from the Anton Chico country. He had a vague recollection of the canyons and the river where the Indians and the New Mexico traders met to do business. It lay somewhere ahead, to the east.

Off to the left he saw what appeared to be a draw, with a thin stand of timber. It might be watered by a spring or a creek. He expected the cart train to turn in that direction, but it did not. This was only the middle of the afternoon. Evidently the men knew of a better place for the night's camp farther on.

January pulled out of the cart's way and waited for Todd and Felipe to come up even with him. He had changed little from when Todd had first known him except that he seemed even shaggier, with gray streaks in his long hair. He rarely smiled, and even when he did there was no humor in it. It usually meant somebody was in for a chewing out.

He drew a rifle from its scabbard beneath his leg.

"Dogie," he said, "take this rifle over yonder and see if you can bring down some fresh meat for supper. Like as not there's deer shadin' up in that scrub timber."

Felipe asked, "What about me?"

"You may be the oldest, but this boy can outshoot you six ways from Sunday. He knows how much I got to pay for powder and shot." He turned back to Todd. "Keep an eye peeled for Indians. We ain't at the tradin' grounds yet."

Riding away, Todd looked back at the procession of ox carts lumbering along a faint trail that years of trader travel had pounded into the prairie sod. Other than Todd, January was the only Anglo there. He had lived among these people so long that for practical purposes he was one of them. They were mostly farmers and sheepmen from the eastern part of New Mexico, descendants of land seekers who had worked their way north from the mother country more than a hundred years before. Long isolated in their native valleys, they had developed a self-sufficient style of life. Almost their only connection with Mexico was through merchant caravans that worked up from Chihuahua through Paso del Norte and across the dry and treacherous Jornada del Muerto, or Journey of Death, to the old town of Santa Fe. Some of these outlying settlements were so isolated that even the tax collectors rarely found them.

They had gradually developed an uneasy but profitable relationship with the Comanches and their Kiowa allies. They carried trade goods out onto the plains to exchange for whatever the Indians had to offer, including cattle and horses taken from Texas settlements as well as from the United States Army. Though these so-called Comancheros dealt in stolen goods, they justified themselves by reasoning that the

Texans, and by extension all Americanos, were the enemy. Had the Americanos not declared war upon Mexico, and had they not taken by force all this land that had long been part of the mother country? Who, the Comancheros reasoned, were the bigger thieves?

Felipe had taught Todd to shoot. He had been such a good teacher that in time the pupil surpassed him. Todd eased his horse into the thin stand of timber, stopping frequently to listen for any sound that might indicate deer up and moving.

Somewhere ahead he heard a snort and a sudden crashing of brush. He thought it must be the largest deer he had ever seen. As his horse splashed across a small pool of water, he saw that he had flushed two young buffalo cows. They broke out of the timber and galloped southward, toward the cart train. With a happy cry, Todd spurred after them.

For a moment it seemed they would break between the strung-out carts before they veered off to the right. Todd closed in on one of the cows, pulling up beside her and aiming for the lungs. Though the muzzle bobbed up and down with the horse's gait, he managed to work up to almost point-blank range and fire. The cow stumbled, got up for a moment, then collapsed, snorting blood. The second cow ran on, alone.

January and Felipe rode out from the train. January took off his hat and scratched his head. "I was thinkin' of somethin' smaller," he said. "This is enough to feed the whole train. I wonder how much I ought to charge them?"

Felipe said, "Why not give it to them? God knows your reputation can stand some help."

Todd held his breath, expecting to see Felipe take the back of January's hand across his mouth. The boy was reckless that way. He often spoke his mind without regard to retribution. Todd envied him his courage.

January said, "I reckon a little charity wouldn't hurt. Maybe they'll quit callin' me gringo behind my back."

Felipe winked at Todd. They would continue thinking it, even if they did not say it aloud.

The cart train halted while the men skinned the buffalo and cut up the meat. Todd heard some squabbling about the division, but most of the men returned to their carts in a cheerful mood. January kept the best cuts. He said, "You boys roll up that hide and put it in the cart. Some Indian will want his womenfolks to tan it."

Todd had not realized how heavy a fresh hide could be. Felipe had to help him lift it. Once dried, Felipe said, it would not weigh nearly as much. He added, "This is the wrong time of the year to make a robe out of it. They will use it for leather, or maybe a tepee skin."

Todd asked, "How come you know so much?"

"This is my third tradin' trip. I have learned about all there is to know."

Todd hoped someday he would have Felipe's self-confidence. He realized it would probably take a couple of more years before he knew everything. By then he would be somewhere around fourteen years old. In this part of the world, that qualified a boy to call himself a man and to chew, smoke, drink, and cuss. He was already ahead in part of that game, for he could cuss in two languages. Being exposed to both the American and the Mexican cultures, he could speak English or Spanish with equal ease.

Cusswords were the easiest to learn. After that, the rest came along in its own good time.

After dropping down into the canyon and moving out onto the flatter ground, he saw that many Indians were already encamped along the river, in the protection of the trees. Because their stay would be short, they had erected tepees smaller than those in which they lived for longer periods. Beyond the camp, perhaps a hundred horses were spread out to graze on the abundant grass. Two wiry-looking boys rode a slow, wide circle around them, giving them room but preventing them from straying.

January said, "The Indians are early. That's a sign they're ready to get serious. Maybe there won't be so much pipe smokin' and big talk before they get down to business." He clearly enjoyed the scene. "Takes me way back to fur-trappin' days and rendezvous. I wasn't much older than you two boys, but I could already hold my liquor. Mankind, what a time that was."

More than a dozen Indian men stood at the edge of the camp, watching solemnly as the carts slowly made their way to their stopping places. Todd felt a shiver run all the way down to his legs. Old images came at him in a rush, most of them frightening.

January noticed. "They scare you, do they, Dogie?"

"A little," he admitted.

"Don't let them see it. Don't ever give them the idea you're afraid, or they'll use it against us. Them heathens will take every advantage to keep from tradin' fair."

Todd thought that was an apt description of January himself.

A large Indian with glittering black eyes took a couple of strides forward, one hand up, the palm out. Recognizing him, Todd shivered again. This was the man who taken him from the family wagon and traded him to January for an old rifle.

January said, "Recognize him, boy?"

"He's the one that like to've cut my throat. I don't remember what he's called."

"He's got a heathen name I can't pronounce. They say it means Two Bulls, in English. He don't look like he's softened up any." January came dangerously near smiling. "If he recognizes you, he's liable to want to buy you back."

"What for?"

"You're gettin' big enough that he could make a warrior out of you."

Todd was not sure of January. Experience had taught him to be cautious, to hold something back, always. "Would you sell me?"

"Depends on what he offered."

January had a twisted sense of humor. Todd could not always be sure whether he was joking or serious. Though he claimed to have brought the boys to handle the stock, it was not beyond belief that he might have included Todd in hope of making an advantageous swap. January always claimed that his middle initial was *P*, for *profit*. *January P. Smith*.

January said, "Don't worry. We won't get around to serious tradin' till tomorrow, at least."

That was of limited comfort. The longer Todd stared at that big Indian, the more disturbing memories crowded his mind. He rarely let himself think anymore of Papa and Mama and Jeffrey, but sight of the Indians took him back to the horrifying day he had purposely done all he could to suppress. He made up his mind to stay out of Two Bulls's sight as much as possible.

That turned out to be difficult. He noticed an Indian woman moving up to look at the cart men. Her gaze lighted upon him and remained there. He remembered her. After six years she had lost some of her youthful beauty and slender figure, but he knew this was Two Bulls's younger wife. Her eyes softened. He realized she knew him. She came up behind Two Bulls and spoke, then pointed at Todd.

Two Bulls had paid no attention to him before, but now he showed a special interest. He moved close and looked Todd up and down, from his face to his feet. He said words Todd could not understand, then made sign talk with his hands. He felt Todd's arms, testing the muscles. He grunted with what Todd took to be approval.

January said, "He says you've growed up to be a man, almost. Wishes he hadn't sold you. Says he never did like that rifle anyway."

Todd tried not to show his uneasiness. "Is he askin' to buy me back?"

"Too early. They won't get down to tradin' yet. Got to have a big doin's tonight to get theirselves worked up. But he's studyin' on it."

The festivities lasted well into the night. Many of the other carts, like January's, had a cargo of whiskey, but nobody offered more than a conservative single round to the Comanches. January said that if given more, too many would be so hung over the next day they might not be in a mood to trade. Besides, they could become dangerous and forget traditional rules of neutrality that were supposed to prevail here.

Todd sidled up to Felipe. "Do you reckon January's really thinkin' about tradin' me off?"

Felipe was of no help. "He was lookin' at the horses the Comanches brought to trade. His mouth watered."

Dread came over Todd as he considered a return to the Indians. He knew the futility of pleading, for when January made up his mind to something, he could be as unmovable as a rock. He told Felipe, "I'm goin' to saddle Beaver and get away from here."

"Do you not remember how far we have traveled? If you got lost on those plains, you would die."

"The carts left deep tracks. I'll follow them back the way we came."

"I would not want to be out there by myself. You will wake up one night and find the wolves chewin' your bones."

Todd weighed the risks. "I'm leavin' anyway while January is celebratin' with the Indians. You don't have to help me. Just keep quiet."

Reluctantly Felipe said, "January may take a whip to me, but I will say nothin'. I am afraid we will come across your dead body out there unless somethin' eats you plumb up."

Todd saddled Beaver and took a goatskin of water, along with some dried jerky. As an afterthought, Felipe brought him the rifle from January's saddle. He said, "You may need this."

"That's stealin', ain't it?"

"How do you think January got it?"

Todd shook hands with Felipe. He eased his way out of camp, walking the horse until he was in the clear, then urging him into a stiff trot and finally a gallop. He slowed again as they ascended the winding trail up onto the escarpment. Once on top, he bare-heeled the horse into an easy lope for a mile or so to put extra distance behind him. Afterward, he slowed to spare Beaver and to keep from losing the cart tracks in the night. At times they were plain. At other times he had to stop and search for them.

Toward morning, feeling confident that January would not chase after him until the trading was done, he stopped, staked the horse, and spread his blanket on the grass. He did not awaken until the brightness of the rising sun penetrated his closed eyelids. He sat up quickly, looking about anxiously for any sign of danger. The open prairie stretched around him as far as he could see in all directions. He heard a faint barking sound. He found that he had spent the last hours of the night in the edge of a prairie-dog town. As he rose to his feet, one of the little animals sounded a signal of distress and dropped into its hole.

He had never eaten a prairie dog. He knew they were a challenge to a hunter's skill. Even if they remained stationary long enough for a rifleman to draw a bead, when shot they would fall back into the hole, beyond retrieval except with a shovel. Digging into the complex of tunnels would expose the hunter to attack by an army of fleas. It might also introduce him to a rattlesnake rankled by being disturbed.

Todd avoided that indignity by chewing on a strip of jerky. Saddling the horse, he said, "There's water up ahead." The plains were dotted with small depressions which became playa lakes after a rain. In some, the water was drinkable enough. Others were heavy with bitter minerals that puckered the lips and set the stomach to churning.

His goal was the draw where he had shot the buffalo. On horseback he was able to cover ground much faster than the carts had done. He reached the place late in the day and pulled off the cart trail. The draw, he thought, should be a good place to lie up out of sight and wait for the return of the caravan. It offered good water for him and the horse. With luck he might bring down a deer or even another buffalo to sustain him for however many days he had to wait.

He was not in a hurry for the reunion. He considered it probable that January would blister him with a quirt. He might have to forgo the saddle and walk for a few days, but whip marks across his butt were preferable to rejoining Two Bulls.

He approached the thin timber with care. Someone or something might be there ahead of him. He heard a rustling of brush and assumed he had flushed some deer. Fresh tracks at the edge of the creek confirmed it. They should be back sooner or later, he thought, and he would eat venison until the carts returned. He staked the horse, giving it plenty of grazing room. He rolled out his blanket and lay on it, resting his head against his saddle. He propped the rifle within reach. Feeling secure, he allowed himself to drop off to sleep and make up for the scant rest he had received the night before.

Awakening refreshed, he chewed more of the jerky, then set out afoot for a quiet exploration of the draw, carrying the rifle at arm's length. Walking along the creek, he examined hoof and paw prints in the muddy edge. He was relieved to find no shoe or moccasin tracks. He had no fear of any four-footed thing he was likely to meet. Even wolves usually gave people a cautious berth. But humans were another matter.

He found no buffalo. Not even a deer showed itself. But out in the grass, away from the draw, he spotted several prairie chickens. He crouched low, moving up on them slowly and carefully. He wished he had a shotgun instead of this rifle. A slug from its barrel would tear a chicken half to pieces. He dropped down on his belly and brought the rifle into position. Then he waited for one of the birds to raise its head and pause long enough for him to aim. A body shot might not leave him much to eat. A head shot was a severe test of marksmanship.

He lay prone for several minutes before the opportunity came. Competition for a bug led two chickens into a squabble. The loser turned and ran, then stopped to look back and see if it was being chased. Todd squeezed the trigger and blew its head off.

He wished Felipe could have seen that shot. At times he seemed irked that Todd had become the better marksman. At others, he boasted of his ability as a teacher.

Ideally Todd would dip the bird in boiling water to loosen the feathers, but he had no container. He skinned it the best he could with his knife. Some pinfeathers remained, but those were singed away when he speared the bird on a stick and roasted it over an open fire. He had seen coyotes devour chickens without regard to the feathers. A few pinfeathers were not going to dissuade Todd from eating, either.

Satisfied, he lay on the blanket again and fell asleep. He had no inkling of time. He was awakened by a loud snort from the staked horse. His first thought was that the cart train had come, but a quick look told him it had not. He had guessed at how long the trading would take, and then the trip back from the canyon. He doubted that the carts could get there before tomorrow or the next day at the earliest.

He patted Beaver to calm him. Carrying the rifle, he made his way through the draw and up the opposite side. He stopped, stiffening. A lone horseman was coming in his direction. Anxiety gripped him as he imagined that January had come to fetch him back. But he soon saw that this was not January, or any other white man. The approaching rider was a young Indian.

He dropped to his knees, hoping to see without being seen. Heart quickening, he fought against panic.

He had never been able to put away completely the image of Mama and Papa falling in that whirlwind attack by the Comanches. He could no longer see their faces clearly in his mind, but he could still hear his mother's scream.

The Indian disappeared in timber to the east. Quickly, Todd kicked sand over the remains of his fire. He saddled the horse and pointed him west, staying within the cover of brush. Maybe the Indian would fail to notice his tracks, or the place where he had roasted the chicken and slept. The lowering sun was in Todd's eyes. Maybe it would blind the Indian if he should turn in that direction.

He dimly remembered his mother teaching him to pray. Felipe's mother had also insisted upon it, though her prayer was in Spanish. He hoped God had learned Spanish, for he spoke Yolanda's prayer as he rode. He had forgotten his mother's.

After a time he heard hoofbeats behind him. Cold dread settled in his stomach as he realized the Indian was searching for him, riding just outside the line of brush. The timber was not heavy enough in most places to hide Todd and the horse. When the Indian came close enough, he would be able to see them.

Todd sought out the thickest cover he could find and dismounted, hoping to present a lower profile. Perhaps the Indian would ride on by. He remembered a trick January had shown him. He covered his horse's nose with his hand to prevent it from nickering at the Indian's mount.

It was not enough. Through the vegetation he saw the Indian stop and look in his direction. He held his breath, trying not to move even a finger. He was convinced the Indian saw him anyway. Slipping down from his horse, the warrior drew an arrow from a quiver slung over his shoulder. He fitted it to a bow and moved cautiously toward Todd.

Todd trembled, his hands slippery on the rifle. His lungs burned. His mouth was full of cotton. He could contain himself no more. He shouted, "Get back or I'll shoot you!"

He realized that was a fool thing to do. If the Indian had had any doubt about just where he was, it was gone now. He could see the grim young face. It was not war-painted, but the eyes seemed to have fire in them. The warrior wanted Todd's scalp to hang from his war shield. It did not matter that his intended victim was still a boy, barely past twelve years old. His brother, Jeffrey, had been only eight-going-on-nine when Two Bulls's band killed him. Todd felt that he was about to wet his britches.

The Indian moved suddenly. Todd heard the twang of the bowstring and the thump of the arrow as it struck a thin limb just in front of him. It was deflected enough that it fell at Todd's feet. The Indian reached back for another. With a shout of desperation, Todd brought the rifle's sights to bear on the warrior's breastbone and squeezed the trigger. The barrel belched fire. The warrior staggered back a couple of steps, then fell. Todd lowered the rifle and stared with burning eyes through the whitish cloud of gunpowder smoke.

The Indian's lips moved as he made some kind of sound. Todd had no idea whether it was a prayer or a curse. He moved closer, for he realized the bow and arrow were no longer a threat. He had not reckoned with a knife in a leather scabbard tied around the warrior's hips. The Indian managed to draw it out, but he could not raise it. He gave up, settling back, slowly going limp. Todd watched the light of life in the black eyes as it slowly dulled, then died.

His knees went out from under him. He sank to the ground, limp as an empty sack. The pent-up tension and fear threatened to choke him. The realization was crushing: he had taken a life. He tried to reason that this was revenge for Mama and Papa and Jeffrey, but that gave him no comfort. The chance was remote that this particular Indian had been part of the group that killed them. Nor did it matter now that this warrior had been trying to kill him. It mattered only that he was dead, and Todd had killed him. He bowed his head and wept.

The initial shock had to run its course before he came around to reason. The Indian had been by himself when he rode into the draw, but was he truly alone? What if he had been scouting ahead for a large party?

Todd realized he had better get away, and fast. His backside prickled as if a thousand needles were sticking him. He took the Indian's knife and rode out of the draw. He had gone perhaps two hundred yards when he heard a horse nicker behind him. Thoroughly frightened, he turned in the saddle, expecting to see a war party in pursuit. Instead, he saw the brown horse the Indian had been riding. It was following him.

In the event he should run into more Indians, he did not want this horse to be with him. Its presence would be like an admission of guilt. He turned and waved his hand, shouting, trying to turn the horse back. It retreated a few feet, then stopped. When Todd resumed traveling, it followed like a pet dog.

He tried again, charging at the animal, using all the best profanity he knew in two languages. The brown would retreat a short way, then come again. He considered shooting it.

I just killed a man. Why not a horse? he asked himself. But he liked horses too well to kill one.

He hoped the brown would grow tired of following and stop to graze, but it did not. Afraid of losing the trail in the darkness, Todd made a dry camp at dusk. The horse was still with him. He noticed that it bore a brand on its left hip. The Indian had not been its first owner.

He felt safer for having put many miles between him and the draw, but he remained vulnerable. He was still in Comanche country. If a pursuing party did not catch up with him, bent on vengeance, he might chance across others willing to lift a scalp anywhere one came handy. He did not build a campfire. He chewed on a strip of jerky and called it supper.

He was up and riding at dawn. He had not slept much anyway, for he kept reliving that desperate moment and seeing the dying eyes. Every mile he traveled put the Indian farther behind him, but the image was relentless. It rode with him all the way. Moving westward increased the time he would have to wait for the cart train to catch up with him, but that was a price he felt he had to pay. He let Beaver alternate between a walk and a trot. Occasionally he gave in to his nervousness and let the horse move into a lope for a mile or so. He realized his mistake when he felt it tiring beneath him.

The Indian horse was still keeping pace. Todd ground-hitched Beaver and moved cautiously to the brown. It eyed him with suspicion, ears poked forward. It backed off a few steps, then stopped and let him approach close enough to grasp a handful of mane.

Todd said, "If you're goin' to stay with us, you'd just as well work a little." Holding on to the mane, he led the animal to where Beaver waited. He transferred his bridle and saddle from one horse to the other. He was pleased that the Indian horse showed no resistance after its first display of shyness. "Somebody gentled you real good," he said. "I think me and you will get along all right." He reached down to pat the horse on the shoulder. "I've got to come up with a name for you. I think I'll call you Comanche."

He found, to his chagrin, that he had lost the rawhide rope with which he had been staking Beaver. He hoped the horse would follow as the other had. Looking back hopefully, he put Comanche into a walk. At first it appeared Beaver was going to remain where it was. But after Todd had ridden thirty yards or so, it trotted to catch up. Perhaps, he thought, it did not want any more than he did to be left by itself on the bald, far-stretching plains.

He came to a place where the flat plains began yielding to broken ground. Not far ahead, the cart trail would branch off into several individual trails. He feared he would not know which to follow. He found a spring where the cart men had watered their animals and filled their goatskins on the way out. This, he decided, would be a good place to wait. He hobbled Beaver. He had no hobbles for Comanche, but he trusted that, because the animal had willingly followed him before, it would not stray now.

He still had a supply of jerky, but he had subsisted on it for so long that the thought of it made him want to gag. He set off afoot to hunt for fresh meat. In a brushy header a mile from camp, he spotted a deer. He stalked it with care, moving only when the doe dropped her head to browse on some low-growing shrub, holding still when she raised her head to look for danger. He managed to approach within fifty yards and reasoned that this was as close as he was going to get. He eased to one knee, steadied the rifle, and squeezed the trigger. For a few seconds the smoke obscured his vision. He thought he had missed, for the deer made a couple of jumps toward thicker brush. Then she went down.

He bled her out and gutted her, then removed the hide. Finding her too heavy to carry for any distance, he trotted back to camp and saddled Comanche. He hoped the wolves would not find the carcass while he was gone. Approaching the deer, the horse snorted and quick-stepped in circles, repelled by the smell of blood. This made it difficult for Todd to lift the carcass up behind the saddle. He heaved and grunted a lot, and did a little cussing.

At least now he would have fresh meat while he waited for the caravan to return.

Watching the horses graze, he studied the brand on Comanche's hip. It appeared to be a combination of the letters *T* and *E*. Though he had not received formal schooling, he had learned enough from Felipe to know his letters and puzzle out printed words if given time. He could read as much as January could. He wondered where the horse had originally come from, and who might have owned it before. It seemed obvious that the Indians had picked it up in a raid, either in the Texas settlements or far to the south, in Mexico. He wondered if the original owner had survived the raid or if his scalp decorated a Comanche lance or shield.

January had counseled against such thoughts, for they were likely to arouse feelings of guilt over possession of a stolen animal.

"What the Comanches do down in Texas ain't none of our concern," he had said. "That's a long way from here, and there ain't nothin' we can do to stop it. Anyway, we don't owe them Texans a damned thing. I was down there one time doin' some tradin', and they stole horses from *me*. So in a way you might say I'm just gettin' back what's rightfully mine. And if there's a profit to be made, so much the better. Profit is what greases the wheels."

Todd was not sure January had the right slant on things, but then, January was a grown man, and Todd was still just a kid of around twelve, give or take a little.

He knew one thing: January would not be pleased about his having gone off on his own.

The horses and cattle, herded separately, preceded the slow-moving carts. Todd watched their approach with mixed emotions, unsure whether to feel relieved or to dread January's displeasure. Felipe was with the horses. Todd rode out on Comanche to meet him. Beaver, prancing with head high, eagerly joined the remuda.

Felipe spoke first, nodding toward Comanche. "Where'd you get the horse?"

Todd did not want to explain twice. He would wait for January. "He followed me."

"The owner may follow you, too, with a gun."

"I don't believe he will."

January rode up looking like a thunderhead full of lightning. He snapped, "Smart aleck, ain't you?"

Todd had rehearsed a dozen times what he would say, but all his preparation disappeared like a puff of smoke. "I didn't want you to trade me off to the Indians."

Exasperated, January said, "Hell, boy, I wasn't goin' to do that. I just dangled you out there for bait. As long as Two Bulls thought he might get you, he would've been easier to deal with on everything else. As it was, he got tougher than a boot. Damned near took all the profit out of the deal."

Todd tried to say he was sorry, but he wasn't, and he could not say so.

January said, "It's a wonder some stray Indian didn't kill you."

Todd shivered. "One tried." He explained what had happened in the draw.

January listened in amazement, then said, "I was fourteen before I killed my first Indian. You're startin' early." He frowned. "You ain't just spinnin' a big windy, are you, boy?"

"That's how I got this horse."

"Are you sure that Indian is dead? I'd hate to have him sneak in at night and cut our throats."

"He's dead, all right. I got him plumb center, like you always told me to."

January appeared satisfied. "You done good, boy. And got us an extra horse in the bargain."

"I kind of figured he was mine."

"You figured wrong. But I'll let you keep ridin' him till I sell him to somebody. That looks fair to me."

It didn't to Todd, but he knew he could do little about it.

January said with satisfaction, "You're learnin' right peart. I can see where you might finally start earnin' your feed."

Most of the caravan had broken up as the traders made their way to their individual homes. January's cart trailed well behind the band of thirty horses he had acquired in trade with the Comanches. In his imagination he was already spending the money he would receive for them. "I'm goin' to buy me a fine pair of boots in Santa Fe, and a suit of clothes to go with them. Been needin' me a new saddle, too."

Felipe asked, "What will you buy for us?"

January seemed surprised, then displeased. "You already got everything you need, both of you boys. What do you want new clothes for? You're both still growin'. Pretty soon you'd be too big for them anyway. Ain't it enough that I feed you and give you a roof over your heads?"

The roof had already been there, thanks to Yolanda's first husband, long before January had moved in. Todd knew it was not good politics to mention that, however.

They were still a mile or so from home when the army patrol suddenly appeared. Todd had seen enough soldiers to know by the insignia that a young lieutenant led the half-dozen enlisted men. He displayed an attitude of superiority.

January muttered, "Damned shavetail, fresh out of West Point. Already knows it all. Give him ten years and he'll wonder what went with all that wisdom."

The lieutenant raised his hand, and his detail halted behind him. He ignored January and the boys until he had given the remuda a quick looking over. Then he demanded, "Where did you get these horses, mister?"

January said, "From the Indians. We're just back from a tradin' trip. I've got a license right here in my pocket." He reached for it, but the lieutenant waved him off.

"Never mind. Every damned Mexican in this valley

has a license to trade with the Indians." He frowned. "You don't look Mexican to me."

"No, sir, I come from Missouri a long time ago. Settled in amongst these people, but I ain't one of them. I'm still white, plumb to the bone."

The lieutenant's sour expression indicated that he thought January had nothing to boast about. "What do you plan to do with these horses?"

"Sell them. Maybe even to your army if they're in a buyin' mood."

"I see three in here that already belong to the army. Surely you have noticed that they bear a U.S. brand?"

January affected a look of innocence Todd had seen many times before. "Is that what the brand means? I never had no idee."

"Surely you must know that the Indians stole those horses, and likely as not all the rest that you have here."

"It's the army's job, not mine, to make the Indians behave theirselves. I traded them a cartload of valuable goods out of Santa Fe and Chihuahua City."

The officer snorted. "I've seen some of the valuable trade goods you and those like you foist off onto the savages. Every last one of you deserves to be scalped or burned at the stake. I should confiscate all these horses and take you to Santa Fe in irons."

January's face was a deeper red than usual. "I got a license."

"Not to buy horses stolen from the army." The officer turned to a corporal. "Cut out those three with the U.S. brand. We're taking them with us."

January seemed to swell up like a toad. "Soldier boy, I call that theft in broad daylight. I'll sue the army."

The lieutenant's frown evolved into a scowl. "Inasmuch as you express contempt for the army, that brings up another question. What are your loyalties to the nation?"

"To the nation?"

"Surely you are aware of the tensions growing between the northern states and the southern. Several states are threatening to secede from the union. In the event that comes to pass, where will your loyalties be?"

January considered. "My loyalty is to me and my family."

Mainly to you, Todd thought.

The lieutenant watched as the soldiers separated the three horses from the rest. He said, "If I were you, sir, I would seriously consider my responsibilities to the nation that has succored and protected me. I would not allow myself to be swayed by ragtag malcontents. They shall be forced to swallow their treasonous words at the point of a sword."

Todd whispered to Felipe, "What is a ragtag malcontent?"

"I don't know. Some kind of a foreigner, I guess."

January cursed as the soldiers rode away. "Damned high-handed way to treat a taxpayin' citizen."

Felipe winked at Todd. Once out of January's hearing, he said, "If he ever paid a tax, it was on whiskey. It could not amount to much. Most of his whiskey comes from a still out in the timber."

"What's that soldier talkin' about, the North and the South maybe bustin' apart?"

Felipe shrugged. "That trouble is a long way from here. In this valley we still belong to Mexico."

7

Sarah Temple poked a couple of pieces of wood into her new cast-iron stove and shook the coffeepot to determine how much was left in it. She said, "I wish you wouldn't go to town today, Matthew. There's a lot of hard feeling about this vote. There's likely to be trouble."

Matthew had a determined look that said he would not be swayed. "Every vote counts if we're to keep Texas in the union."

"People around here know how you feel, and a lot of them don't like it. Like as not somebody'll want to fight you."

"Somebody like Nash Wickham? I can whip him with one hand tied behind me."

"That's no fit talk for a man of the cloth."

"Sinner or saint, a man ain't worth a continental if he won't stand up for what he believes in. I'm goin', and I'm takin' Jeffrey."

Jeffrey looked up in surprise from his breakfast plate of salt pork and scrambled eggs. "Me?"

Sarah gave the boy an anxious look. "Why Jeffrey? He's just fourteen years old. He can't vote."

"This'll be a day he'll want to remember. It could be a turnin' point in his life. In all our lives."

Sarah's expression was as determined as Matthew's. "Then we're taking the wagon, and I'm going with you."

Matthew said, "Women can't vote."

"No, but maybe I can keep you out of trouble."

Sitting with his legs hanging off the end of the wagon, Jeffrey marveled at the crowds. He had never seen so many people in town before, not even on a court day. Citizens all over Texas were voting on whether to secede from the union. People around Weatherford, as everywhere else in the state, had been arguing over the matter for weeks.

He said, "I don't understand what *secede* means. They can't pick up the state and move it somewhere else. Everything will still be in the same place whichever way the election turns out."

Matthew had been troubled since he had learned of plans for this vote. He said, "Surely the people of Texas have the good judgment not to choose secession. We fought hard to become a state. To throw it all away now . . ." He shook his head.

Jeffrey had heard just enough conversation about trouble back east to leave him confused. People spoke of places like Washington and Philadelphia, Richmond and Atlanta, but those were just names to him. He had never seen anything except a little of Arkansas and a little of Texas. Whatever lay beyond the bounds of his personal experience was as vague as last night's dream. He had heard talk about slavery from people who didn't own any, and about state's rights from people who did what they jolly well pleased without asking permission of anybody, local, state, or federal.

It seemed to him that everything was all right as it stood. People should leave things the way they were and not try to make changes where changes were not needed. Life had been good for him with Matthew and Sarah Temple. They weren't Mama and Papa, but they had treated him as their own. They had fed and clothed him and seen to it that he received some schooling. He could read a newspaper when one came his way, and he could do ciphers well enough to catch a merchant trying to squeeze a little extra from an account.

He asked, "What does Fletcher say?" He regarded Fletcher Knight's opinion as the final word in almost any situation.

Matthew replied, "Fletcher doesn't say much. I don't know whichaway he'll lean, but I hope he's on our side."

Sarah said, "Even if he isn't, he's been too good a friend to let a matter like this come between you. It'll all blow over in due time."

"I wouldn't be so sure. It could lead to a war."

"God forbid."

"Sometimes God gets disgusted and leaves us to our folly."

A crowd had gathered on the courthouse square. Hearing a loud and insistent voice, Jeffrey wondered if some itinerant preacher might be delivering a sermon. Drawing closer, he saw an agitated Nash Wickham standing in the bed of a wagon, poking a stubby finger at the sky. Wickham declared, "Must we continue to tolerate the heel of northern oppressors on our necks? Must we continue to stand for hell-bound abolitionists trampling upon the Bill of Rights for which our ancestors gave their all? Nay, I say. It is time we declare ourselves free of these New England radicals. They seek to destroy our freedoms and lay their heavy yokes upon our suffering shoulders."

Matthew spoke up, perhaps more loudly than he intended. "Sufferin'! The only burden on that old miser's shoulders is all the money he's piled up and stashed away."

The words evidently carried to Wickham, for he turned his round, red face toward Matthew and pointed that stubby finger. "And what say you, Brother Temple, to those who would dictate how we are to live, what we may do, and what we may not?"

Matthew lowered his head and gave every appearance of wishing he could simply disappear. Wickham kept badgering him. "Speak up, Brother Temple. Or have you left the service of the Lord and aligned yourself with the devil's disciples?"

Reluctantly Matthew rose from his seat in the wagon, even as Sarah tried to pull him back down. His years of lay preaching had given him an easy way with words. "I say this, Nash Wickham, that we ought to scratch our heads and think before we go off half-cocked. Fifteen years ago I marched with Zachary Taylor and his army into Mexico. Some good men died there, but we got the job done. After that I pitched in to help make the Republic of Texas a state. We've prospered right well under the union banner. I fought for that flag, and I'd be a yellow dog to turn my back on it now."

Wickham chewed on that for a moment, then said, "I have always suspected that beneath that saintly manner lay the conscience of a cur."

Matthew exploded. He jumped down from the wagon and rushed toward Wickham, ignoring Sarah's pleas to come back. "I'm tellin' you to your face, Wickham, you are a shameless liar and a hypocrite in the eyes of the Lord."

Wickham sputtered, his face scarlet. He climbed heavily down from his wagon, clenching his fists. "I am at your service, sir. You may have your choice of weapons."

Matthew said, "I am not a duelist, but I'm willing to wrestle you anytime and anyplace, or fight you bare-fisted, no rules."

Jeffrey held his breath, fearful that Wickham might shoot Matthew then and there. The butt of a pistol showed plainly in the man's broad waistband. Matthew carried a rifle in the wagon, but he would be dead before he could turn around to fetch it.

Fletcher stood there tall and strong. He moved quickly, placing himself between the two. He said, "Men, there's no call for a fight. Against the whole of Texas, our puny little vote here won't amount to a spit in the lake."

Matthew argued, "Maybe not, but we'll live a long time with the consequences of it."

Fletcher said, "In this country every man has a vote, and the majority rules. The votes don't always go our way, but we have to make the best of it, however it comes out."

Sarah had left the wagon. She gripped Matthew's arm. "Come on, let's get away from this crowd. Half of them want to whip you."

Matthew resisted. "Maybe the other half will help me."

"You're a preacher. The last thing you want is a riot that'll get a lot of men hurt. Come on, turn the other cheek and walk away from this."

Matthew grimaced. "That's not fair. You're usin' the Scriptures against me."

She scolded, "They make more sense right now than you do." She held to Matthew's arm and thrust her chin toward Jeffrey. "You take the wagon around to the other side of the courthouse. We're going in so Matthew can cast his vote. Then we're getting out of town as fast as we can."

Wickham's face was still flushed. His eyes bespoke murder, but Fletcher blocked him against any further move toward Matthew. He said, "Nash, you had the freedom to speak your mind. So did Matthew. The sun will rise in the mornin' no matter whichaway the vote turns out. Why don't me and you go have us a drink?"

Wickham only grunted, but his heavy shoulders slumped. He turned his back on Matthew and Sarah. Several friends gathered around, congratulating him on his stand. When they quieted, he said, "We'll wait till Texas is free and independent again. Then we'll tend to the traitors among us." He glanced at Fletcher. "And them that take their side."

Jeffrey felt a chill. He flipped the reins and started the wagon around the courthouse, as Sarah had told him to do. He found an open space and stopped there to wait. He watched two men square off and start pummeling each other. A third man struck one of the combatants across the head with the long barrel of a pistol. The victim went to his knees, quivering.

Jeffrey knew little about politics, but he could see that it would be a poor choice for a long career. Around here, it could be dangerous.

Matthew and Sarah came out through a door opposite the one by which they had entered, avoiding further contact with Wickham. Some of Wickham's friends jeered the couple. Matthew's expression was grim, Sarah's determined as they climbed into the wagon. An egg came sailing from somewhere and spattered against a sideboard. Matthew took the reins. Jeffrey sat again with his legs dangling off the rear of the wagon. He sensed that this was not a time for questions, so he asked none. They were half a mile from town before anyone spoke.

Sarah finally said, "If it hadn't been for Fletcher, Wickham might've shot you."

"That's the only way he could've beaten me."

"It's not worth your life just to make a point."

"Men've died doin' that."

"Well, I don't want *you* to. You're more important to me than Texas or the union or anything else."

"You wouldn't want me to tuck my tail and run from what I believe in."

"I would if that was the only way for you to stay alive." Sarah glanced back over her shoulder. "Jeffrey lost his real parents. What would he do if he lost you, too?"

"He's as old as I was when I was thrown out on my own. He'd find his way."

It would be days, perhaps weeks, before results of the statewide vote became widely known. The local result was revealed within a short time. A majority supported secession. The news threw Matthew into a state of anxiety Jeffrey had not seen in him before. Matthew's mood cast a cloud over the household. In contrast to his usual talkative manner, he said little more than was necessary to get the chores done. Pleading illness, he avoided going anywhere, even to preach. Sarah was also quieter than normal. Few friends stopped by, though the town road was nearby and carried its usual amount of horse, wagon, and buggy traffic. Fletcher was one of the few visitors. Matthew eagerly asked him what news he had heard.

Fletcher said, "There's been blood spilled already between secessionists and them that voted for the union. There'll be men killed over it, I'm afraid. It's just as well you stay low till the weather clears."

Jeffrey developed a sense of foreboding. Matthew had said secession would bring changes, that nothing would ever again be the same.

Sarah asked anxiously, "What'll we do if it comes to war? Matthew's too old to go and fight."

Fletcher's face was grim. "But he's not too old to run. He may have to go to Mexico if hotheads get the upper hand."

Matthew asked, "Why Mexico?"

"You wouldn't want to go north or west. That's Indian country. Go east and you'll face a thousand miles of secessionists."

"What would I do in Mexico?"

"Stay alive. That could get hard to do around here if Nash Wickham and his kind take over. Better to be alive in Mexico than dead in Texas."

Matthew mused, "I reckon I could find my way around in Mexico. I've already been there once, durin' the war. Even had a young lady teach me some Spanish." He added quickly, "That was before I knew you, Sarah."

Sarah said, "But we have our home here, this farm. We couldn't just go off and leave it."

Fletcher said, "It'd still be here when you got back. At least you'd better be thinkin' about it, and makin' ready. War makes people do awful things they wouldn't otherwise consider, or gives them an excuse to do what they always wanted to but were scared to try. Wickham has had it in for you ever since you settled on the land that he wanted for himself."

Matthew's eyes were sad. "It's a hard thing you've proposed, Fletcher."

"It's for you to decide. You're a free man. I just want to see you keep bein' a live one."

Sarah said, "Maybe we're borrowing trouble. Maybe none of this will ever come to pass."

Matthew said, "I'll pray hard, but not every prayer gets answered the way we want it to. We've got to brace ourselves for whatever comes."

Jeffrey saw a profound sadness in Matthew's and Sarah's eyes as they watched Fletcher ride away. Matthew said, "I wonder whichaway Fletcher voted."

Sarah said, "It doesn't matter. He's almost the only dependable friend we have left."

News about the war's outbreak spread across the land like a wind-driven wildfire, touching off violent confrontations between some who had favored secession and some who opposed it. Though weeks of somber talk had led Jeffrey to expect trouble, this was more than he was prepared for.

He had finished the evening milking and was carrying the bucket to the house when he heard a horse running. Fletcher reined to a quick stop, a small cloud of dust drifting past him. His face flushed, he demanded, "Where's Matthew?"

Jeffrey had heard Matthew chopping wood. "Out by the woodpile."

"You better come along, Jeffrey." Fletcher put the horse into a trot. Jeffrey followed him in a run, splashing milk from his bucket. He heard Fletcher's urgent voice. "Forget about the wood, Matthew. You have to hide, and do it quick."

Matthew resisted. "I've got things to do."

"Nash Wickham and his bunch are comin'. They just killed one Union man in town. You're next on their list."

Jeffrey's sense of dread was so intense that he could taste it. It was like the day he'd watched Comanches overrun his parents' wagon.

Sarah heard the commotion and stepped out onto the back porch. "What's this all about, Fletcher?"

"There's no time to talk. You've got to hide Matthew someplace. Wickham has got blood in his eye, and he's not far behind me."

Matthew appeared confused. "Hide where? Anyway, I'm not afraid of Wickham."

"Today you'd better be. He's on his way and got some hard men to help him. He intends to make an example of you."

Sarah hurried down from the porch and ran toward the barn. "Come on, Matthew. We'll cover you up with hay."

Matthew argued, "But they'll search this place till they find me."

Fletcher said, "Not if they think you've run away. I'll head south and make sure I leave plenty of tracks for them to follow." He turned to Sarah. "I know it's against your religion to lie, but you'd better lie to Wickham and make it sound good."

He swung back into the saddle. "Matthew, you'd best leave as soon as it's good dark. If I was you, I'd sure be thinkin' about Mexico."

"I can't go off and leave Sarah and Jeffrey."

"You have to. They can follow you. I'll help them."

Fletcher left at a run. Jeffrey was frozen in confusion, watching him go. Sarah grabbed his arm. "Come on, Jeffrey. We have a job to do."

She led him into the barn. "Matthew, you burrow into that pile of hay. Jeffrey, take the pitchfork and cover him up good."

Jeffrey did as he was told, throwing hay over Matthew until he protested that he was being smothered. Better than being hanged, Jeffrey thought. He went back outside and retrieved the milk bucket, which he had forgotten in the excitement.

Fletcher had not exaggerated. Nash Wickham arrived with seven men, their horses glistening with sweat. Wickham had the same grim look as when he had come in pursuit of the horse thief. Jeffrey shuddered, remembering what had happened to that luckless man. Wickham's malevolent gaze landed first upon Sarah. "Mrs. Temple, we are here to talk with your husband."

Her voice was as stern as his. She said, "You've just missed him. He got wind that you were coming."

"Now, who could have told him?" Wickham's eyes narrowed. "Fletcher, perhaps?"

"We haven't seen Fletcher in days." She made it sound so truthful that Jeffrey would have believed her had he not known different. She added, "I don't see a badge on any of you."

"We are patriots. That gives us all the authority we need to deal with the traitors in our midst."

Her voice dripped sarcasm. "I wonder how many of you fine patriots are going to volunteer for the Confederate army?" Her sharp gaze cut from one to another. "Not many, I would judge."

Wickham said, "Each of us serves in his own way. We are not all privileged to join our troops in battle."

One of Wickham's followers had ridden ahead, examining the ground. He returned, pointing south. "Fresh tracks goin' off yonder-way. They show that he left at a run."

Wickham took the news with a scowl. "Then let us be after him while the trail is hot." They left, stopping for a moment to look at the tracks Fletcher had left, then moving into a long trot.

Jeffrey instinctively turned toward the barn. Sarah caught his arm. "Wait till they are out of sight. We can't give them any reason to get suspicious."

They waited several minutes in the kitchen, Sarah trembling with anxiety. Jeffrey felt his back prickling. Sarah said, "Step outside and make sure none of them have dropped back."

Jeffrey saw no sign of Wickham's men. Fletcher was doing a good job of leading them astray. Sarah said, "There is always a chance someone is watching. We'll have to wait until dark before we do anything out of the ordinary. You go out and feed the stock. Make sure Matthew's best horse stays in the pen."

By the time Jeffrey was finished, the sun had sunk behind clouds low on the horizon. Yet, it seemed that night came on as slowly as Christmas. That prickly feeling stayed with him until full darkness.

Sarah said, "Saddle Matthew's horse." She carried a rolled blanket and a sack of food to the barn. Jeffrey tied them to Matthew's saddle while Matthew crawled out from beneath the hay. He tried to dust himself off and complained that he would probably itch for a week.

Sarah asked him, "Have you decided what you're going to do?"

Matthew said, "You know where my cousin Eli lives, down on Bull Creek close to Austin. I'll wait for you-all there. Come with the wagon when you think it's safe to move. Then we'll decide what to do next."

She said, "They'll probably watch us for a few days, waiting to see if you come back."

"Take your time. I'll cut east from here so I don't run into them. Somewhere below Fort Worth I'll turn south toward Austin."

"But what about the farm?"

"It'll still be here when we can afford to come back. I doubt this war'll last long. Cooler heads will prevail."

Jeffrey was becoming tall enough that Matthew did not have to lean down far to hug him. "Boy, you look out for Sarah. I'm dependin' on you. And take care of yourself, too."

Jeffrey tried not to choke. "I will."

Tears glistened on Sarah's cheeks. Bitterly she said, "Damn the secession. Damn Nash Wickham. And damn Texas."

Matthew said quietly, "Don't damn Texas. It's been good to all of us. Just damn the fanatics that stir up trouble where there wasn't any."

"I don't know what I'll do without you."

"You'll make out fine. You've got Jeffrey here to help you."

Matthew embraced Sarah. He gave her a long kiss, swung into the saddle, and put the horse into a run.

Worriedly Jeffrey asked, "You think Wickham'll come back?"

"They'll track Fletcher till dark, then likely wait for daylight so they can see the trail again. They'll come dragging back tomorrow, lookin' for somebody to blame."

"They wouldn't hurt a woman, would they?" Such an idea was virtually inconceivable to Jeffrey.

"You can never be sure what a man like Wickham might do in a fit of anger."

"Wickham already suspicions that Fletcher told Matthew to get away."

"Fletcher knows how to take care of himself. Wickham'll bluster and make a lot of noise, but the dog that barks the loudest is generally the first to run away."

Jeffrey and Sarah sat down to a belated supper. She ate little, poking at her plate, her head down. Her thin shoulders trembled with silent sobbing. "It's not fair," she said. "We don't hardly know what the war is all about. We've got nothing to gain and a lot to lose. Why couldn't they just leave us alone?"

"Some folks ain't satisfied unless they're messin' in other people's business."

Sarah stared at Jeffrey. "Be glad you're not of age to go fight."

He said, "I wouldn't know which side to fight for. I don't understand any of it."

"Neither does hardly anybody else. But the war wind is blowing. God knows where it'll take us."

As he was about to go to bed, Jeffrey heard someone knock on the door. He thought of Wickham and felt a jolt of fear.

A muted voice said, "It's me, Fletcher."

Jeffrey's heart pounded. He opened the door just enough that he could see out and be certain before he swung it wider to let Fletcher enter. Sarah recognized the visitor and quickly blew out the lamp.

She said, "Somebody may be watching the house."

Fletcher said, "I don't think so, but it's good to be careful."

She demanded, "Why did you come back here? Wickham suspects that you warned Matthew."

"I thought I'd better be here when that bunch comes back empty-handed. You may need some help."

"Even if Wickham wanted to, I don't think those men would let him hurt a woman."

"But he could burn you out and run off your stock. So I'll stay here and sleep in the barn. Have you got a blanket to spare?"

"Of course." She considered for a moment. "People may talk, you staying the night here with Matthew gone."

"That's better than havin' them talk about you bein' burned out of your home."

"I don't want to believe he would do that."

"Wickham would, except he's afraid I'd kill him too dead for the resurrection. Matthew will understand. Nobody else matters."

"You're a real friend, Fletcher, maybe too much for your own good."

A look came into Fletcher's eyes, warm yet at the same time sad. "You . . . you and Matthew . . . have always been good friends to me."

It was the next afternoon before Wickham and his followers returned, droop-shouldered and walking tired horses. Wickham's eyes were red from fatigue and dust. Frustration was in his voice as he confronted Sarah and Jeffrey in front of the house. Sarah's arms were folded in an attitude of defiance. The shotgun was leaned against the wall close behind her.

No one needed to tell Jeffrey that the posse had been unable to catch up with Matthew.

Fletcher walked around the corner of the house, a pistol in his waistband. Wickham stiffened at the sight of him. He said, "I suppose you know you have thwarted the will of the people."

Fletcher said, "The will of some people. Not every-body. Looks to me like you've got enough to do just tendin' your farm and countin' your money. You've got no call to be chastisin' people who see things dif-ferent than you do."

"Don't think I'm going to forget your part in this." Wickham glanced at Sarah. His eyes narrowed. "But I can see a reason for it. Everybody knows you'd like to have her for yourself. With her husband gone . . ."

Fletcher clenched his fists. "Climb down here and I'll teach you to have some respect for a good woman."

"I always respect a *good* woman."

Fletcher took two strides and grabbed Wickham's shirt. Eyes frightened, Wickham managed to jerk his horse around and break free, though the shirt ripped and a couple of buttons popped loose. He pulled back out of Fletcher's reach. "You helped a traitor to escape. I would be justified in killing you right here."

Fletcher's face was scarlet. "If you had the guts to try. In front of all these men, I'm givin' you a chance. See if you can shoot me before I can shoot you."

Wickham breathed hard. Sweat rolled down his face and cut tracks in the dust that clung there. Cau-tiously keeping his hand far from the pistol on his hip, he said weakly, "I will tend to you at the proper time and place. Right now I am worn and tired. You have me at a disadvantage."

Jeffrey saw disgust in several faces as the men real-ized Wickham was not going to accept the risk.

Wickham turned and put his horse into a trot in the direction of town. Some of his men followed, but a pair broke off from him and traveled eastward. An-other held back to tell Fletcher, "I'm sorry I let that old windbag talk me into this. If I was you, I wouldn't let him slip up behind me. And I wouldn't let this lady stay here."

When they were gone, Sarah came down from the porch, her face fearful. "Fletcher, he'll get you sooner or later."

"No, he won't. I'm fixin' to leave."

"Where to?"

"I've joined a frontier rangin' outfit to scout for Indians. It's a way to serve without goin' east to fight against the Union."

"That could be dangerous."

"It's got to be done. The Comanches won't be long in figurin' out that a lot of men have gone off to fight the Yankees. They'll commence to testin' our defenses."

"What about your blacksmith shop?"

"I sold it to Adam. Wickham doesn't know about it yet." Fletcher turned to Jeffrey. "You help Sarah gather up everything you'll need for a long trip. You-all can travel a good ways before daylight."

Sarah asked, "What about you?"

"I've got a few things to take care of. I'll be back to help you load the wagon after dark." He caught up his horse and left, following the tracks left by Wickham's men.

Sarah stared regretfully at the house. "I hate to leave here. God knows where we'll end up."

Jeffrey said, "There's a chance they'll burn this house."

Sarah's lips pinched. "It's just a house. We can build another."

They gathered blankets and clothing, kitchen utensils and tools, stacking them just inside the back door. Sarah studied her near-empty kitchen cabinet. A set of china remained. "They were my mother's," she said. "I'm afraid they'll get broken if we try to take them."

Jeffrey said, "And stolen if we don't."

Sarah said, "Empty the wood box. We'll put them in it and bury them. They'll be here when we come back. If we come back."

"Fletcher said he doesn't think the war will last long. Both sides'll get tired of the foolishness. I'll bet we'll be back here before Christmas."

He buried the box behind the barn. He and Sarah ate a cold supper while waiting. Darkness came, and with it Fletcher, leading a packhorse with a large bundle on its back. Jeffrey hitched the team and brought the wagon up beside the back door. With Fletcher helping, they quickly loaded everything Sarah had set aside to take. With a short rope, Jeffrey tied the milk cow to the rear of the wagon. He tied longer lead ropes to Matthew's remaining horse and mare.

Fletcher said, "Time to go. I'll ride with you a ways to see you get started all right."

They left before moonrise, heading south.

8

Jeffrey hunched on the wagon seat, the reins in his hands. Sarah sat with him. Fletcher rode alongside, leading his packhorse. Worried, Jeffrey said, "These wagon tracks will be easy to follow."

Fletcher said, "We'll cut into a main road as soon as we can. Your tracks will be lost amongst so many others."

Sarah said quietly, "Leave it to Fletcher. He always knows what he's doing."

Fletcher heard. "I wish that was the truth. Half the time I wonder what I'm goin' to do next, and if it'll be the right thing when I do it."

That admission troubled Jeffrey a little. He had always regarded Fletcher as self-assured and capable of anything he set his mind to. It was unsettling to consider that Fletcher might be more like Papa than he had imagined, vulnerable to making mistakes like most everybody else.

He had only a vague sense of time. He knew they

had been under way most of the night before he began feeling drowsy. He slipped into short moments when he was more asleep than awake, though he felt the vibration of the wagon as it rumbled over rough ground. He would come awake with a start, then slowly drift again. Sarah gently took the reins from his hands. "Climb back into the wagon and find a place to lie down," she said. "I wouldn't want you falling off and letting the wheels run over you."

Fletcher said, "Best you stop and both rest awhile. You'll be fresher tomorrow."

Sarah said, "We haven't gone all that far yet."

"Horses and mules have to rest, and so do people."

Jeffrey thought it ironic that it was harder to go to sleep after they stopped than when he had been on the wagon. But he eventually dropped off, awakening when he heard Fletcher breaking up wood to build a fire. The sun was red at the horizon but barely able to break through layered clouds.

Fletcher said, "I was fixin' to wake you. Looks like it might rain later on. We'd better rig a tarp under the wagon bed and load it with dry wood so you won't have a cold camp tonight."

Jeffrey had seen wagons with a cowhide slung beneath to carry firewood, or dried cow and buffalo chips if wood was not available. He helped Fletcher with the tarp, letting it sag enough that it could accommodate a decent load. Then he gathered wood until Sarah called him to breakfast. He had learned to drink black coffee despite her warning that it would stunt his growth. He was already five feet tall and growing, so he considered coffee no threat.

He kept looking to the north, half expecting to see Nash Wickham and some of his cohorts. Fletcher noticed. He said, "Wickham looked like he was worn down to a nub yesterday. I doubt he's fanatic enough to go out on another chase today."

Jeffrey felt reassured.

Breakfast finished, Fletcher said, "It's time for me to leave you. I've got a ways to travel."

Sarah's voice was regretful. "I wish you could go with us all the way."

"I promised to report to camp by nightfall. You know the way from here on, and I don't think you'll need to worry about Nash Wickham."

The two looked at each other for a long moment, both plainly wanting to reach out but determined not to do so. Fletcher moved quickly into the saddle. Jeffrey handed him the packhorse's lead rope. Fletcher said, "There'll be a better day," and rode off to the west in a brisk trot.

Sarah said, "I wish I knew when that will be."

The clouds thickened as the morning moved toward noon. To the south they were a dark blue, almost black. Jeffrey said, "Somebody's gettin' a frog strangler."

The clouds overhead began to boil. Sarah wrapped a blanket around herself and Jeffrey as rain began to fall, a sprinkle of large drops first, then a heavier downpour. She said, "We'll keep travelin' while we can. Once this road gets good and muddy, we'll have to stop."

On the off chance that Wickham *was* still following, a heavy rain would wash out the wagon tracks, Jeffrey thought. Getting wet would be a small price to pay for peace of mind.

A while later Sarah said, "Bridge ahead. Take one of the horses and lope up to see if it looks safe to cross."

Jeffrey found the water running high and brown with mud, lapping against the bottom of the bridge. Some of it splashed over the top. A couple of wagons were already stalled on the near side and one on the far side, their occupants unwilling to risk the crossing. A large canvas was tied to one of the near wagons and spread out to provide a cover against the rain. A campfire blazed just beneath the edge.

Returning to Sarah, he said, "We'll have to wait with the rest of them for the water to run down."

As Jeffrey pulled the wagon up close to the bridge, a man stepped out from under the tarp. He looked like a farmer. Beckoning, he shouted, "You folks come over and get out of the rain."

Jeffrey told Sarah, "You go on and get dry. I'll unhitch the team and take care of the stock."

Sarah insisted on helping him before seeing to her own comfort. A young man came out to lend a hand. Cold and wet, a young woman huddled beneath the shelter with two small children, near the fire. A middle-aged man and woman greeted the newcomers. The man said, "Sorry we've got such poor accommodations, but at least it's pretty dry under here. You-all come far?"

Sarah was hesitant in answering. Jeffrey figured she didn't want to be specific, at least until she determined these people's political leanings. "Far enough to get wet," she said.

"How much farther you got to go?"

"To kinfolks south of here."

The man stood just inside the edge of the canvas, looking at Jeffrey's wagon. He said, "Just you and your son, travelin' all by yourselves?"

"He's not—" Sarah broke off, then said, "He's pretty handy at takin' care of things. We get by all right."

She gave Jeffrey a frowning look that warned him against telling too much. The man's questions might be innocent, or he could be an informant for the new Confederate state government. They seemed to be everywhere these days. First Matthew, then Fletcher, had warned that one of the war's results was a strong attitude of distrust, even among friends. One guarded his opinions until he was certain about the company he was in.

Jeffrey decided his best course would be to keep quiet. He doubted that anyone would ask for his opinion anyway.

The man introduced his family. "I'm Ephraim Baines. This here is my wife, Emily. The young feller is my son, John, and the pretty young lady with him is his wife, Amity. The two young'uns are theirs. It's a lucky man I am to have such a family. We're headin' south."

The man's wife gave him a silent frown like the one Sarah had given Jeffrey. It was a hush-up signal.

He added, "We got burned out by the Indians, you see."

Jeffrey thought the two wagons appeared heavily laden for a family that had endured a burnout. He suspected these people were Union sympathizers trying to escape persecution, but it was not his place to question strangers.

Ephraim was unable to restrain himself long. Talking appeared to be a compulsion with him. He said, "Too bad about this rain. We'd figured to be a good ways further on by now."

Sarah observed, "It appears to be letting up some. Maybe after a while the water will run down enough that we can get across."

Jeffrey discerned a touch of anxiety in the young

woman's face, mirrored in her husband's. "We do certainly hope so," she said.

Ephraim said, "It's a devilish poor time to be travelin'." His inflection made it seem more a question than a statement.

Sarah said simply, "Sure is."

"We had a hard time gettin' a fire started, the wood bein' so wet."

Jeffrey pointed. "We've got dry wood in a tarp under the wagon. I'll fetch some over."

The heat soon dried Jeffrey's clothes, and he enjoyed the warmth. He only half listened to Ephraim's talking. Sarah nodded a lot in response. At length Ephraim said, "I notice you ain't asked about our politics."

Sarah said, "I figure that's your own business."

"And it should be, but no matter where you turn, there's folks that think it's their business, too. They get almighty serious about it."

"So I've seen."

"We come from up near the Red River. We talked against the secession vote, and now there's some hotheaded heathens got their knives sharpened up for us. That's why we're travelin'. All we want is to mind our own business and stay out of trouble."

Sarah said, "That's what I want, too."

Ephraim gave a sigh of relief. "I'm tickled you feel that way." He turned to his wife. "Woman, don't you think we ought to get some supper started? Them kids are bound to be hungry."

Sarah said, "I'll help. We've got provisions in our wagon. We'd be glad to share."

They were halfway through supper when Jeffrey heard horses. Uneasy, he picked up his plate and walked to the edge of the overhead tarp. "Somebody's comin'."

Sarah stiffened. "Nash Wickham?"

Jeffrey squinted. "I don't think so. They look like strangers."

Ephraim turned grim. "Not to me, they don't. John, reach into the wagon and hand me my rifle." His son hesitated, then complied. Ephraim said, "They'll listen better when they see me holdin' this. You let me do the talkin'." He glanced at Sarah and Jeffrey. "This is our affair. You don't owe us nothin'."

Looking concerned, Sarah beckoned Jeffrey to her side. John's wife huddled with her two children.

Five riders approached the wagons. Most still wore slickers, though the rain had stopped. One, a sturdy dark-complexioned man of belligerent countenance, moved out into the lead. He dismounted and handed his reins to the nearest horseman without even looking at him. He had the air of a man very much in charge. The other men got down from their horses. Two drew their pistols.

Sternly the visitor said, "Well, Ephraim, looks like old Mother Nature is sidin' with the Confederacy. I'd near given up on catchin' you and John. I doubt we would've if the river hadn't stopped you."

Ephraim's eyes smoldered. "You've got no business with us, Lockwood, and we've none with you."

"That's where you're wrong. We warned you—especially John—about that treasonous talk. It's time you learn a lesson about loyalty to your country."

"The United States is our country. Them that've turned their backs on it have got no call to preach to me and mine."

Lockwood stepped close and punched a finger against the younger man's chest. "John, we gave you a choice. You could join the Confederate army, or you could stretch a rope. You chose to run."

John's face paled, but he did not reply.

Lockwood said, "You've still got that choice. We'll take you back to join the regiment, or we'll leave you hangin' from one of those trees on the riverbank. Which'll it be?"

Blanching, the young woman rushed forward to clutch her husband's arm. "No! You can't take him away from us."

Looking ready to wilt, John took her in his arms and held tightly. "They give me no way out. I've got no choice but to join the regiment."

Raging, Ephraim shouted, "Like hell!" He brought the rifle to his shoulder. But Lockwood was faster. He drew a pistol from his waistband and fired. Ephraim's rifle roared and put a hole in the canvas overhead. He stumbled backward and fell.

John dropped to one knee beside his father, crying "Pa!" Several of Lockwood's men swarmed in and grabbed him. Lockwood pointed to the animals staked beyond the Temples' wagon. "Go fetch one of them horses. We'll put him on it and take him back to do his duty."

They were about to take one of Matthew's horses. Jeffrey protested, but none of the men paid any attention to him. When he stepped in front of the one who led the horse, the man roughly pushed him aside. Lockwood glowered. "Careful, boy, or we may decide you're old enough to make a soldier, too."

Jeffrey saw the futility of further argument. He just wished they had taken the mare instead of the horse. She was not much of a prize.

The three women knelt beside the fallen Ephraim. His breathing was raspy and irregular. With each heartbeat, blood pumped from a wound in his shoulder.

Ephraim's wife cried, "Hold on, Ephraim." She

threw herself down over him. John's wife shouted angrily, "The war won't last forever, Lockwood. When it's over, we'll remember you."

Lockwood said, "Keep talkin' and you'll hang your husband. Come on, men, let's go home before we have to shoot the womenfolks, too."

Sarah told Jeffrey, "Run to our wagon and get some towels." She managed to pull Ephraim's wife back enough that she could examine Ephraim. She folded one of the towels Jeffrey brought and pressed it against the wound in an effort to stop the blood. John's wife stood beyond the shelter, weeping as she watched Lockwood and his men take her husband away. At least they did not carry him to the trees.

Sarah said, "I wonder how far it is to a town. Ephraim has got to have a doctor."

Jeffrey said, "I see a church steeple across the river, but nobody can get across that bridge right now. The last town we passed was five-six miles back."

Emily Baines said, "Then let's get him into the wagon."

Jeffrey wished Fletcher were there. He helped Sarah and Emily lift Ephraim into one of the wagon beds while John's wife, Amity, quickly gathered up the camp equipment. Jeffrey hitched their teams.

As they started to leave, Sarah expressed her sympathy. Emily Baines said, "We hoped we'd left the trouble behind us. But once trouble takes ahold, seems like it never lets go."

Sarah asked, "What'll you folks do now?"

Emily looked at her daughter-in-law. She said, "There ain't no point in us goin' on south. We done it mainly to get John away from Lockwood and them. We'll find Ephraim a doctor. Then, live or die, I reckon we'll head back home." She knotted a fist. "I don't

know when or how, but the day of judgment will find
Lockwood on his knees beggin' for the Lord's mercy.
There ain't goin' to be any."

The two women turned their wagons so that they
pointed to the north. Jeffrey watched them sadly, in
shock over how rapidly everything had happened. He
wondered how men probably otherwise honest and
upright could let politics bring them to such extremes
of violence.

He said, "I can't hardly believe what just happened."

Sarah said, "But it did. War can bring out the worst
in men's nature, or it can bring out the best."

"I've seen some of the worst. I'd like to see what
the best looks like."

"You've seen Matthew, and you've seen Fletcher."
She touched his shoulder. "You've shown some of it
yourself. You've handled responsibility awfully well
for a boy of fourteen."

"Goin' on fifteen," Jeffrey said.

He walked to the edge of the bridge. The water
roared, but it had receded some. He went back and
reported to Sarah. "Maybe by mornin' it'll be down
enough to cross over, if it doesn't take the bridge out."

Sarah's eyes were bleak. "It can't happen too soon
for me. I want to put this awful place behind us."

That night, Nash Wickham invaded Jeffrey's dream
and awakened him with a start. He fantasized about
Wickham being caught on the bridge just as it was
swept away, like Matthew's story about Pharoah's
soldiers who drowned trying to overtake Moses and
the children of Israel. But that had been a long time
ago. Miracles like that did not happen anymore.

As Jeffrey hoped, the water was much lower by
morning. One of the bridge supports appeared to have

been knocked out of alignment, but as far as he could see, the rest were still where they should have been. Sarah prepared a hasty breakfast.

The people who had been waiting on the far side were making preparations to move. Sarah said, "Let's get the team hitched. If that wagon makes it across all right, we'll start."

Tensely Jeffrey watched the oncoming wagon. He half expected the bridge to collapse, but it held. The northbound travelers seemed much relieved as they came abreast of the Temple wagon. A man and a woman were on the seat. The woman was on the verge of crying. "Thank God we made it," she said. "I thought I felt the bridge start to move while we were on it."

"Your imagination," the man said. "We done just fine. You folks fixin' to try it now?"

Sarah said, "We are."

The man said, "We heard a little shootin' over here last evenin'. Trouble?"

"Trouble enough." Sarah showed that she did not want to talk about it.

The man did not press her. "We'll watch to be sure you make it across all right."

Jeffrey did not see how that would help much if they went into the roiling water. It was still swift enough to sweep them downstream.

"Let's go," Sarah said. Hands shaking, Jeffrey started the team. The milk cow and the mare followed behind the wagon. The mules' hooves sounded like gunshots as they struck the wooden planking. The bridge groaned under the weight. Jeffrey was certain he felt it shift.

Sarah's voice reflected fear. "Keep moving."

The advice was unnecessary. He had no intention

of stopping. Instead, he put the team into a stiff trot to get across as quickly as possible.

As the wagon cleared the wooden structure, Jeffrey heard a crunching sound. Looking back, he saw the bridge begin to move. It seemed for a moment to buckle, then much of it collapsed into pieces. The debris tumbled away in the swift and muddy current.

He held his breath until his lungs burned. He tried to speak but seemed to have lost his voice.

They traveled a hundred yards before Sarah spoke. She said in a low whisper, "Like the children of Israel, the Lord has delivered us."

But to what? Jeffrey wondered.

9

Relatively isolated for generations, the Spanish villages of northeastern New Mexico were only occasionally affected by the excursions and alarms that bedeviled other parts of the country. The American invasion that had made them citizens of the United States had but a marginal influence on day-to-day lives. The people still spoke the unique Spanish dialect that had evolved during long years of limited contact with their mother country. They tilled their small plots of farmland and herded their sheep and cattle as they had from the time of first settlement. They tolerated the small influx of gringos in the same way they tolerated the winter snows, the summer droughts, the seasonal infestations of crop-eating bugs.

They tried to ignore the American Civil War. After all, it was a long way from New Mexico, and gringo against gringo. What had it to do with *gente de razón*, the people of reason?

Todd was aware of the war but felt that it was too far away for concern. He had observed no sign of it in the valley, though he had heard talk and had seen United States soldiers on his infrequent trips to Santa Fe as January's ward.

The autumn Comanche moon had come and gone. The Indians had made their final raids into the Texas settlements before the onset of winter and had booty to offer to the likes of January. So now Todd was on his way home from the plains with January and Felipe. The three, along with a couple of temporary hired hands, were driving a herd of cattle and more than forty horses acquired from the Comanches. They had cost January a cartload of trade goods and three boxes of obsolete European rifles smuggled up out of Mexico. He made up for that expense by paying his help a pittance. Local wages were traditionally low. January always said it ought to be a jailable offense to upset tradition.

January rode among the horses once they were away from the Indian camp, watching for injuries or faults he might have overlooked before. He appeared satisfied. He said, "You got to watch them Indians every minute. Some people set out on purpose to cheat you."

Felipe gave Todd a wink.

January said, "I ought to do all right, sellin' these to the army. When soldiers go into battle, horses get killed. The price of fresh ones goes up."

Todd said, "People get killed, too."

January dismissed the comment with a shrug. "People die from one thing or another every day. War just rushes it up. And it's good for business."

It never seemed to bother January's conscience that the Indians had stolen the animals he traded for. He said, "It ain't for me to tell the Comanches about the Ten Commandments. They got their ways, and I got mine." He had been careful not to accept horses carrying the U.S. brand, remembering that the army had confiscated three from him once.

Todd said, "Yolanda says it's a sinful thing to be makin' a profit off of people dyin'."

"Women don't understand the ways of the world. I figure on takin' my share. If I don't, somebody else'll get it. The biggest dog don't always get the bone. Lots of times it goes to the smartest and the fastest."

"Like you?"

"Damn right. This war may not last long. The time to fish is when the fish are bitin'. These horses'll fetch me a good price from them yellow-leg soldiers in Santa Fe."

"The rebels might pay more."

"Maybe, but they ain't here. Besides, they got enough sorry land in Texas. What would they want with New Mexico?"

Todd could not remember enough about Texas to make any judgment one way or the other. All he knew of it was the open plains, and the Indians had full control there. That region might as well have belonged to France or England, for all the good Texas got out of it. January said he hoped it would stay Indian forever. Todd figured he must be amassing a small fortune from the Comanchero trade, for he spent no more than he had to on his adopted family. Every so often January would carry away a leather bag heavy with coins. When he reappeared, he no longer had the money. Felipe and Todd had tried a few times to follow him, but he was as elusive as a will-o'-the-wisp.

Felipe sometimes fantasized aloud about finding where January buried it. "When I do," he said, "I will take my mother to Mexico. Her and me and you, we could live like a Spanish governor down there. Maybe even a king."

"Till somebody stole it all," Todd replied. "Then we'd just be some more poor peons."

"That's all we are now, livin' with January. *Mucho trabajo, poco dinero*." Much work, little money. "We ought to go join the army, maybe."

"We're too young. Anyway, it's a gringo army. I don't know if they take Mexicans."

"The Mexican army, then. They've always got a war down in Mexico. They don't care how young we are."

Todd resisted the notion though it had some appeal for him. He knew Felipe was simply venting his frustrations by talking so boldly. He would probably spend his whole life right there in northeastern New Mexico, like the generations before him. He said, "Maybe we'll go someday when we're older and bigger. January ain't much, but right now he's all we got."

When they dropped down into the valley, it struck Todd that he saw almost nobody. That seemed strange. Usually people would be working in the gardens and fields or herding sheep out on the grassy fringes.

January noticed it, too. He said, "Maybe somebody brought the smallpox in here while we been gone."

Todd ventured, "Maybe it's Indians."

"Indians don't mess much with this valley. They need somebody to trade with. You and Felipe stay with the stock. I'll lope off down there and find out what's goin' on."

Felipe appeared a little spooked. He said, "Maybe everybody is dead. They say in Mexico whole villages have died out. There wasn't enough people left to bury them."

Todd pointed. "Everybody ain't dead. I see old Bonifacio with his sheep, over yonder along that gully."

"Bonifacio's been dead for years. He just won't lay down. He must be a hundred and six."

Todd watched January ride up to Bonifacio and engage him in conversation. The old man gestured vigorously, pointing southward, then to the north. January returned after a time, his expression sober. He said, "A bunch of Union soldiers been through here, lookin' for volunteers and grabbin' up horses for the army. He says there's talk that Tejanos are fixin' to invade down in southern New Mexico. May already be there."

"Texans?" Todd asked.

"I don't know what in hell they would want with this godforsaken part of the country, but the report has got the people around here boogered. Most everybody is stayin' out of sight and hidin' their stock, afraid the army will confiscate it."

Todd looked about as if he expected to see an army riding over the hill. "If they're grabbin' horses, they're liable to take these away from us."

"They can lord it over these poor Mexicans, but they won't do it to old January. Let's head these horses north. I know a little box canyon where we can hide them till the yellow-legs agree to pay my price."

"And if they won't?"

"Then the rebels will."

"How do you know they'll ever come here?"

"They're Texans. When they set their minds to somethin', they get it. Dogie, bring your blanket roll. You may be campin' awhile."

It was a small canyon, boxed in on three sides by heavily timbered hills. A tiny creek snaked down the length of it on its way to join a river farther to the south. The cured grass was boot-top high, showing no sign of recent grazing. The only animal tracks Todd saw were from elk.

January said, "Let them scatter. I don't think they'll stray far into that timber, not with plenty of water and grass where they're at. Boy, you'll set up camp here at the south end and watch that they don't leave the valley till I come to get them."

"By myself?"

"You're old enough to earn your keep."

"When'll you be comin' back?" Todd asked.

"How should I know? You just stay and do what I tell you."

January had left the carts and the cattle stopped back on the trail, several miles to the south. He untied two cloth sacks from the big horn of his Mexican saddle and handed it to Todd. "Here's some flour and salt. For meat, you've got your rifle. You're big enough to take care of yourself." He turned and rode back toward the herd.

January hollered for Felipe, who said, "I better go. When he gets mad at me, he takes it out on Mama. Good luck. Watch out for bears."

Todd camped at the edge of the timber at the southern end of the valley, blocking any horses tempted to wander off in that direction. None showed an inclination to stray far into the timber. He took stock of the grub January had left with him and decided he couldn't live long on flour and salt. He decided to see if he could shoot something.

He entered the timber on foot. In a while he managed to stalk a doe and bring it down. He gutted her and walked back to camp to get his horse, Comanche.

He fried a piece of backstrap for supper and was grateful to be away from January for a while. He almost hoped the man would never come back. But he knew better. January would keep coming back a month after he was dead.

A week turned into two, then into three. He had a hard time keeping warm, though otherwise he enjoyed the solitude. He dragged deadfall timber down into camp to build a crude shelter against the bitter north wind and the occasional flurries of snow.

Felipe came once to bring him more food. Todd appreciated the brief break in his solitude. "Anything happenin' down in the valley?" he asked.

"War talk. The army pushes on January for horses, but he won't admit he's got any. He waits to get his price. You may have to spend the winter up here."

"It's not that bad most of the time. Beats havin' January around all the time, tellin' me what to do."

Felipe said, "Me and you, we're big enough to take these horses and sell them ourselves. Maybe we could join the rebels and take back the land the Americanos stole from us."

Todd pointed out, "The rebels are gringos, too."

Felipe stewed over that. "You're right. Whichever side wins, we lose." He brightened. "Unless they all kill each other off."

January came, eventually, bringing Felipe along to help. He had little to say until he had ridden the length of the canyon, counting the horses. He told Todd sternly, "Damn good thing you didn't let any of them get away."

Todd's face stung, and not altogether because of the cold.

Felipe shrugged. "You expected him to say thank you?"

January heard and reacted angrily. "I don't owe you boys no thanks, either one of you. You're gettin' fed, ain't you? You've got clothes on your back, ain't you? It's you that ought to be thankin' *me*. Come on, now, there's a soldier boy waitin' to pay me cash money for these horses."

It was almost night when they reached the farm. January loped ahead and opened a gate into the largest corral. The horses entered without resistance. Their gentleness told Todd that they had been used to this kind of handling before the Indians had taken possession.

"You boys fork out some hay," January ordered. "I'm tired." He unsaddled and walked to the house. Shortly he was back out on the porch with a jug.

Felipe carried a forkload of hay from a stack and pitched it into a rack. "Don't that gringo war have somethin' to do with slaves?"

Todd said, "So I hear."

"Maybe when it's over, we'll be free."

January said the soldiers would be out in the morning to take possession. After breakfast, Todd suggested, "Maybe me and Felipe ought to go feed those horses some more hay."

January shook his head. "They'll belong to the army in a little while. Let the soldiers feed them. Hay costs money."

It had not cost January anything except Todd's and Felipe's sweat. They had raised the crop, cut and stacked it.

Todd said, "Well, I'm goin' to feed Comanche, anyway."

"Not much," January warned. "A fat horse is a lazy one."

Toward midday, Todd was in a small corral with

Comanche when he saw the soldiers approaching. There was no question who was in charge. A bewhiskered man in a tailored blue coat with a lot of braid raised his arm in a slouchy salute. *"Muchacho, habla inglès?"*

"Sure I speak English," Todd replied.

The officer looked surprised. "Damn near everybody I've seen around here is Mexican. It's a pleasure to find somebody who speaks God's language."

It had never occurred to Todd to wonder what language God spoke.

The officer said, "I assume these horses belong to your father."

"They belong to January, but he ain't my father. He ain't no kin at all. He just claims to own me."

"Am I correct that these are the ones he is offering for sale?"

Todd nodded. "Anything January has got is for sale if the price is high enough. He even tried to sell me a few times."

The officer grunted. "You're too light-complected for that. Mind if we look through the horses?"

Todd was unsure about taking the responsibility upon himself, but January had acquired them to resell. "Help yourselves."

The officer and a couple of his men walked among the horses, studying them slowly and carefully. "Most of them have brands," he said. "Where did they come from?"

Todd hedged. "The people January got them from picked them up one place and another."

The officer made a good guess. "Mostly from the Texas settlements, I would wager. In the light of the moon."

"I don't know, sir. I wasn't there."

"It doesn't matter. Texans threw in their lot with the rebels, so I have no sympathy for them."

"We heard the rebels are comin' into New Mexico."

"They've moved into the Mesilla Valley and taken Fort Fillmore, but they won't hold it long. We'll send them running back to Texas with their tails between their legs."

Todd asked, "How much do you figure them horses are worth?"

"That is a question Mr. January and myself will have to work out. Value is decided by the most one side will give and the least the other will take."

"January ain't cheap. He'll take all he can get."

"I'll have to appeal to his better nature."

"If he's got one, he keeps it buried someplace. I ain't never seen it." Todd almost added, "like his money," but he caught himself. January would not want strangers to know his banking habits.

January had seen the soldiers. He walked up from the house. "Howdy, Lieutenant. Did you bring the money?"

The officer hedged. "I know we agreed upon a tentative price, but I was hoping I might appeal to your patriotism."

"Patriotism is all right as long as it don't get in the way of business. Our agreement was cash on the barrelhead. Gold or silver, none of this paper money or scrip. I like to keep everything straight and aboveboard."

"You're a hard trader."

"It's a hard life."

They began the task of counting out forty head, examining them one at a time. After the officer rejected three for what he perceived to be faults, he had chosen thirty-nine. He said, "We're one short. How about that sorrel in the pen yonder?"

January said, "That's my own horse. Couldn't sell him." He looked about for Todd. "Dogie, go bring that Comanche horse in here."

Todd felt alarm. "But he's mine."

"There ain't nothin' around here yours. I told you when you got him that he would be for sale sooner or later."

Todd protested again, until January raised a hand as if to strike him. "Boy, I said go get that horse!"

Wanting to cry, Todd went into the small pen where he had fed hay to Comanche. He left the gate open and drove the horse out to join the thirty-nine. The officer gave Comanche a long look before nodding with approval. "He'll do just fine."

Todd's voice broke. "But . . . he's my horse."

The officer seemed not to hear him, and January gave him a hard look that threatened retribution. Comanche stood still while Todd put his arms around the animal's neck. Tears were warm on Todd's face.

The officer brought a cloth bag that had been tied to his saddle. "Here's what we agreed upon."

January said, "Let's count it."

"You don't trust me?"

"I trust my own count."

By rights, Todd thought, a little of that money should be his, though it would take a lot more to buy Comanche if he had his way. He watched the two men spread the coins in a feed trough and count them. As the last coin went back into the sack, January nodded in satisfaction. "They're yours," he said. "Where are you goin' with them?"

"Southwest, to Fort Craig. General Canby is organizing a reception there for the Texans, if they ever get that far."

"These horses ain't been fed today, so I'd advise you to let them spread out and graze awhile before you leave the valley."

The lieutenant glanced at the haystacks. "You didn't feed them?"

"They're your horses."

The soldiers pushed them out of the corral and set them off at a trot. January watched, clutching the bag of coins to his chest as if it were a beloved pet. Finally he turned to Todd, his face contorted. "Don't you ever do such as that again. When men are tradin', boys keep their mouths shut."

Todd could not help feeling defiant. "You oughtn't to've sold Comanche."

"I'll sell whatever I damn please. As long as you're eatin' and sleepin' under my roof, all I want to hear from you is, 'Yes, sir.'"

It was not really January's roof, Todd thought. By rights, it was Yolanda and Felipe's. January had simply moved in and taken over. However, pursuing that argument would have been as futile as trying to stop a prairie fire with a leaky bucket and just as likely to get him burned. "Yes, sir," he said.

Yolanda walked out of the house and shouted, "*Comida.*"

Sadness lay heavily on Todd. He had no desire to eat. January started toward the house, then turned to look back. "Ain't you comin'?"

"I don't feel like it."

"That leaves more for me." January went on to the house.

Todd slumped on the edge of the feed trough, his

head down. He felt like weeping but made up his mind not to. He was getting too big for that. He fantasized about ways to impose hurt on January, including having him run over by all forty horses.

He could still see the remuda moving down the valley. The horses had left in a gallop, eager to exercise their legs after a night confined to the corral. Now they slowed and stretched out in a long line, mostly three or four abreast.

Suddenly Todd sat up straight, jolted by an idea. The Indians had stolen these horses. Why couldn't he steal one, too?

He looked toward the house. January was inside, filling his belly at Yolanda's table. Afterward he would probably take a long siesta, a habit he had picked up from the Mexican people. It would be a couple of hours, at least, before he stirred. By then Todd could be a long way from there.

He weighed his chances and saw that the odds did not favor him. Much could go wrong. January might catch up to him before he could retrieve Comanche, or the soldiers might discover him trying to take the horse. He would have no food with him, no blanket, no rifle. These were formidable obstacles, but all he could see was that the soldiers were moving away with his horse, and he had to get him back.

He considered taking one of the horses the officer had turned down but decided they had been rejected for good reason. His gaze moved to January's favorite, in a pen by itself. If he was going to steal one, he might as well steal the best, he thought.

But taking this one meant he could not come back. In the first place, January would sell Comanche again. In the second, the punishment might be more than he was willing to bear.

He lost little time in making up his mind. He had long intended to leave the farm as soon as he felt competent to take care of himself. He had reservations about his ability to do that yet, but this was a crisis situation. If he could take care of the here and now, the future could take care of itself.

Saddling January's sorrel, he realized he should go to the house for dinner first. He was leaving with an empty stomach and no prospects for his next meal. But the thought of losing Comanche overrode other considerations. Yolanda always said God would provide. He regretted leaving without saying goodbye to her. She had been like a mother to him, or at least an aunt, helping to make up for January's exploitation.

He would, however, say goodbye to Felipe, and Felipe would convey his thanks to Yolanda. He rode to where he knew Felipe would be with his flock of sheep.

Felipe's eyes were wide with curiosity. He asked, "You're ridin' January's horse. He'll skin the hide off of you."

"He sold Comanche to the soldiers. I'm goin' to get him back."

"Those soldiers will take you for a Mexican horse thief and shoot you. They always look for an excuse to kill a poor Mexican."

"I don't intend to get caught. Anyway, I'll leave them January's horse. They may never notice the difference."

"Think what January will do when you come back."

"I ain't comin' back."

Felipe looked him over critically. "You got no gun. You got no blanket. I'll bet you got no food either."

"I'll make out." Todd felt his throat tighten. "We've

always talked about leavin' here together someday. How about you goin' with me?"

Felipe's eyes brightened for a moment, but he sobered quickly. "I can't leave my mother. Without me, all she has is January. I will stay here till I am big enough to whip him. I will throw him off of the place. Then my mother can find a better man."

Todd understood. "She's already got a better man." He shoved out his hand. "Tell her I'm sorry to leave this way, without thanks or nothin'. Tell her I'll be back someday when *I'm* big enough to whip January."

"*Adiós*," Felipe said as Todd turned away.

The tracks were plain. Forty horses would not be difficult to follow.

Todd toyed with several ideas. One was to ride boldly up to the Union officer and propose a swap, January's horse for Comanche. After all, the man had offered to accept that horse before Comanche had been considered. But the officer might sense that Todd had taken the sorrel without permission. He would probably arrest Todd as a thief, then wait for January to catch up and retrieve his property.

It was a cinch that January *would* catch up. He set a lot of store in that horse. Though he traded with thieves who stole from others, he had no tolerance for anyone who stole from him.

Todd decided his best chance was to sneak in during the night, make the exchange, and ride on.

By late afternoon he was catching up. A little before sundown, he saw the horses a few hundred yards ahead, moving slowly. The soldiers were letting them graze as they went along. He thought they would probably be herded under guard after dark, but at dusk the troops turned them into an old sheep-and-goat pen. That way the soldiers would not have to herd them, but they would almost certainly post a guard. Outsiders soon learned, if they had not been warned ahead of time, that property not guarded in that part of the country could easily become property lost.

Shortly, Todd saw the flicker of a campfire. The soldiers were cooking their evening mess. He needed no reminder that he had eaten nothing since breakfast. His stomach reproached him with gurgling and cramps. He loosened the girth and tied the horse, then sat on the ground. He watched the fire and felt sorry for himself. He imagined what Yolanda must have set on the table tonight. He even considered slipping into the soldiers' camp and helping himself to some of their rations. But that would be foolhardy. He faced risk enough just in getting his horse back.

Despite his best intentions, he dozed off. He awakened with a start and wondered how long he had slept. January had taught him to tell time by the stars. They told him it was well past midnight. If he was to lay his hands on Comanche, he had best be getting at it. He tightened the cinch, mounted, and started walking toward the corral, hoping to make little noise. To him, the squeak of his saddle sounded as loud as the cry of a hawk protecting its nest. The hoof beats were like a whole remuda on the move. He decided to dismount and lead the horse. Maybe that would make less sound.

He paused, knowing there would be at least one guard. Watching and listening, he determined that one stood outside the corral, halfway around. Before dark he had spotted what passed for a gate, a couple of horizontal poles that could be slid back to make an opening. He headed for it, his nerves tingling.

At night every sound was magnified, the occasional stamping of a hoof, the distant cry of a coyote, two voices in quiet conversation where he had seen the guard. His heart beat like an Indian drum.

He reached the gate and cautiously slid back the top rail. He moved the bottom one just enough to leave a little clearance. He held his breath and listened. He heard nothing. He led the horse into the corral and took off the saddle, blanket, and bridle. In the darkness all the horses appeared to be the same color, black. He feared he would not be able to pick out Comanche. He moved carefully among them, carrying the bridle.

He heard a faint nose-rolling sound, and a horse stepped up to him, nosing his shirt pocket. He had often given Comanche a bite of whatever he had with him. Joyfully Todd whispered, "Good horse." He rubbed Comanche's neck, then put the bit in his mouth and slipped the bridle over the animal's head. He led him toward the gate, where his saddle lay.

He had almost reached it when a harsh voice demanded, "Who goes there?"

Todd froze. He saw the dim figure of a man standing where the bars were slid back. The voice came sharper. "Speak up, or I'll shoot."

Todd's heart was in his throat. He raised his hands and managed to plead, "Don't." He trembled all the way down to his boots.

The voice shouted, "Corporal of the guard!"

Todd could see him now, a soldier with a rifle pointed straight at him. The man said, "Come here, you. Leave that horse." He poked the rifle into Todd's stomach, but not very hard. "You ain't bigger than a pine knot. Come on, I'm showing you to the lieutenant."

The soldier walked Todd out through the opening,

then paused to slide the top bar back into place so none of the horses would stray. "Down yonder," he said, "to the camp."

The campfire had been kept alive through the night, though it had burned down considerably. Todd saw a couple of tents. The soldier called for the lieutenant. A gruff voice answered. Shortly the officer emerged, wearing trousers but no shirt. His underwear reflected the reddish yellow of the campfire's flame. "What is it, Smith?"

"Caught me something, sir. I don't know if it's a Mexican or an Indian or what, but it lacks some being full-grown."

The lieutenant took Todd's arm. "Come on up to the fire where I can get a look at you," he said. "Smith, did you check him for weapons?"

"He ain't got as much as a pocketknife."

Another soldier brought a lantern and held it close enough to Todd's face that he felt the warmth. The lieutenant said, "I believe I've seen you before. Aren't you that boy of January's?"

Todd nodded reluctantly. "He's not my daddy, though. He's no kin at all."

"What are you doing here?"

Todd struggled for the strength to speak. "I come to trade horses. You took mine."

"January said it wasn't yours."

"January don't always tell it straight."

"You say you meant to make a trade?"

"I didn't come to steal. You liked January's horse. I brought it to swap for Comanche."

"I don't suppose you had January's approval?"

"I didn't ask him. He'd've said no."

The lieutenant considered that, then chuckled. "How were you going to explain this to him?"

"I wasn't figurin' on goin' back."

"Aren't you a little young to travel about the country on your own?"

"Some wean quicker than others."

The lieutenant gave him a long study. "I'm inclined to believe you. If we find forty-one horses in that corral at daylight, besides our own, we'll concede that you didn't steal anything. At least from us. January might take a different view."

"Yes, sir. He's liable to come lookin' for his horse. I don't want to be here when he does."

"We'll discuss that in the morning's light, after we've counted the horses. Now, there's still some night left. Smith, get him a blanket. And see that he doesn't decide to forgo our hospitality."

Todd said, "Don't worry. I ain't leavin' without Comanche."

His stomach growled. He considered asking if they had anything he could eat, but he decided that might be stretching his luck. Surely they would let him share their breakfast. He moved near the fire and rolled up in the blanket the soldier had given him. When he opened his eyes, the sun was rising. He smelled bacon frying and coffee boiling.

The officer lifted the pot away from the fire and poured in a cup of water to settle the grounds. He said, "Good. You're awake. We'll have breakfast shortly."

The only thing Todd had taken off was his boots. He pulled them on, then folded the blanket and looked about for the soldier who had lent it to him. The officer said, "Keep the blanket. You're likely to need it. It appears you left home without much preparation."

"I didn't have the time. The notion hit me all of a sudden."

"I am curious about you. How did you happen to fall into the clutches of a man like January if you're not kin to him?"

Todd explained that Indians had killed his family, and that January had bought him from the Indians with the intention of getting a reward. When that failed, he had tried to sell Todd, again without success. "He's been stuck with me, and me with him, ever since."

"I'm sure he's gotten his money's worth out of you." The officer sipped his coffee while giving Todd a thoughtful study. "I wish we could take you along and find you a suitable home, but sooner or later we're likely to have a fight with the Texans. A battleground is no place for a boy."

"I'm bigger than I look."

"In terms of experience, you're already a grown man. But in years, I'm afraid nature can't be rushed. You're still a boy. So eat your breakfast, then we'll go count the horses."

At the corral, Todd pointed out January's sorrel. He said, "That's the one I brought to trade for Comanche. You ain't losin' nothin'."

The lieutenant smiled. "It seems a fair trade to me. Go catch your horse."

Todd retrieved his bridle from where he had left it the night before. He walked among the horses until he came to Comanche. He slipped the bridle over his head and led him out to where the saddle lay.

The lieutenant asked, "Do you have any idea where you're going?"

"I ain't goin' back to January, that's for sure. I'll be lookin' for a job someplace so I can take care of myself. I don't suppose I could join your army?"

"Ask me again in two or three years."

"Maybe I could go to California and dig for gold."

The officer shook his head. "Many have searched, but few have found it. You'd best locate a poor but honest farmer who needs help, who can put a roof over your head and feed you three meals a day."

"January did that, but I can't say much for his honesty."

They walked back to the camp, Todd leading Comanche. He rolled the blanket and tied it behind his saddle. One of the soldiers brought a sack. "Lieutenant said to give you some vittles to take along."

The officer asked, "If January shows up looking for his horse, do you have any message for him?"

"I can't think of a thing." Todd let Comanche pick his direction. He headed southwest.

10

At midmorning Todd was still chilled from sleeping on the ground, wrapped in the single army blanket with his saddle blanket beneath him. He had already found several reasons to regret having left the farm so suddenly and so poorly prepared. He had no coat, no gun, no money. He had only a little of the food the Union officer had given him, barely enough for a lean noon meal. At least he had Comanche.

Santa Fe offered the most likely opportunity for him to find work, and he knew the town. He had been there several times. But to go to Santa Fe carried the risk of encountering January. He considered riding west as far as Albuquerque instead. He had never been there, but he had heard talk about it. From Albuquerque south, down the Rio Grande, lay several villages of varying sizes where someone might have a place for a boy willing to work.

He felt winter's sharp breath on the north wind. He thought of Yolanda and Felipe, envying them a little despite the fact that they were still under January's thumb. At least they were warm and had food in the house. But he was not cold enough or hungry enough to go back.

He was traversing a region he had not seen before. Its cedar- and pine-covered hills and narrow valleys appeared drier than the valley where he had lived the last few years. They were much different from the open plains to the east, where the Comanches still held full control. He was uneasily conscious that this region was subject to periodic raiding by Apaches and Navajos. They had never gone in for trading on a scale to match the Comanches, and they felt no compunctions against hitting the scattered Mexican farm settlements. The American army had done what it could, but much of it was infantry, next to useless in a pursuit. Moreover, now that Texas Confederates had invaded the southern part of the territory, it was likely that the troops would have to concentrate their attention on that threat.

He began to notice a scattering of sheep. His first thought was that if he could find the herder he might get some hot food and warm himself at a campfire. It gradually dawned on him that the sheep seemed to be drifting aimlessly in several directions. A responsible herder would let them disperse only so far, allowing them room to graze but not enough to risk losing them.

What if Indians had killed the herder? he worried. If Navajos, they would probably have taken the animals with them. They had a reputation for appropriating sheep to drive back to their mountain strongholds. He did not know much about Apaches except that the Comanches hated them. The two tribes seemed to enjoy any chance to kill one another. He wanted to shout, but caution prevailed. He looked to the sky for buzzards, then realized most of them had drifted south for the winter. Smart birds, he thought. Maybe he ought to follow them. But going south, he would risk running into the invading Texans. For all he knew, they might be worse than January. Most people around there regarded them as having horns and a forked tail.

He rode around the perimeter of the sheep band until he heard what he first took to be bleating, then decided that it was a human voice. It came clearer as he rode toward it. *"Ayúdame."* Help me.

He found a boy, not much older than himself, lying on the ground, dark face contorted in pain. In Spanish, Todd asked him what the trouble was. The boy pointed to his right leg. Broken, he said. He had been trying to chase a coyote away from the sheep. A rock had shifted under his foot, and he had fallen. Sheep ambled around him now, pausing to browse on brushy plants, oblivious to his plight. Only his dog showed concern. It barked distrustfully at Todd but made no hostile move.

Todd had never treated a broken leg. He started to feel the injured limb, but the boy cried out at the first touch. Todd jerked his hand away. He asked, "Where do you live?"

Gritting his teeth, the boy pointed westward. The house was out of sight behind a hill, he said. He had brought the sheep out for the day's grazing. He was to loose-herd them until time to return them to the safety of their pen at dusk.

Todd said, "I don't know how to treat your leg. But if I can get you up on my horse, I'll take you home."

"Mil gracias."

Todd led Comanche as close as he could, then got behind the boy and tried to helped him arise. The herder cried out in pain. He looked as if he might faint. Todd eased him back to the ground. "You are not able to ride. I'll go to your house and bring help."

The boy spoke softly, almost in a whisper. "My grandfather will know what to do."

"What's your name?" Todd asked in Spanish. He might need to know to convince the grandfather that he spoke the truth. There was always distrust among these people when an Americano spoke. They had heard too many lies.

The youth said, "I am Ricardo. My grandfather is Fernando Garcia."

"My name is Todd. Some call me Dogie."

"Dogie? That has a strange sound. It is gringo?"

"It means an orphan calf or lamb."

"I am orphan, too." Cold sweat broke out on the boy's face and ran down into the collar of his dusty shirt. Shock was setting in. "If the coyote comes back, I cannot protect my grandfather's sheep."

"I'll come back out and pen them for you."

For a moment, Todd entertained a guilty thought: he might get a job herding these sheep. He was immediately ashamed of himself. To benefit by someone else's misfortune was the sort of thing he would expect from January.

The house was a small adobe like dozens of others he had seen, high on a rise overlooking a narrow creek. To fetch a bucket of water meant a fifty-yard trip down and back, but that was better than to risk floodwater surging into the house, melting the adobe walls like a cake of sugar. Beyond the humble dwelling were rickety sheep pens built of tree limbs jammed tightly together, and a long, low shed to protect animals from snow or cold rain. Cactus plants encircled the pen, a deterrent to any hungry coyote tempted to invade the sanctuary. He saw a two-wheel cart beside the house and a mule grazing below the shed. Farther away was a hog pen. A goat with a bell on its neck watched Todd's approach, then turned and ran. The bell's tingling made the mule look up and poke its long ears forward.

The front door opened. A man with gray hair and beard peered out cautiously, as if prepared to slam the door and bar it in a hurry. Todd reined up and said in Spanish, "Hello, Grandfather. I bring bad news. Your grandson is hurt."

The old man moved more quickly than Todd had expected. In an instant he was at Todd's side, asking questions. Todd pointed in the direction from which he had come and explained that the boy's leg was broken. "I could not get him on my horse. We will need that cart to bring him home."

"You stay here," Fernando Garcia said. "I will bring the mule."

The mule acted as if it did not want to come. Todd listened to the old man's brisk language as he persuaded the animal to turn and enter a corral. He heard no words he had not heard from January and the Comanchero traders, but he thought Garcia put them together better than most. In short order the grandfather had the mule in harness and was hitching it to the cart. He hurried into the house and brought out a couple of blankets.

"Take me to Ricardo," he said.

Todd rode ahead, pointing the way. The cart bumped over rough ground. Todd wondered that it did not break apart. It appeared none too sturdy.

The injured boy seemed to have difficulty focusing on his grandfather. The old man sized up the situation in a glance. "Before we move him, we must straighten the leg," he said. He pointed to some dead scrub cedars. "Find for me a couple of straight limbs."

Todd found none that he considered straight, but he brought the best he saw. The grandfather said, "Hold him. This will hurt."

Todd held Ricardo while the old man pulled the leg straight. The boy cried out, then fainted. "It is just as well," the grandfather said. "He will not feel the pain when we place him in the cart." With gnarled hands he used strips of leather to bind the wood to the broken leg. He said, "Help me lift him."

The grandfather had more strength than Todd would have expected in a man whose shoulders were thin and bent. They laid Ricardo on the blankets in the bed of the cart. The old man pointed. "There is a bit of a road yonder."

It hardly qualified as a road. Todd would have regarded it as a wagon trace at best. But it was gentler than the way they had come. Ricardo was conscious again. Todd could tell that he was grinding his teeth to keep from crying.

He helped carry the boy into the house and place him atop a goatskin on a handmade wooden cot. The grandfather said, "I will go for a *curandero*. Will you wait here and watch Ricardo?"

Todd knew about *curanderos,* the healers. In many mountain and valley villages they provided the only medical service the people had, beyond what they could do for themselves.

He asked, "What about the sheep? They will stray."

"Ricardo is worth more than all the sheep. I have little enough left of my family."

"When you come back, I can ride out and bring them to the pen."

The old man gave him a questioning look. "You

know sheep?" The implication was that gringos did not.

"But of course." He had often taken Felipe's place when January needed the older boy for some other chore.

The old man remained unconvinced. "We shall see. If you are hungry, there are tortillas and beans in the kitchen. And roast pig." He unhitched the mule from the cart and rode away on it, bareback.

Todd went immediately to the kitchen. The food was cold, but he ate as if it were a feast. Satisfied, he sat in a chair beside Ricardo's cot and watched the boy go in and out of a fitful sleep.

The grandfather returned with a man riding a burro. The *curandero's* beard was longer and grayer even than Fernando's. His comments indicated that he was going to reset the broken leg. Todd did not care to watch, for in his imagination he could feel the pain. "I will bring in the sheep," he said.

The dog followed him. It was protective of the little flock and growled as if it distrusted Todd's motives. Todd sought out those sheep that had strayed farthest and turned them back, then made a semicircle around the rest, bunching them. The dog began to help, bringing in stragglers. When one stamped its foot and resisted going, the dog rushed in and bit it in the flank. Given the sheep's inherent fear of canines, that was enough.

At January's, Felipe had a dog, but it was too stupid to herd sheep. It was more likely to chase them away than to bring them in.

A belled ewe led the bleating flock to the corral and through the gate. Todd closed the opening, careful not to rub against the cactus that lined the fence. A coyote would have to be hungry to challenge that thorny barrier. The gate was vulnerable, but even it was built solidly enough to make entry difficult for a predator. Todd suspected the dog offered an extra measure of protection.

Fernando Garcia walked out with the aging *curandero* and quietly indicated his approval. "Someone has taught you well," he said to Todd. "I have not seen you before. Where do you come from?"

Todd jerked his head to the northeast.

The old man said, "Too many times I have seen boys like you, far from home. You have run away from your father, no?"

"No, sir. I have no father. I have been living with a man named January. He sold my horse, so I traded his and got mine back."

The *curandero* reacted to the name. "I have heard talk of this Enero, this January. I am told he is not a man to be trusted. Like so many Americanos, he has been known to lie."

Todd agreed. "Yes, sir. Even when he talks in his sleep."

That brought a chuckle from the grandfather. "So now you cannot go home again because you are considered a horse thief."

"That is how January would see it."

Both old men examined Comanche and seemed to approve. The grandfather asked, "How did a boy your age come by such a horse?"

Todd feared they would not believe him, but he told of the trip he had made with January to trade with the Indians, and how he had killed one in self-defense. The expression on the two men's faces indicated that they suspected January had coached him well in the liar's art. But they did not challenge his story.

Fernando asked, "Do you think you are far enough away that the January will not find you?"

"I did not leave much of a trail for him to follow."

"You are welcome to stay with us until Ricardo is able to tend the sheep. But we have no money to pay you."

The chilly north wind cut through Todd's thin shirt and reminded him he had no coat. "I don't have to have money, just enough to eat and a place to sleep where it is warm. And a coat if you have an old one to spare."

"We have one that is too small now for Ricardo. You may have to mend it. Did the January teach you how to do that?"

"No, but Yolanda did. All our clothes have had to be mended."

The *curandero* said, "It is a curious thing to find an Americano boy who speaks the mother tongue as you do."

Todd explained that it had been necessary for him to learn. For most people in the valley, Spanish was the native language. He told how he had been coached by Felipe, Yolanda, and some of the Comancheros. Even January had taught him a little, though his accent was not the same as everyone else's. He was branded as Americano the moment he opened his mouth. Todd could not judge his own accent. As far as he knew, he had none.

The *curandero* said, "The young learn easily."

Fernando said with regret, "But they do not remain young long. How old are you, *hijo*?"

"I cannot say, exactly. Twelve, perhaps thirteen. I do not know how old I was when the Indians killed my real family. That was six years, and a little more."

Fernando said, "I have seen many boys your age

making their own way because their families cannot
feed them, or they have been orphaned. Such is the
case with my grandson. Ricardo's mother and father
died of the fever. My wife and I raised him together
until the smallpox took her. Now there is only myself,
and him."

"That is still a family. It is more than I have."

"We are fortunate. We have this farm that my
father's grandfather received from Spain. We have the
sheep and goats, some chickens, and some pigs. Life
is good."

Not all that good, Todd thought, looking around.
Everything about the place bespoke poverty. But
what was poverty to one person might seem prosper-
ity to another. He had heard it said that to one who is
barefoot, the man who has shoes is rich.

Fernando said, "We have so much more than those
before us. None of this was here when my father's
grandfather came. He had to build it all with his
hands."

Almost everything Todd could see was constructed
of wood, mud, or stone, materials available on the
land. Little had the look of something bought and
paid for.

Fernando said, "There is much to enjoy in small
comforts. When one does not ask for too much, one
is not often disappointed."

After promising to return tomorrow to check on
Ricardo, the *curandero* got on his burro and quirted
its rump with a switch. He took with him two chickens, their legs tied together. People there lived mostly in
a barter economy, trading goods or services for what
they needed. Little cash was exchanged: few citizens
had any.

Watching the departure, Fernando said, "Many Americanos do not believe in the powers of the *curandero*. Do you?"

"I doubt that a gringo doctor in Santa Fe could have done more. At least he didn't dance around and shake a rattle."

"There is much in this world and beyond that we are not meant to understand. We need only to know that there is a kindly God who watches over us."

"How come he lets such bad things happen sometimes?"

"Iron cannot be shaped until it has been through fire. The trials we endure shape us and make us strong."

Todd could not accept that without question. "Not everybody endures. My folks didn't."

"But you have, and you are the stronger because of it. You had to be brave to leave the January. You were secure so long as you stayed with him, but you were not happy."

"I am not happy now."

"You will be, when you find your way."

Todd quickly fell into the daily rhythm of the Garcia farm, which included saying grace before each meal. Yolanda had done that, too, but January had always gone ahead and started eating. He once said, "Why should I give thanks to the Lord? It wasn't him done all the work, it was me." The meals at Fernando's were simple and limited compared to what had come from Yolanda's kitchen, but the atmosphere at the table was peaceful. January had dominated the talk that went on at mealtime, much of it heavy with criticism of Todd, Felipe, Yolanda, or the world in general. Here, the conversation was low-key and pleasant.

Todd had always thought January would be critical of heaven, should St. Peter be so careless as to let him in. The odds against that, however, were formidable.

He took the sheep out each morning to graze and brought them back to the pen by supper. He often had time on his hands during the day. Some passing missionary had once left a Bible at the Garcia home. Because it was in English, neither Fernando nor Ricardo could read it. Todd took it along most days and struggled with it during slack periods when the sheep were staying within bounds and coyotes out of sight. His forefinger laboriously tracing each line, it took him three weeks to work halfway through Genesis. Even after so much hard study, he was not sure he understood it all. He envied youngsters who were able to go to school on a regular basis. He would bet the big words didn't bother them.

Ricardo was soon moving about the little house on crude tree-branch crutches shaped by his grandfather, though there was no thought of his going back out to herd sheep, not for a while yet. Todd didn't wish him bad luck, but he hoped this job as a substitute herder would last at least until spring brought warm weather.

Evenings, the old man often brought out a fiddle he said had been made by his grandfather. The design was crude but the music pleasant to Todd's ears. He had heard little music at January's except Yolanda's humming while she worked.

There were days when snow lay heavily on the ground, and the sheep had to remain in the pen. He forked hay to them and broke ice on the water trough.

He kept a wary watch for coyotes. At this time of year, when small game was scarce, grumbling bellies drove them to take chances they would otherwise avoid. Todd practiced the use of a slingshot until he could hit a coyote at thirty yards or strike close enough to send it running.

One afternoon he saw a coyote sneaking up at the far edge of the grazing flock. The distance was too great for the slingshot. The dog was with him but had not spotted the predator. Todd said, "Coyote!" and pointed. The dog snapped to attention, saw the coyote, and went barreling after it, cutting through the flock, scattering sheep in its wake. The coyote fled, the dog close on its heels.

Watching the chase, Todd became aware of three men walking northward, across country. He shouted, but they went on their way after a brief pause to watch the coyote and the dog. That surprised him. Most people passing through would stop to ask about the way ahead or to take a simple meal at Fernando's table. Fernando enjoyed company, once he saw that they meant no harm.

Dark clouds covered the sun. Todd smelled snow in the crisp afternoon air. The dog returned from its chase, and he sent it around to gather the sheep. As he pushed them into the pen for the night, he saw two men hunkered at the end of the low shed, out of the chill wind. He closed the gate and waited, hesitant to approach them. Fernando had little worth stealing, but some thieves were willing to take whatever there was, no matter how trifling, and administer punishment to the victim for not having more.

The two men wore disheveled uniforms, but they were not American soldiers. Neither had shaved in days. Walking to where Todd waited, one said in

Spanish, "We wish no harm. We have come a long way, and we are hungry. Whose farm is this?"

Todd studied them with suspicion before he answered, "It is Fernando Garcia's."

"A countryman. But you are Americano. Why are you here?"

"I have a job tending his sheep."

The two men looked at each other, doubt in their eyes. "A gringo boy working for a Mexican? That is not the usual way."

"It is a way for me to survive the winter."

"A runaway, then. Or an orphan."

"Both, you could say."

"You could say we are runaways also. We are of the New Mexico militia. We left Fort Craig to save our lives."

Fort Craig. Todd recalled that it lay somewhere to the south. It was where the American officer was taking the horses he'd bought from January. He asked, "What happened at Fort Craig?"

"The Texans came. At Valverde they had a terrible battle with the American soldiers. Many of us in the militia chose to flee. The fight is not ours. It is between the Texans and the Americans. Why should we shed our blood for foreigners?"

"Where are the Texans now?"

"They are coming this way. We believe they intend to take Santa Fe and Albuquerque."

Coming this way. The thought made Todd uneasy. He suggested the two go with him to the house. Fernando would want to know about this.

The old man was sympathetic to the militiamen. "It was right that you left. The fight does not concern you. No matter which side wins, they will continue to oppress us."

One man had not spoken more than to give his name. He busied himself putting away as much roast goat as he could, along with a second helping of beans. The other paused in the middle of his meal to say, "Uncle, it might be wise for you to leave here before the Texans come." *Uncle* was a term often used for older people, related or not.

Fernando was disturbed. "I cannot. I have my sheep and goats, my pigs and chickens."

"The Texans will eat them all anyway. They seem to devour whatever is in their path."

Todd suggested, "The Texans will probably stay on the trails. I could take the sheep and goats up into the hills where they would not be found."

The militiaman frowned. "Can any gringo be trusted? Even a boy?"

Fernando considered. "I have confidence in this one. But it would be dangerous to go up into the hills in a winter so hard. One might freeze in the snow." He looked at Todd. "The coyotes are always hungry at this time of year. You could not fight off all of them. They would eat the sheep. And when they finished them, they might be hungry enough to eat *you.*"

The militiaman warned, "The hills might not be so dangerous as the Texans."

Fernando's voice was firm. "We have had to face danger since the time of my father's grandfather . . . the weather, the Indians, the political thieves in Santa Fe, the American invaders. We have always survived. We will again. Our veins carry the blood of the conquistadores."

Mine don't, Todd thought. He felt cold, just thinking about the Texans.

11

Todd had mixed feelings when Ricardo dropped his crutches in favor of a walking stick. On one hand, he was glad his friend could soon go back to herding sheep, a job Todd was finding more and more monotonous. On the other, he feared that Fernando would decide he was no longer needed. He might be left out on his own again, with winter's end nowhere in sight.

For days, moving with the grazing flock in the narrow valley and up the hillsides, Todd saw small clusters of men working their way northward afoot. Most gave him little notice but passed on by as if hard-pressed, though some stopped briefly at Fernando's house and took advantage of his hospitality, humble though it was. The majority were Spanish-speaking militiamen, fleeing the invaders they feared were not far behind.

A small detachment in American military uniforms stopped to water their horses in the creek. One rode to where Todd was trying to watch the soldiers and the sheep at the same time. He had the stern appearance of an officer. He spoke a poor grade of Spanish, stumbling over words unfamiliar to him as he attempted to piece together a question.

Todd tried to put him at ease. He said, "I can speak English."

Startled at hearing a local speak his own language, the officer took a closer look. "Damned if you ain't American."

"I ain't real sure what I am. Mexicans call me a gringo, and some Americans take me for a Mexican. I don't rightly fit noplace."

"What is an American boy doing in this godforsaken part of the country?"

"Herdin' sheep for Fernando Garcia."

"Working for a Mexican? Your mother and father must not be very proud of you."

"I ain't got any folks. There's just me."

"Even so, you ought to raise your sights higher than this." The officer frowned in disapproval. "Have you seen any Texas soldiers pass this way?"

"I don't know what a Texas soldier looks like. About all I've seen has been militia, headin' north and tryin' not to get caught up with."

"Militia!" The officer's mouth twisted as if he tasted bitter medicine. "Not worth the powder it would take to blow them to hell. Half of them turn tail and run at the first shot."

"They don't see where it's any of their fight. They're Mexican."

"They don't want to acknowledge that they're Americans now."

"Most gringos don't seem to think they are, either."

In Santa Fe, Todd had observed Americans treating the native people as if they carried a communicable disease.

The officer said, "They were more hindrance than help at Valverde. We were glad to see them desert. You'd better watch out that these people don't turn you into a Mexican, too." He frowned again. "You're certain you've seen no Texans?"

Todd resented the man's condescension. "If there's been any passed this way, they didn't come and tell me about it."

"We're probably still ahead of them. We're on our way to join the troops in Santa Fe. Then we'll make those Texans wish they'd never left home."

Todd let sarcasm seep into his voice. "If they whipped you at Valverde, do you think you'll do better someplace else?"

The officer's eyes narrowed. "If you were older, I'd arrest you on suspicion of being a Southern sympathizer." He looked suspiciously toward the adobe house. "What are your boss's sympathies?"

"He's got no sympathy for either side."

The officer turned abruptly to the enlisted men who waited for him. He signaled for them to move out, then warned, "Tell Garza or Gonzales, or whatever his name is, he'd better not give any aid and comfort to the enemy. Otherwise, there'll be a reckoning when this is over."

That's only if your side wins, Todd thought.

He had the good judgment not to say it aloud.

After penning the sheep that evening, he told Fernando the gist of what the officer had said, leaving out the disparaging comments. The old man shrugged and said, "We have suffered from invaders before. Like the smallpox, they stayed awhile, then left. And when they were gone, we were still here. We will always be here."

The Texans' coming was announced early one morning by an excited neighbor, vigorously applying a switch to his resistant burro and shouting as if the devil grabbed at his shirttail. "*Los Tejanos!* They are just behind me."

Standing in his snow-covered yard, Fernando accepted the news with little emotion that Todd could see. He tightened a woolen blanket around his thin shoulders and asked the frightened man, "Are they killing people?"

"I don't know. I did not wait to see."

"Sounds carry far in this valley. I have heard no shots."

"Perhaps they are killing with their sabers. You can still escape if you hurry."

Fernando shook his head. "I am too old to run. My grandson can walk again, but he cannot run. As for this boy Todd, he may run if he chooses."

Todd said, "I wouldn't know where to run to."

The neighbor said, "It is your choice, but if they murder all of you, don't complain to me." He rode on, whipping the overburdened burro into a reluctant trot.

Fernando watched him, then turned back to the house. "Let us eat some breakfast. It will leave that much less for the foreigners to steal."

Todd asked, "What about the sheep? If I take them out, maybe the Texans won't see them."

"There is too much snow. We will have to feed them in the pen."

"The invaders may take all your animals."

"They may eat the chickens and perhaps the pigs. I doubt they will want the sheep. Those move too slowly. And the mule is old."

Todd fretted. "But Comanche's not. I'm going to hide him in the brush."

"Eat your breakfast first. It is not good to be out in the cold with an empty stomach."

The neighbor need not have abused his burro. The Texans did not arrive until late afternoon. Fernando tried not to look worried, but Todd saw it in his eyes. The old man said, "You will have to tell me the meaning of their words."

Walking out into the snow with Fernando and Ricardo, Todd saw a small company, some horsemen, some infantry, trailed by two wagons. Only a couple of the men wore what he recognized as uniforms. Except for a long campaign's wear and tear, most looked like the general run of Americans he had seen on the streets of Santa Fe. They wore whatever suited their fancy or, more likely, their financial ability.

A man in a fraying gray uniform raised his hand as a signal for the others to stop. He said, "I hope there's somebody here who understands English."

Todd said, "I'm the only one that can. Mr. Garcia wants me to do the talkin' for him."

The Texan had the same look of surprise as Todd had seen in the Union officer. He said, "I didn't expect to find a white boy amongst these Mexicans. Where are your folks?"

"Ain't got any. I take care of Mr. Garcia's sheep."

The officer's expression indicated that he did not approve, though he did not give voice to his concern. He said, "Tell Mr. Garcia that we need to buy some provisions."

"Buy?" Todd had expected him simply to take whatever he needed.

"We've had very little meat except what game we could find along the way, and no eggs at all. We'll pay a fair price for some pigs and chickens."

Todd translated for Fernando. The old man seemed as surprised as Todd at the prospect of payment.

The officer said, "We don't have any cash, but we are authorized to issue scrip."

Todd did not know what *scrip* meant. The officer explained, "It is like a promissory note, backed by the full faith and credit of the Confederate government."

That sounded shaky, but Todd recognized that he knew nothing about finance. He explained to Fernando the best he could, then told the officer, "He says that'll suit him all right. Folks around here are used to the army just takin' what it wants."

"The Yankee army, not ours. Tell the old man my company needs to bivouac here for the night. We'll want one of his pens for the horses. The men will sleep under that long shed yonder, out of the snow."

Todd repeated this in Spanish. Fernando was pleased that they did not intend to confiscate everything. He invited the officer into the house, where he could warm himself.

The Texan smiled. "Tell him I'm much obliged. I'll be in after I've seen to the horses, and to my men."

Back inside, Fernando said, "Perhaps they are not devils after all."

Todd fretted. "You know what that American officer said about aiding and abetting the enemy."

"His enemy, not mine. I have no enemies except those who would hurt me. The Tejano at least offered to pay for what he takes."

"You might have to go to Texas to collect anything on that scrip."

"It is better than to be robbed outright."

Todd did not see a clear difference.

He looked out the door a bit later. Three campfires blazed in the dusk as the soldiers began cooking supper. He saw several chickens being plucked and heard the squealing of a pig in the process of being slaughtered. The officer came back into the house and warmed his hands at Fernando's fireplace.

Todd said, "Mr. Garcia invites you to share supper with us."

The officer nodded in Fernando's direction. "Tell him I'm much obliged, but it'd look bad if I ate separate from my men. I wouldn't want them to think I'm puttin' on airs."

The men didn't know how poor a house this was, Todd thought, or how simple a meal it would be.

The officer said, "They elected me lieutenant before we left San Antonio. They could unelect me just as easy."

Todd had assumed that officers were chosen by somebody way up in the government, like the president, perhaps. "You mean they vote on who gets to lead them?"

"That's how we do it in the Texas army."

Todd explained to Fernando. The old man betrayed some doubt. He said, "I served once as a soldier for Mexico. The officers were as far above us as the clouds in the sky. They thought they were appointed by God."

The Texan's name was Orville Sanderson. He said he had been a farmer and cotton broker before the war. Todd had seen cotton, but the word *broker* was new. To him, it seemed to indicate financial difficulty.

He said, "You been in some fights with the Union soldiers?"

"We haven't had to fight much so far. They have given up pretty peart or run away when we've braced them. Our General Sibley is marchin' now on Santa Fe. Things could get a little scrappier there."

"I ain't never heard of him, but there's a lot I ain't heard of."

"He ranked high in the Union army before the war broke out. Now he's a Confederate brigadier general in charge of the New Mexico campaign. Frankly, though, he's a bit too fond of the bottle. I don't suppose a youngster like you would know much about that sort of thing."

"I used to live with a feller named January. He always favored his whiskey, only he never drank much when he was tradin'. He let the other feller have most of the bottle. Made him easier to skin."

"Shrewd man."

Todd didn't know what *shrewd* meant, but he assumed it had something to do with staying sober.

Mention of January aroused Sanderson's curiosity. Warming to this easy-smiling Texas officer, Todd told him what little he could remember about his parents, about the Indian attack, about his ending up with the trader.

Sanderson asked, "This January, is he a Southern man?"

"I've heard him say he came from Missouri."

"Bein' from there, he could lean in either direction."

"I reckon he leans whichever way the wind blows. If you-all win the war, it's apt to blow from the south."

The Texan said, "I suspect from the way you talk that you're a Southern man yourself."

"I don't recollect much about my real pa and ma except they came out of Arkansas."

"That makes you a Southerner. If you were a little older I'd be pleased to recruit you into the service of the Confederacy."

Todd wondered how it would feel to be a soldier. It ought to be better than taking orders from January. It might even be better than herding sheep in the wintertime. "I'm twelve or thirteen. Ain't sure, exactly. How old would I have to be to join your army?"

"I reckon you could be a drummer boy, if we had a drum. Only we don't." Sanderson considered for a minute. "You could be of help, though. I don't have a man who can talk Mexican. You could go along and do the talkin' for us, like you've done here."

The thought stirred Todd's imagination but also aroused some doubts. "I've got a job."

"Not much of one, from what I can see. I bet you're not even gettin' paid. We'd pay you—a little bit."

"A feller could get killed, soldierin'."

"You wouldn't do any fightin'. First sign of trouble, we'd send you back out of the way."

Todd's pulse quickened. He had never given serious thought to being a soldier. Of course he would not be a full-fledged one. He realized he would be more like a mascot, or a civilian employee. Maybe if he liked it he would become a real soldier once he was a little older.

Fernando and Ricardo looked puzzled, not understanding any of the conversation. Todd explained it to them.

Fernando asked, "You would leave us?"

"Now that Ricardo has healed enough to take care of the sheep, I am a burden to you. I would not be a burden to these soldiers. I would earn my keep."

"Sometimes soldiers die."

"He says they would send me away from the fighting."

"Many times I have fought the Indians. Often there is no place to get away."

"Then I'd dig a hole and cover myself up." Todd paused, studying the old man's dark expression, uncertain what it meant. "I will not go if you do not approve."

Sadly Fernando said, "It is not for me to approve or disapprove. In years you are still a boy, but in experience you are old enough to decide for yourself what you will do. This war is not ours, but you are Americano. Perhaps it is yours."

Todd told Sanderson, "I'll go with you."

"It's still a long walk to Santa Fe. Got a horse?"

Todd smiled. "I hid him out. Afraid you'd take him away from me."

"Not without payin' for him. We're honorable people. Mostly."

Up before daylight, Todd walked out through fresh snow to where he had staked Comanche on a long rope within a thick growth of scrub timber out of sight from the trail. Coiling the rope, he said, "We're travelin' again, old friend." The horse snorted, its warm breath condensing in the cold air.

Todd ate a hasty last breakfast at Fernando's table, trying not to dwell on the concern he saw in the old man's eyes. He said, "Maybe I'll get back down this way sometime when the war is over."

Fernando shook his head. "I am an old man. I may not be here. But Ricardo will make you welcome."

Ricardo simply nodded. He had not spoken three

words that morning. Todd thought he saw a tear in the youngster's eye, and he felt a stinging in his own. He said, "Lieutenant Sanderson says the war will be short. He says the Yankees showed at Fort Fillmore and Valverde that they have no stomach for it."

Fernando said, "We did not think they had the stomach for it in 1846, when they took Santa Fe from General Armijo. We were wrong."

The Texans moved together in some semblance of a formation. Todd had seen enough military in Santa Fe to know that these men were not professional soldiers. Tired, their clothing tattered and torn, they showed the debilitating effects of long months on the campaign. They would have been farmers, merchants, laborers of all kinds, enlisted on the promise of adventure and a chance to whip up on some Yankees. Though they must have departed San Antonio with a light step and high spirits, they appeared to have left most of their enthusiasm back along the trail.

Todd, however, felt his pulse quicken at the prospect of watching two armies clash with rifles blazing and cannons belching fire.

"*Adiós,* Fernando," he shouted. "*Adiós,* Ricardo." He beat his heels against Comanche's sides and moved up to join Lieutenant Sanderson, impatient for the adventure to begin.

12

Turning in the wagon seat, Jeffrey looked back at the collapsed bridge, most of it now a pile of wreckage tumbling downstream on turbulent waters the color of chocolate. He felt a tightness in his chest. His nerves were still jangled after the tension of taking the wagon across even as the timbers began to shift under the power of the flood.

He glanced sideways at Sarah. She was still biting her lip, her eyes pinched in the aftermath of fear.

He said, "It's all right now. We were lucky."

Her voice was strained. "It wasn't just luck. I was praying with every turn of the wheels." She looked back at the trailing mare and cow. The cow was pulling hard against the lead rope, trying to break loose. "Old Brindle didn't want to go," she said. "If the wagon hadn't dragged her, she'd still be on the other side of the river."

The mare, too, was frightened, eyes wide and rolling, ears working briskly back and forth. Jeffrey brought the mules to a stop. "Maybe we'd all better see if we can get our breath back." He looked again at the surging stream behind them. Even if he had known how to swim, he would not have been able to fight that powerful current.

Sarah said, "I doubt that Wickham followed us. Even if he did, he wouldn't be man enough to cross until the water goes down." She continued to tremble. "I wonder where Matthew has got to by now . . . if he's at his brother's place yet."

Jeffrey could only guess how much farther it must be to the farm on Bull Creek, where Matthew Temple had said he would wait. He said, "He won't be happy when we tell him that feller Lockwood took his horse. Pity he couldn't have taken that no-account mare instead."

Sarah touched Jeffrey's hand. "He'll be so tickled to see us, he won't bother about a lost horse." She bit her lip again. "I hope he hasn't run into somebody like Wickham or Lockwood along the way. You know Matthew. He'll tell them what he thinks whether they like it or not."

"There's nothin' shy about him."

"I can't wait till we see him and know he's all right."

Matthew has always been able to take care of himself, Jeffrey thought. *After that bridge, I'm not so sure about us.*

The waterlogged road slowed their movement. Mud tugged at the wheels. The mules pulled hard to keep the wagon moving. Jeffrey stopped often to allow them to rest.

Early in the afternoon, while they paused for sake of the animals, Jeffrey saw two horsemen coming up from the south. Except for a farmer and his son, these

were the first people they had met since crossing the
bridge.

"What do you think?" he asked Sarah.

"Coming from the south, they can't know anything about us. If they were coming from the north,
I might worry a bit." But he noticed that she reached
down and touched the rifle beneath the wagon seat.
She seemed reassured by its presence.

The two seemed to be carrying enough equipment
for a long trip. Each had a canvas war bag suspended
from the saddle horn. One's blanket was rolled in a
careless manner and tied behind the cantle, hanging
down farther on one side than the other. The horses'
legs were spattered with mud. The men had a grimy
look and carried several days' growth of whiskers.
One wore a shapeless woolen hat, the other an old
black cap with a frayed bill. Sarah stiffened, watching
them. Jeffrey sensed her fear. It was contagious.

The man with the wool hat removed it and made
a sweeping gesture. He grinned, showing a wide but
uneven row of tobacco-stained teeth. "Howdy, good
lady. What're you doin' out on such a mean and
muddy road?"

"Traveling," she said, biting the word short.

"So it appears." The man's gaze swept over the
wagon. He could not see what was beneath the canvas sheet stretched over the hoops, but his curiosity
was obvious.

Jeffrey asked, "How is the road ahead of us?"

Wool Hat shifted his attention momentarily to Jeffrey, but his companion continued to stare at Sarah.
He said, "About the same as what's behind you. If
you didn't like that, you'll not like what's to come."
He looked back at Sarah. "Your son seems a likely

lad, but you should have a man with you to do the heavy liftin'. Where's your husband?"

"Just behind us," Sarah said. "He stayed back to help pull my brother's wagon out of a mud hole. They'll all be along pretty quick."

Jeffrey remembered Fletcher's telling Sarah that lying for a worthy cause was no sin. She was getting good at it.

The man made as much of a bow as he could without leaving the saddle. "Then we'll bid a good day to you, lady, and wish you a better road ahead. Come along, Simon."

Sarah did not look away from them until they had gone a hundred yards up the road. "We'd best be moving," she said. "They'll know I lied when they don't find anybody coming along behind us."

"You think they mean us harm?"

"They were looking us over like a coyote looks at a rabbit. They may think we're carrying valuables in this wagon."

"We're not, are we?"

"I hid most of our money in the bottom of the flour barrel."

Jeffrey shouted at the mules and put them into reluctant motion. They traveled a couple of more miles, struggling with every step. Jeffrey was glad when Sarah said, "They're about given out. It's early, but we'd just as well stop and make camp."

"Yes, ma'am." He looked back. "I don't see any sign of those fellers. Maybe we were worried over nothin'."

"Maybe." She pointed to a small depression in the ground where rainwater had collected. "I hope that's not too muddy for the mules. After they've watered, you'd better feed them. They've earned it."

The mules smelled the water, refusing at first to

drink it. Thirst won out after a minute or two. Afterward, Jeffrey poured oats into two canvas morrals and slipped the straps over the mules' heads so they could eat. Sarah started a fire with dry wood from the cowhide beneath the wagon bed. Jeffrey was leading the mare out to stake her on grass when she jerked her head up and pointed her ears toward the back trail. He missed a breath.

The two scruffy men they had met earlier were almost upon them. Sensing that they were up to no good, Jeffrey shouted a warning to Sarah and made a run for the rifle. The man in the woolen hat spurred his horse and beat Jeffrey to the wagon. He jerked the rifle free as Jeffrey reached for it.

"Now, sonny," he said, "a boy your age ought not to mess around with guns. They can get you bad hurt." Lifting his foot from the stirrup, he gave Jeffrey a hard shove, slamming his head against the wagon wheel. Jeffrey swayed, stunned.

Sarah rushed to place herself in front of Jeffrey. "You've got no cause to hurt him," she cried. "Take whatever you've come for and leave us alone."

The man in the cap gave her a wink. "I reckon we'll do both, in our own good time."

Wool Hat said, "It ain't ladylike to lie like you done. Me and Simon rode a ways and didn't see nobody. Looks to me like you ain't got no husband."

Sarah said, "If there's anything in the wagon you want, take it. Then go. We won't try to stop you."

"Oh, I imagine we'll be takin' some things along. Some groceries, money if you've got any, and them mules. They ought to fetch us a few dollars, next town we come to."

Sarah's voice began to break. "You can't take our mules. We'd be stranded here."

Wool Hat said, "Simon, get up in that wagon and see what you can find." The grimy partner climbed up under the canvas. He said, "Ain't much we can use. Found a bag of coffee. And here's a purse. Bet it's got money in it."

"Fetch it, then. And throw out a blanket."

Simon climbed down. Wool Hat reached into the purse and found a few silver coins. Frowning, he said, "That ain't much for folks that're travelin'. You sure you ain't got some more hidden in there?"

Sarah's voice quavered. "That's all there is. Now leave us alone."

"We ain't quite done. Simon, spread out that blanket." He grabbed Sarah's wrist and pulled her up against him. Bending her backward, he tried to force a kiss on her. Sarah screamed, beating at him with her fists.

Shouting, Jeffrey sprang to help her. From the corner of his eye he saw Simon swing a pistol. The barrel struck him across the side of his head. He fell against the wagon wheel again, a riot of color flashing before his eyes. He slid down the wheel until his face was in the mud.

He heard Wool Hat say, "Simon, you better tie that boy's hands to the spokes." Jeffrey felt his wrists being bound, though he could not clearly see the man doing it. He heard Sarah struggling, crying, the men laughing. He tried to pull himself up, but he fell back, his face in the mud again.

The men's laughter was soon mixed with curses and grunts. Cries of anguish came from Sarah. Eventually her crying dropped to a whimper.

Wool Hat finally said, "Come on, Simon, let's go grab them mules."

Simon replied, "You sure we ought to take them? They'll slow us down."

Wool Hat argued, "Them mules are money. Get that mare, too."

The sound of hooves told Jeffrey that the two men were traveling westward, taking the mules. He struggled to raise his head. All he could see was blurred and discolored, swinging back and forth like a pendulum. Nausea made him want to throw up, but he could not. As his vision began to stabilize, he saw Sarah lying on the crumpled blanket, weeping. He wanted to call out to her, but he could not find his voice. All that came from him was a weak cry.

Sarah heard and raised up. Her dress was torn away from her shoulders, her hair disheveled. Her cheek was bruised and turning blue. Pulling her skirt down to cover her bared legs, she struggled to rise. She stumbled toward Jeffrey and dropped to her knees in front of him. Gently she took his chin between two fingers and turned his head so she could see where he had been struck.

She said, "They could've killed you."

He demanded, "What did they do to you?"

"Don't ask me. Don't ever ask me." Trembling, she untied his hands. She said, "I'm sorry you saw it."

"I didn't," he said. "I couldn't see."

"That's something to be thankful for." Tears shone in her eyes. "Stay where you are. I'll wash the mud from your face and see what I can do about that wound." She climbed into the wagon and returned with cloth and a wash pan. She dipped water from a wooden barrel strapped to the side of the wagon and cleansed the area where the pistol had struck. "It's stopped bleeding now."

Jeffrey said, "You better take care of your own self. That bruise is gettin' dark, and it's bled some, too."

He had not been able to see, but he had heard enough. He burned with guilt that he had not been able to stop them, any more than he had been able to stop the Indians from overrunning his parents' camp. Anger rising higher, he declared, "I wish I could kill them both."

She shuddered. "It wouldn't change what's already done."

Jeffrey managed to get to his feet. He held on to the wheel to steady himself as a wave of dizziness passed over him. He walked slowly around the wagon, holding on to it while trying to control his legs. "At least they didn't take the cow," he said.

He paused where the blanket lay twisted on the ground. He tried awkwardly to fold it.

Sarah's voice was sharp. "Don't put it in the wagon."

"What do you want me to do with it?"

"Take it to the fire and burn it."

"It's a good blanket."

"Burn it!"

He had to stoke the fire and put more wood on it. The woolen blanket smoked and gave off a pungent odor as it slowly yielded to the flames.

Sarah climbed into the wagon. When she reappeared, she was wearing a different dress, an old one drab and gray. She handed Jeffrey the torn one she had removed. "Burn this, too."

It seemed a shame, he thought. She had few dresses to begin with.

Presently he caught a movement to the south. "Somebody else comin'," he said. He forced his legs into a painful trot toward the wagon.

Sarah said, "No use looking for the rifle. They took it."

They moved together apprehensively. She placed her arm around his shoulder while they waited.

As three horsemen neared, Jeffrey saw the shine of a badge. The wearer was middle-aged and blocky, with a heavy, graying mustache. His manner was all business. "Good day, ma'am," he said, touching fingers to the brim of his hat. "I'm Sheriff Honeycutt. We're on the trail of two robbers. Seen anybody pass this way?"

Her lips tightened. She tried but could not speak.

Jeffrey said, "We sure did. They hurt Sarah. Then they stole our mules and left us stranded here."

"How long ago?"

Jeffrey was unsure about the time. He had been groggy through some of it. "Maybe an hour."

The sheriff dismounted and moved up for a close look at Sarah. Without her telling him, he seemed to recognize what had happened. His face darkened with fury. "A man who'd do this to a woman . . . he ain't no man. He don't count even for a cur dog." He glanced at a tall, sandy-haired man still on horseback. "Claypool, you stay here and see what you can do for these folks. Me and Ferris will go on till we catch those sons of bitches. I hope they'll decide to put up a fight."

Jeffrey told him the two had gone west.

The sheriff said, "Tryin' to hold on to the mules, they'll be easier to catch up with." He took his seat in the saddle and looked again at Sarah. "I'm sorry we came too late to prevent this. I promise you, though, somebody is fixin' to bleed for it."

He and the other man rode westward in a stiff trot.

They would have no difficulty following the muddy tracks.

Sarah turned her back and leaned against the wagon. Jeffrey burned with a wish that he could somehow ease her misery, but he knew nothing to do. Claypool beckoned him with a gesture. "Come on, boy, leave her be for a while."

They moved away from the wagon as Sarah walked around to the other side and seated herself on a three-legged milking stool. Claypool said, "Right now I doubt that she wants to talk to anybody, or see anybody. Best thing is to give her time and room to sort things out for herself. Let's see if we can't boil us some coffee."

Taking the coffeepot, Jeffrey fetched water from the keg. It was near where Sarah sat, but she did not raise her head to look at him. She covered her eyes with one hand.

Stirring the fire, the deputy said, "There's always been thieves and renegades, but it seems like there's more of them nowadays. They've been crawlin' out from under the rocks since the war started. Chances are these two didn't want to go into the army. They decided to light out, grabbin' whatever they could get along the way. It was this lady's bad luck to come along at the wrong time." He grimaced. "It'll be their bad luck when Sheriff Honeycutt catches up with them. At heart he's a good man, but with that sort he'd rather go to a funeral than a trial."

Jeffrey said, "The sheriff told us you-all were trailin' those men. What else have they done?"

"Robbed a farmer way down at the far end of the county. Pistol-whipped him might near to death. They tried to grab hold of his daughter, but she got her hands on a gun and scared them off. They didn't figure we'd find out about it so quick. Else they'd be in a bigger hurry." He examined the wound on Jeffrey's head. "I don't like the looks of that. It's a wonder the brains ain't oozed out."

Jeffrey's head still pounded as if cannons were going off inside.

Claypool asked, "How old are you, boy?"

"Fourteen."

"Then you're old enough to know about things like this."

"I know about them. I don't understand them, though."

They passed the rest of the afternoon mostly in silence. Sarah did not come back from the other side of the wagon. Claypool built up the fire and brewed another pot of coffee. Jeffrey drank it black. It seemed to give him strength.

He said, "I ought to've been able to do somethin'."

Claypool replied, "I expect you gave it the best try that you had in you. Don't fret yourself over what you couldn't help."

"But this ain't the first time when I couldn't do anything to help."

"You're expectin' too much for a boy of your age."

"I'm goin' on fifteen. That ought to be old enough to do better than I've done so far."

"Don't get in a hurry. You'll be an old man soon enough."

Jeffrey heard the horses before he saw them. Three men came from the west, driving two mules and the mare ahead of them. Claypool stood up, looking relieved. "It's the sheriff and Ferris. Looks like they've got a prisoner."

"Just one?" Jeffrey asked.

"Ferris is leadin' a horse. Appears there's a man tied across the saddle." Claypool walked out to meet the oncoming riders. "Howdy, Sheriff. I see you got your men."

Jeffrey recognized one of the three riders as Wool Hat. The man's face was streaked with blood, his head bare, his shoulders slumped in defeat. The other robber was tied facedown across his saddle. Jeffrey saw a dark stain on the saddle skirts.

Sarah came around the wagon and waited while the sheriff and his deputy dismounted. The prisoner remained in the saddle until the sheriff reached up and grabbed a handful of his shirt. "Come down from there."

Wool Hat appeared on the verge of collapse, his legs wobbling. His hands were tied in front of him. The sheriff gripped his arm and roughly pushed him toward Sarah. The prisoner kept his head down.

Honeycutt ordered, "Raise up."

Wool Hat did not comply. The sheriff gave him a hard shake. "I said lift your head up. Look this lady in the eye."

Reluctantly Wool Hat raised his chin. His face was bruised. Blood had caked on his cheeks and jaw.

The sheriff asked, "Is this one of the men?"

Sarah stared, not replying. Then, hatred boiling in her eyes, she raised her arm and slapped Wool Hat with all her strength. His head snapped back. She doubled a fist and flattened his nose for good measure. It bled. Tears welled in his eyes.

The sheriff seemed pleased. "The other one took a shot at us. He never got a chance to try a second one. This snivelin' coward fell on his knees and begged us not to shoot him."

Sarah turned away from Wool Hat, trembling.

The sheriff said, "What he did to you is a hangin' offense. But you'll have to stay around and testify to the court."

Sarah gasped. "Tell it all, in front of a crowd? I couldn't."

"If you don't, the worst he'll likely get is some prison time, and then he'll be on the loose again."

Sarah swallowed. "Haven't I been shamed enough already? I just couldn't."

Disappointed, the sheriff said, "I can understand how you feel. But there's another way to put an end to it." He lifted his pistol from its holster and held it out for her. "You can use this. We'll all take an oath that he was shot resistin' arrest."

Wool Hat's eyes bulged in terror. He cringed and tried to turn away.

Sarah took the pistol in both hands and aimed it at Wool Hat. He raised a plaintive cry for mercy. Her hands shook as she tried to pull the trigger. She gave the pistol back to the sheriff and said, "I wish I could, but I can't."

Honeycutt shrugged. "Then we'd best be gettin' to town before it's plumb dark. Claypool, you stay and help the folks break camp. We'll go on ahead."

Claypool harnessed the mules while Jeffrey tied the mare and the cow on their lead ropes behind the wagon. Sarah took her place on the wagon seat, her jaw set like granite. Jeffrey put the mules into motion. Claypool rode alongside. He asked, "Are you all right, ma'am?"

"No," she said. "I wish now that I'd pulled the trigger."

They had gone half a mile southward when Jeffrey heard a gunshot from somewhere ahead, followed in a moment by another.

An ironic smile crossed Claypool's face. "Sounds like the prisoner tried to escape."

The outlaws' end had probably been preordained the moment Sheriff Honeycutt took their trail, Jeffrey thought. He glanced at Sarah. She looked straight ahead. Her face betrayed no emotion, but her thin shoulders quivered. She said, "It should have been me who shot him. Next time I will."

Jeffrey said, "He ain't got any next time."

"There may be another like him. Or worse."

13

The sheriff and Deputy Ferris waited at the edge of town. In the dusk, Jeffrey saw two men tied across saddles of the led horses. Sarah glanced at the dead men, then turned her head away. Jeffrey gave them a longer study, feeling he should be gratified. Instead, his stomach threatened to turn over.

Claypool said, "Justice can be rough, but there's times the situation calls for it."

Jeffrey was not impressed by the town. He saw a modest stone courthouse, three saloons, one church, a couple of stores, and a few other small business buildings. Two or three dozen plain frame houses were scattered about.

The sheriff pointed. "You can camp your wagon over at the barn yonder. There's pens and feed for the stock. Sorry, but nobody's seen fit to build a hotel."

Sarah asked, "Is there a place where I can get a bath? I feel so dirty."

Honeycutt nodded. "I'll take you over to my house. The missus'll heat up some water for you. We've got an empty room with a bed in it. You'd be mighty welcome to stay." To Jeffrey he said, "We don't have a bed for you, but you can roll out your blankets on the parlor floor."

Claypool offered, "I've got an extra cot in my shack. The floor can get awful hard in the wee hours of the mornin'."

"I'm obliged," Jeffrey said.

Sarah said, "Sheriff . . ." She hesitated, anxiety in her eyes. "Do you have to tell Mrs. Honeycutt everything?"

"There's no reason to. Ferris and Claypool know how to keep their mouths shut. We won't even need to bring you into this. After all, we were huntin' those tramps for that other robbery. All anybody needs to know is that they've gone where no slick lawyer can sweet-talk a jury into settin' them loose."

Jeffrey found it difficult to reconcile the sheriff's compassion for Sarah with the remorseless killing of the two fugitives. He knew he was a long way from understanding the contradictions of the world. Maybe when he got a little older . . .

Claypool had described his home properly when he called it a shack. He said, "There's hardly room enough to cuss a cat, but I don't get to spend much time in it anyhow." He lighted a lamp. "First thing, let me take a look at where you got hit on the head."

Jeffrey had been unable to wear his hat since Sarah had wrapped a bandage around his wound. Claypool unwrapped the cloth and whistled under his breath. "I've seen hills that wasn't much bigger than the knot on your head. How does it feel?"

"Like there's a war goin' on inside. I saw double for a while, but there's just one of you now."

Claypool said, "I know a man who got kicked in

the head by a mule. He ain't been quite right since. You'll bear watchin' for a while." He rewrapped Jeffrey's head with the same cloth he had removed. "We don't have a real doctor in town, but I could fetch a feller that's pretty good with horses."

"Thanks, but I suspect we'll move on come mornin'." It was likely that Sarah would want to leave this place behind as quickly as she could. Putting the dark memories behind her would be more difficult.

Claypool built a fire in a small cast-iron stove and set about frying bacon. "I've got cold biscuits in the cabinet yonder, left from breakfast," he said.

Jeffrey ate a little, but he had no appetite. The images of the day haunted him, including the sight of the two robbers tied dead across their saddles like deer brought down for camp meat. He asked, "Don't it turn your stomach, seein' people die that way?"

"With renegades like those two, it don't bother me any more than the killin' of a mad dog. They ain't worth one tear in a good woman's eyes."

"They put tears in Sarah's eyes."

"Save your sympathy for her. The outlaws've got none comin'."

Jeffrey frowned. "I don't know if I could ever be a lawman and have to witness things like what happened today."

"You don't know what you could do if you were provoked enough. Me, I was just a button when a feller shot my daddy in the middle of a cornfield just to steal his mule. But I taken our old shotgun and followed him to where he thought he was safe. I wasn't but eleven years old, but I got that mule back."

"What about the man?"

"Not even his mother came to the funeral." Claypool

poured himself a second cup of coffee. "When circumstances force your hand, you can do things you never thought you could."

Claypool was rattling around before daylight, but that did not bother Jeffrey. He had slept little anyway. Claypool baked a fresh pan of biscuits and fried more bacon for breakfast. He said, "Can't set you out on the road with an empty stomach. You'd better eat more than you did last night."

"I'm obliged for the cot, and for the vittles."

"You're welcome. I hope the rest of your road is smoother than what it's been so far."

"We've still got a ways to go."

He pulled the wagon up in front of the sheriff's house and found Sarah waiting. She stepped out onto the porch, the sheriff and his wife just behind her. Mrs. Honeycutt followed Sarah to the wagon. She said, "If you ever come this way again, you'll find the door wide open to you."

Jeffrey leaned down and extended his hand, helping Sarah up onto the wagon seat. She thanked the Honeycutts for their hospitality and said with urgency in her voice, "Let's be going."

As they moved down the street, she looked back once. In a strained voice she said, "She knows. Nobody told her, but she knows."

Jeffrey was at a loss to reply.

Sarah said, "I guess it shows, somehow. Maybe it'll pass before we reach Matthew. Please, Jeffrey, don't tell him about this."

"I won't."

"Can't these mules move any faster?"

"The road's still muddy."

Sarah hunched in the seat, her head down. She said nothing more the rest of the morning. About noon they came within sight of a village. She said urgently, "Can we go around? I don't want strangers looking at me."

"The trail goes right through. We're liable to get stuck if we get off of it."

"Very well, but I'm going back under the wagon sheet till we're on the other side."

Jeffrey had never seen Sarah act this way, as if frightened by the thought of meeting people. It troubled him. He said, "We're liable to go through some more towns before we get to where Matthew is."

"You don't understand," she said. "You couldn't."

He thought it might seem odd to bystanders, a boy his age passing through by himself in a covered wagon with a milk cow and a mare tied on behind. He received a few passing glances from people on the street, but nobody stopped him to ask questions. It dawned on him that nobody really cared much. Most people were too involved in working out their own problems to take more than passing interest in others'.

He said, "It's all right now. We've put the town behind us."

Sarah climbed out from under the wagon sheet and took a worried look back. "Did you see anyone who looked suspicious?"

"They were just everyday folks, mindin' their own business and leavin' us to ours."

They pulled off the trail at noon to rest the animals. Jeffrey said, "I'll build a fire and make you some coffee. Maybe you'll feel better."

She said, "I doubt it, but go ahead."

Jeffrey searched the wagon, then remembered. "Those thieves took our coffee yesterday, and we never got it back. Looks like we'll have to stop in the next town we come to and buy some."

"No," she said quickly. "We can do without."

In the aftermath of yesterday's ordeal, he could appreciate Sarah's fear that other renegades might lie in wait. He could not quite understand her sense of shame, however. Nothing had been her fault. She had fought that grubby pair with all the strength she had. By now they had had dirt shoveled in their faces and could never hurt anyone again. But he realized the hurt they had already done might be painfully slow to heal.

Mrs. Honeycutt had given Sarah a sack containing freshly baked bread, smoked ham, and cookies. Sarah tried but could eat very little. Jeffrey's appetite had returned with vigor.

He thought he heard voices. He moved next to the wagon, where he could quickly reach the rifle. In a minute he saw a ragged column of men walking in single file, headed by a man in a gray uniform riding a black horse. Sarah started to climb up into the wagon.

Jeffrey said, "Looks like soldiers to me, probably marchin' off to the war. They ain't goin' to hurt us."

"Just the same," she said, "I don't want a bunch of men looking at me."

The officer saw the wagon and loped ahead of his troops. He gave Jeffrey a looking over and asked, "What are you doing on the trail all by yourself, young fellow?"

Jeffrey did not want him to look in the wagon and upset Sarah. It seemed a good time for a harmless lie. "My pa is out huntin' for meat."

"Are you out of provisions?"

"No, sir, except for coffee."

"I think we can spare you a little. The supply wagon is just behind us."

Jeffrey counted thirty men afoot. None wore a uniform like that of the man on horseback. They carried a mismatched assortment of weapons from long rifles to shotguns, muzzle-loading pistols, and frog-sticker hunting knives. All gave him a once-over as they passed by. He said to the officer, "I suppose you-all are on your way to the fightin'."

The officer nodded. "We've just organized this little company. We only hope we won't be too late. We fear the Union army may surrender before we reach the field of battle."

"It might be best if they did."

"And deny us a chance to test our steel? No, sir, there is no thrill to compare with charging headlong into the enemy, braving the fire and smoke of the battleground, proving to ourselves that we are men."

The well-framed words had a stirring ring. Jeffrey suspected the officer had memorized them to recruit soldiers for the company. But proving one's manhood could get a person killed.

The supply wagon stopped, and the officer handed Jeffrey a small bag of coffee beans. He said, "You had best treat these as a Sunday luxury. The war is likely to make them scarce soon, along with much else."

"My pa will be obliged."

The officer added, "It's a pity you are so young. It's unlikely you will get a chance to fight, because we're going to make short work of this war."

Probably the same thing they're saying up north, Jeffrey thought.

The supply wagon moved on, and the officer galloped ahead to take the lead as the column disappeared over the hill.

Sarah came out of the wagon. She said, "They don't realize what they are getting themselves into. But Matthew knew. That's why he left."

Perhaps if Matthew had not left, or if he had been with them yesterday, Sarah would not have had to endure her ordeal. Or, if Fletcher had remained with them, the robbers would have passed them by. Jeffrey permitted himself a moment of resentment against both Matthew and Fletcher before acknowledging that Matthew had seen no acceptable alternative to flight. Otherwise, by now he would have been forcibly recruited into the army and marched off to war like the little company that had just passed by. Or a mob of zealots headed by Nash Wickham would have hanged him. As for Fletcher, he had answered the call of duty as he had seen it.

The real blame lay with Wickham, Jeffrey thought. Or perhaps it went further, to the hard-headed leaders on both sides who refused to seek a middle ground and demanded their own way without compromise, ignoring the probable consequences. He realized he was not yet mature enough to think on the leaders' level. He could judge only by what he could see. He had seen enough to know how much misery people could mindlessly inflict upon one another.

He said, "At least now we've got coffee."

But Sarah did not want any.

They passed out of the open, rolling country with many of its valley bottomlands already taken up by farms. They moved into a more broken region of rough hills, caliche outcrops, and cedar thickets numerous enough that the wagon trail had to wind in, out, and around them. Even here, Jeffrey saw that diligent farmers had cultivated small fields wherever they found soil deep enough between the rock-strewn

hills. They were eking out a living against strong odds
in a stubbornly resistant land.

The water keg was low. While Sarah hid herself
beneath the wagon sheet, Jeffrey hailed a passing
horseman to ask how far it might be to a creek. The
man spoke a language Jeffrey could not understand.
His efforts at communicating yielded only confusion.
After the man rode on, Sarah said, "Many German
settlers have come into this part of the country. A lot
of them haven't learned English."

"With different languages, how do people get
along with one another?"

"There is one thing they understand in every language. Buying or selling, they all count their money
the same way."

The trail took a tangent to the west. That puzzled
Jeffrey at first, until it led him to a spring bubbling
from a broken outcrop of granite. He saw a tent and
found two men camped there, studying him with suspicion. They had not seen Sarah. She kept out of sight
when they met anyone.

"Howdy," Jeffrey said, a little uneasy. Both men
carried firearms, one a rifle, the other a shotgun. He
asked, "You-all talk English?"

A lanky young man with a dark black beard did
not accept the question in good grace. "Do we look
like Dutchmen to you?"

"I don't know what a Dutchman looks like."

"Not like us, for damn sure. The country's overrun
with them. Are you sure you ain't one yourself?"

"I don't guess so. I'm from North Texas."

"As far as I know, they've spread everywhere . . .
Austin, San Antonio, and most of the settlements in
these hills. We ought to run them back to where they

come from before they ruin this country with their foreign notions. Majority of them voted against secession."

"I don't have any foreign notions. I just wanted to ask if I can water the stock here, and fill up our water keg."

"*Our* water keg? I don't see anybody but you. Is somebody hidin' in that wagon?" The man started in Jeffrey's direction, raising a shotgun.

Sarah appeared behind the wagon seat, pointing the rifle. The man began backing up. "Now look, lady, I didn't mean nothin'. I didn't know but what there might be a robber hidin' in there. You-all help yourselves to all the water you want. Me and Jess will even fill the barrel for you."

"There's no need for that. Just remember that we keep our eyes open, too."

Jeffrey filled the keg first, then led the mules to a narrow stream that flowed from the spring. Once they were satisfied, he watered the mare and the cow.

The two men stood back, watching. They had laid their weapons down. One said to Jeffrey, "You folks act mighty touchy. Can the lady really use that rifle?"

Jeffrey said, "I've seen her notch a squirrel's right ear without touchin' the left one." It was a lie, but this trip had been an education to him.

The man appeared to accept the statement at face value. "You've got nothin' to fear from us, but you'll want to stay watchful. There's people runnin' away from the war, takin' whatever they can lay their hands on along the way. These are dangerous times. Especially for a lady travelin' with nobody to protect her but a half-grown boy."

"I'm grown enough." Despite his bluster, Jeffrey knew better, for he had already failed Sarah once.

As they pulled away from the spring, Sarah looked back with apprehension. "Do you suppose they might follow us?"

Jeffrey was inclined to believe the pair harbored no bad intentions. "Not everybody is like those two we met the other day."

She admitted, "I had my hand on the trigger. I was ready to shoot if he came much closer to the wagon."

That thought disturbed Jeffrey. "You might've killed an innocent man."

"I'm beginning to wonder how innocent *any* man is when he faces temptation enough and doesn't think he'll suffer any consequences."

Sarah was torn when they came to a fork in the road. She said, "Matthew brought me here once to visit his brother. I know we're close, but I don't know which of these roads we should take. They both look alike."

Jeffrey said, "The mules need a rest. Why don't we wait here till somebody comes along that can tell us?"

Sarah seemed uncomfortable with the idea. Jeffrey said, "We've run into quite a few people since we started this trip. Except for two, nobody's tried to do us any harm."

Sarah said, "The next one may be different."

Though nervous, she managed to stay on the wagon seat while a rider approached on the left-hand fork. She held the rifle on her lap. The horseman gave the weapon a long look before he asked, "You folks need any help?"

Sarah said, "We're not sure which way to go from here. We're on our way to John Temple's place."

He gave her a long, suspicious study. "I'm not sure

I can be of any help to you. What do you want to go there for?"

"John Temple is my brother-in-law."

He asked her name, and she told him. He said, "Maybe you don't know it, but there's been a little trouble around here. Some unfriendly people have been lookin' for John Temple's place lately."

"Why?"

"Because he's got pro-Union notions. A lot of folks here do, but not everybody goes around preachin' their ideas out loud the way he does."

Sounds like Matthew, Jeffrey thought.

The rider added, "He's spent a lot of his nights sleepin' out in the cedarbrakes, where he ain't easily found. Now, if you're really his sister-in-law, tell me what his wife's name is."

"Auralee. She was a Benton before she married."

The man eased. "I reckon you're who you say you are. I just didn't want to send John any extra trouble. For all I knew, you could be markin' the way for some unpleasant people." He pointed to the left-hand road, over which he had just come. "About five miles down thataway you'll come to an old wagon wheel layin' on the left-hand side of the road. About twenty or thirty yards past that, keep your eyes peeled for a dim trail leadin' off east. It ain't easy to see, which has been a good thing lately. Don't be scared when you're met by a bunch of loud hound dogs. They keep anybody from slippin' up on John."

"I suppose you're for the Union, too."

"No, ma'am, I voted for secession. But John's an old friend of mine. I want him to still be alive when this war is over with."

Moving on, Jeffrey said, "See what I told you? There's still lots of good people."

Sarah did not reply.

Jeffrey might have missed the trail that turned off had he not been told where to watch for it. He heard the dogs before he saw the farm. Half a dozen came at a run, ears flopping, each trying to bay the loudest. They circled the wagon, exciting the mules and the mare. The cow tried to hook at them, but the lead rope caught her up short.

"What a racket," Sarah said.

Jeffrey nodded. "Nobody's apt to sneak in."

The dogs escorted them all the way, like an jubilant reception committee. A black man stood in the front yard, waiting for the wagon. He appeared to be six feet tall, and as broad as an ox yoke across the shoulders. "You dogs," he commanded, "git!" They scattered obediently, a couple going under the porch, others to the barn. One, however, remained at the big man's side, looking up at him expectantly as if awaiting further orders.

The man's guarded expression betrayed nothing of his thoughts or attitude. Jeffrey assumed he was a slave. He said, "We're lookin' for the John Temple place. Is this it?"

The man did not answer directly. He said, "You-all got business with Mister John?"

Sarah spoke. "I'm Sarah Temple, John's sister-in-law."

The black man made a tentative smile. "Then you're the one they been lookin' for, I expect. Let me go call Miz Auralee." He stepped up onto the porch and knocked on the door. The dog followed closely.

The frame house was modest, overdue for fresh paint but fronted by wide and colorful flower beds. In its simplicity it resembled the house that belonged to Matthew and Sarah. Beyond it, past the barn and a set of livestock pens, stretched a field of corn and cotton. The corn was tall enough to hide a man. Jeffrey suspected it probably served that purpose from time to time.

A woman came to the door. "What is it, Boley?" The black man said something in a low voice. She stepped out onto the porch and cried, "Sarah! Get down and come in this house." She hurried out to the wagon. She was shorter and heavier than Sarah, gray streaking the hair gathered by a ribbon at the back of her head and hanging down almost to her waist. She had a smile that seemed a yard wide.

"We've been waiting and watching for you," she declared. She looked at Jeffrey. "I suppose this is the boy Matthew told us about?"

"I'm Jeffrey," he said.

Auralee and Sarah hugged each other. Auralee asked, "Did you have any trouble on the road?"

Sarah held her answer for a moment. "Nothing to talk about." Her voice became anxious. "Is Matthew here?"

Auralee's smile faded. "He was, but he's gone. Him and John both."

Sarah was visibly distressed. "Gone? But we've come so far . . ."

"I'll tell you about it in the house." Auralee put her arm around Sarah's shoulder and escorted her to the porch.

Boley asked, "You want I should unload the wagon?"

Auralee replied, "No, only what they need right away. They won't be here long. None of us will."

That puzzled Jeffrey. He started to ask but decided he would find out in due time. At the moment he was glad to get his feet on the ground and stay in one place at least a little while. The dog nosed around his legs, evidently trying to decide whether to approve of him.

Boley asked Jeffrey, "How old are you, boy?"

"Fourteen. Goin' on fifteen."

"Is that old enough that I ought to call you *Mister*?"

"Jeffrey's fine. Ain't nobody *mistered* me yet." He frowned. "I wonder what she meant about us not stayin' long."

"I don't reckon the missus will mind me tellin' you. Home guards come around lookin' for Mister John. They mistaken his brother for him, and there was a considerable fight. Them no-goods left but said they'd be comin' back with a hang rope. Two of them, one apiece. Wasn't nothin' to do except leave, so Mister John and Mister Matthew, they taken off for Mexico. Said as soon as you-all got here, you and Miz Auralee and her children was to take your wagons and follow after."

"Women and children? All the way to Mexico by theirselves?"

"I'm supposed to go, too, to help out. I'm strong. I can lift one end of a wagon off of the ground if it ain't too heavy loaded."

Jeffrey believed it. Boley was about as big a man as he had ever seen close-up. He would make two of Fletcher.

Boley said, "I ain't real keen about goin' to Mexico. I don't know how they'll treat black folks like me."

"I've heard that they don't allow slavery. Soon as you cross into Mexico you'll be free."

"I'm free now. I saved up and bought myself. Old master signed the papers and everything before he died."

The dog rubbed his shoulder against Jeffrey's leg and looked up, inviting Jeffrey to pet him.

Boley smiled. "Looks like you passed muster with Old Flop. He's good at readin' folks. If he thinks you're all right, that's enough for me."

They unhitched the team, turning them, the mare, and the cow into a pen and closing the gate. Jeffrey looked toward the field. "If everybody leaves here, what'll happen to the crops?"

"There's some neighbors that'll come and harvest them. For theirselves, of course. At least it won't go to waste."

"Seems a shame to go off and leave it all."

"Better for Mister John to go this way than at the hands of them home guards. The war gives them an excuse to let their natural meanness rise to the top like clabber in a milk jar."

"If they're so keen about the war, why don't they go fight in it?"

"It's safer to stay home, where they can do their devilment and not worry much about somebody shootin' back. Be glad you're young, or they might come after you."

In the house, Jeffrey found Sarah weeping in disappointment. She said, "It's been such a hard trip. Now I find that it isn't over yet. I don't know if I can face it."

Jeffrey said, "What happened before won't happen again. And this time it won't be just me and you. There'll be a bunch with us."

He met Auralee's children. Harry was about eleven, freckle-faced, a strong hint of red in his thick mop of hair. Lucy was thirteen, skinny but starting to show the first bloom of womanhood. Her features were pleasant. Her blue eyes sparkled with life. Jeffrey found himself looking at her more than at Harry, and she was staring back.

She did not hide her curiosity. She asked boldly, "You ain't really kin to us, are you?"

"I'm not blood kin to anybody that I know of. After the Indians killed my folks, the Temples took me in and treated me like I was theirs."

Lucy said, "I'm glad you're not real kin."

Jeffrey asked, "How come?"

"Because I couldn't marry you if you was."

Taken aback, Jeffrey said, "Ain't you too young to be thinkin' about gettin' married?"

"If I start thinkin' about it now, I'll be ready when the time comes."

"Why pick on me?"

"You're the only one around here."

It struck Jeffrey that if Todd were alive he would be near Harry's age and size. He had managed for some time not to dwell on the loss of Mama and Papa and Todd, but seeing Harry brought it all back in rush. He fancied how different his life might have been were it not for that Indian raid. Papa, coming from Arkansas, would probably be a staunch Confederate, and they wouldn't be worrying about home guards and reprisals against Unionists. He and Todd would be hunting and fishing together and enjoying an innocent boyhood.

Harry said, "I ain't never seen a real live Indian. What're they like?"

"Scary," Jeffrey said.

"I'll bet we look scary to them, too."

"I suppose." The subject was painful, so he changed it. "Got any good fishin' around here?"

"Sure. You want to go?"

"Later, maybe, if we've got time." Perhaps it would

bring back the good feeling of the old days in Arkansas. Or, as likely, it would simply bring back the pain of loss.

Lucy came from the kitchen. "Supper's about ready. You-all had better wash up." She lingered, watching Jeffrey. "The wash pan is on the back porch."

Jeffrey had his hands in the water when he heard the dogs making a racket again. He dried on a rough cloth towel. Boley's voice came from the front porch. "Miz Auralee, it's them home guards again. They ain't give up yet."

Harry declared, "I'd like to shoot them, if Mama would let me."

Auralee heard. She said, "It'd be like shooting one wasp out of a nest. The rest would come get you."

Jeffrey followed Harry through the house and onto the front porch. Sarah remained in the house, a handkerchief to her face. Boley was on the ground, standing protectively between the four horsemen and Auralee. She stood on the porch, her arms folded in defiance.

The spokesman looked nothing like Nash Wickham except for the malice in his eyes, Jeffrey thought. He said, "Miz Temple, we've got no business with you today. We've come to talk to John Temple and that brother of his."

Her voice was crisp. "You may search the premises to your heart's content. The rest of us are about to have our supper."

"Got a place set for John Temple?"

"Come and see, if you're of a mind to."

"You wouldn't say that if he was here, so I take it that he ain't. Just where is he?"

"Somewhere this side of hell's half acre."

Jeffrey admired the little woman's spunk. Her jaw

looked as solid as stone. These men would do nothing to hurt her, however. Not even the veneer of patriotism would shield them from the stigma of injuring a woman.

The men pulled away, separating to search the barn and fields. They went about it half-heartedly, going through the motions as if resigned to the fact that their quarry was not there.

Auralee said, "Come on in, boys, and let's have supper. They can waste their time without our help."

Boley said, "Me and Old Flop'll watch that they don't carry off nothin'." He remained outdoors. Jeffrey guessed that Auralee fed him on the porch anyway, when the rest of the family had finished. It was not customary for blacks to sit with whites at a meal.

Sarah seemed distracted, leaving half the food on her plate and getting up from the table while others were still eating. Auralee watched her with concern. Later, she beckoned Jeffrey out onto the porch as she carried food to Boley.

Frowning, she said, "Sarah is a troubled woman. I think it's more than just not finding Matthew here. Something happened on the way down here, didn't it?"

Jeffrey stalled. "We had a lot of trouble, what with the mud and all. It was slow goin'."

"It was more than that, I think. Somebody did something to her."

Jeffrey felt hemmed in. "It ain't my place to say. You'll have to ask her."

Auralee seemed to sense the truth, just as Sheriff Honeycutt had done. She said sternly, "It won't happen on this trip. I'll kill the man that tries to touch her."

"That's what the sheriff did. He killed both of them."

"Both?" Her lips tightened. "No wonder she's disturbed."

Jeffrey's conscience kicked in. "Don't tell her I told you. I said more than I meant to."

"I won't mention it, but it's a good thing to know. It explains a lot."

14

Todd knew from the Mexican farmer's belligerent expression that this was not to be a pleasant encounter. He had realized early that most native New Mexico people had little use for Americanos, whether Union or Confederate. Now it had become a test of wills between them and the Texas foragers, whose needs at times approached desperation. The invading force had used up most of what it had brought, and preconceived notions of living off the land had proven to be too optimistic in an arid region whose people were perpetually poor. The Texans subsisted largely on supplies taken from Union garrisons and what they could buy, borrow, or confiscate from the citizens.

Lieutenant Sanderson told him, "Kid, we've got to have feed for the horses, or they won't carry us much farther. Tell this Mexican we'll pay him a fair price."

Payment, however, would be in Confederate scrip. The government had issued General Sibley no cash to support this expedition. Civilians feared the scrip was not worth the paper it was written on, a doubt Todd had come to share. His conscience pained him when he had to voice a confidence he did not feel. These were his people, to the extent that he had any people.

He repeated in Spanish what the lieutenant had told him. The farmer's response was a stern refusal. He wanted silver, either Mexican or American. The paper, he declared stiffly, was not good enough to wipe himself with.

Sanderson had become increasingly impatient with local Mexicans as Texas troops had moved northward. He had hoped the Confederates would be seen as liberators, for the people there had chafed under the rule of the Union government since Kearney's victory over the Mexican military in 1846. Instead, they resented both armies, considering them foreign invaders to be resisted wherever possible. The few who accepted the Tejanos found themselves ostracized by a majority of the population. Most spoke the word *Tejano* as an epithet.

The farmer declared, "The little I have is for my family and my animals."

Todd said, "If you do not sell, they will take it anyway. The Texans say that once they win the country, they will redeem their scrip with Union silver."

"*If* they win," the farmer snorted. "Look at these you ride with. They look hungry, and they are without feed for their horses. An army cannot fight if it has nothing to eat."

"This is just a small detachment, and it is away from the main army. The lieutenant says once they take Fort Union they will have plenty to eat, and enough to feed the animals."

"I think they will never take Fort Union. The American eagle will tear the Tejano sparrow to pieces."

Sanderson understood none of the conversation. He cut in, "Is he goin' to sell willingly, or not?"

"Not willingly, sir."

"Unwillingly, then." He called, "Sergeant Willingham."

Todd had noticed that it seemed to be the sergeant's job to relay the lieutenant's orders to the men. Willingham had no uniform to distinguish him from the other men, but they obeyed him without question, just as he obeyed the lieutenant.

Sanderson said, "Detail several men to search the sheds for stored grain, and anything else we might need."

"Yes, sir," Willingham said, and hurried to carry out the order.

Sanderson scribbled several lines on a sheet of paper and handed it to the farmer. "Tell him when we've set up a provisional government, he'll get his money."

The farmer accepted the paper with resentment. As the lieutenant turned away, the Mexican asked Todd, "How is it that you speak like one of us, but you are gringo?"

"Have you heard of a man named January?"

"Yes, but nothing good." The farmer looked as if he smelled a dead skunk. "I suppose he is your father?"

"No. He bought me from the Indians when I was little."

"A poor bargain, if you willingly travel with the devil Tejanos." The farmer turned his back, cursing the soldiers who removed grain from his shed, and chased a lean steer across an arroyo.

At first the idea of soldiering with the Texans had struck Todd as a chance at grand adventure. The reality had been long scouting forays, exhausting night marches in bitter cold, missed meals, and occasional thirst that cut like a sharp knife shoved down his throat. Moreover, he had faced hostility in most of the people they had come across, resentment over the taking of supplies, or simply over the presence of an invading force. The Texan leaders had misjudged the natives' reception. They had found the land inhospitable and often barren, grass sparse, water chancy, the weather hostile. It seemed that when the wind was not stinging the men's faces with sleet or snow, it was biting them with blowing sand. More Texans had died of pneumonia than from Yankee bullets.

Sanderson ordered the patrol to make camp. The soldiers caught and killed the steer, long of legs but short of flesh, its foreshoulders narrow and hip bones sticking out far enough to hang a hat on. They roasted it over an open fire and ate it without salt, without bread, and without coffee to drink. Willingham cut off a strip and extended it to Todd. "Here, kid, you look like you could use a decent meal. This ain't exactly it, but maybe it'll pad your ribs for a little while."

Todd expressed his thanks. Willingham smiled and said, "You're a good lad."

Todd warmed. January had never treated him with this kind of respect.

A dyspeptic-looking soldier named Prentiss complained, "Damned poor grade of cattle they raise here, nothin' like we've got in Texas."

Sanderson said, "Things'll get better when we rejoin the main force. They took a wagon train of supplies from the Yankees in Albuquerque and Santa Fe."

Todd accepted his small allotment of meat. It awakened his appetite without satisfying it. He wished he were back herding sheep for Fernando Garcia. He had not gotten fat there, but he had never been this hungry.

Prentiss said, "We made a mistake comin' into this godforsaken country. The whole of New Mexico ain't worth the life of one Texan, and we've already buried too many good men."

Willingham said, "Quit your bellyachin', Private Prentiss." He bore down on the word *private*. Prentiss had been a corporal until he was busted for cowering in a ditch during a skirmish with federal troops near Fort Craig. "You volunteered for this mission. You signed up for better or worse."

"This is a hell of a lot worse than I figured on."

"We've won every contest so far. When we take Fort Union, the whole of New Mexico will be in our hands. The lieutenant thinks General Sibley's next step will be to take Colorado. The Confederacy has lots of allies there."

Prentiss argued, "I'll bet it's got lots of Unionists, too. They ain't goin' to just faint and fall over."

"The Colorado mines will give us the money to go on west from Tucson and take California. There we'll have the goldfields, and we'll have open seaports. The federals can't blockade them all."

A soldier named Brown said, "We hear rumors that the Yankees are gettin' reinforcements out of Colorado. Fort Union may not be easy pickin's like the officers claim."

Prentiss said, "Especially General Sibley. He's been laid up sick or drunk, or both, half the time since we left Texas. What the hell does he know about anything?"

Willingham said, "This army's got good officers like Lieutenant Sanderson, and like Pyron and Scurry.

When we're drinkin' California wine on the shores of the Pacific, you'll see. Now, those of you not on guard had better turn in. Lieutenant says we'll rejoin the main column tomorrow. Then it's on to Fort Union."

The soldiers began rolling up in their blankets as near the campfire as possible. The night air was so crisp that Todd felt his toes freezing in his shoes.

Sanderson told him, "I wish I could speak the language like you do. I'd explain to this farmer why the Confederacy will be good for the people here. They'll have a government that asks them what they want instead of just tellin' them what to do."

Todd said, "January says the only government people these folks ever see are tax collectors."

The patrol pulled onto the old Santa Fe trail, which merchant and immigrants wagons had traveled for decades to and from Missouri. The men joined the main column and received a hot meal shortly before reaching a place someone called Johnson's ranch. Excited couriers brought word of a battle being waged by forward units farther ahead in Glorieta Pass.

Flushed with anticipation, Sanderson said, "Kid, we're ordered up to join the fight. The wagon train is to remain here, where it'll be safe. I want you to stay with it, out of harm's way."

Todd thought he heard cannon fire somewhere ahead. "What if you need me to talk Mexican for you?"

"Any talkin' done up there will be with guns. I'll send back for you when we've whipped the Yankees." He turned to Sergeant Willingham. "Let's go."

Willingham seemed cheered by the prospect of a fight. "Yes, sir."

Sanderson rode off with the men of his unit, spurring his horse into a stiff trot. Todd watched with a disturbing sense of abandonment, a bit like the feeling he had when January rode away and left him on the square in Santa Fe. A foreboding came to him that this fight could go badly wrong.

Because the ranch was far from the scene of battle, only a token guard was assigned to stay with the supply train. Many who remained were the sick and wounded, and five Union prisoners taken earlier. There were more drivers than battle-seasoned soldiers. Some complained about being left behind when all the action was taking place miles up the trail.

Todd understood their disappointment, for he shared some of it. He had seen little action other than a couple of brief skirmishes that Sanderson had ordered him to observe from out of range. He imagined the exhilaration of being in the middle of a pitched battle. But that image was compromised by an underlying sense of dread. He had been chilled more than once by the sight of dead and wounded men carried to the rear in wagons, their bodies bloody and broken.

A six-pounder fieldpiece had been set up on a hillside. Several hundred horses and mules were left behind in the ranch's corrals at the edge of the trail.

With time on their hands, some of the men napped or played cards. Others built fires and cooked a hot meal. Todd moved from one group to another, sampling their food. The moodiness left him as he truly filled his stomach for the first time in days.

Warmly contented, he staked Comanche out to graze and spread his blanket on the ground so he could nap near the embers of a dying campfire. He dozed, dreaming of a banquet table sagging under the weight of food. He was awakened abruptly by men shouting in excitement. He flung the blanket aside and blinked, trying to determine what was happening.

"Yankees!" someone yelled. "Up yonder on the mountain."

He saw them, a long line of men making their way afoot through the pine trees, hurrying down the mountainside. A rattle of gunfire began to reverberate in the canyon. Bullets kicked up puffs of dust. Todd's heart was suddenly in his throat.

They're trying to kill us, he realized.

The Texans' one cannon blasted, the echo bouncing along the canyon. Vastly outnumbered, most of the soldiers panicked and fled up the trail toward the main force at Glorieta, away from the attackers, or west toward Santa Fe.

Todd lost whatever little enthusiasm he'd had for battle. He made a run for Comanche. The horse was plunging against the picket rope, trying to break loose. Todd grabbed his bridle and tried to pull it over the horse's ears, but Comanche was too frightened to hold still. Before Todd could calm him, he found himself staring into the muzzle of a rifle.

A grizzled man in civilian clothes shouted, "Put them hands up, Reb."

Todd quickly raised his hands, letting the bridle fall to the ground. Around him he heard only sporadic shooting. Comanche managed to pull the picket pin out of the ground and lope away, dragging the rope.

Several Texans, not yet overtaken by the federals, quickly gathered what loose horses and mules they could muster in a hurry and sent them galloping up the canyon toward Glorieta Pass, safe from the Union soldiers. Comanche went with them.

The man with the rifle moved closer and gave Todd a severe scrutiny. "Hell," he said, "you ain't a soldier. You're just a pup."

Todd was unable to answer at first. His throat seemed to have swollen shut. Finally he managed, "Where'd you-all come from all of a sudden?"

"We're Colorado militia," the man said. "Pike's Peakers."

The rumor had been true. Colorado volunteers had come to join the federal troops. Todd felt renewed fear for Lieutenant Sanderson.

The militiaman said, "We cut across the mountain to bite you rebs in the ass. Didn't figure to run into a whole supply train. That's what this is, ain't it?"

Todd did not reply. It was not his place to confirm the Coloradoan's guess, correct though it was. Prodded by the muzzle of the rifle, he joined other prisoners. The five Union men cheered as their allies set them free.

The firing soon stopped. It had hardly qualified even as a skirmish, for the Texans had been caught by surprise and overwhelmed before they had time to mount any concerted defense. Todd wanted to turn away but felt compelled to look at a few Texans who lay dead. All up and down the line of wagons, he saw men with their hands raised. Militiamen were methodically collecting weapons and herding their captives into one group. The wounded and sick who had been carried in the wagons were brought together, joined by bleeding men wounded in this surprise attack.

Todd heard a loud shout and turned to see what he first took to be a giant. A tall, barrel-chested, bewhiskered officer in full uniform stood near the gathered prisoners, yelling orders in a voice that might have reached to the top of the mountain. "Guard these rebels closely. Let no man escape."

A junior officer asked, "Major Chivington, they'll be a burden if we go back over the mountain like we came."

Major John Chivington's black eyes were alive with excitement in the aftermath of battle. "We may be obliged to shoot them should Texas forces threaten us. Otherwise we would probably face them again."

The younger officer seemed astonished. "Shootin' prisoners doesn't seem like a Christian thing to do."

"I'll be the judge of what is Christian. The Lord has given it to us to smite the heathens. We are here in his service."

"If it comes to that, are we to shoot the wounded, too?"

"Wounds heal. They'll pick up a rifle again if we let them rejoin Sibley's brigade."

Another officer pointed to the horses and mules remaining in the corrals. "There are too many for us to take back over the mountain. What'll we do with them?"

Chivington gave but a moment's attention to the animals. "We cannot let them fall into Texan hands again. Kill them."

The officer argued, "That will burn up a lot of ammunition."

"Use your bayonets. Get it done, and quickly."

The major's flushed face was fearsome as he turned it once more upon the prisoners. The soldier who had captured Todd said, "Major, this boy is too young to be a soldier. We'd ought to spare him."

Todd shrank away from the officer's fiery gaze.

The major declared, "A boy now but a fighting man tomorrow. He cast his lot with the enemy. If need be, he will die with them."

Todd shuddered all the way to his toes. He shared

the contagion of fear spreading among the prisoners. He sensed that Chivington meant what he'd said.

He heard the screams of horses and mules as the militiamen moved among them, plunging bayonets into their throats. He imagined the same thing happening to him. He wanted to cry.

The major asked, "How many wagons?"

A subordinate said, "I rough counted upwards of eighty, sir. They're packed with all kinds of supplies. Powder and ammunition, too."

"Burn them!"

"We could use some of this stuff ourselves."

"We might not be able to hold it if attacked in force. Destroy it all."

The prisoners were herded away from the wagons. The militiamen set about putting the torch to all the rolling stock, even to the harness. Todd ducked instinctively as a wagonload of ammunition exploded, shaking the ground, showering fire and debris.

The major exulted to one of his officers, "At best I had hoped to strike the Texans from the rear and harass them a bit. But the Lord showed us the way to cut their jugular without losing a man of our own."

The enormity of what had happened was slow to soak in, but Todd gradually began to see it. This wagon train and its supplies were lifeblood to the Texans. The loss would leave them painfully handicapped a thousand miles from home in a barren and hostile land.

Chivington moved out of Todd's sight. He heard a voice say, barely above a whisper, "Hey, boy. Come here." The soldier who had captured him beckoned with a slight movement of his finger. Todd went to him. The soldier said, "If it comes to us havin' to shoot the prisoners, I ain't goin' home with you on my conscience.

While the major ain't lookin', you scoot yourself into them cedars yonder."

"He said not to let anybody escape."

"He said *man*. You're just a boy. Run as far away from here as you can. Git!"

After a quick look to be certain the officer was still out of sight, Todd sprinted for the cover of the brush. Heart racing, he paused for a few seconds to be sure there was no outcry over his escape, then moved on quickly, crouching low. His conscience troubled him, leaving the other prisoners to whatever fate Chivington might choose, but not enough to tempt him into going back.

He worked his way around the edge of the mountain until he felt he was clear of the Colorado volunteers, then dropped back down into the Santa Fe trail. He heard no gunfire ahead and assumed the battle in Glorieta Pass was over, or at least interrupted by a cease fire for removal of wounded and dead. He wondered who had won, if anybody.

He realized all too well who had won at Johnson's ranch. He sensed that no matter what had happened in the pass, the Texans had been placed in desperate straits by loss of the wagons and the vital supplies they carried. They would never take Fort Union now that the Coloradoans had reinforced Canby's Union forces. They would be fortunate if they even made it back to Texas.

He heard no firing behind him. He surmised the prisoners had not been shot. That, at least, was to the good.

Without food, without a blanket, at dark he pulled back from the trail to be certain Chivington's men would not retake him in case they should come up that way toward Glorieta. Cold, but without a fire or any way to start one except by rubbing sticks together, he went through a miserable night with little sleep. As far as he knew, nobody had passed by in the darkness. He had no idea where Chivington had gone, if indeed he had gone anywhere.

Weary, hungry, cold, at daylight he trudged on toward the pass, wondering whom he might meet first, Texans or Union soldiers.

He came, after a long time, to a Texan outpost. Two soldiers met him, rifles in their hands, challenging him to identify himself. Then one recognized him. He said, "He's that boy that's been talkin' Mexican for Lieutenant Sanderson. How's things back down the canyon, kid?"

Todd shook his head. "Bad. Do you know about the wagons?"

"We've already heard. Seen the smoke, too. Did they really burn them all?"

"All that I saw."

The two soldiers looked gravely at each other. "Goin' to be short rations from now on," one said.

"Or no rations at all. Hell of a note this is. We stomped the Yankees real good and drove them back toward Fort Union. Then they snuck around behind us and burned up our wagons." He spat. "Damn that Sibley, he ought to've been here, but he's back in Albuquerque. Probably got a bottle in one hand and a fork in the other."

Todd asked, "Have you seen Lieutenant Sanderson?"

"Seen him once in the thick of the battle. Ain't seen him since."

Todd's stomach rumbled. He said, "I don't reckon you'd have anything to eat?"

One of the soldiers reached into a knapsack lying

beside the trail. "Just a little hardtack. Don't bust your teeth on it."

When Todd reached the main body of troops, he found most in high spirits over their victory. He thought that they probably did not yet grasp the gravity of Chivington's flanking maneuver. So far they had won every battle they had fought in New Mexico, only to lose the war in what amounted to no more than a light skirmish.

Todd felt sickened by the number of wounded he saw in camp. He soon found Sanderson among them, lying on a blanket. The lieutenant had taken a rifle ball in his thigh. His face was pale, and he was running a fever. He tried to grin at Todd, but he hurt too much. He said weakly, "I was afraid they got you, kid."

Todd explained about the kind Coloradoan who had helped him escape. "A major by the name of Chivington was talkin' about killin' all the prisoners, but I don't think he did it."

"He might've remembered that we have some of theirs." Sanderson tried to change position but groaned and gave up. "I think gettin' the bullet out butchered me up worse than the bullet itself." His face twisted as he endured a spasm of pain. "Did you walk all the way?"

"My horse got loose. Last I saw, he was runnin' in this direction."

"Go look at the corrals. Might be somebody found him and brought him in."

Todd did not see Sergeant Willingham. He asked about him.

Sanderson's face was grave. "He died chargin' into the Union guns. He was a soldier to his last breath."

Todd was saddened. Willingham had talked to him

as if he were an adult. He asked anxiously, "How about you? You goin' to be all right?"

"If I live long enough." Seeing the worry in Todd's face, he added, "I'm from Texas. I don't intend to let a little old Yankee bullet kill me before I get home."

"Do you think you'll be startin' home now?"

"The officers are still talkin' it over, but I don't see where they've got a choice. We'll soon be out of anything to eat, to feed the stock, or even to fight with. We've already used up about everything in Santa Fe and Albuquerque." His eyes were sad. "Looks to me like the only thing we can do is head back for Texas."

"Maybe get a fresh start and do it over?"

"I doubt you could get most of these men to come back. They've seen all they want of New Mexico. I have, too."

"What about the Colorado goldfields, and California?"

"They're too damned far from Texas."

Weary, Todd sat down to rest and to consider his situation. He could walk away from the Texans and fade into the native population. He could go eastward and join the Union forces, offering them the same translator service he had given the Texans. Or he could follow the Texans' retreat, fetching and carrying for the wounded lieutenant.

One option he thought of but quickly dismissed was to go back to January. As the crow flew, it should not be far to the farm.

Sanderson called, breaking Todd's concentration, "Would you mind bringin' me some water? I'm burnin' plumb up."

Todd trotted to Sanderson's side and felt the lieutenant's forehead. It was hot. He picked up the canteen and ran in search of water. He brought it back, still at a run. Sanderson took several long and desperate swallows, as if he could not get enough. He gripped Todd's arm and rasped, "Kid, you're a lifesaver. Don't leave me."

Todd no longer had to worry about making a decision. It had been made for him. He said, "I won't."

15

Todd thought it strange that the two sides could fight viciously, then declare a temporary truce to exchange prisoners and wounded, and to bury their dead. They turned from being warriors to being gentlemen, then turned to warriors again. He could not imagine Indians doing that, at least not the ones to whom he had been exposed. With them, the enemy was always the enemy, to be fought as long as the heart kept beating and breath remained. There might be retreat, but not a truce.

The battle in Glorieta Pass had left many dead. Under a white flag, both sides took time to bury them. That sad task done, the battered federal forces moved back toward Bernal Springs, partway to Fort Union. The Texans began a slow retreat toward Santa Fe.

As Sanderson had suggested, Todd retrieved Comanche from among the corralled horses. The brown had lost the picket rope somewhere along the way. Todd had no saddle and blanket but quietly appropriated replacements from those belonging to men who had fallen in the fight. He helped place Sanderson among other wounded in a wagon, then followed it as it lumbered to the western entrance to the canyon and ultimately to Santa Fe.

At Johnson's ranch, he gazed solemnly upon the cold, dark ashes of what had been a wagon train. Only the fire-blackened iron remnants remained, like the ribs of an animal devoured by wolves. Chivington had left the most badly wounded Texans behind, along with a few of his own too hurt to retreat over the mountain. Both sides acknowledged an obligation to take care of enemy wounded just as they would their own. These would be transported to Santa Fe, where a hospital had been set up to treat Union soldiers and Texans alike.

A sickening stench arose from the corrals, where the slaughtered horses and mules lay in large black patches of dried blood. Todd patted Comanche on the neck, thankful that he had not been among them.

The Texas cannon that had boomed a few times at the start of the skirmish lay where the federals had left it, spiked, its wheels smashed as they had rolled it down a hillside.

He heard men mutter about the desolation they saw around them, speculating on what it portended for their futures.

He rode up to the wagon that held the lieutenant, crowded among several other wounded. "Anything you need, sir?" he asked.

Sanderson's voice had no strength. "We'd be obliged if you'd fill these canteens. We've drunk them dry."

Todd complied and wished he could do more. Whatever romantic notions he might have built up about soldiering and fighting had been turned inside out by the misery and death he had witnessed. He had heard ministers and priests talk of hell as a place of eternal fire. He knew better now. Hell was a battle-field.

In Santa Fe, Todd was amazed to find that Mrs. Louisa Canby, wife of the Union commander, had organized a group of local women to help tend the sick and wounded without regard to whether they were federal or Confederate, on the grounds that all were "sons of some dear mother." He remained as close as possible to Lieutenant Sanderson, running errands for the women who cared for him and the others. During the long days in Santa Fe he heard many rumors. The Texans were going to try again to take Fort Union. The Texans were *not* going to try to take Fort Union. The federals, augmented by a large force of Colorado volunteers, were descending upon Santa Fe. A large force was *not* descending upon Santa Fe.

The truth seemed to be that both sides were licking deep wounds and were not eager to march too soon into full-scale hostilities. Certainly, Todd hoped they would not. He had seen more than enough.

He remained close to the hospital most of the time, trying to be as useful as possible, seeing to Sanderson's personal needs, fetching and carrying for the medical volunteers. He stood with his back to the wall, staying out of the way and watching helplessly as a dying man cried for relief from his pain. He was sent to fetch the ambulance driver and stood by while the man's body was carried away to be buried with the many others who had died there. He wanted to cry, but he had used up his tears.

To get away for a while from the hospital's depressing atmosphere, he wandered to the familiar plaza in the center of town. Local people seemed to be going on with their lives. They tried to avoid the fray as much as possible, not overtly aligning themselves with either side. Young men and young women met one another and walked around the plaza while older people watched, critical of any improprieties they saw or imagined. Todd had heard a lot of soldier talk and understood what those improprieties were. His relatively brief time with the Texans had given him a broad education in the ways of war, and the ways of men and women.

Watching the young people helped take his mind off the tragedies he had witnessed. He found girls more interesting than they used to be. Perhaps, given his tender age, he was rushing things a bit, but he supposed war had a way of doing that to people.

He concentrated his attention in particular on a dark-eyed girl not many years older than he. Flirting with the young men, she had a smile he could see across the plaza. He was not aware that someone had walked up behind him until a familiar voice grated on his ear.

"How do, horse thief. I thought you'd plumb left the country."

He did not want to look, but he was compelled to turn. He felt a jolt of fear as he saw January standing over him, hands on his broad hips, bewhiskered face twisted into a scowl.

"Damned smart aleck, ain't you, takin' my best horse and runnin' off like a chicken-stealin' coyote."

Warmth rose in Todd's face. "You sold my horse. I traded yours to get mine back."

"He belongs to me, like everything else you've got. Where's he at?"

Comanche was corralled with the other Texan horses, but Todd had no intention of telling January that. He lied. "He got shot in the fight at Johnson's ranch."

"Serves you right. At least I got my horse back. Had to bribe that damned Union officer an extra fifty dollars to get him. Where you been all this time?"

"Been workin' for the Texans."

"Have they paid you?"

"Some." Todd shoved his hands into his pockets as if to protect what was in them.

"Give it here."

Todd backed away, but January grabbed him by the shoulders and gave him a brisk shaking. "Hand it to me."

Reluctantly, Todd brought several pieces of paper from his pocket. January gave them a quick glance and cursed. "Scrip! Is that all they gave you, scrip?"

"It's all they've got. They promised it'll be good."

"Good for nothin'." January threw the paper on the ground. "The rebels are whipped. Don't you know they'll be goin' back to Texas now with their asses draggin'? A wagonload of that paper wouldn't buy a shot of whiskey."

Todd could not meet the man's smoldering gaze. "I don't drink whiskey anyhow."

"Well, maybe you've learned your lesson. You don't do nothin' for nobody unless you know they're goin' to pay you. So come on back to the farm. There's plenty of work waitin' there for you."

Todd knew the answer before he asked the question. "You goin' to pay me?"

"Pay you? Ain't it enough that I feed you and give you a place to sleep? You damned ungrateful pup, I could go off and leave you here, like I ought to've done the last time."

Todd began to take courage. He had survived

worse things than January could do to him. In a burst
of defiance, he said, "You'd just as well do that. I ain't
goin' with you."

January was as outraged as if Todd had struck him.
"You'll do what I tell you to."

"You ain't my daddy. You've got no say over me.
Maybe I owed you for takin' me away from the Indians, but I worked that off a long time ago. I'm old
enough to get along by myself, and you can go to
hell."

January's face was crimson. "You'll starve to
death. When you do, don't come crawlin' to me." He
drew back his hand as if to strike, then lowered it and
turned away, growling. Watching him leave, Todd felt
an exhilarating sense of liberation. He picked up the
scrip and put it back in his pocket. It did not matter
whether it would ever be worth anything or not. He
was free from any bond to January. That was worth
more than a wagonload of money.

He returned to the hospital feeling much better
than when he had left it.

Though his wound was far from healed, Sanderson
was impatient to be back on his feet. Crutches were in
short supply, so Todd crafted a pair from tree limbs,
padding them with cloth to reduce irritation under
the arms. Sanderson insisted upon trying them when
a doctor wasn't looking. He fell a couple of times.
Todd worried that the wound might bleed again. So
far, it had not.

Nobody told him, but he reasoned from what
he saw that the Texan forces were preparing to retreat, first from Santa Fe, then from Albuquerque.
He warned Sanderson, "If they decide you're not in

shape to make it home, they're liable to leave you here. The Yankees'll move in as soon as this outfit pulls out. You want them to get you?" He still felt cold every time he thought of the day Major Chivington contemplated shooting prisoners to prevent their falling back into Texan ranks.

Sanderson shook his head. "I just want to go home. No tellin' how long the Yankees would hold me."

Todd felt awkward about giving advice to a grown man, especially one who held the rank of lieutenant. Everybody was calling him "kid," and he knew the name fitted. He said, "Good thing the doctor didn't see you fall."

The supply situation had been improved by discovery of hidden federal stores in Santa Fe, but this would afford only temporary relief. General Sibley came up from Albuquerque, appraised the condition of his Texas troops, and decided to vacate the New Mexico capital. Rumors abounded that Canby was bringing a federal contingent north from Fort Craig to reinforce those at Fort Union, and that he would soon advance on Santa Fe and Albuquerque. Sibley was still expressing confidence that he would receive reinforcements and supplies from Texas. Then he could try again to challenge Fort Union. He planned to retreat southward to safer ground and wait. Short of ammunition, he ordered the secret burial of eight brass howitzers to reduce the burden on the draft animals.

Sanderson was ordered to remain in Santa Fe with more than a hundred other wounded. Within their means, both sides had been humane in their treatment of enemy wounded. But Sanderson wanted no part of Union captivity.

"I'm goin' home," he declared, "if I have to walk

every step of the way on these damned crutches, by myself."

Todd had Comanche. He could ride along with the troops. He wished he could offer the horse to Sanderson, but he felt that the lieutenant was in no condition to sit in the saddle. He knew also that the officer would be fortunate to endure even a mile afoot.

He approached the driver of a supply wagon with a proposition. "If you'll take him, the lieutenant will buy you a wagonload of whiskey when you get back to Texas."

That was a tall but empty promise. Todd had no authority to speak for Sanderson.

The driver said, "What kind of whiskey?"

Todd did not know one whiskey from another, but he had learned the high art of lying by observing January. "The best there is."

"The lieutenant is supposed to stay here. If I take him, the higher officers are liable to raise hell."

"They do it anyway, don't they?"

The driver could not argue that point. He said, "Smuggle him under the canvas when you know there's no officers watchin'. I ain't takin' no responsibility. If you get caught, I'll swear I never seen that lieutenant in my life."

Todd told Sanderson what he had done. "You'll have to lay low till we get far enough that they can't send you back."

"Kid, I hate havin' you lie for me, but I don't know what I'd do without you."

"I'm glad to be gettin' away from Santa Fe myself." He had not told Sanderson about his encounter with January or about a nagging fear that January might show up again and carry him away by force.

He was strong for his age, but not strong enough to fight January.

He watched the soldiers load the wagons with all the supplies they could carry. When he sensed that they were almost ready to go, he looked up and down the line for any officer who might interfere. Seeing none, he hustled Sanderson to the chosen wagon and helped him climb painfully up over the tailgate and under the canvas. He tossed in a blanket. "Better cover up with this. Otherwise, anybody pokin' around the back end of the wagon is liable to see you."

The driver made it a point to keep his back turned until an order came down the line for the wagons to move. He said quietly to Todd, "Remember now, a whole wagonload of whiskey. Kentucky, not some cheap Mexican rotgut."

"Kentucky," Todd agreed. He would not know Kentucky whiskey from pickle juice.

Comanche was rested and seemed to enjoy escaping the confinement of the corral. He pranced, his head bobbing up and down. Todd patted him on the neck and looked back at the sprawling brown adobes, relieved to be leaving the town. He could remember little good that had happened to him there. He knew the Texans felt the same way.

This invasion of Union territory, launched with high hopes and boundless ambition, had degenerated into the kind of bad dream that makes a person wake up in the night drenched with cold sweat. Sibley had addressed the men with an air of confidence that they would soon return. Next time they would carry the Confederacy all the way to the Pacific. Todd had sensed the emptiness of the words.

A number of civilians accompanied the southbound

army. Todd understood that they were Confederate sympathizers who feared ill treatment from the federals. Among them he particularly noticed a nice-looking older woman—he figured she must be at least thirty—riding in a wagon alongside a Mexican woman. At second look, he was sure he had seen her before. She had been a volunteer in the makeshift hospital in Santa Fe. In the wagon were a couple of trunks and several boxes. The Yankees were certain to confiscate anything she had been forced to leave behind.

A sandy road made for hard pulling and slow going. When the column halted for the night, Sanderson wanted to get out of the wagon and stretch his legs. Todd worried, "If anybody sees you, we'll both be in trouble. They'll probably send you back."

"How? I can't ride a horse, and they can't spare a wagon."

"They might leave you here and figure the Yankees'll pick you up when they come along. *If* they come along. If they don't, you could starve to death." Todd frowned. "*We* could starve to death. I'd have to stay here with you."

Sanderson reluctantly accepted Todd's counsel. "I couldn't be responsible for lettin' that happen to you. I'll stay put a little longer. But if I don't get on my feet and move around pretty soon, this hip is liable to lock up. I'd never walk normal again."

Todd ate only enough supper to keep his stomach from rumbling. He smuggled the rest to the lieutenant.

Sanderson said, "There's a wide crack in the wagon bed, so I managed to take care of one problem while we were travelin'. But I've got another."

Todd nodded. "I'll bring you a bucket."

By the second night they had gone far enough that it seemed unlikely the officers would try to send Sanderson back to Santa Fe. After dark, the lieutenant climbed out of the wagon with Todd's support. The wagon driver refused to help. He would not even stay and watch. He said, "What I don't see, nobody can accuse me of knowin' about."

Sanderson held on to the wagon until Todd handed him the crutches. He fitted them under his arms and took a few tentative steps. He said, "It doesn't hurt like I thought it would. Maybe I'm goin' to heal after all."

Todd suspected he hurt more than he admitted.

A captain walked down the line of wagons and stopped in surprise, watching the lieutenant move around on the crutches. "Sanderson," he exclaimed. "I thought the wounded that couldn't walk were supposed to stay in Santa Fe."

"I never heard any such order." That was not quite a lie, Todd knew. Sanderson had heard about the order secondhand but had not heard it actually delivered.

The captain asked, "How long before you think you can ride horseback?"

Todd took that as an implication that if Sanderson couldn't ride, he would be left behind.

Sanderson said, "I'm about through with these crutches. I'll be in the saddle tomorrow."

Todd felt misgivings, but it would have been futile to voice them. Sanderson would ride—or try to—even if it crippled him for life.

After a hasty breakfast the next morning, Todd managed to wangle a horse and saddle for the lieutenant. Sanderson attempted to lift his left foot to the stirrup, but he grimaced in pain and gave up after a couple of tries. Todd improvised a set of steps for him by placing one ammunition box on the ground, then stacking two more next to it. With some trembling and struggling for balance, and with Todd's support, Sanderson managed to stand atop the pair of boxes and slide his right leg over the cantle. His face was contorted and shiny with cold sweat as he settled into the saddle. Todd feared he would fall, but he managed to stay in place.

The captain who had challenged him said, "I admire your courage, but I despair over your lack of judgment. This journey may kill you."

Sanderson said, "If it does, bury me in Texas."

Todd asked, "What do you want me to do with the crutches?"

"Throw them away."

Watching Sanderson ride, twisted off-center in the saddle to favor his hip, Todd decided to stow them in the wagon instead. The lieutenant might be glad to have them after a few hours on horseback. As they moved ahead, Todd tried to stay close without being obvious about it. He did not want to wound Sanderson's pride. One wound was enough.

Passing through Albuquerque, then following the Rio Grande in a southerly direction, the battle-weary Texans were glad to be putting northern New Mexico behind them. Though General Sibley preferred to refer to the move as a change in tactics, Todd knew it was a retreat. Just about everybody in the command knew it, though some would not admit it aloud. They sensed a constant threat from Union soldiers following somewhere behind them.

The Texans camped at the farming village of Peralta, near the river. Advance forces had set up a strong line of defense there within a complex of irrigation ditches. The next morning, the unexpected sound of Union bugles caused a rude awakening in the Confederate camp. Todd hesitated when Sanderson told him to catch the horses. Hobbling along without crutches, Sanderson said, "Hurry up. Looks like we've got to give them another whippin'."

Todd wished he could share the lieutenant's optimism. He saddled the officer's horse, then Comanche. Sanderson warned him, "Take your horse and get in one of those deep ditches, kid. Stay back from the fight. If things go sour, get on that horse and run like hell."

As the lieutenant rode to join his men, Todd shouted, "Watch out they don't put a bullet in the other hip." He doubted that Sanderson had heard him. Even if he had, he would not flinch from what he saw as his duty. To Todd, even a victory today would seem a futile gesture in the face of eventual defeat.

Though Sibley had ordered the burial of howitzers in Santa Fe, he had kept as a trophy of war six Union artillery pieces taken in the battle of Valverde. These weapons were quickly brought into firing position against the advancing federal soldiers. Todd hunkered down in a ditch deep enough to hide Comanche. He listened to the duel of the big guns and cringed as bullets kicked up dust on the ditch bank. The seesaw battle continued for what felt like hours, though the sun had not actually moved that much.

The firing died down. Todd sensed that the Texans had held their ground for the most part. Canby's Union troops withdrew out of rifle range. Both sides had had enough fight for the time being. Sanderson rode back to where Todd waited. He was weary and in pain, but he had no new holes in him.

Relieved, Todd asked, "Don't you think you ought to get down and rest?"

He helped Sanderson dismount. With his feet on the ground, the lieutenant leaned against his horse for support. He breathed heavily. Todd could only imagine how that hip wound was hurting him. The man had no business being on horseback, but to tell him so was a waste of time.

Sanderson said, "Seems like we surprised them about as much as they surprised us. I think they captured one detachment, but we managed to push them back."

Todd said, "Maybe they'll give up and retreat to Albuquerque."

Sanderson shook his head. "I wouldn't, if I was them. They'll want to make sure we keep movin' south."

"How far is it to Texas?"

"A long ways. We'll be in a bad fix for supplies. This country has already been picked over for everything it's got." Sanderson frowned. "You don't have to go with us. You could drop out here and mix in with the town folks. The Yankees wouldn't need to know you've been with us."

Todd had already thought about it. Going on with the Texans would carry him into a new environment, to a different sort of people. He would be much more at home if he remained in New Mexico. But, on the other hand, he faced the possibility that sooner or later he would fall back into January's clutches. For all he knew, January might be following after the federal troops, hoping for a chance to drag him back to that farm and make a workhorse of him again.

Besides all that, Sanderson needed him, even if he didn't know it.

He said, "I reckon I'll string along with you. Texas must not be too bad, the way everybody's itchin' to get back there."

He saw a spot of fresh blood on the lieutenant's ragged trousers. He said, "I'm afraid that wound has busted open. I'll see if I can find a doctor to come and take a look."

Sternly Sanderson told him, "No. He'll order me to stay behind, and leave somebody to make sure I do."

Todd thought of the woman. "I saw a woman doin' nursin' work in the hospital in Santa Fe. She's here with the other civilians. Maybe she'd take care of you and not say anything about it."

Sanderson remained adamant. "No woman is goin' to see me with my pants down. I'll take care of myself, thank you." He looked about to see if anyone was watching, then unbuttoned his trousers and slipped them partway down. The bandage was two days old and showing fresh blood.

Todd said, "I'll go to a hospital wagon and see if I can swipe some fresh wrappin'."

"Don't get caught. They'll ask too many questions."

"I was taught by as slick a thief as ever lived."

He knew of at least one wagon that carried medical supplies. He watched for a chance when no one was watching, then climbed in. He got away with bandages and a bottle of antiseptic. On his way back, he saw the woman. He noticed this time that her hair was the color of straw, her features pleasant for an old woman of thirty or so.

Sanderson was not going to like this, but Todd felt that it was necessary. Nervously he approached the woman and said, "Ma'am, didn't I see you in the hospital back in Santa Fe?"

"I was there. I don't remember you being a patient, though."

"I wasn't, but my lieutenant was. He's down yonder

a ways, wounded." He pointed. "He needs better care than I know how to give him. Reckon you could . . ."

"Of course. Lead the way."

Walking beside her, Todd said, "One thing: he doesn't want anybody to know. He's afraid they'll make him stay behind. He doesn't want to be a Yankee prisoner."

She smiled. "I wouldn't either. That's why I'm with this wagon train. Don't worry. It'll be just between us rebels."

Sanderson reddened when he saw Todd bringing the woman. "Dammit, kid, I told you. It's not decent, a woman seein' me half naked."

She said sternly, "I volunteered in the hospital. I saw a lot of men half naked. Anyway, I was married for seven years. There's nothing you can show me that I haven't seen before. Now, let's take a look at that bullet hole."

Sanderson resisted at first but then relented, glaring at Todd. He lowered his trousers just enough to expose the wound and nothing else.

She said, "That bandage is rotten. It'll be a wonder if your hip isn't rotten, too." She removed the wrapping and washed the area around the wound with antiseptic. Sanderson clenched his teeth to keep from crying out.

Todd asked, "Does it burn?" before he realized how silly that sounded.

Sanderson rasped, "Hell no, it feels fine." He then apologized to the woman for using profanity.

She said, "I've heard a lot worse, coming down the Santa Fe trail with a bunch of mule skinners. Hold still while I put a fresh wrapping on." As she bandaged the wound she asked, "What's your name, Lieutenant?"

"Orville Sanderson. What's yours?"

"Ella Hawkins."

"You said you used to be married. What did you do, kill him with that stuff you just poured on me?"

"No, he died of typhoid fever two years ago."

Sanderson's voice softened. "I'm sorry. I had no call to say what I did."

"No offense taken. We'd brought goods from Missouri and set up a store. He went back to buy more merchandise and must've drunk some bad water along the way. Teamsters buried him on the trail."

"So you weren't with him?"

"It was a week before I even knew. Never got to say goodbye to him."

"Many a Texan has died on this campaign. A lot of women are widows but don't know it yet."

She nodded. "There should be a better way than war to settle an argument. I wasn't mad at anybody. Now I don't know who to be the maddest at." She tied a final knot to keep the bandage stable. "There, that's finished. But you shouldn't be riding a horse for a while."

"Got no choice. They'll leave me if I don't."

She pointed with her chin. "My wagon is a little way back yonder. The boy knows where. If you get tired, you can ride with María and me."

"Who's María?"

"A woman I knew in Santa Fe. She's on her way to join relatives in El Paso del Norte."

"I'm much obliged for the offer, Mrs. Hawkins. It'd be a pleasure."

Sanderson watched her as she walked away. He said, "Kid, I ought to tan your hide, but I won't. She's a fine-lookin' woman."

"I guess, for somebody that old."

Sanderson grinned. "Old? She's hardly shed her baby teeth yet. I wonder if she knows anybody in Texas." He considered for a minute. "She's goin' to know *me* before this trip is over."

In the dark of night, the Texans crossed over to the west side of the river, coming out cold and wet but putting distance between themselves and the federals before daybreak. As soon as it was light enough to see, Todd began looking behind him with apprehension. The sandy road made for slow traveling, especially by the heavier wagons and the artillery pieces. The column was dangerously strung out, many of the draft animals weak from overwork and poor forage. It would be a tempting target for a flanking maneuver, yet the Union troops made no such attempt. The forerunners of their column appeared on the east bank and rode along paralleling the Texans, keeping the river between them.

Todd asked, "Why don't they cross over and hit us? Looks to me like we'd be easy to take right now."

Sanderson said, "Maybe they've decided we're on our way out anyhow, so why get more of their men killed? What would they do with us if they captured us all? They'd have to feed us. I'll bet they're on short rations, too." He shifted his weight in the saddle, grimacing as pain lanced his hip. "Like as not they'll keep doggin' us at a distance. They won't want to let us stop and take up a position anywhere."

The wind rose strong and cold. Blowing sand stung Todd's face like needles. From time to time the column came upon flat stretches of alkali crust. The hooves and the iron-rimmed wheels crushed it to powder that blew into the travelers' eyes, burning like pepper. Its taste was as bitter as gall.

Camped for the night at the junction of the Rio Grande and the Rio Puerco, Todd was aware that the officers were holding council. He could not hear the words, but at times he could hear voices rising in argument. In the darkness, he saw Union campfires across the river. They were a grim reminder that death lay in wait a few hundred yards away, dependent only upon a decision by the Union commander.

The nearness of the federals played upon the Texans' nerves. Some wanted to cross the river and attack. After all, they had won every major battle so far, only to be undone by a critical shortage of supplies. They should have been able to overwhelm the enemy there, then march on south to the federal outpost at Fort Craig, bypassed during the Texans' northward drive earlier. More than likely that fort was well supplied with foodstuffs for the men and feed for the animals. It was there for the taking.

But General Sibley thought otherwise. He decided a confrontation at Fort Craig was too dangerous. He had personally helped fortify that post before he resigned his commission in the Union army to take up a command for the Confederacy. He was well aware of how formidable it would be, how difficult to overwhelm. For all he knew, Union colonel Canby was there now, and he might have ordered Colorado volunteers to reinforce the garrison.

No, he decided, the wisest thing would be to return to Texas, regroup, reoutfit, and come back with a much stronger force, better supplied and more adequately financed than before.

That much Sanderson told Todd when the officers'

conference was over. He said, "Sibley's right that the best thing is to get back to Texas. As for makin' another try at takin' New Mexico, I'm afraid he's just whistlin' in the wind."

"Then they've whipped us?" Todd had begun to think of the Texas army in terms of *we* and *us*.

"It's not the Yankees that's whipped us. It's that we've never had supplies enough. We've tried to live off of the land in a country where even buzzards starve to death." His voice had a bitter edge. "Flags wavin' and bands playin' . . . we let them shine and blind us back in San Antonio. But our eyes are open now." He turned away until his emotions cooled, then said, "I think I'll go see how Mrs. Hawkins is farin'."

The lieutenant had spent a lot of time seeing to Ella Hawkins's welfare. She, in turn, had bandaged his wound every night, taking her time about it. Todd noticed that when the two were together, the Mexican woman would leave the wagon and go for a long walk.

Sanderson had said he was fighting for his country's freedom, but it appeared to Todd that he might be on the way to losing his own.

16

Auralee had already selected most of the things she wanted to take. They were stacked along the walls, ready to be loaded into two wagons. She thought Sarah needed a couple of days to rest before beginning another journey. Jeffrey helped Boley bury valuables, as had been done with Sarah's china. They covered the burial place with hay.

Jeffrey asked Boley, "What about all those hound dogs?"

"They'll have to stay. They're pretty good at takin' care of theirselves here at home. I don't know as we could feed them on the road."

"And Old Flop?"

"Flop'll do whatever pleases him."

The morning came for departure. Jeffrey was to drive his wagon. The other two would be handled by Auralee and Boley. Lucy and Harry were on horseback, bringing along half a dozen extra horses and mules as well as Matthew's mare. Sarah sat beside Jeffrey but left it to him to handle the reins. He had not seen her smile in the days they had been there. Jeffrey had begun to worry that she might be about to take down sick on the trail.

"Are you ready?" he asked her.

She nodded without speaking, her gaze fixed on Auralee's wagon ahead. Auralee cracked a whip over her mules' heads. Jeffrey set his mules into motion, following. He had long since stopped thinking of them and the wagon as being his property. In his mind, everything belonged to the family. He looked back to see if Boley had started.

Lucy, riding sidesaddle, shouted to start the loose stock moving parallel to the single-file wagons. Harry put his horse into a gallop and tried to make the mules run so he could chase them. Auralee shouted at him to ease off. "We want to get to Mexico with all of them," she said.

Jeffrey wondered what they would do with the extra horses and mules when they crossed the border. Sell them, perhaps, or trade them for supplies. Of one thing he was certain: they would be stolen if left behind, unattended. More than likely, the house and barns would be ransacked, emptied of anything that might have value. When and if John Temple's family returned, they would have to replace most of their belongings.

Two milk cows plodded along behind Auralee's wagon on short tethers. The Temple cow was tied behind Jeffrey's wagon.

Boley had to stop and order the dogs back to the house. The rest went reluctantly, but Old Flop never left Boley's wagon.

Jeffrey found himself watching Lucy as she followed the loose stock. Her blond hair was done up in pigtails that bounced with the movement of her

horse. He imagined she must feel awkward and un-
balanced, riding half sideways with her leg crooked
over the horn of the sidesaddle. Yet, she sat firmly
and appeared to be at ease. Her long gray skirt covered everything but the toes of her lace-up shoes. The
proprieties were fully met even under the stress of a
forced move that carried her away from home.

After they had settled into a comfortable pace,
Jeffrey attempted to make conversation. He hoped
he could encourage Sarah to break her silence. He
said, "Travelin' is a lot easier now with the mud all
dried up."

She nodded but offered no other response.

He said, "I've heard a right smart about San Antonio. Reckon we'll be goin' through there?"

Sarah said only, "Ask Auralee."

He gave up trying to get Sarah to talk. At the
noon stop he asked Auralee. She said, "No, there's
too much Confederate military in San Antonio. We
might get more attention than we want. We'll travel
farther west of there, through some of the German
settlements. Most of them are opposed to secession.
Several counties down that way have been declared
to be in rebellion against the state."

"I thought the whole idea of this trip was to get us
away from the war."

"It is. But if you can't dodge a prairie fire, you
work your way through the thinnest part of it the
fastest way you can."

The trail led them through an increasingly hilly
region of cedar and live oak and outcrops of lime-
stone ledges. They did not lack for fresh meat. Each
evening, Jeffrey took the rifle and worked his way
through the thickets afoot, bringing down a white-
tail deer almost every time. The region abounded in

springs and narrow creeks. Grassy, open flats were interspersed between the rough hills.

The country appealed to him. He told Sarah, "I think I could live here someday and like it."

She gave him a questioning glance. "You'd leave us?"

"I'll have to go on my own eventually. I'm grown, pretty near."

"You're a boy. Enjoy it while you can. You'll be an adult soon enough, and things'll look a lot different."

It was the most he had heard her say in a while. He plied her with questions, trying to keep the conversation going, but she was done with talking. She answered him with a word or two, a nod, or a silent shake of her head. He gave up after a while and went back to watching Lucy.

His best guess was that they were averaging ten miles a day or a bit less. They could travel no faster than the milk cows could walk. Boley joked that making them trot would cause them to give buttermilk. Milking Auralee's two cows was one of Boley's daily chores. Their production was declining under the exertion of travel.

"Time we get to Mexico, we'll be givin' *them* milk," Boley said.

One afternoon, as the trail topped a hill and started on a downward slope, Jeffrey saw a town ahead. Shortly afterward, Auralee stopped her wagon because a large tree branch had fallen across the ruts. Jeffrey climbed down and helped Boley move it so the wagons could pass.

"Wonder what town that is," he said.

Auralee replied, "My map says it's Kerrville. We'll need a few supplies, so we'll camp there tonight, on the Guadalupe River."

"Guadalupe," Jeffrey said. "Funny-soundin' name."

"Spanish. But I've heard the town's pretty heavy German. I hope we find a storekeeper who talks American."

At the edge of town they were hailed by a man whose English was all too easy to understand, as well as his motives. He said to Auralee, "If you folks are lookin' for a place to put up for the night, I can show you to a nice wagon yard. There'll be feed for the stock and cots for yourselves. You can sleep under a roof. You won't need to worry about the rain."

The sky had been clear all day. Auralee said, "How much for all that service?"

"Seein' as you look like good, honest folks, we'll figure the cost right down to the bone. Ten dollars for your stock, two and a half for five cots." He pointed his thumb toward Boley. "I'm not countin' him. He'll have to find himself a place under the trees down on the river."

Auralee said, "We can all find ourselves a place down on the river and camp for nothing."

"I might refigure it a little."

"Good day, sir." Auralee had a firm way of demonstrating that a conversation was over. She turned her head away from him and started the team into motion. On the main street she brought the wagon to a stop in front of a large store. She climbed down and walked back to stand beside Sarah. "Towns'll be a little scarce from here on. I'm going to pick up a few things we're short of. Would you like to go in with me?"

Sarah shook her head. "Too many people. I'll stay where I am."

Auralee gave her a look of regret and entered the store.

Two horsemen approached the wagons. One wore an ill-fitting gray suit with braid that indicated it was meant to be a uniform. He had the all-business look of a man accustomed to giving orders. The other wore civilian clothes and hung back half a length, as if accustomed to following orders. The officer looked the wagons over, then reined up beside Sarah. He said, "I don't see any menfolks except that boy."

Jeffrey assumed he was the boy in question until the man pointed at Boley. If Boley was a boy, he thought, he was the biggest one Jeffrey had ever seen.

Sarah did not reply. The man persisted, "Are your menfolks in the store?"

Curtly she said, "We have no menfolks with us. We're all women and children . . . except that boy." She nodded toward Boley.

"You don't sound Dutch." The man studied her for a moment. "I guess you ain't. Didn't mean to bother you, ma'am, but these Dutchmen around here need a lot of watchin'. Been some of the young ones taken off to Mexico, lookin' to join the Union army. You can't blame us for bein' suspicious of everybody till we've checked them over."

Curious, Jeffrey asked, "How could they join the Union army in Mexico?"

"They could go to the Mexican port and take passage on an American ship. Or they could travel all the way up the river to New Mexico, if the Indians didn't get them."

"Either way would take a long time, wouldn't it? I keep hearin' people say this war'll be over in a little while."

"The way our troops been whuppin' up on them Yankees, they'll be hollerin' for a settlement pretty soon. Them Dutch boys will find themselves stranded in some far-off place and wish they'd never left home." He tipped his hat. "Been nice talkin' with you, ma'am."

Sarah had not spoken more than a dozen words to him, and she had said very little more to Jeffrey.

Watching the two men ride away, he said, "That must be what passes for the Confederate army around here."

She just nodded.

They camped for the night beneath cypress trees along the river, putting up a tent for the women's privacy. Jeffrey, Harry, and Boley would sleep outdoors. A couple of other wagon camps were nearby. Jeffrey noted that the pair of Confederate soldiers gave those a brief inspection before stopping in the light of the Temples' campfire. The officer tipped his hat to the women but looked mostly at Sarah. So did the other man. "Evenin', ladies. Is there anything the army can do for you-all?"

Auralee answered quickly so Sarah would not feel pressured into doing so. "Not a thing, but thanks for asking."

"We were a little concerned, you-all not havin' any menfolks to help you."

Auralee sounded confident. "With so many men gone off to war, women have learned how to manage right well by themselves."

"These are troublesome times indeed. Should you need help of any kind, don't hesitate to send for us." The officer touched his hat brim again, and the pair disappeared into the night.

"He's suspicious," Auralee said quietly. "I suppose there's been other families gone to Mexico after their men."

Jeffrey asked, "Do you think he'll follow us?"

"Awhile maybe, till he's satisfied that our menfolks aren't going to join us."

"Maybe we ought to get an extra-early start in the mornin'."

"No, he can't do us any harm. Like as not, John and Matthew are already in Mexico. It might be good to have those two following behind us in case we run into trouble."

"You think they'd come and help?"

"It's in their raising to respect women and take care of them. And I think they both might be a little taken with Sarah."

Sarah flushed. "Why would you say that?"

"It's in their nature. You're still a good-looking woman."

Sarah's voice was bitter. "That kind of attention is the last thing I need. When a man looks at me like those did, I want to kill them."

As they traveled southward the next day, Jeffrey occasionally glanced back. He did not see the two soldiers.

Shortly after they crossed a small, clear creek, shaded by tall cypress trees, Auralee's mules stopped suddenly and reared up in the traces. One squealed in fright. The contagion spread quickly to Jeffrey's team and to Boley's, though Boley was strong enough to keep his under tight control. Old Flop bounded away, barking fiercely.

Holding the reins tightly, Auralee shouted at her team, then exclaimed, "My God, what is that?"

Jeffrey fought his team, trying to prevent it from running. He caught a glimpse of something moving ahead. He blinked, not quite believing what passed before his eyes. Three large, strange creatures he had never seen before moved along at a steady clip. Their necks and ungainly legs were long. Each had a large hump on its back.

He remembered pictures he had seen in books. These were camels.

The loose stock caught wind of the beasts and took flight, Lucy and Harry trying hard to keep up with them.

Auralee's team broke into a run, making a tight circle that threatened to flip her wagon. Jeffrey was unable to help because he had his hands full with his own. Sarah held to the seat with both hands. Auralee screamed at her mules and sawed futilely at the lines.

From somewhere behind, two horsemen came at a dead run. They pulled in on either side of Auralee's team and got hold of the bridles. Hollering at the mules, they gradually muscled them to a stop.

The blood had drained from Auralee's face. She exclaimed, "Thank the Lord."

Thank the Confederate army, Jeffrey thought. The rescuers were the two who had checked the family camp the night before.

The camels moved on, unperturbed by the excitement, though one kicked at Old Flop and missed. Jeffrey brought his team under control and pulled up close to Auralee's wagon. Her mules dripped sweat, their eyes still rolling in the aftermath of fright. Boley ran from his wagon and wrapped his strong arms around one mule's head, forcibly holding it still as the soldiers backed away.

Sarah jumped down and ran to Auralee's side. "Are you all right?"

Auralee was breathing heavily. "I reckon. Just had the daylights scared out of me. What in God's name was that?"

The officer smiled. "You've just made the acquaintance of Jeff Davis's camels, ma'am. They've frightened many a horse and mule, and they've even reformed a few drunks who thought they'd stumbled onto the devil."

Jeffrey was having trouble getting his breath. "But what're they doin' here? This ain't no desert."

Several hundred yards away, Lucy and Harry were getting the runaway loose stock under a semblance of control. The officer looked over the wagons and nodded in satisfaction. The contents of Auralee's wagon had been bounced around and scattered somewhat, but no irreparable damage had been done.

He said, "When Jefferson Davis was secretary of war, he got the notion that camels might be good to carry freight on the western deserts. They could pack more than a mule, and they could go a long time without water. He imported a boatload and had a big camel corral built a little ways up the creek here from Camp Verde. When the war came on, people lost interest in the camels. A lot of them were turned loose to wander. Most of the Ay-rabs that came with them went home. Nobody else knows how to handle them." He smiled. "There's a bright side to this. You got to see the circus without paying for it."

Auralee said, "We almost paid for it. They came close to tearing up three good wagons. It's lucky you happened to be coming along behind us."

"To tell you the truth, ma'am, it wasn't luck. You-all have the earmarks of a family tryin' to get to Mexico. We figured your menfolk might've circled around town to meet you on this side. So we followed you."

"Looks like you figured wrong."

"Not about you headin' for Mexico. I still suspect that part is true, but we can't afford to go any farther in hope of catchin' up to your men. We'll have to bid you *adiós*." He paused. "Do you know what *adiós* means?"

"Can't say as I do."

"You'd best learn that and a great deal more if you're goin' to Mexico. They don't talk much American down there." He took off his hat and looked at Sarah. "I hope you understand that we are just doin' our duty. We've got nothin' against two such lovely ladies. We hope all goes well with you on the rest of your journey."

The pair headed toward Kerrville. The officer turned in the saddle a couple of times, looking back toward the wagons.

Auralee said, "Sarah, I think you charmed him."

Sarah said, "I certainly did not intend to." She seemed to draw herself into a knot.

As Auralee had said, they traveled well to the west of San Antonio. They had passed over the Lampasas, the San Gabriel, the Colorado, the Frio, and smaller creeks and streams. Several more days brought them to the Nueces River.

Jeffrey said, "I'm beginnin' to get web feet. We've already crossed so many rivers. How many more are there goin' to be?"

Auralee said, "The next big one will be the Rio Grande."

Jeffrey looked at her hand-drawn map. Texas did not appear so large on a sheet of paper, but on the ground it had turned out to be formidable. They had already traveled most of the way across it from north to south, and the map indicated that they were still a few days short of reaching Brownsville.

Auralee said, "From what Matthew told me, the ground is fixing to get flatter, brushier, and an awful lot dryer. We've got to be sure we fill the water barrels every chance we get."

Jeffrey had seen much to like about the hills west of Austin. What he saw now looked more like a desert, sand and cactus and brushy plants with all manner of thorns that tried to reach out and grab him, or so it seemed. "Looks like an outlaw country to me," he said.

"John says from here to the border it *is* a haven for outlaws from both sides. If the law gets to pressing them, they can pull back into the brush, or they can cross the Rio Grande. With a war on, I doubt there's enough law left to do much about them."

Sarah had had little to say, but she commented, "I don't like it here. I feel like a bandit is waiting behind every bush."

Jeffrey noticed that she hid the rifle behind a box of supplies. It remained within easy reach but would not be obvious to someone not seriously searching for it.

He said, "If a bandit should happen to show up, it'd be his own fault."

17

An hysterical Mexican girl burst suddenly out of the brush, almost as much a surprise as the camels had been. She ran to Auralee's lead wagon, waving her arms and crying, startling the mules. Auralee fought to keep her team under control. She demanded in a high-pitched voice, "What is it, girl? What are you trying to say?"

The words spilled in a torrent. Jeffrey understood none of it. He guessed she was speaking Spanish. She was young, her black hair disheveled, her plain cotton dress torn, her brown face and arms scratched and bleeding from fighting her way through the thorny brush.

The girl kept babbling, crying, pointing back westward, where the brush was thickest. Auralee said, "Girl, I haven't got the slightest notion what you're talking about." She shouted, "Boley, come up here and see if you can make any sense out of what she's saying."

Sarah hurried to the girl's side and took a grip on

her shoulders. Sympathetically she said, "Easy now. We're here to help you."

Fearful, the girl shrank away from Boley as he approached, Old Flop at his side. Jeffrey figured Boley must look like a giant to her. In a deep but gentle voice he said some words Jeffrey did not understand. The girl's fright gradually eased. She replied to him excitedly. Boley listened, then said, "I just get a word here and there. Best I can figure out, she got away from a bad man out there someplace. She's afraid he's comin' after her."

Sarah's eyes flashed with anger. "We're not going to let anybody get her. Tell her that."

Boley tried. Jeffrey was not sure the message came across.

Auralee said, "She's not but a slip of a girl. I can't imagine any man trying to hurt her."

Tight-lipped, Sarah said, "I can."

Auralee motioned for the girl to join her on the wagon seat. Jeffrey held out his hand to help Sarah climb back up beside him. Color had risen to her face. She reached down and touched the rifle as if to reassure herself that it was there.

They moved on. The Mexican girl kept watching the brush and looking back anxiously. Jeffrey asked, "What'll we do if somebody comes to get her?"

Grimly Sarah said, "Whatever we have to."

They had traveled a couple of miles when the girl stiffened in fear. Jeffrey turned to see what had frightened her. A man on horseback overtook Boley's wagon at a long trot. As he passed Jeffrey and Sarah, he shouted at Auralee, "Haul up there! You've got somethin' that belongs to me."

The girl threw her arms around Auralee as the lead team stopped. Auralee held her protectively. Boley came running on foot, Old Flop beside him. Jeffrey jumped down and joined them.

The rider was American. He looked as if he had been out in the brush for weeks, hair shaggy, whiskers long, skin darkly weathered by sun and wind. He wore stained cotton britches. His homespun shirt was ripped in several places, probably victim to hostile thorns. He looked into the defiant faces and declared, "What're you doin' with that girl? She's mine."

Auralee asked, "Is she your daughter? Or maybe your wife?"

"None of your business what she is. I own her, and I want her."

"It doesn't appear that she wants you. From the bruises, it looks to me like you've been beating on her." The girl still clung desperately to Auralee. "If she's not your daughter or your wife, I don't see where you've got any claim."

"She's my property. I bought her."

"Bought her?" Auralee's voice rose in anger. "Human beings aren't for buying and selling."

The man jerked his head toward Boley. "No? What about him?"

"Boley's a free man. And this girl is free, too."

The man grabbed the girl's arm and roughly jerked her away from Auralee. He said something in Spanish and flung her to the ground.

Near Jeffrey's wagon, Sarah raised the rifle. She fired a shot that cut through the edge of the man's ear. "Back off," she shouted. "The next one goes between your eyes." She rammed another cartridge into the breech.

Startled, the rider grabbed at his ear. He cursed, and tugged on the reins to control his frightened horse. "Dammit, you could kill a man."

Sarah said, "Damned right I could."

A trickle of blood ran down the man's neck. "It ain't none of your affair."

Sarah leveled the rifle. "Between the eyes."

The man looked at the blood on his hand and backed his horse a few steps. "Damn you, she belongs to me, body, soul, and all the rest of her." His gaze was concentrated on Sarah's rifle.

Auralee said, "The law would see it different."

"Possession is the only law that counts around here."

Sarah said, "Well, you don't possess her anymore."

"I'll be back."

Auralee warned, "I wouldn't, if I were you. Just because we're mostly women here, don't think we're helpless."

Boley hissed to Old Flop, "Sic him!"

Flop tore after the man and the horse. They disappeared quickly into the brush, the man still shouting curses. Flop returned shortly, looking pleased with himself.

Jeffrey was a moment in getting over his surprise. He saw a strength in Sarah that he thought she had lost after her ordeal with the two outlaws. He leaned down and helped the girl to her feet. He had not seen her so closely before. He guessed that she was not much older than he, but her haunted eyes and a dark bruise across her cheek spoke silently of abuse he could only imagine.

Sarah walked up, still carrying the rifle. She hugged the girl and asked, "What's your name, child?"

The girl did not understand. Boley spoke, and she replied, "Dolores."

Boley said, "That means 'sadness,' or 'pain.'"

Auralee said, "The child looks as if she's had a lot

of that." She glanced in the direction the rider had taken. "We'd best be moving."

Toward dusk, they came upon several freight wagons already camped for the night, their tongues pointed southward. Each bore a cargo of baled cotton. Auralee motioned for the girl to climb back beneath the wagon sheet, out of sight. She said, "We don't know what manner of men these may be." The comment was unnecessary, for the girl could not understand the words. But she hid herself.

A burly man with graying whiskers walked out to meet the oncoming wagons. He cradled a rifle in muscular arms that looked as if they could wrestle a mule to the ground. "Who you be?" he asked warily.

"Just travelers," Auralee said. "Mostly women except for two boys and a freedman. Who are you?"

"Freighters, on our way to Brownsville. Name's Jack Fountain."

He gave the three wagons and their occupants a quick looking over. "Sorry to be suspicious, but it pays in these parts. The brush is infested with the worst outlaws of two countries."

Auralee said, "So we're told. Reckon you'd let us camp here close to you-all? We'd feel safer with some menfolks nearby."

The freighter nodded. "You'd be welcome. I can guess why you women are travelin'. You ain't the first I've seen doin' the same. But don't be afraid I hold anything against you for it. I stay clear of politics."

Auralee smiled. "And I'd guess you're hauling that cotton to Mexico to get around the Yankee blockade. I can't say I hold anything against you for that, either."

The freighter broke into a grin. "Looks like we're all a desperate lot of lawbreakers, me in Union eyes and you to the Confederacy. Camp anywhere you feel like, ma'am."

Auralee hesitated. "Do you talk Mexican?"

"Fair to middlin'. You have to, down in this border country."

"I've got somebody I'd like you to talk to after a while. She doesn't talk American, and we don't talk Mexican."

"I'll come over to your camp after supper."

"Come *for* supper if you'd like."

"I'd be tickled. Ain't often I get to break bread with two nice-lookin' ladies."

Auralee smiled. "Don't forget that we're married."

"So am I, but my eyesight's still fair to middlin'."

When he came to the camp later, he was clean-shaven and wore a fresh shirt. The Mexican girl watched him fearfully. He spoke in a calm, sympathetic voice that gradually wore down her misgivings. With prompting from Auralee, he asked questions. Hesitant at first, she eventually began to talk at length, pausing from time to time to weep quietly.

Fountain turned to Auralee and Sarah. He said, "She comes from a village south of the river. You ain't seen poor folks till you've seen poor Mexicans. Her mama and daddy died of the fever, and their kids were scattered out with relations. An uncle took her but treated her like a slave. He finally traded her for a mule to a gringo named Catlett. The gringo treated her like a dog. Even . . . well, I don't like to speak of such things to ladies like yourselves. Anyway, she ran away last night while he was dead drunk. She's scared to death he's goin' to come and take her back."

Sarah gripped the girl's trembling hand. Tightly she said, "He's already tried. He left in a right smart of a hurry."

Fountain said, "I know about this Ward Catlett. He ain't exactly overrun with scruples. Was I you, I wouldn't give him a chance to get the upper hand. I'd shoot him on sight."

Jeffrey asked, "What about the law?"

"Most of it has gone to the war. Ain't enough left around here to do you any good, or any hurt, either. Just kill him and be done with it." He considered for a moment. "I might be able to spare a man, if you'd like me to send one with you."

Auralee said, "We wouldn't want to impose on your good nature. If it comes to trouble, I expect we can manage for ourselves. We have so far." She tilted her head toward Sarah. "This lady is a devil of a good shot. Mr. Catlett has already found that out."

"That bein' the case, he'll try to take every advantage and hit you where you're not lookin'. So be on the *cuidado*."

Sitting in the flickering light of a dying campfire, Lucy studied the Mexican girl with curiosity. She leaned toward Jeffrey and whispered, "She looks a little older than us."

"I suppose she is. Or maybe a hard life has made her look that way."

"She's too old for you, don't you think?"

"I hadn't thought about it." He eyed her curiously. "How come *you* thought about it?"

"You can't marry both of us."

"I wasn't figurin' on marryin' anybody. And even if I did, I ought to be shavin' first."

The subject made him uncomfortable. He left the fire and went to the place where he had spread his blankets on the ground. Boley followed him, grinning. "You better be watchin' out," he said. "Whatever Miss Lucy wants, she generally gets it."

Jeffrey's face warmed. His embarrassment was made worse by the fact that he could think of no proper response.

He wanted to sleep, but too much was running through his mind. He tried not to think about the Mexican girl and the man who seemed hell-bent on taking her back, but the images persisted. When he became too restless to lie still any longer, he arose and picked up the rifle. Boley's blankets lay rumpled on the ground. Jeffrey saw him, a dark shape leaning against a wagon near the women's tent. Moving quietly, he took Boley by surprise. The black man whirled, a knife in his hand. He lowered it and whispered, "Boy, you like to've got a blade in your brisket."

Jeffrey's heartbeat quickened as he realized what could have happened to him. "You thought I was that feller Catlett?"

"Yes, and I was about to gut you like a fish."

"I couldn't sleep. I thought I'd just as well be up keepin' watch."

"That's what I'm doin'. You'd best go back to bed. You ain't big enough to tangle with a man like that anyway."

"I've got the rifle. That'll make us even. What were you goin' to fight him with?"

"Miz Auralee's bullwhip. Or this knife, if he got too close."

Jeffrey did not see Old Flop. Usually he was not far from Boley. He asked, "Where's the dog?"

"Out prowlin' around. I don't expect he'll let a stranger sneak in without raisin' a holler."

No one did. The next morning, Jeffrey was feeling sluggish from lack of sleep, but he went about his routine chores, preparing to break camp and move on southward. He had a hunch no one else had slept much better except perhaps Lucy and Harry. They had been pushing the loose stock along some distance from the wagons when Catlett had appeared. They had missed seeing him and hearing his threat.

Jack Fountain came around as the women were putting away the skillet, plates, and cups used at breakfast. He said, "Your wagons will travel faster than mine, so it's better that you start first. Sure you don't want me to send a man with you?"

Auralee said, "Thank you kindly, but we can handle it."

Sarah did not speak. As Fountain walked back to his wagons, Auralee said, "Despite their rough edges, most men turn out to be pretty good old boys."

Sarah's eyes were grim. "But a few need killing."

Catlett's return was bolder than anyone expected. Harry came pounding toward the wagons, his horse on the run. He was shouting before he was close enough to be understood. He rode straight up to his mother's lead wagon and cried, "He's got Lucy."

Auralee's jaw dropped. "Who are you talking about?"

"He rode up and lifted Lucy right off of her horse. He's comin' this way now, bringin' her."

Jeffrey stopped his team. Sarah grabbed the rifle and jumped down, circling around to hide herself behind the wagon. Jeffrey remained on the wagon seat until he saw the rider approaching, carrying Lucy in front of him. He dropped to the ground, wishing he had a rifle, too. He could not see the Mexican girl. He assumed she was hiding in Auralee's wagon.

Catlett stopped twenty yards out. He had one arm

around Lucy. The other hand held a pistol. He called, "I've come to make a swap."

Jeffrey could see Lucy's eyes, wide in fear. Old Flop circled the horse, barking a challenge.

Auralee demanded, "You turn my daughter loose."

"I told you, I'm here to trade. Your girl for mine."

He looked around cautiously, counting the wagon people. "There's one of you missin'. Where's that other woman?" He held the muzzle of the pistol against Lucy's head.

Sarah showed herself but without the rifle. Catlett was not close enough to read the hatred in her eyes, but Jeffrey saw it.

Catlett moved a little closer. "How about it? You goin' to swap, or not?" When no one answered, he said, "I'd as soon keep this girl. She's white, and she's fresh."

Dolores came out from beneath Auralee's wagon sheet and slowly climbed down. She walked slowly toward Catlett, sobbing. He said, "That's better. You people are startin' to show some sense."

Auralee said angrily, "It's her doin'. I didn't ask her to give herself up."

Catlett released Lucy so he could reach down for Dolores. As Lucy slid to the ground, she turned quickly, flaring her long skirt and shouting at Catlett's horse. The surprised animal stepped backward, throwing Catlett off-balance.

Boley shouted, *"Flop! Sic him!"*

The dog nipped at the horse's legs, startling it into a frenzy. Lucy grabbed Dolores's arm and ran to Auralee's wagon.

Cursing in Spanish, Catlett fired the pistol, but missed. Auralee rushed out and grabbed the girls, whirling around to place herself between them and Catlett.

Sarah stepped back to where she had left the rifle at the side of the wagon. Bringing it to her shoulder, she shouted, "Damn you, you'll not do to Lucy what was done to me!"

Catlett fired first. Sarah jerked, but she squeezed the trigger. Catlett slumped, dropping his pistol. His horse began pitching. Catlett flew from the saddle, landing on his hands and knees. He felt around on the ground, urgently searching for the fallen weapon.

Jeffrey reached it first. Catlett was bleeding from a wound in his shoulder. He extended a bloody hand forward. Jeffrey pulled back out of his reach, holding the pistol.

He heard Auralee cry, "Sarah's been shot."

Sarah lay motionless on the ground.

Catlett groaned. "Stupid damned woman." He brought his hand up to his wound. Blood flowed between his fingers.

Auralee knelt beside Sarah and cried, "Oh my God. She's dying."

A terrible fury swept over Jeffrey. He leveled the pistol at Catlett. The man's mouth dropped open in horror, and he raised a crimson hand, as if it could ward off a bullet. He cried, "Don't."

Jeffrey fired. Catlett screamed as the bullet raised a puff of dust from his shirt. Jeffrey fired again and again until Catlett pitched forward on his face. The pistol jammed, but he kept trying desperately for one more shot.

Boley gently touched his arm. "Ain't no use shootin' him anymore. I believe he's dead."

Jeffrey threw the smoking pistol at the body and

staggered to where Sarah lay. The two girls had joined Auralee there. Auralee cried, "Sarah, hold on."

Sarah struggled to keep her eyes open. Her lips moved, and Jeffrey bent closer to hear. She rasped, "Tell Matthew . . ." She grasped Jeffrey's hand. "Tell him . . ."

Her hand fell limp. Jeffrey continued to grip it. Tears burning his eyes, he murmured, "I'll tell him."

He would tell Matthew of Sarah's courage, but never would he tell what else had happened to her.

Auralee was devastated. "Matthew is waiting for her down in Mexico somewhere. How can we break this to him?"

"It's this war," Jeffrey cried. "Without it, she'd still be back on the farm. So would Matthew."

The weight of loss bore down heavily upon him. He had helped bury his own mother. Now he would have to bury a woman who had become a second mother to him.

Boley's voice was calm. "You'd best put the blame where it belongs, on him." He pointed at Catlett's body. "He ain't got nothin' to do with the war. He's just a bandit. I'll bet the devil is stokin' up a special hot fire just for him."

Jeffrey realized he should feel remorse. He had never killed a man before. The outlaw's death should be troubling him, but he could feel nothing for Catlett. His grief was only for Sarah. He turned so the others wouldn't see the tears that scalded his cheeks. He rubbed them away onto his sleeve and looked at the fallen outlaw.

He declared, "I'm glad I killed the son of a bitch."

Boley touched Jeffrey's shoulder. "Me and you had best be diggin' a proper grave for that poor woman. I'll fetch a shovel."

Jeffrey asked, "What about Catlett?"

Boley shook his head. "We'll let him feed the coyotes. That's as good as he's got comin' to him."

They had almost finished the grave when Fountain rode up in advance of his cotton wagons. He reacted with concern when he saw the quilt spread across Sarah's body. "Been somebody killed?"

Jeffrey said, "It was Sarah. And Catlett." He explained as briefly as he could.

Fountain removed his hat. "Poor lady. Never got to see her husband again. Who killed Catlett?"

Jeffrey took a deep breath. "Sarah put the first bullet in him. I finished the job."

Fountain blinked in surprise. "You're too young to have a dead man on your conscience."

"My conscience is not hurtin' me one bit. I wish I could've killed him a dozen times." Jeffrey frowned as a disturbing thought came to him. "I suppose the law will bear down hard on me for this."

"Not if the law doesn't know about it. I'll take Catlett off into the brush and dump him. Nobody's goin' to worry about him disappearin', except maybe some he owes money to. I ain't goin' to talk about what happened to him, and I'm sure you folks won't."

Catlett's horse had strayed a hundred yards or so. Fountain rode out and brought it back. "Would you-all help me throw Catlett over his saddle?"

Boley lifted the outlaw and laid him across the nervous horse. Catlett's pistol still lay where it had fallen. Fountain picked it up. He asked, "Was this his?"

Jeffrey nodded.

Fountain extended it toward him. "You'd just as well have it."

"I'd always remember this is the gun that killed Sarah."

"A gun is just a tool, like a hammer or a saw. It carries no guilt. You may have need of it someday."

Reluctantly Jeffrey accepted the pistol. Fountain led the animal and its burden out into the chaparral. In a while he returned.

Jeffrey asked, "What did you do with his horse?"

"Unsaddled him and turned him loose. Maybe he'll drift back to wherever Catlett stole him from."

The cotton wagons were lumbering into view. Fountain told Auralee, "There's a fair to middlin' campground a little farther along. You-all are welcome to share it with us."

She said, "We've got to give Sarah a decent buryin' before we move on. Pity we don't have a preacher to read over her."

"When I come back next trip, I'll see if I can fetch one up here from Brownsville."

"Maybe that'll put her soul to rest. Mighty little rest it's had till now."

They wrapped Sarah in Auralee's quilt. Boley gently eased her down into the grave. Auralee read from a Bible and said a prayer. Boley took a board from his wagon's tailgate and set it up after Auralee scratched the words *Sarah Temple* on it. "Seems a pity to bury her way out in the middle of nowhere," she said. "But the Lord'll know where she's at."

She suggested that they move on to where the cotton wagons camped. She said, "I don't think any of us could sleep if we stay here."

Lucy lingered at the new grave. Jeffrey said to her, "That was a brave thing you did, boogerin' Catlett's horse."

"It was all I could think of to do."

"He tried to shoot you."

"I thought about that afterwards. I didn't at the

time, so I guess I wasn't really brave after all. Just dumb."

As they made camp near the Fountain wagons, the wagon boss came over. He asked Auralee, "Everybody all right?"

Auralee looked at Jeffrey. "I guess we're all shook up pretty bad."

"I don't envy you, havin' to break the news to the lady's husband. I suppose he's waitin' in Brownsville?"

"Across the river in Matamoros, him and my husband both. At least that's been the plan."

"Livin' in Mexico will be different from what you're used to. Think you're ready for it?"

"I wasn't ready for this stupid war, but we've learned to live with it. I guess we'll survive in Mexico."

"When you get to Brownsville, ask for directions to my wagon yard. Talk to Tiburcio Valadez. He'll send a message across the river to let your men know you've arrived."

"We're much obliged for all you've done."

"It wasn't much. If there's ever anything more I can do for you, I'll be in Brownsville when I'm not on the road." He looked toward Dolores. "What you goin' to do with her?"

"I've got no idea."

"I've been thinkin'. My wife's been stove up lately and needin' help. We'd be glad to take the girl in."

"That's kind of you."

Fountain walked to where Jeffrey was feeding the mules. He said, "You seem to be a good hand with a wagon and team."

Jeffrey said, "I can think like a mule when I need to."

"Good help is hard to find. If you need a job, I

could use you and your wagon in my freightin' business."

"You think I'm old enough?"

"I was skinnin' mules when I was ten. You're old enough to do the job but young enough to come and go on the Texas side of the river and not be bothered by home guards."

Jeffrey admitted, "I've been worryin' about how I'd fit in Mexico. I've never been anywhere but Arkansas and Texas."

"Think about it. I'll be in Brownsville till I get this cotton delivered and pick up freight to go back to San Antonio."

"I'll see how things stand when we get there. I may come lookin' for you."

Valadez led them through the streets of Brownsville and past long rows of cotton bales, bringing them finally to the ferry. Struggling with the language, he told them he had sent a messenger ahead to inform the Temple men of their coming.

The ferry was simply a flat wooden boat with protective rails, propelled across the Rio Grande by heavy ropes. Jeffrey reasoned that it must be safe, for it made many crossings every day and had never sunk, so far as anybody had said. Nevertheless, it bobbed up and down, giving him the same queasy feeling he had encountered on the collapsing bridge weeks ago. Harry did not help by asking, "Do you know how to swim?" He seemed just as uneasy.

The ferry was not large enough to carry all three wagons at once. Boley remained behind to follow on the next trip with his wagon and the extra animals.

Halfway across, Auralee was already asking, "Can you see them? Are they waiting there?"

Harry's eyes were the sharpest. He said, "I see Daddy. And I think that's Uncle Matthew there with him."

Auralee and Lucy left the ferry the moment it touched the dock. They ran into the waiting arms of a man Jeffrey assumed was John Temple. Reluctantly Jeffrey stepped off, steeling himself for the sad duty to come. Matthew hurried to meet him, smiling broadly and pumping his hand with vigor. "Sure good to see you, boy. You look like you've gotten older since I saw you last."

"I feel like I have, too. A lot."

Matthew's gaze eagerly searched over the wagons. "Where's Sarah?"

Jeffrey swallowed a lump that had risen in his throat. "We lost her."

"Lost her?" Matthew's smile vanished. "What do you mean?"

"She's dead." He almost choked. "A bandit shot her. We buried her alongside the trail."

Matthew turned away and leaned against the wagon. His shoulders trembled. "A bandit? Why?"

Fighting tears, Jeffrey explained. "She was tryin' to protect a Mexican girl she didn't hardly even know."

John and Auralee came over to share Matthew's grief, and Jeffrey's.

The ferry operator was impatient to clear the deck so he could take passengers back to the Texas side. Jeffrey dreaded another trip across that rolling river, but he did not want to stay there and go through a new round of mourning. He said, "I'd best go back and help Boley with the stock."

Matthew and John had rented a couple of small
stone houses at the edge of town. John said apolo-
getically, "It's nothin' like home, but it'll have to do
for a while."

His description was an understatement. The houses
were cramped and devoid of comforts. Each had but
two rooms and a fireplace for cooking. Water had to
be carried from a community well down the street.
John said, "We've been boilin' the water before we
use it. Last thing we want is to come down with chol-
era or somethin'."

Auralee asked, "Have you and Matthew found any
kind of work to do?"

"Not much. He's done some preachin' to the American community. I've helped load freight wagons carryin' goods across to Texas."

Jeffrey thought of Fountain. "What kind of goods?"

"Mainly guns and other military stuff."

"Guns?"

"Wagons bring Texas cotton to sell to English buy-
ers on this side of the river. They send it out of a Mexican port because the Union blockade can't touch
foreign ships. The cotton buys rifles and munitions
for the Confederacy. American authorities can't do
much except stand by and watch." He frowned. "I'm
ashamed to say I've had a hand in that, but there's
little else to do here. A man has got to make a livin'."

Auralee said, "It's just one little old river, but it sure
does make a difference."

John said, "I think this game will soon be up. We've
heard rumors that the Union is fixin' to send an invasion force into Brownsville and shut down the trade."

Auralee frowned. "What'll that mean to us?"

"If the Union does invade, it means we won't have
to worry about the Confederate authorities anymore

We can go over to Brownsville. Like as not the Union army will have work for us to do."

Matthew had been a silent, brooding presence since learning of Sarah's death. Jeffrey shared one of the small houses with him and was aware that Matthew sat up most of a long, dark night, staring at the bare walls. Harry came over at daybreak and invited them to share breakfast in the other house. Hollow-eyed, Matthew picked at the food on his plate but ate little.

He said, "I've spent the night thinkin' and prayin' over what to do. I intend to take the next American boat I can catch. I'll sail back around to where I can join the Union army."

Auralee frowned. "You're too old to be a soldier."

"Maybe they'll need a chaplain. There's bound to be somethin' I can do." He nodded toward Jeffrey. "One thing worries me, though. I can't take the boy."

John said, "Don't bother yourself about that. We'll care for him, me and Auralee."

Jeffrey said, "You won't have to. I'm old enough to take care of myself."

He thought it best not to reveal that he already had an offer of a job. Matthew would not like the idea of his helping freight goods for the Confederacy.

Matthew appeared to have reservations, but he said, "I guess you're of age to make your own decisions. I was doin' it by the time I was as old as you are. I reckon we've taught you about all we can, me and Sarah." He choked on his wife's name.

Jeffrey said, "I'll be all right."

Matthew pondered awhile, regaining his composure. He turned to his brother. "John, I want you to go with me and talk to that American lawyer we met. I want him to draw up a paper showin' that Jeffrey owns half interest in the farm. And if I don't come back when the war's over, it's all his." He raised his eyebrows. "Is that all right with you, Jeffrey?"

Jeffrey swallowed. "You'll be comin' back. Everybody keeps sayin' the war won't last long."

18

Todd was walking, leading Comanche to ease stress on the horse as they worked their way up a rough mountain trail ahead of the wagons. General Sibley had ordered the column to leave the river and cut across the mountains, partly in hope of avoiding conflict with a larger Union force and partly because the river road's deep sand severely hampered movement of the wagons. They had been falling farther and farther behind, the teams worn out, starving for both forage and water. Many wagons had been abandoned, their contents left behind or packed on mules already nearing the limits of endurance.

Men had been left behind, too, the sick, the wounded, the exhausted. Some would die on that rugged trail. A column a mile long when it started in the morning would gradually stretch out to several times that, vulnerable to flanking attacks by federals or Indians.

Todd kept an anxious eye on Sanderson, afraid some officer of higher rank might declare him unfit to go on. Down on the river, those who stayed behind could reasonably count on the federals' finding them and giving them such care as was available. Up here on the mountain route, they might not be found. As far as Todd could see, Union troops had made no effort to follow the Texans to higher ground.

Sanderson appeared to be holding up as well as most. Like Todd, he was periodically dismounting and leading his horse, though his limp was worrisome. Only a couple of times had he taken advantage of Ella Hawkins's invitation to ride with her in the wagon, and then for only a short while. He said he did not want to appear more privileged than his men. The Hawkins wagon was trailing behind like the others, severely challenged by the harsh terrain.

Sanderson said, "Kid, I want you to go back and stay close to Mrs. Hawkins. If she needs more help than you can give her, come up and get me."

Todd had noticed that many men showed a willingness to help her, so it was unlikely he would have to fetch the lieutenant for anything less than a complete wreck. He was torn between the woman and Sanderson. She warmed him with an easy smile. The Mexican woman fawned over him, telling him in Spanish what a good boy he was, a credit to his parents.

He did not feel like a boy anymore. The hardships of recent weeks had toughened him. Witnessing so much death had given him a keen awareness of his mortality, and everyone else's. Constantly remaining alert for danger had sharpened his senses. Union troops were not the only thing to worry about. The Texans were edging into Apache country. Those Indians liked to pick off stragglers. Union or Confederate, it mattered not to them.

He remembered little about his mother and father

except for the violent way he had seen them die. He recalled vividly, however, his terror when the Comanches picked him up and carried him away from the smoking carnage. He reasoned that there was probably a big difference between Comanches and Apaches, for they often warred against each other. But the two tribes were equally to be dreaded by the white man.

Ella Hawkins greeted him as he rode back to her wagon. She looked thinner than when he had first seen her, her dusty face drawn, her dull eyes making a lie of her forced smile. To reduce the weight her team had to pull, she had dumped most of the goods she had brought from Santa Fe. She said, "Hello, kid. How did you leave Lieutenant Sanderson?"

"He's wore out, like everybody. He told me I should stay back here in case you need help."

She glanced at her servant. "That makes us feel a lot better, doesn't it, María?"

The Mexican woman was slumped on the wagon seat, too weary to do more than nod.

Todd realized Mrs. Hawkins was teasing him, but it was a gentle sort of teasing, not malicious or condescending. He felt that he could hold his own if trouble came from outside. He had picked up a rifle and a pistol discarded by exhausted soldiers trying to lighten their loads. The mountain trail behind the column was strewn with abandoned equipment, dead and dying animals. A few fresh graves, too.

Mrs. Hawkins asked, "Has anybody said how much longer we'll be on this trail?"

"I ain't sure anybody knows. Seems to me like we're just pickin' our way across. Lieutenant says we'll swing around Fort Craig and leave it be because we don't know how big a force the Yankees have got there.

We'll probably cut back down to the river farther south and hope they don't ambush us."

"I don't know how much longer my team can hold up to this."

"I wonder how much longer any of them can. The men, either."

Todd had to reach up and grab his hat as a gust of wind tried to tear it from his head. On top of the other discomforts, the wind whipped like an angry beast on the mountain. It threatened to suck the breath from him. The two women bent into it, their heads down. It was a long way from the New Mexico Todd had known, the land of pine trees and green valleys, of sparkling streams and wild game. If Texas was going to be like this, he thought, he might better have stayed with January. At least January was quiet at times, when he drank enough to put him to sleep.

The long column gradually pulled together to camp among the cedar trees. After seeing to his men, Sanderson came to Ella Hawkins's wagon. Todd had dug a fire pit for her and started flames licking at dry cedar limbs. Wood was plentiful enough here, though water was not.

Sanderson asked, "Is the kid takin' care of you all right?"

She replied, "The young man has done right fine." She put emphasis on *the young man*. That set well with Todd. He felt that the recent weeks' experiences should qualify him for that higher status. A kid would not have endured this far.

Sanderson studied the lines of fatigue in the woman's face. He said, "You might've been better off if you'd stayed in Santa Fe. This trip has been hard, and there's still more ahead."

She said, "I couldn't stay."

"Why? The Yankees wouldn't do anything to a woman."

"You think not?" She glanced uneasily at Todd, as if she wished he would wander off out of earshot. He had no intention of doing so. This sounded too interesting.

She said, "There was this federal officer . . . he . . ." she looked at Todd again, "made advances. When he grabbed me, I struck him with the first thing I could lay my hands on, a poker. I think I broke his nose. He swore he'd see me tried as a Confederate spy. You Texans came, and he retreated with the rest. But I knew he'd be back."

Sanderson said, "Maybe we shot him at Glorieta."

"I doubt it. He's the kind who would stay in the rear, out of harm's way. That broken nose is probably the worst injury he's suffered, more's the pity."

"But you had to go off and leave just about everything you owned."

"They would've confiscated it anyway. I brought out what silver I had, Yankee and Mexican. It'll help me start over again somewhere."

"Texas would be a good place to do that, once you learn your way around."

"I learn fast."

Sanderson flexed his hands several times, his face furrowed in thought. "I've got a place of my own . . . some cropland, some grazing. I have a notion you'd like it there."

Todd thought he saw a flicker of light in her eyes. "Orville, are you proposing to me?"

He mumbled uneasily, "I reckon I am, in my own awkward way."

"We only met a few days ago. You don't really know me yet."

"Time is in short supply when there's a war on."

She touched his hand. "Let's think about it till we get somewhere that we can stop a few days. We can decide then."

Sanderson shrugged. "I've already decided. But it takes two to make it official, so I'll wait."

Todd felt warm inside. This was the only good thing he had seen come from the long, tedious retreat. From the whole war, for that matter.

The journey across the mountains was a brutal test of endurance for men and animals as well as for wagons. By the time the column dropped back down toward the Rio Grande, it had spent nine days laboring through a wilderness of peaks and canyons, rocky hillsides, poor grass and little water, leaving a trail of broken wagons, dead and crippled animals to mark its passing. The exhausted Texans met a detachment bringing welcome news that a relief train was on its way north from Mesilla to meet them, bringing food and supplies.

Sanderson had thinned, his cheeks drawn taut, his roughly mended uniform hanging loose on his shoulders. Some of the loss came from the slow healing of his hip and some from short rations, barely above starvation levels.

The soldiers cheered as they caught sight of the shining river after the ordeal of crossing the arid mountains. Todd was too tired to cheer. He looked forward to a nighttime bath in the Rio Grande. After a meager supper, he waded in with his clothes on, for they needed washing as much as he did. Late April had brought warm weather, though the water was still cold. He did not stay in it long. Shivering, he hurried to a campfire.

The soldier Prentiss teased him. "You look ten pounds lighter than before you went into the river."

Todd said, "Dirt was all that held my clothes together."

Though he had never had any excess flesh, he had lost weight. He could feel the bones in his hands and arms.

Rested, the column moved south again and met the promised commissary train. For a while, at least, the men had food enough to fill their bellies. Feeling that the Union troops were well behind, Sibley ordered his men to cross over to the east side of the river. Wagons that had survived the rigorous retreat were floated across on hastily built rafts. The howitzers had remained loaded in case of Union attack and had to be fired to prevent the powder from becoming wet in the crossing. The loud reports created a desperate stir among the men, who had not been advised in advance. Some quickly rallied in a defensive posture to meet the enemy. No enemy appeared, however, and the tattered remnants of the Texas army crossed the river.

That evening Sanderson went to Ella Hawkins's wagon with a message. "General Sibley is fixin' to leave in the mornin' and hurry on down to Fort Bliss. A few civilians will be goin'. I want you to go with them."

Fort Bliss was in Texas but barely out of cannon range from the New Mexico line.

She protested, "We ought to be safe enough now. We haven't seen any federals."

"The general with a few light wagons can travel faster than this column. You'll be more comfortable at Fort Bliss. You can rest up, and you might get enough to eat, for a change."

"What about you?"

"I can't leave my men. I'll get there when they do." He looked at Todd. "I wish you'd take the kid with you."

Todd objected. "I'm doin' fine right where I'm at. Besides, you need somebody to look after you."

"We've still got a ways to go, kid. It ain't goin' to be sweet milk and corn bread just yet."

"I've been with you since way back last winter. I've made it as good as most of the men I've seen around me, and better than some. I'm stayin' put."

Sanderson shrugged. "I'm too worn out to argue." He turned back to Ella Hawkins. "I'll see you when we get to Fort Bliss."

"I'll be waiting."

He kissed her without regard to how many men might be watching. Anyone who didn't already know how they felt about each other had not been paying attention, Todd thought.

Having fresh supplies and seeing no sign that Union troops were pushing for an attack, the Texans took time to rest themselves and what remained of their horses and mules. They scattered among native settlements along the river but gained little in the way of forage for the animals. The local people, poor to begin with, had already yielded up most of what they had. Secure in the conviction that the Confederates were about to vacate New Mexico, they became openly hostile to further confiscations.

The Texans spent several days making a slow descent downriver to the point where the Rio Grande touched the Mexican border and bent southeastward to the old Mexican town of El Paso del Norte. A small, mixed American and Mexican adobe hamlet had developed on the Texas side of the river, next to a spartan army post with the hopeful name of Bliss. Few would have described it as blissful. "Forlorn" would be more like it.

Todd's reaction was that the town looked much the same as other venerable settlements he had seen along the Rio Grande as it made its way southward through New Mexico. High, dry mountains had dominated the area east of the river most of the way. Where there were not mountains, there was sand, and lots of it. Here, tall, shady cottonwoods swayed in the wind. Farmers diverted river water through a complex of ditches to irrigate small fields, vineyards, and orchards that could not have lived on the scant rainfall. A small dam diverted the river's flow to power a flour mill a little way from the village.

Sanderson told him, "Don't judge Texas by what you see here. It wouldn't have been much of a loss if we'd let Mexico keep this part of the country. The town on the other side of the river has mainly been a stoppin' place for travelers on the road from Chihuahua to Albuquerque and Santa Fe. They didn't tarry long, and neither will we."

"We'll be goin' on pretty soon?"

"The general's gettin' reports about a California column on its way to reinforce Canby's federals. They'll be comin' down the Mesilla Valley before long. By then we'd best be out of their reach, on our way to San Antonio."

Todd had no concept of Texas geography. "Is it as far as we've already come?"

"Farther, I'm afraid. But at least it's ours. Ours and the Apaches' and the Comanches'. We're not apt to run up against any of those so long as we stay in sizable bunches. They'll just stand off and watch, hopin' to catch somebody laggin' behind. Don't let it be you."

"I don't aim to let them catch me again. I've still got a couple of scars from the other time."

"The one on your arm?"

"No, I've had that one about as long as I can remember. Best I recall, I stumbled and fell into a fireplace. I was little then, and my recollection's not clear."

"You still can't even remember your name?"

Todd shook his head. "I wish I could. I used to tell people my last name is January, but I've quit that. Every time I say the word, I imagine I can see him standin' in front of me. It ain't a happy sight."

"I suppose not." Sanderson studied him for a minute and asked, "What do you think you'll do when we get to San Antonio?"

"Go with you, I suppose."

Sanderson frowned. "That may not be practical. I'll still be in the army. After a little leave time, they'll probably send me to wherever the fightin' is, back in Virginia or someplace."

"What about Mrs. Hawkins? You figure on marryin' her, don't you?"

"I do. I'll send her to my farm to wait till the war is over. It looks now like that's goin' to take longer than most of us thought. You could go there with her if you want to."

"I'll think on it." Todd was not all that well acquainted with Mrs. Hawkins. As far as he had seen, she seemed a nice woman, but he didn't want her bossing him. He didn't want anybody bossing him. He had had his fill of that with January.

Mrs. Hawkins was not difficult to find. Todd recognized her tent, set up next to her wagon near the fort. Sanderson had already seen it, for he left his troops and loped on ahead.

Private Prentiss snickered. "The lieutenant ain't goin' to get much sleep tonight."

Todd knew the risk in criticizing his elders, but he said, "You've got a dirty mind, and a mouth to match it."

Prentiss was unrepentant. "You don't know nothin', kid. You wouldn't have any idea what to do if you was to lay up next to a good-lookin' woman. But you can bet the lieutenant does."

Todd had to fight down an impulse to hit him, for he knew the consequences. Prentiss had hidden in a ditch rather than face the federals' guns, but he would be brave in striking a youngster. Todd simply said under his breath, "Go to hell."

He followed Sanderson to the tent. He saw the couple embracing and tried not to watch. He watched in spite of himself. When they pulled apart, Ella Hawkins smiled at him and said, "Looks like you took good care of him for me, Todd."

"Done the best I could," Todd replied. "He's healed up, pert near."

Ella's warm gaze went back to Sanderson. "He looks fine to me."

Sanderson said, "The question is: what do we do now? From what I hear, we'll soon be marchin' east for San Antonio."

She said, "I've located an American preacher. He said he'd be glad to marry us, if you still feel that way about it."

Smiling, Sanderson asked, "Are you proposin' to me?"

She mimicked what he had said when she had

asked the same question once before. "I suppose I am, in my own awkward way."

"There's no tellin' where I'll be goin' once we get to San Antonio. To some other part of the war, most likely."

"All the more reason to marry now. We should take advantage of whatever time we're given together."

Sanderson said, "Let's hitch your team and go find that preacher. Come along, kid. You can be a witness."

Todd was not sure whether to laugh or cry. He felt glad for the couple. They would be happy together, at least for a time. On the other hand, he felt an ache of loneliness, a sense of being cut loose on his own, as he had been so many times before. Sanderson would not need him anymore.

He could stay here, perhaps across the river in Mexico, where the federals could not reach him. His ability to speak Spanish would stand him in good stead. Or, he could go on with the retreating forces and see what fate might await him in Texas.

The west wind hit him in the face, stinging him with sand. It was blowing toward the east. He took that for an omen. San Antonio it was.

The eastward retreat in Texas was as crushing an ordeal as the one they had just endured in New Mexico. General Sibley stayed to see most of the troops get started, then hurried on toward San Antonio in a fast-moving carriage. The command was divided into smaller units, so only a limited number would converge on a watering place at one time. Rations continued to be short because merchants across the river in Mexico refused to accept scrip. To take supplies by force, done often in New Mexico, could cause an international incident, which the Confederacy did not want.

It was early June, and the extreme heat of western Texas was as painful as the winter cold had been to the north. Spring thaw had put the Rio Grande in flood, spreading water across the valley and forcing the retreating soldiers to remain well north of the river, in deep, hot sand that made every mile a struggle. Comanche had thinned. Todd could feel him tiring much too early in the day. Scarcity of forage was sapping what strength remained in horses and mules that had survived this far. The walking infantrymen trudged along, forcing themselves forward step by step on blistered feet, buoyed only by anticipation of getting home. They waved their arms and slapped at swarms of gnats, which added to the misery.

One by one they passed the watering places, so widely scattered that the men suffered severely in the long stretches between. There were Fort Quitman, Eagle Springs, Van Horn's Wells. Far ahead lay Dead Man's Hole. Men dropped out of the march to rest, a few to die. Some who remained on the march did so in a half-conscious state as if hypnotized, oblivious to what was going on around them, their bleary eyes seeing little except tracks left by the men ahead.

Todd walked and led Comanche most of the time, trying to spare him. Todd's tongue was swollen, dry, and immobile. He was so dehydrated that he no longer sweated. His head felt as if it were cooking. He recognized symptoms that threatened sunstroke but could do nothing to alleviate them. He strayed from the road and found himself entrapped in the needle-sharp clutches of a catclaw bush. He tore his already tattered clothes a bit more in the struggle to break free. Twice he went to his knees and brought himself back to his feet by force of will.

He heard men ahead trying to cheer, though their efforts were hampered by a deadening thirst. Todd's vision had narrowed as if he were looking down an open shotgun barrel. He had to blink several times before he could see a wagon coming to meet the column. It had gone ahead to Dead Man's Hole and had brought back barrels of water. Todd impatiently awaited his turn in line, then drank feverishly until Sanderson stopped him.

"Easy," he cautioned, a thick tongue making his voice sound unnatural. "Wait a little while, then drink some more." Sanderson's lips were dry and cracked, and so were Todd's.

When Todd was able to speak, he asked about Ella. Walking along with his aching head down and eyes half closed against the bright sunlight, he had lost sight of her.

Sanderson said, "She's bearin' up." He had tried to persuade her to board a stagecoach leaving Fort Bliss for San Antonio, but she had refused to leave her husband. She remained in her wagon, at the rear of the strung-out column.

Thirst momentarily satisfied, Todd gave Comanche what water the officer in charge would allow, then lay down to rest. He was weary to the bone but knew he was no worse off than the rest and better than many. At times he regretted not staying behind in El Paso del Norte, though he knew the futility of thinking about it now. He had to muster whatever internal strength remained and complete the trip. No matter what awaited him at the end, it must surely be better than this.

Ahead, he saw distant low peaks that a soldier said

were the Davis Mountains. Somewhere among them lay Barrel Springs, and beyond that, Fort Davis. From there, the soldier said, conditions should gradually improve as the trek continued to San Antonio.

Fort Davis was an oasis, built on an open stretch of ground towered over by a high, fluted wall of weathered and broken stone. Limpia Creek flowed nearby. Though water was plentiful there, rations remained short. Men and wagons followed the creek as far as possible, then climbed up through a high pass and stretched out across a dry, dusty plain to old Fort Stockton and Comanche Springs. Todd was told the springs had been a watering place for raiding Indians as far back as anyone knew. The men were careful not to let themselves drop behind. They knew Indians could be biding their time on these greasewood flats, hoping to lift the scalps of stragglers.

Comanche Springs gushed a generous flow of cool, sweet water. The men rested awhile in and around the vacated adobe buildings of the old frontier fort. It had been placed there to guard the springs and protect travelers on the long trails that stretched across the vastness of western Texas. From there, the men made a long, dry march to the brackish Pecos River. They followed the Pecos to a former Union post at Fort Lancaster, toiled their way up a steep wagon trail to higher ground, then labored on to Beaver Lake and beyond, day after painful day.

Through the shimmering heat waves Todd saw something far ahead that he could not identify. His initial reaction was fear that this might be a band of Comanches. He had already seen more of those than he wanted to. In a while, however, the outlines became clearer. This was a string of wagons, moving west in the direction of the Texans. He made out two horsemen loping ahead to meet the soldiers. Soon he heard a whoop and a holler from the head of the column.

The word rapidly swept back through the long line of men. These were relief wagons, bringing food, water, and supplies gathered by sympathetic citizens of San Antonio and other towns to the east.

"Thank God," Todd murmured, his mouth too dry for him to say more. His eyes burned as he looked about for Sanderson and Ella, wondering if they had heard. They were coming along slowly, far back. They leaned together on the wagon seat, Sanderson's horse tied on behind.

Todd had harbored doubts, but now his confidence began to rise out of the gloom. *We've been through hell and high water, but maybe we'll make it after all.*

19

Jeffrey was as skittish as his mules, riding the ferry across the Rio Grande from Matamoros to the Brownsville side of the river. The vessel bobbed up and down, the current slapping at its sides. He held tightly to the near mule's bridle, patting the animal on the neck and hoping it would not panic. A mule could be steadier than a horse under most circumstances, but there was little limit to the damage it could do if frightened.

The day before, Jeffrey had bade goodbye to Matthew Temple as his foster father took a Mexican hack out to the port to board an American vessel. In deep grief over Sarah Temple's death, Matthew had taken the first step toward his stated intention to sail around to a northern port and offer his services to the Union cause. Entreaties by his brother and sister-in-law, Auralee, had not changed his mind. Jeffrey had not tried to dissuade him. Sarah's death lay heavily on his thin shoulders. He understood Matthew's grief, though he did not share the intensity of Matthew's partisan feelings.

As for himself, he dreaded the prospect of idling out the war on the Mexican side of the border. He had found Matamoros foreign to everything he knew. He did not speak the language or understand the customs. Maybe it was all right for Lucy and Harry—they were younger and more adaptable—but he wanted to be doing something to keep his hands and his mind busy. He had declared his intention of working his way back to the farm, and Matthew had given his blessing.

In the wagon were Jeffrey's few personal possessions and a tombstone for Sarah's grave.

He pulled the team to a stop in front of Jack Fountain's barn. Tiburcio Valadez seemed not to recognize him as he came out through the big open door. "Boy, you want something?"

"Mr. Fountain offered me and my wagon a job. I'm here to take him up on it."

Valadez studied Jeffrey with doubting eyes. "You are how old?"

"Old enough to handle a team. Old enough to pack my own weight."

"That is for Mr. Fountain to say. See him at the warehouse." He pointed. "He loads freight for San Antonio."

"Much obliged." Jeffrey set the team to moving, stopping just short of a long line of freight wagons. Some were already loaded, some waiting. Jumping down, he wrapped the reins around the brake and gave the mules a moment's attention. They appeared to have recovered from the nervousness that had beset them on the ferry. Unlike Jeffrey, they had no objection to standing idle. It was their preferred position.

Fountain, sleeves rolled far up on his muscular arms, was directing a crew in loading a stack of long wooden boxes into a large wagon. "Careful now," he cautioned, "don't drop it. They won't pay a plugged peso for busted rifles." Seeing Jeffrey, he stepped forward, his big hand outstretched. "Howdy, boy. Did you think about my offer?"

Jeffrey winced under the crushing handshake. "Yes, sir. Me and my mules and my wagon, we're rarin' to go to work."

Fountain's eyes narrowed. "Are you sure you've thought this through? You know what we're haulin'."

"Yes, sir, military stuff."

"For the Confederate army. I had the notion that your family opposes the Confederacy."

"I don't know much about politics. I just know that I want to get away from here."

The truth was that Jeffrey had struggled with his decision, weighing one side against the other, making up his mind, then changing it. If he hauled munitions in his wagon, they would be used against Union forces. Conceivably, that could include Matthew Temple.

Fountain sensed Jeffrey's ambivalence. He said, "If you don't haul it, somebody else will. It'll get to where it's goin' no matter what you do or don't do."

"I was thinkin' maybe I could haul somethin' besides war stuff. Maybe I could take on some of your supplies, like feed or vittles or barrels of water. Stuff that wouldn't be goin' to kill somebody."

"Somethin' that wouldn't aggravate your conscience?"

"That's my thinkin'."

Fountain nodded. "I've studied on it myself, many times. I don't like this war, but I didn't start it. I know this cargo is on its way to kill men that never did anything to hurt me. But what difference would it make if I quit? It'd get there anyway. Maybe this hellish stuff will help make people get a gutful of the killin' and put a stop to the war."

"That's one way to look at it," Jeffrey admitted.

"You have to look at it that way, or you'll lay awake at night with it chewin' on you like a blanketful of bedbugs."

"I just don't want to haul anything that'll kill somebody."

"All right, no guns. Go down to the foot of the line. We'll load your wagon when we can get to you. If everything goes accordin' to plan, we'll be on the road by daylight tomorrow." He paused. "You didn't ask me about pay."

Jeffrey shrugged. "I haven't worried about it. I figured you'd be fair."

"I try to be. What's more, I deal in silver, not Confederate paper. Silver will spend anywhere."

Jeffrey did not intend to spend more of it than necessary. When he had earned enough, he intended to return to the farm, to work it and have it in good condition for Matthew's return after the war. Rolled up in his blankets was the paper Matthew had signed giving him half interest, willing it all in the event that he never came back.

Jeffrey's was a sturdy farm wagon but not as large or heavy as most of Fountain's, built to haul freight. As he moved it up to the warehouse, Fountain looked it over carefully, examining the undercarriage, the wheels. "It'll take a moderate load," he said. "You'll be haulin' part of our rations and cookin' supplies."

Jeffrey was glad he would not be hauling munitions. He helped with the loading, accepting floubarrels, bags of beans, and kegs of tamales sealed in lard as they were handed up to him one by one. When the loading was completed, he spread the canvas sheet over the hoops to protect the goods in the event of rain.

Late in the afternoon he saw a wagon driven by a middle-aged woman. The Mexican girl Dolores sat beside her. Household goods were stacked and tied in the wagon bed.

"My wife," Fountain said. "I'm movin' her to San Antonio. I don't want her to be here if the federals move in on Brownsville."

Jeffrey thought about it. "If that happens, you won't be able to freight cotton down here anymore."

"We'll just cross the Rio Grande farther up, then bring the wagons down on the Mexican side." He smiled. "I'll bet we'll hear the Yankees cuss clear across the river."

Jeffrey's attention went to an oncoming wagon flanked by four armed guards. He heard Fountain groan, "Aw hell. I was bettin' Old Man Remick wouldn't be ready before we left."

A fifth horseman, bearing no firearms that Jeffrey could see, greeted Fountain with a curt nod. He wiped a neckerchief across his sweaty face and into his gray hair. He said, "I hope you intend to live up to your promise."

Fountain said, "Dammit, Remick, I hoped you'd find somebody else. This'll draw raiders like a dead mule draws buzzards."

"I'm sending four extra guards to help you. We can't afford to keep sitting on this government silver. If the Yankees come, they'll take it all."

"But my wife'll be with me on this trip. This puts her in extra danger."

"I'm sorry, Fountain, but in these times we have to think of our country before ourselves."

Fountain looked at Jeffrey. "Son, you may want to reconsider goin' with us. If the word gets out that we've got a load of silver with us, we're liable to have a fight."

Jeffrey considered for only a moment. "I've got nothin' to stay here for. I'm goin'."

Fountain shrugged. "Suit yourself. Just so you know."

By nightfall all the freight wagons had been loaded. The teamsters gathered in a shed where two Mexican cooks had prepared supper. Jeffrey watched the men wrap tortillas around pieces of goat meat and tried to emulate their ease. Half the meat fell out of the open end and landed in the dirt the first time he tried. He looked about self-consciously to see if anyone laughed. All pretended they hadn't seen, but he knew they had.

Fountain sat beside him, biting into a green pepper, then taking a bite of beans. He asked, "Have you got a rifle?"

"Yes, sir, the one Sarah kept in the wagon."

"Good. All kinds of bandits work the road from here to San Antonio. Mexicans, white, some you can't be sure about."

"Like Catlett?"

"As bad or worse. They don't often bother us when we haul cotton except to try and take our stock. Stealin' cotton bales is too much heavy work. But they get interested when we haul guns and ammunition. They'll be even more interested if they find out what else we've got."

"Maybe they won't know."

"Half the town probably knows already, so we'll have to keep our eyes open and our powder dry."

"Looks like the army would protect you, since you're haulin' for the government."

"There ain't enough soldiers to go around. Them that's here have to stay ready in case the Yankees come in from the Gulf. So you see, we're all soldiers in a way. We've got our own war to fight right here in South Texas."

After dark, Jeffrey rolled out his blanket beneath the wagon. He spent the night turning restlessly, kept on edge by fleeting dreams about a thousand raiders coming to take his wagon.

Brownsville was largely Mexican, though American merchants had put up many substantial buildings to support the trade they did on both sides of the border. This had been the jumping-off place for the Mexican war, and a Union military presence had remained here until Texas secession. Now the fort was home to a limited force of Confederate volunteers. Several of these sat on horseback at the edge of town and watched the line of wagons pass by. Jeffrey was surprised to see that all were of Mexican blood. He had not considered that some of the local native people would be sympathetic to the Confederacy.

Fountain told him, "There's a whole company of them under the command of Santos Benavides. If the Yankees do land, they'd better be prepared to fight the Mexican war all over again."

Mrs. Fountain's wagon led the procession, for teamsters farther back down the line were likely to eat dust. The freighters moved at a slow and deliberate pace. Fountain did not want to overtax the teams. Under weight of the cargo, the iron-rimmed wheels left deep tracks where the ground was soft. The trail leading to San Antonio had been beaten out by many decades of trader and immigrant traffic. Jeffrey remembered this part of it from the Temples' trip south. He was pleased to see armed outriders paralleling the train. Fountain himself rode a big black horse, frequently dropping back to check the rear.

The wagons came to the place where Sarah was buried. An end-gate marker had been left there, but it leaned badly. Tufts of hair on the edge indicated that stray cattle had rubbed against it in an attempt to ease their itching. Sight of the grave brought harsh memories rushing back. Jeffrey's eyes burned as he and a husky teamster set the tombstone in place.

True to his promise, Fountain had brought along a minister to say some words over Sarah. He was a gangling, rawboned man of stern countenance. Jeffrey took him to be a circuit rider, carrying a light bedroll tied behind his saddle and a large black-bound Bible in his saddlebag. He removed his hat and waited for Jeffrey, the Fountains, Dolores, and several teamsters to gather around. He recited from his open Bible without having to look at the pages. He reminded the Lord that Sarah had been a righteous woman, a good wife and mother, cut down in the prime of life by one of the devil's own, who the minister hoped was now and for all eternity roasting in hell.

Tears on her cheeks, Dolores made the sign of the cross.

Jeffrey blinked to clear his eyes. All in all, he considered it an excellent service. Matthew would have been pleased.

Fountain said, "That's a nice stone. It does her proud."

The bandit who had killed her would never have

a stone, or even a grave. Jeffrey hoped he had made a good meal for the buzzards so that at least some good had come of his existence.

Fountain said, "You're not fixin' to cry on me, are you?"

"No, I'm done with that. I was just thinkin' about the outlaw that shot her. I'd like to kill him all over again, and all the others like him."

"You're not old enough to study on killin'. Too much of such thinkin' can poison a young man's mind."

"There's people in this world that need killin'."

"Don't be in a hurry. Maybe you'll be lucky and somebody else will do it before you have to. I'll admit to puttin' a few men under. I'm not proud of it, but the world is a better place without them in it."

Fountain escorted his wife and Dolores back to their wagon at the head of the line. Jeffrey climbed onto his own and took a long, melancholy look back at the grave. He knew it was unlikely he would pass this way again.

The trouble came early. In camp that night, as the teamsters gathered around the cook wagon for supper, one of Remick's guards fired a pistol into the dusk. Instantly two guns blazed, and the guard went down.

Someone shouted from out in the brush, "Everybody lift them and stand easy where you're at. Anybody else who reaches for a gun won't get to finish his supper."

Along with all the teamsters, Remick's three remaining guards raised their hands.

Jeffrey glanced at his wagon and thought about the

rifle hidden there. It might as well have been back in Brownsville for all the good it would do. He looked to Fountain for guidance. Fountain wore a pistol on his hip, but he showed no sign that he might reach for it. His hands were at shoulder level. Frightened, Mrs. Fountain and Dolores moved to him. He stepped in front of the women, shielding them.

Fountain muttered to the nearest guard, "Damned poor protection you-all are."

The guard said, "It ain't our silver. We ain't dyin' for two dollars a day."

Several horsemen emerged from the brush, all brandishing pistols or rifles. Two were Mexican. The rest appeared to be Anglo. One of the Mexicans dismounted and moved among the teamsters, taking from them any weapons he saw and pitching them into a pile well out of reach.

The invaders were led by a thin rider who might have weighed a hundred thirty pounds. His sharp face looked a little like a fox's, but his eyes were more like a wolf's. He said, "Ain't no need anybody gettin' hurt unless they ask for it."

Fountain stared at him. "Seems to me like I know you."

"You ought to. Name's Johnny Diamond. Last time I tried to raid your train, you put a bullet through my arm. Damned thing still hurts."

"My aim ain't what it used to be. Gettin' old, I guess."

"Don't do anything that'd keep you from gettin' any older. Remember, I owe you for this sore arm."

It seemed to Jeffrey that Fountain was taking this calmly, considering all the guns pointed in his direction. He supposed the freighter had been caught up in situations like this before. Or perhaps he did not want to start a fire that might get the women burned.

Fountain asked, "Do you expect to get all these wagons back down to the river?"

"Wish we could, but we've just come for one. It ain't yours anyway, so it oughtn't to pain you much. Once we're clear, you can go on up the road with your outfit."

"Old Man Remick'll sic the soldiers on you."

"Not if you take your time in lettin' him know about it. Just to be sure you do, we'll take one of your people with us." The outlaw looked over the teamsters and stared for a moment at Mrs. Fountain and Dolores. He said, "That young Mexican gal is likely-lookin'. Reminds me of one Ward Catlett had the last time I saw him. But I'm afraid she'd get my crew to fightin' amongst theirselves. So I'll just take this boy." He pointed at Jeffrey.

Jeffrey felt his heart skip.

Fountain said, "I'd rather you took me instead. He's just a boy. There ain't no harm in him."

"All the more reason for me to take him. With you, I couldn't look away for a minute."

The minister took a step forward. "Me, then. I'm not armed. All I've got is my old Bible."

"Who would give a damn about a hellfire preacher? There's too many of them as it is. I need somebody that'll make people think twice before they try me." Diamond jerked his head. "Come here, kid."

Reluctantly Jeffrey stepped toward him, feeling sick at his stomach. He glanced back but knew Fountain could do nothing to help him. Neither could the minister, beyond offering up a prayer.

Diamond said, "We'll let him go at the river. He can catch up to you before you get to San Antonio."

He frowned. "But if we run into trouble, things might not be real good for him."

Fountain's face was flushed. "If anything happens to that boy, Texas and Mexico together won't be half big enough to keep me from findin' you."

"Then don't do anything that'll get him hurt. Just go on your way like nothin' happened. And next time you see Old Man Remick, tell him we're much obliged."

Two of the raiders hitched a team to Remick's wagon. They brought a horse for Jeffrey but no saddle. Diamond said, "I hope you can ride bareback, boy. I figure you'll be too busy hangin' on to give us any trouble."

Under the circumstances, Jeffrey doubted he could give them much trouble with or without a saddle. Diamond waited until all his men were ready to move, then told Fountain, "I'm leavin' a man close-by to watch you for a while. If you send somebody south toward Brownsville, you can write it down in your book that this boy'll suffer for it."

Fountain looked at Jeffrey with regret. "Sorry, son. You do whatever he says and don't try anything." He turned to Diamond. "Remember what I told you. Hurt that boy and you can write it down in *your* book that my next bullet won't hit you in the arm. It'll go right between your eyes."

Diamond shrugged. "If nothin' goes wrong, this boy can live to grow a gray beard so long that he'll trip on it."

One of the outlaws turned Remick's wagon halfway around and set the team onto a dim trail that led into the brush. Diamond jerked his head at Jeffrey. "Mount up, kid. We're movin'."

Jeffrey grasped the horse's mane and sprang up

onto its back. He cast a last, anxious glance back over his shoulder at the Fountains and Dolores and the teamsters. He caught a glimpse of the fallen guard and saw him move a little. At least he was not dead. The minister moved out and dropped to one knee by the wounded man's side.

The wagon moved at a fast pace the first mile or so, then slowed when Diamond warned the driver, "These mules have got to last awhile. We can't kill them at the start."

Diamond had a lieutenant whose face Jeffrey could not see because of all the whiskers. The man asked, "When're we goin' to take a look and see what we've got?"

"Wait till daylight. We'll need to rest the mules by then anyway. Right now we'd best put some miles behind us. Chances are that Fountain sent somebody back to Brownsville, in spite of what I told him."

"You think he knew you were lyin' about leavin' a man to watch him?"

"He's no fool. Who in this bunch would've stayed behind and taken the risk of losin' his share?" Diamond turned in the saddle to address Jeffrey. "Are you keepin' up, boy? If you've got any notion about slippin' away, you better forget it."

Jeffrey saw no chance of doing that, at least not for the first couple of hours. Then the wagon bogged to a standstill in a deep pit of loose sand. The driver cracked a whip. The mules struggled but could not make the wheels turn.

Diamond cursed. "Why in the hell didn't you watch where you were goin'?"

The driver responded angrily, "How the hell am I supposed to see in the dark? You ought to've had somebody out in front, showin' me the way."

The two exchanged more angry words, which did nothing to free the wagon from the sand. At last Diamond ordered, "You sons of bitches get down and push."

The men became so involved in trying to move the wagon that for the moment nobody thought to watch Jeffrey. He backed his horse quietly away from the crowd, then turned and heeled it into a run, tearing through the chaparral. It clutched at his clothing, ripping his trouser leg, stinging his skin. In the rush of excitement he barely felt any of it. His heart pounded with exhilaration.

Then a rawhide loop sailed past his head and dropped over his shoulders. Before he could stop the horse he hit the end of the rope and was jerked roughly to the ground. He lay coughing, trying to get his breath. His hip ached where he had fallen on it, but that did not hurt as much as his disappointment in not getting away.

One of Diamond's Mexicans sat on a horse, calmly coiling his reata. "*Hijo,*" he said, "better you don't go noplace."

Jeffrey's horse had stopped and stood watching impassively as the Mexican rode up to it and grasped the trailing reins. With a motion of his head he indicated that Jeffrey should climb back up. When Jeffrey was seated on the horse's back, the Mexican loosened the reata enough to raise the loop from the shoulders and settle it around Jeffrey's neck.

"You run again," he said, "you choke pretty good."

The rope had been used enough to make it slick, though it still chafed. Jeffrey swallowed hard.

The men had freed the wagon. Diamond gave Jeffrey a quick looking-over and said, "You've got guts, kid. Maybe after this you'll have better sense, too."

He turned to the Mexican. "Careful you don't strangle him. Jack Fountain would cut out your guts and hang you with them."

Fountain's lieutenant said, "Damned kid's more trouble than he's worth. I say we shoot him." He drew his pistol and leveled it at Jeffrey's head.

Diamond ripped the gun from the man's hand and knocked him to his knees with it. He demanded, "You want to spend the rest of your life lookin' back over your shoulder for Fountain? Use your head for somethin' besides a place to put your hat." He stuck the pistol into his waistband. "Better I hang on to this for a while." He looked at Jeffrey. "You all right, kid?"

Jeffrey mumbled, "I guess so." Dejected, he took a little comfort from the fact that Diamond seemed to intend him no harm. He wondered whether the outlaw was softhearted or just afraid of Fountain's vengeance.

Diamond's anger had arisen in a flash and evaporated just as quickly. He whistled a merry tune as the bandits made their way through the brush. After a time he pulled his horse in beside Jeffrey's. He said, "Kind of young, ain't you, to be wrestlin' mules for Jack Fountain? What did you do, run away from home?"

"I've got no real folks. I'm tryin' to make my own livin'."

"I started young myself. Got tired of doin' without. You're a likely lad. I could show you a thing or two."

"About bein' an outlaw?" The thought was repugnant. It reminded Jeffrey of the two who had abused Sarah, and the one who had killed her.

Diamond said, "Whatever it takes. You've got to watch out for yourself, because nobody else will."

That had not been Jeffrey's experience. Every time he had needed help, somebody had befriended him.

The trail, faint to begin with, faded and disappeared. The riders and wagon kept moving across country, through chaparral, around occasional mesquite thickets and thick tangles of prickly pear. The eastern sky began to lighten. Diamond told his lieutenant, "We'll stop and water the team at the Sanchez place."

The lieutenant nodded sullenly, evidently still nursing a grudge.

As the first fingers of daylight spread across the low brush, Jeffrey saw a small rancho ahead, a couple of adobe buildings and some brush corrals. Diamond signaled to the Mexican. "Go tell Sanchez and his family to stay in the house. The less they see, the less they can tell. Make sure they understand."

The Mexican lifted the loop from around Jeffrey's neck and recoiled the reata as he put his horse into a long trot toward the house. Jeffrey rubbed where the leather had burned him. That made it burn more.

Diamond suggested, "First chance you get, rub some bacon grease on it. Or axle grease if you've got no bacon. That'll help ease the bite."

A gringo bandit unhitched the mules and pumped water into a short wooden trough. He cupped his hands and drank from the spout.

Diamond's lieutenant demanded, "When're we goin' to open them strongboxes?"

Diamond looked at the expectant faces that surrounded him. "I reckon now is as good a time as any. From here we can each carry some of the silver and leave the wagon. We'll move faster that way."

Two men struggled to lift the two boxes. One slipped from their grasp and fell the last couple of feet to the ground. Jeffrey had not seen the boxes before. They were secured by the largest padlocks he had ever seen. Diamond drew his pistol and said, "Stand back, all of you. Don't want anybody hit by a ricochet."

He had to fire three times before the first lock finally broke open. Eagerly he pulled it away and opened the heavy lid.

The lieutenant leaned down for a close look. "Silver bars!"

Diamond doubled his fist and cursed. "Silver bars hell! Take another look. It's lead bars."

"Lead?" the lieutenant declared in astonishment. He lifted one from the box and swore, "Damned if it ain't." He swung around angrily to face Diamond. "Fountain done a switch on us."

Diamond's face was flushed with anger. "It wasn't Fountain. It was Old Man Remick hisself. Son of a bitch didn't figure anybody would find out till the wagon got to San Antonio. That'd give him plenty of time to get away with the silver."

"Where do you reckon he went with it?"

Diamond stewed. "If it was me, I'd take it across the river to Mexico and catch a boat for South America."

"What can we do now?"

"Ride like hell for Matamoros. Maybe we can overtake him before he gets to that boat. Water your horses, boys, and let's travel."

The lieutenant jerked his head toward Jeffrey. "What about the boy?"

"We don't need him anymore. Kid, you can take this wagon back to Fountain and tell him it's a gift from Johnny Diamond and Old Man Remick."

A voice spoke from the brush. "You can tell me yourself."

Fountain and four other horsemen held rifles pointed at the raiders. Jeffrey had to blink to recognize them against the glare of the sun rising behind them.

Diamond's jaw dropped. "Where the hell did you-all come from?"

Fountain said, "From hell, if any of you wiggles a finger. Now it's your turn to throw your guns into a pile." He beckoned to Jeffrey. "Step away from them, son."

Jeffrey's heart skipped again, this time from relief. He quickly joined Fountain's men.

Fountain said, "Now, Diamond, you-all put that silver back in the wagon."

Diamond said, "You'd better take a look. It ain't silver."

Fountain blinked. "Certainly it's silver."

"That's what Remick told you. But sometimes a man will lie. Even a nice old man like him."

Fountain motioned for Diamond's men to back away, then moved up and looked into the open box. "Lead?"

"Put in there for the weight. Good for nothin' except moldin' bullets. I'd like to mold one for Remick."

It was Fountain's turn to curse. "Damned greedy old reprobate, he put my wagons and my people at risk, just so he could steal the government silver."

"I figure he's probably in Mexico, tryin' to catch a boat. Me and my boys had figured on tryin' to reach him before he gets his feet wet."

"I wish I had time to do it myself."

Diamond said, "Let me and my boys do it. You couldn't hold all of us anyhow. We'd find a way to get loose from you before you ever got us to San Antonio."

Fountain considered. "I ought to shoot the lot of you."

Jeffrey feared he meant it. He pointed to the lieutenant. "That man yonder was fixin' to shoot me. Diamond saved my life."

Fountain shook his head. "Don't worry. It's against my religion to shoot an unarmed man."

Diamond said, "I've got a lot of respect for religion. Used to practice it myself."

Fountain said, "I'll make you a deal. You can go if you'll agree from now on to let my wagons be."

"I'll shake your hand on that."

"Forget the handshake. Just go get the son of a bitch."

The bandits picked up their weapons and grabbed their horses. In a minute they were away at a gallop.

Jeffrey said, "I didn't think you'd just let them go."

"Like he said, we'd have our hands full tryin' to hold them. And maybe they'll catch Remick. He's due some retribution."

"Whether they get him or not, the silver is gone."

Fountain shook his head. "It ain't enough to make a big difference in the war. We'll water the horses and start back. We've lost a day of travel."

Jeffrey said, "You took a big risk, comin' after Diamond's bunch."

"You didn't think we was goin' to stand back and let them take you to God knows where, did you? We figured to bust you loose one way or the other. *And* get the silver back."

"Diamond was goin' to turn me loose anyway. I reckon he ain't too bad, for an outlaw."

"Yeah," Fountain said dryly. "Probably sends money home to his mother. But I'll bet he don't tell her where he got it."

The horse and wagon tracks were easy to follow until they cut into the trail Diamond had used. The procession came in sight of Fountain's wagon camp in late afternoon. Fountain said, "The womenfolks'll be real glad to see you're in one piece. They were fit to be tied when Diamond took you away."

"What about that wagon? It's Remick's."

"He ain't got any more use for it. So now you own two wagons."

Jeffrey grinned. Two wagons. He was already feeling richer than when he had started, and Fountain had not even paid him yet.

20

Jeffrey thought the stone warehouse looked like a prison, its side walls long and featureless except for one large door, its front windows barred. Armed soldiers slouched about, some leaning against the wall as they watched the freight wagons pull in. Most of Fountain's teamsters had been there before and knew the routine. Jeffrey kept his seat on the wagon, watching Fountain and the other teamsters for a cue.

Fountain addressed two soldiers at the door, then went inside. Shortly he reappeared with a man who wore a sweat-dampened white shirt, his string tie hanging loose. Fountain presented a sheaf of papers to him. In a short time, a crew of mostly Mexican laborers began unloading the wagons and carrying the cargo into the dark and cavernous warehouse.

Fountain walked down the line of wagons, pausing to speak to Jeffrey. "Well, boy, what do you think of San Antonio?"

Jeffrey hoped the warehouse was not representative, but he said, "Looks pretty good after the long trip up from Brownsville." His rump felt numb after so many days sitting on the flat wagon seat.

Fountain said, "We'll take a few days of rest before we start south with another load of cotton. I've got to get Mrs. Fountain settled somewhere."

Jeffrey had been considering his next move. Though he could use the money, he was in doubt about making another trip down the trail. He had lain awake at night, thinking about the farm, wanting to get back to it. He was hesitant to tell Fountain. He felt his obligations to the big man had not been fulfilled.

It seemed to him that the wagons were emptied faster than they had been loaded, perhaps because much care had been taken to balance each piece of cargo. He dreaded telling Fountain that he planned to leave. He wanted to postpone it as long as possible.

As the job neared completion, Fountain sat on a rifle crate and motioned for Jeffrey to sit beside him. He said, "I don't suppose you know anybody in San Antonio?"

"Never was here before. The Temples circled around when we were comin' south."

"You'll need a place to stay while we're here. I'll be puttin' the missus up at the Menger Hotel till I find her a house. You can stay there if you're of a mind to."

"I've got used to not havin' a roof over my head. I'd just as soon put up at a wagon yard. It'd be cheaper."

"You're a man, pretty near. You can make up your own mind." Fountain reached into his pocket and brought out a small record book. "You've got some money comin' to you. I promised it'd be in silver, not paper."

"I'm much obliged."

"Another thing: you've got two wagons on your

hands. You can't drive them both. I'll buy that older one from you."

Jeffrey was torn about selling. This was the wagon his parents had brought all the way from Arkansas, the one the Indians had tried to burn, the one he and Sarah had used on their flight southward. He said, "I think I'll keep the old wagon. I'll sell you the bigger one. It'll suit your purpose better anyhow."

"Done." Fountain stood up. "I've got paperwork to sign. Then we'll go to supper."

Jeffrey did some mental calculations. With his wages and the price of the wagon, plus a little money Matthew had left him, he would have enough to cover expenses in going back to the farm and probably some to tide him over once he got there and made a crop.

Fountain's face was grim when he returned. He gathered the teamsters around him. "Boys, it'll be a while before we hit the trail with another shipment of cotton. Somethin' has come up, somethin' a lot more urgent. I've just been told that we've got a lot of soldier boys makin' their way back from the fightin' in New Mexico. They're hungry and half naked, and they've been starved for water much of the time, workin' across the desert.

"Good people around here have been gatherin' up food and clothes and stuff for them. I've volunteered my wagons to go meet the soldiers and give them as much relief as we can carry. We won't be alone. There'll be other wagons. There won't be any wages, but it's mighty little sacrifice compared to what our soldier boys have gone through."

Jeffrey's gaze searched the teamsters' faces. Most showed enthusiasm. A couple appeared less than happy, but they went along rather than be shamed by the rest.

Fountain nodded with satisfaction. "I was sure you'd feel that way. Supper will have to wait. We'll load wagons tonight and get started early in the mornin'. Every hour we lose is another hour those boys will have to suffer."

Jeffrey's stomach growled with hunger. But he had been hungry before. It had not killed him yet.

An old wagon road led west from San Antonio. Jeffrey had been told it meandered from one watering place to the next on its tortuous way to El Paso del Norte, hundreds of miles away. As his wagon bumped along the rough trail, he listened to water sloshing in the wooden barrels that made up his load. His rump ached.

They met an army ambulance the second day, several sick and wounded men inside. Their clothing was tattered, their faces dusty, gray, and bewhiskered, reflecting the misery they had endured. Watching them wolf down bread and dried meat and gulp water until they nearly choked, Jeffrey felt sick himself.

The ambulance driver said, "We're a ways ahead of the main bunch. They're strung out from hell to breakfast. You think these men look bad? You ain't seen the half of it yet. We've left fresh graves all the way from Santa Fe to Comanche Springs."

Jeffrey had thought he had seen war in the actions of the Confederate zealots and home guards against men loyal to the Union. He realized these men had been through far worse. If there were others more in need than the occupants of the ambulance, he dreaded seeing them, yet he itched to be moving on down the road to help. He was relieved when Fountain gave the order to roll the wagons.

Toward evening, they met another weary group

of retreating soldiers, most afoot. The few who had horses were walking and leading them, for the animals looked as miserable as the men. The men swarmed around Jeffrey's wagon, dipping cups into a barrel of water, spilling it on themselves in their eagerness.

He noticed what he first took to be a small man but soon realized was no more than a boy, a gaunt figure leading a gaunt brown horse. His face was blistered and drawn, his eyes dull and tired. His clothing was torn and dirty. He imagined the boy might be twelve or thirteen, though hardship had lined his face and made him appear older. Jeffrey was immediately drawn to him. He could only guess what trouble those hollow eyes had seen.

The boy was drinking water in big swallows, as if this were his last chance. Jeffrey feared he was about to hurt himself. He caught the thin, shaking hand that held the cup. "Slow, kid. It'll go down the wrong pipe and drown you, drinkin' that fast. Take a few breaths and let it settle."

The boy coughed and looked up from the cup. "Thanks, mister. I do believe you've saved my life."

"After I've saved you, I don't want to see you kill yourself takin' on too much water too quick." Jeffrey studied the face. He had an odd feeling he had seen it before. He said, "You're not old enough to be in the army. What're you doin' with these soldiers?"

"I'm workin', talkin' Mexican for them. Was, anyway."

Jeffrey was intrigued. "You can talk Mexican?" He had not learned more than a dozen words.

"I've been in New Mexico about as far back as I can remember. I'd've starved to death if I couldn't talk Mexican."

"How come you left there?"

"The war. I went to work for the Texas soldiers to get away from the man that owned me."

"How could somebody own you? You're white."

"Indians had a hold of me. They sold me to a trader. He said I'd belong to him till I got grown, but I showed him different."

"What'll you do when you get to San Antonio? You got folks there?"

"My folks are all dead. I don't belong to nobody but me."

"I'm in the same shape myself."

The boy drank more water. Jeffrey said, "I'll bet you're hungry. I'll get you some bacon. You can fry it when you stop for the night."

"I ain't waitin' that long." The boy took a knife from his pocket and cut a chunk out of the slab Jeffrey gave him. He wolfed it down raw.

Jeffrey almost gagged, watching him.

One of Fountain's teamsters said, "Don't be so surprised. Men that've been starved have a strong cravin' for fat. I've seen them eat lard straight out of the bucket."

Jeffrey said, "I've never been that hungry."

"Count yourself lucky. These poor devils have marched through hell and out the far side."

The boy said, "Much obliged for the bacon. I'll save the rest for supper. Do you reckon you could spare a little water for my horse? He's about done in."

Jeffrey dipped water into a bucket. The boy lifted it, and the horse dropped his head into it, drinking as eagerly as the boy had.

Jeffrey said, "Good-lookin' horse. All he needs is some green grass to fill him out. Where'd you get him?"

"From an Indian. I call him Comanche."

The name brought terrible memories rushing back to Jeffrey, of the raid on the family wagon, the murder of his parents and little brother. He said, "I'd've named him somethin' different."

"It seemed to fit, since it was an Indian I got him from."

"What did you have to give for him?"

"Nothin'. The Indian was dead."

"Somebody killed him?"

"Me. He was fixin' to put an arrow in my heart."

Jeffrey's memories brought up a long-buried anger. "I wish somebody would shoot them all."

The boy shrugged. "They ain't all bad people, once you get used to them. They killed my folks and carried me off with them, then sold me for an old rifle. January—he's the man that bought me—took me on tradin' trips into the Indian country later. I got to where I wasn't scared of them anymore. Not much, anyway."

Jeffrey heard a cry from up the line of wagons. The signal had been given to move on. He shook the boy's hand. "Good luck. Maybe I'll run into you in San Antonio."

"I don't know how long I'll stay there. I've got to find me a payin' job someplace. Much obliged again for the water and the bacon."

As the wagon began moving, Jeffrey looked back once. He saw the youngster walking eastward, leading the horse.

For a while he was troubled, still feeling that something about the boy's face seemed familiar, yet knowing it was unlikely. He had never been in New Mexico.

Just at sundown Fountain called a halt for the

evening. The wagon train had encountered another cluster of soldiers, most walking, a few leading horses too worn out to carry them. The scene was much the same as before, men rushing for the water wagon. The teamsters began building campfires and cooking supper for the famished soldiers.

To his surprise, Jeffrey saw a woman walking toward his wagon, carrying a bucket. Like the men, she looked dusty and tired. Her face was sunburned despite the slat bonnet she wore. She extended the bucket toward Jeffrey and said, "I've got some sick men in my wagon. They need water."

"Yes, ma'am." He hurried to fill the bucket. "I'll carry it for you, ma'am. Just show me the way." He followed her to a wagon where three men lay on blankets. They reached eagerly for the cup.

The woman told them, "Drink slowly. There's plenty to go around."

Jeffrey said, "If you empty this bucket, I'll fetch some more."

The men passed the cup around as Jeffrey filled it again and again. Not until the men had drunk did the woman take her first sip of water. He asked her, "Are you a nurse?"

"Not by training, but I do the best I can. My name's Ella Hawkins. I mean Sanderson." She made a tentative smile, then winced as her sun-cracked lips gave her a moment of pain. "I haven't been married long enough to be used to my new name."

He nodded toward the sick soldiers. "Is one of these men your husband?"

"No. Lieutenant Sanderson is down the line somewhere, seeing to his troops. Some are straggling behind."

Jeffrey could hear bacon sizzling over several fires

and smell camp bread being fried in skillets. He said, "These men'll feel a lot better once they get enough to eat. Looks like they've had a hard time of it."

"It's been awful. But it'll be over soon." She studied him with steady blue eyes that he realized were pretty, like Sarah's had been. She said, "You seem young to be traveling with these relief wagons."

"Not as young as a boy I saw a while ago, with the soldiers."

"That would be Todd."

The name startled Jeffrey. "Todd? That's what he's called? I never thought to ask him what his name was. I had a brother by that name."

"Had? What happened to him?"

"Indians killed him, along with my ma and pa. He wasn't but about five years old."

Ella frowned. "That's odd. Todd said they killed *his* parents. His brother, too."

A chill ran down Jeffrey's back. "Did he tell you what the rest of his name was?"

"He said he couldn't remember. *Todd* was all he knew."

Jeffrey tried to remember what little the boy had told him. He had said the Indians had carried him off. But that couldn't be. He had seen Todd buried alongside his mother and father. It was a memory he had tried for years to keep shoved to a far, dark corner of his mind.

Then he remembered something else. His rescuers had not let him see the body. They had wanted him to remember his brother as he had been, not in the mutilated condition in which they had found him.

What if the boy they had buried had been someone else?

He gave a sudden cry that startled the woman and

the men in the wagon. "Todd! My brother Todd!" He set the bucket down with a thud and went running, shouting, "Mr. Fountain. Mr. Fountain."

Jack Fountain stepped out from behind a wagon. "What's the matter, boy? You look like you saw a h'ant."

"I think I did. I think I've seen my brother."

"But Indians killed him a long time ago. You told me so."

"Maybe I was wrong. The boy we saw today with the soldiers, his name was the same as my brother's. Everything fits."

"I'm afraid you're imaginin' things. You could be lettin' yourself in for a terrible disappointment."

"I've got to overtake him and find out."

His eyes full of doubt, Fountain said, "We need the water that's in your wagon."

"But I can't afford to let him get to San Antonio ahead of me. I might lose him there and never find him again."

Fountain's face twisted as he considered. "I guess we can transfer most of the water to another wagon." He laid a heavy hand on Jeffrey's shoulder. "I'm afraid you're chasin' after a shadow. But God go with you."

Ella Sanderson watched as Jeffrey hitched his team. She said, "Todd is a good boy. We've talked about taking him to Orville's farm. He needs family of his own after being alone so long. I hope he *is* your brother."

Jeffrey said, "I felt somethin' when I first saw him. Felt like I knew him, but I didn't know what to make of it."

"We'll be in San Antonio in a couple of days. Wait and let us know what you find out."

"I'll have to stay anyway till Mr. Fountain gets back. I've got wages comin'."

Though the sun was low, he did not have the patience to wait until morning. He was determined to travel as long as he had enough light to backtrack the wagons. He set the mules into a pace he thought they could sustain and held them to it until full darkness. He made camp but ate little and slept less, his backside prickling with impatience. Old memories kept haunting him. He kept seeing his mother and father. He remembered fishing with Todd and having to forcibly stop his little brother from throwing stones into the creek, frightening away the fish. He remembered the time Todd tripped and fell into the fireplace, deeply burning his arm.

At first light, he harnessed the mules again and started, without taking time for breakfast. He chewed on a piece of yesterday's bread and drank water from a keg as he traveled.

Refreshed by food and water, the soldiers had made relatively good time. It took Jeffrey well into the morning to begin overtaking stragglers by ones and twos. Some tried to hide, fearing he might be an Indian. Once they saw he was not, they crowded around the wagon for another drink of water.

It was early afternoon when he saw the boy leading his brown horse a couple of hundred yards ahead. He pushed the mules into a long trot, the remaining water kegs rocking and bumping upon the wagon bed. The boy heard the rattle of trace chains and stopped, looking back as Jeffrey passed by a cluster of walking soldiers and drew up even with him.

The boy grinned. "You got any of that water left?"

"More than you can drink." Jeffrey jumped down

from the wagon and removed the lid from a keg strapped to the side. He handed the boy a tin cup. He watched as Todd swallowed eagerly. Trying to remember how his brother had looked before the Indian raid, he made mental allowances for changes that the years would have brought. The light-colored hair had darkened. The baby fat was gone. Sun-blistered skin was drawn tight across the cheekbones. Nothing was the same except perhaps the eyes. They were the eyes of Jeffrey's father.

He said, "They tell me they call you Todd."

The boy nodded. "Some do. Most just call me kid, or 'Hey, you.'"

"What's your last name?"

"I've tried a long time to remember. It never has come back to me."

"Does Barfield sound familiar?"

Todd thought about it. "I don't know. Seems like I heard it somewhere, but I can't remember for sure."

"Do you recall havin' a brother?"

"Yes, I remember him, all right."

Jeffrey's heart raced. "Was his name Jeffrey?"

Todd's eyes widened. "It was."

"Do you remember fallin' into the fireplace and burnin' your arm?"

"That's somethin' you don't forget." Todd pulled up his torn sleeve. "That's where I got this scar. But how come you to know all that?"

"My name's Jeffrey. I pulled you out of the fireplace. I'm your brother."

Todd's jaw dropped. "But the Indians killed him."

"Remember Old Brownie, the dog? I was out huntin' for him, and they never saw me. They carried you off, and the militia found the body of a boy they killed. We thought it was you."

Jeffrey and Todd were both trembling. Todd said, "I remember. They'd captured another boy. He kept cryin', so they beat his brains out. They kept me till old January came along and bought me." Tears began to cut through the dust on his face. "All this time, I thought I didn't have no kin left anywhere in the world."

"I thought I didn't, either."

Both crying, they fell into each other's arms. Dust rose as Jeffrey slapped Todd on the back. When he could bring his voice back under control, he said, "You know, you were a pesky little brother. I hope you've changed."

"I can still be pesky when it's called for. Just ask old January." Todd pulled back. "We've found one another. Now what're we goin' to do?"

"I've got a farm. Half of one, anyway. Soon as I tend to business in San Antonio, I'm goin' back to it. I'd be real tickled to take my little brother with me."

"This tired old horse and me, we've traveled a long ways. How far is it?"

"Up in North Texas. We've got several rivers to cross between here and there."

Todd patted the gaunt horse on the neck. "Me and Comanche have done crossed many a river. I reckon we can wade a few more."

Forge

Award-winning authors
Compelling stories

· ·

Please join us at the website
below for more information
about this author and other great
Forge selections, and to sign up for
our monthly newsletter!

· · · · **www.tor-forge.com** · · · ·

Forge Books by Elmer Kelton